This Love's not for Sale

This Love's Not for Sale

ISBN: 1492253286
ISBN 13: 978-1492253280

DEDICATION

To my husband and my daughter whose patience is wearing dangerously thin with my writing obsession, but still they remain loving and kind. For how long? Only time will tell…

ACKNOWLEDGEMENTS

To family, friends and coworkers for their support.

To my loyal readers.

To Mallory, my sometimes assistant and sounding board for my ideas.

To Kendra & Chris for allowing me to borrow "don't be a weenie your whole life"

To Tad Anderson for use of his finely tuned "ewww"

To my wonderful beta readers who help make sense of my thoughts.

To Beautifully Bound for their talents and the Bondage Bear

CONTENTS

CHAPTER 1

"Tucker McGrath!"

Lilliana's secretary had poked her head into her small office and shrieked with such intensity and ear-piercing deafness, it startled her and damn near made her piss herself.

"What the Kegel muscles, Dana?" She asked with her own still contracted from their unexpected work-out.

After calming herself, Dana proceeded to tell her that there was an emergency consultation being requested on none other than the man whose name she had screamed out like a giddy schoolgirl. Apparently there had been an altercation and Tucker was on his way in.

She hurriedly got her station set up to inspect the damage while the secretary placed a phone call to the dentist on-call. Her job as a dental hygienist was fairly mundane from day-to-day so when there was an emergency, she felt the rush of adrenaline and welcomed the change of pace.

As Dana stood waiting for some kind of reaction, she looked up at her unimpressed. Being so new to the area, she had no idea who Tucker McGrath was. Dana rolled her eyes and informed her that Tucker was, in fact, a scrumptious package of masculinity who was single, and quite well known throughout the Tri-State area for his many business ventures and sizeable wealth. Apparently it was also no secret that he had been married multiple times and was a womanizing player whose reputation preceded him. Lilliana remained unfazed and shrugged her shoulders as she continued setting out more equipment.

She was still adjusting to her new surroundings and job. It had been over a month since the death of her beloved Auntie Margo and the notice had came as a shock to her. She had spoken to Margo only a few days before her death and she was so cheerful and full of life, it was hard to believe that she was *really* gone. Her mother had died when she was nineteen and Margo had been her closest confidant after her mother's passing.

She recalled sitting stunned and with tears streaming down her face as she listened on the phone about Margo's sudden heart attack. Margo's lawyer spoke softly and tried to console her, but she was too upset to hear his sympathetic words. Margo was very thorough and all of her funeral plans were set up in advance, leaving only the details of the will to be dealt with upon her arrival to Bridgeport The astonishment of being told she been left the sole heir of her Auntie's estate and all of her personal belongings was still fresh in her mind.

Margo had always been very charitable with her modest wealth and Lilliana thought for sure Margo would've just donated her land and possessions to some needy foundation.

While she prepared her work station, she thought back to her last conversation with her Auntie and tears wet her eyes. She would forever miss the closeness and the bond they shared. Other than a few distant second cousins, she was completely alone now and without a soul to rely on.

Her sadness was interrupted when she heard a commotion at the front desk and a man's booming voice. She quickly put on a disposable gown, mask, scrub cap and sterile gloves.

She smelled the infamous Tucker McGrath before she saw him. A subtle, clean, citrus scent wafted into the room and her belly fluttered. She missed the smell of a man. Only a few seconds later, Tucker staggered in.

She immediately looked him over. She did a guesstimate and averaged his height to be just less than six feet tall and slightly taller than her ex-husband. He was holding a bloodied towel to his mouth and his expensive, tailored business suit was disheveled with his white shirt sporting blood stains, and his jacket revealing a ripped lapel.

Tucker stood before her, boldly intimidating, and she pointed him towards the dental chair.

He promptly fell into it, laid his head back and grumbled, "Thucking thell."

"There's no need for that kind of language, Mr. McGrath," she scolded him.

She was well versed in the language of Dentalese and she knew immediately he had said *fucking hell.*

His mouth tightened before he barked even more obscenities at her.

"Yes, yes, I understand; you're hurt and angry. Now let me see what's going on inside that potty mouth of yours."

Clenching his jaw, Tucker narrowed his eyes, expressing his disdain with her condescending attitude. Dana and two of the dental assistants were waiting just inside the door ogling him and obviously amused with the way she was handling him. When Lilliana heard them giggle, she dismissed one of them, but motioned to the other assistant with a wave of her hand.

She placed suction and water into his mouth and rinsed it clean of all traces of blood. She then placed a soft bite block and looked into his mouth with a mirror. Tucker groaned and winced, and she broke the news to him.

"Okay, the good news is that all of your upper and lower central and lateral incisors appear to be intact. Now for the bad news: your left upper first and second molars appear to be damaged along with the gum tissue. Of course, we'll check to be sure that there's no damage to the bone by doing an x-ray."

"Thucking theak Engith," he snorted.

"Fine, in English, two of your back top teeth are cracked. The dentist is on his way in now so he can get you patched up."

Lilliana regarded Tucker curiously. His eyes were framed by dark lashes and she was instantly struck at the lusty shade of brown staring back at her. She noted his set face and his fixed eyes as he watched her closely. She studied his hair, noting its darkened copper shade frosted with streaks of silver scattered throughout. He was definitely handsome. No – more than that, he was stunning.

She peered back into his mouth and was also taken at how perfectly straight his teeth were. She had always been a sucker for a nice set of chompers and she couldn't help but comment on them.

"Did you have orthodontia?"

He shook his head with an air of complete unconcern.

"*Really*? You have the most amazing molars I've ever seen," she responded dreamily as she gazed into his exposed mouth.

***

Tucker had never heard something so medical sound so oddly sexual. Who was this feisty female behind the mask? He scanned her face trying to make out her features, but all that could be seen were her bright hazel eyes hidden behind sweeping lashes.

His eyebrows went up when their eyes met and his expression held a note of mischievousness as an ember of sexual attraction sparked between them. One corner of his mouth twisted upward in a mocking smile when he saw the tops of her cheeks, warm.

She took in a deep breath and looked away quickly. Anxiously, she proceeded to shuffle the dental equipment and clean and suction his mouth again.

"You seem a little old to be involved in schoolyard fights, Mr. McGrath," she stated flatly without making direct eye contact.

Her imperviousness was slightly amusing if not unnerving. Most women cowered or swooned in his presence, but this woman did neither. He started to mumble something back, but the dentist arrived and cut him off. She stood to speak with the dentist and Tucker craned his head to the side to try and get a better look at the shrouded female. He found her quite intriguing and could see that, despite her wearing an oversized isolation gown, she was quite shapely by her silhouette. She looked to be a little shorter than his ex-fiancé, or around 5'4"ish.

She kept glancing at him time and time again as his eyes moved up and down her veiled body. When he realized he had been caught mentally undressing her, he winked and attempted to smile. A fleeting look of irritation crossed her face and she rolled her eyes, turning her back to him while she and the dentist continued their conversation.

Damn that gown. Tucker wanted nothing more than to get a good look at her ass. He could deal with a boring personality, in fact, he had on many occasions, but having an unattractive ass was a deal-breaker for him. It must be round, firm and bounce in time to each of his thrusts or else there was just no hope for things to work out. He tried to envision what was hidden behind the throw-away gown and wondered what kind of mystique her ass held.

He wondered, too, if she was married. He didn't need another ass whooping like the one he had just received.

A tall blond-haired assistant moved in next to him and attempted to strike up a polite conversation. By her body language, it was obvious that she was interested in him, though she seemed a little juvenile for his tastes. He had already had his share of pretty young things and they turned out to be more trouble than they were worth, in his opinion. His second wife was proof of that. As for his *almost* third wife, well, he didn't want to think about her right now.

The pain in his jaw was throbbing and so was the ache in his groin from gaping at the hygienist as he tried to picture what the hazel-eyed temptress looked like au natural.

If she liked his molars, she should see his di... His lascivious thoughts were interrupted when the tall man wearing a white coat approached and sat next to him. He didn't pay much attention to what the dentist was saying because he was too busy concentrating on the masked women hovering over his shoulder.

"It would do you well to pay attention to what Dr. York is telling you, Mr. McGrath," she chastised when she, again, caught him eye fucking her.

That woman was something else. Any other time or situation, he would've taken her into a private room, bent her over his knee and showed her just who was in charge and what would do *her* well. Yes, that's what she needed – a good bit of discipline.

After receiving x-rays, getting a minor patch up on his cracked molars and packing for his cut and swollen gums, Tucker was finally released from the dental office. To his dismay, the femme fatale in desperate need of a spanking was nowhere to be found.

When he was picked up by his business partner, he caught a glimpse of himself in the mirror and was horrified at his own reflection. He had a black eye, a swollen jaw and his hair and clothes were a wreck. It was no wonder the hygienist hadn't shown any interest in him; he wasn't on his best game.

"I have good news," Marco told him.

"What? That douche nozzle who punched me is in jail?" He snorted sarcastically.

"No, but he will be just as soon as you file a police report about the incident. Just a word of advice: the next time you decide to sleep with a woman, you should probably make sure she's not married first."

"Where's the fun in that?" He countered as he continued to look in the mirror and inspect the damage done by the jealous husband. "So what's the good news?"

"I have the information on that property you've been interested in on the edge of town. It turns out the owner died recently and her niece is now the sole owner."

"No shit? That is good news. Maybe the niece will be more reasonable. That stubborn old woman wouldn't even consider talking to me about selling her land. What's her name and where's she from?"

"Lilliana Norris. She's from the Midwest somewhere but she's relocated here recently."

"For what? Fuck. I hope she's not planning on taking up permanent residency in that house. I need to talk to her right away. Get me her number. No. Fuck that. I'll get changed and pay her a visit myself. I prefer to do business face-to-face anyway."

Looking over the rims of his glasses, Marco raised his eyebrows and smiled ironically, "Yes, I can see that."

CHAPTER 2

After stopping to buy groceries, Lilliana made her way to her new home. She was still in the process of unpacking her belongings and going through the last of her Auntie's memorabilia. Margo had been very organized and kept her home in perfect order, making it easy to sort through things, but she was finding it difficult to actually get rid of anything without going into an emotional meltdown.

She had no sooner put her provisions away when she heard the unfamiliar sound of another car driving up her long driveway. She peered out her large kitchen window to see a black, four door Maserati pulling around her circular driveway.

She was bewildered, wondering who the hell would be visiting her. In the month she had lived there, not one single person had paid her a call. She quickly made her way to the front door and stepped out onto her front porch, watching with interest as the shiny, diplomatic vehicle parked. When the door opened, loud music came from the car to the tune of *Koop Island Blues*. She was charmed to hear such an obscure song that she absolutely adored, being played. She smiled, but her grin promptly faded when out of the car stepped Tucker McGrath.

Her belly did a flip-flop and her nether regions began contracting. Irritated with her bodily response, she stepped off the landing and approached him, ready to swiftly kick him off her property. She knew he was a realtor and it didn't take a genius to figure out why he was there.

Tucker walked to the front of his car where he met her. His desirous eyes moved over her body unabashedly and a small smirk stole onto his face. He furrowed his eyebrows and scratched his chin while continuing to take inventory of her.

She took the moment to do her own inspection of him now that he was cleaned up and more presentable. Aside from his blackened and swollen eye, Tucker was striking beyond comparison. He had skin a warm shade of praline;

slightly long, wavy hair the color of dark chocolate with silver undertones; a rugged, handsome face that revealed a square chin with a hint of a dimple in his left cheek, and a wicked mouth that she was sure he had done sinful things with. He had a straight Grecian nose, eyes that a girl could get lost in, and a smile that could bring her to her knees.

As for his body - sweet heavenly sculptors had done a number on him. He was superbly proportioned, firm and solid without being too muscular, with massive shoulders that filled out his expensive white button down shirt, a broad chest and long, lean legs. The way he stood as if he prided himself in his good looks and carried himself with an air of confidence, it was no wonder he had bedded so many women. How could they resist his demigod facade?

"Have we met before?" Tucker asked as his eyes roamed over her.

It was apparent he had the feeling of déjà vu, but he couldn't quite place her, and Lilliana was pleased he didn't recognize her.

"Yes," she stated mysteriously without further elaborating or telling him that she had her hands in his mouth not two hours ago.

***

Tucker's stance shifted and he stood quietly appraising Lilliana while he rubbed his chin, trying to place the dark-haired beauty whose eyes seemed familiar to him. He gave her body a raking gaze and a lascivious thought came to mind that perhaps he had fucked the woman before. He was annoyed with himself that he couldn't remember if he had his cock in her or not because surely he would've remembered dicking such a lovely specimen.

He eyed the small, curvaceous woman with wispy, short hair the color of onyx, taking a mental snapshot of her features. Her face was arresting with hypnotic and deceptively colored eyes that appeared brown at first glance and malachite in the direct sunlight. He was mesmerized by the delicate and ethereal quality about her. She had a small snub nose and a lightly tanned complexion with flushed pink skin set against high cheek bones. But her most appealing feature was her mouth. Fuck yes, those lips – heart-shaped, generously curved and the color of amaranth.

"Did we..." He trailed off as he waggled his eyebrows suggestively at her.

She immediately picked up on his lewd insinuation and was appalled. "Have you been with so many women that you can't recall whom you've been with?" She wrinkled her nose.

Tucker's head cocked to one side and he grinned, "Maybe."

"That's disgusting," Lilliana replied snottily.

"If you say so," he answered, fighting the urge to laugh.

"What are you doing on my property?"

"That's what I'm here to discuss," he answered with a cool nod.

She waited for the rest of his reply, but he stood watching her without a sound, enjoying keeping her in suspense.

She shook her head impatiently at him. "Are you just going to stand there or tell me what you're here to discuss?"

Suddenly, he had the strange urge to tease her, though he didn't know why. "You're an impatient little thing, aren't you?"

"I don't have time for this," she rebuked, turning to walk away.

When Lilliana didn't give into his kidding, he got straight to the point. "Your property, Ms. Norris, is what I'm here to talk about, and how I want to buy it."

She spun on her heel to face him again with a contemptuous wrinkle in her brow. "You don't have enough money to buy my property," she sneered, looking away from him and into the grassy field that stretched out behind him.

"Oh, I have enough money. In fact, I have more than enough. You just need to tell me your price."

He was defensive and quickly becoming irritated with her insolence. Twice in one day he had a vision of a woman bent over his knee with red ass cheeks. Was it a coincidence or just the fact that he hadn't had a female spread across his lap in more than six months? Probably the latter, he guessed. The image was so vivid in his mind it was as if he could feel the tingle in his palm. Even his cock twitched while thinking about spending some quality time in his time-out room while teaching this little girl how to behave. He tried to clear his wayward thoughts and focus on the task at hand, which was to put Lilliana Norris in her place.

"You're not understanding me. What I'm saying is: even if you have enough money, you don't have enough money. To. Buy. My. Property," she declared scornfully.

He took a slow, deliberate step toward her and narrowed his eyes, barely able to contain the impulse to pull her over to him, shove his tongue down her throat to shut her smart-ass mouth up, and then spank the living daylights out of her. Gritting his teeth, he tried to withhold his overwhelming frustration and arousal.

"Everything has a price, Ms. Norris. *Everything*," he growled as he continued to move slowly and gracefully, like a wolf stalking its next meal.

Her eyes rounded and she took a step back. He hadn't felt the uneasiness of a beautiful woman in a very long time and he found it enthralling that she could at least recognize his animalistic intentions and power, despite her willfulness and disobedience. However, his elation was soon shot down when she responded.

"This might come as a shock to you, but not everything is for sale," Lilliana huffed back, her tongue heavy with sarcasm. She pretended not to understand his look of agitation and refused to back down despite their physical proximity and the hungry look in his eyes.

He tempered his agitation the best he could. "I have yet to find something or *someone* that isn't."

"Well now you have. I'd appreciate if you and your amazing bicuspids would leave now," she stated, waving her hand in dismissal.

Who the fuck did this woman think she was to try and dismiss him so easily? He seethed. Just as he opened his mouth to voice his plans to paddle her backside, her statement struck a key and it suddenly dawned on him who the sassy-mouthed, cock-tease was.

"I thought it was my molars that you liked?" He smirked as her jade-flecked eyes widened with surprise.

***

Tucker's picture-perfect face split into a large, crooked grin in an attempt to disarm Lilliana with his dazzling smile. She raised her eyebrows at him as his realization of who she was hit her. While she found his grin sexy as hell and his manly features damn near impossible to resist, she wasn't about to give in to his obvious attempt at manipulation. He not only had sizeable wealth, but an ego the size of Texas.

Her pulse rate was still elevated after her near show-down with him. The way he had moved toward her as if he was about ready to make a meal out of her still had her on high-alert, but it still didn't stop her from attempting to deliver another blow to his fat ego.

"It just so happens that I admire all of your teeth, but it's your ass I want off my property," she responded in an unaffected, controlled voice.

Completely ignoring her flat tone, he asked, "Are you seeing anyone?"

She was shocked at his bluntness and caught off guard by the sudden vibrancy in his voice. "And why the hell is that any of your business?"

"I suppose technically it's not, but seeing as I plan on banging you six ways to Sunday, I thought it would be polite to ask," he rejoined, pushing his hair back and revealing his devilish, whiskey-brown eyes.

She gaped at him, astonished at his unpredictability. The burning flame she saw in his eyes startled her and she doubted he knew anything about being polite. She was even more aghast than before at his audacity and sheer lack of verbal restraint.

"I'm surprised you can stand upright or walk with a set of balls that big. If you hadn't just had dental work, I'd slap that filthy mouth of yours," she scolded him, casting her angry eyes on him and pouting her bottom lip.

***

Tucker chuckled out loud while he watched Lillian's mouth, fascinated with the luscious shape of it. She had no idea the size of his testicles and the lengths he would go to get his way. Every curve of her body spoke defiance, but if she thought being rebellious was going to deter him, she was dead wrong. Stubbornness had never stopped him before from pursuing what he wanted, and this little succulent tart with a fierce tongue and ass that begged to be swatted sure as hell wasn't going to send him running the other way.

He suddenly wondered what it would feel like to have those full lips wrapped around his shaft and that sharp tongue licking his *big balls*. He bet her smart-ass mouth would look absolutely divine glistening with his warm come.

He showed no signs of relenting. "Although it's polite of you, there's no need to restrain yourself on my behalf. Just for future reference, Ms. Norris, I'd love to put my filthy mouth all over every inch of you." Though Lilliana was obviously becoming incensed, he was quite enjoying their verbal foreplay.

"Dream on. And just for future reference, Mr. McGrath, I don't fuck. I make love," she gave him a roll of her eyes and turned her body sideways away from him.

The position of her body gave him a perfect view of her slender figure, the curve of her ass, and her voluptuous breasts as they hung and jiggled with her movements. Her nipples stiffened in response to the cool Connecticut breeze, and he clenched his jaw as he fantasized about rolling them through his teeth and plucking at them with his fingers.

Strangely enough, he was aroused by her mulishness and she only seemed to give him what he wanted by persisting with rejecting his attempts at winning her over. Inexorable, he continued, "That's unfortunate to hear because a good hard fuck is exactly what you need, Little Girl," he answered ferociously as he slicked his tongue across his mouth like a hungry wolf.

***

The sight of Tucker's wet tongue poking out momentarily shook Lilliana. Feeling her lower belly ache with sexual tension, she did her best to quickly regain her composure, even if he was slightly correct in his assumption. Though she didn't *need* a good hard fuck, she sure as hell *wanted* one.

"How dare you presume to know my needs. You have no idea what makes me tick. I'm no *little girl*, Mr. McGrath. I'm a grown woman with desires you'll never comprehend. It's very obvious to me that from your attitude, I doubt you know what *any* woman needs."

Tucker moved in closer. "Why don't you educate me then, Sweetheart," he simpered, clearly trying to ignore the sting of her harsh words.

She had heard more than enough. She was getting nowhere with this ridiculously handsome, egotistical fat-head. "Are you done? Seriously, you just don't know when to stop, do you?" She snorted as she backed away from him.

"When I see something I want, no, I don't."

She placed her hands belligerently on her hips. "Are you referring to my land or me?"

He raised his right eyebrow mischievously and spoke in amused contempt. "Both, of course."

She had grown intolerant of this man. She lifted her chin, meeting his pompous gaze straight on. "You can't even begin to fathom the amount of fucks I don't give about what you want." She pointed toward the road where he had come in. "You know the way out."

He threw his hands up in the air in fake resignation, but smirked derisively. "Until later then, Little *Woman*?"

"Not if I can help it," she pursed her lips.

Tucker got back in his car at a snail's pace and fumbled around before closing his door. As he drove away, she stood watching his expensive car leave a trail of dust in its wake. Something on the ground where he had been parked caught her attention. It was his business card. She stared at it a moment before picking it up. As she walked back to her home, she laughed at his image obnoxiously portrayed on the front. He was so full of himself. When she flipped it over, his personal number scrawled on the back. That man was one sneaky son-of-a-bitch.

Back in her kitchen, she tried to calm her rapidly beating heart but it was no use. Tucker had a physical effect on her that she was finding exasperating. Displeased with herself, she threw the card into the garbage. She stood looking at it for several seconds, mulling over whether or not to remove it and stow it away for a horny rainy day. He would at least be good for an occasional *bang* should she get the itch. Against her better judgment, she removed it from the trash and hung it on her refrigerator, if not for any other reason but to remind herself that a man still found her desirable.

***

Coming to the main road, Tucker paused and looked in his rear-view mirror trying to get one last look at the hellion who was wreaking havoc on his emotions. She was already out of sight and he considered turning his car around, busting in and taking what he wanted. There was no doubt she, too, felt the sexual tension flickering between them, but he'd been wrong before and he didn't want that scene played out again.

He scanned his surroundings - the lush green fields, a small picturesque lake nearby, half a dozen large outbuildings, and a fenced in area that once held horses. There had to be at least 100 plus acres of land going to waste. Oh, the things he could do with the goldmine the saucy Lilliana Norris was sitting on. He could split it up into residential tracts and make upwards of 500 million dollar, easy. Maybe more. It was just close enough to town that he could even make it an industrial park if he chose.

His mind was busy thinking about where the parking garage would go, where the new ten story complex would be located, and how much green he would be rolling in if he went in that direction. Hell, there was enough land he could make part of it residential and part of it industrial with a small strip mall or shopping plaza.

He was getting ahead of himself. First and foremost, he needed to win over the smart-mouthed tease. After a little background check, he would find out exactly what her needs were and go from there. He sped off with a new purpose: to win over the obstinate Lilliana Norris at any cost.

CHAPTER 3

Lilliana's night was long and restless. As she lay tossing and turning, trying to think of everything but Tucker, her mind drifted to her last encounter with her ex-husband.

She remembered how just moments after finding out about her Auntie's death she had run a hot bath, just wanting to soak away her woes. While the bathwater was running, there had been a knock on the door. Only wearing a towel, she had peered through the peephole and was irritated to see her ex-husband on the other side. When she opened the door, he had pushed his way past her without being invited in.

"I just heard the news, Lil. This is awful. When do we leave?" She recalled him saying.

As usual, Adam had been presumptuous in his assertion that she would take him along with her.

"*We're* not going anywhere. I'm leaving tomorrow morning," she had stated plainly as her annoyance bubbled over. "How did you find out when I just found out myself only an hour ago?"

Adam looked hurt and sighed loudly. Lilliana knew that look all too well. He was pouting and her tolerance level was wearing thin.

"I called your office to ask when you were scheduled next and they told me."

"You shouldn't have called them and you shouldn't have come here."

"I thought maybe you needed to talk to someone and..."

She cut him off. As usual, Adam had been thinking only of himself. He truly was the most selfish man she had ever known.

"I don't need a sympathy fuck," she had told him blandly.

He feigned shock and huffed at her, "That's not what I was thinking about."

His words were unconvincing as evidenced by his body language and the fact that he wouldn't make eye contact with her. They had been divorced for almost two years and he was still sniffing around trying to get into her panties. She had found it ironic considering that when they were actually married, he was *banging* everyone in town more often than he was putting out for her. When she had found out about his numerous infidelities, she promptly packed up the few belongings she had and left him.

She knew Adam had always thought she would go running back to him, but when he received the divorce papers in the mail, she found it amusing that he was appalled that his money couldn't keep her. She was even more pleased at how utterly stunned he had been when she didn't ask for one red cent of his family fortune when they divorced.

She recalled how he had stood in the middle of the living room pacing while she replayed their bad breakup. She never did have much patience with him and he never could take a hint.

"You need to leave, *now*," she had told him firmly.

"Precious, please. Let me buy the airfare and we can go to Connecticut together," he had pleaded with her.

Like hell he she would've allowed him to buy the airfare. It would have been just like Adam to hold it over her head like a crazed loan shark who would later threaten to lop off one of her tits when she didn't repay him with sex or whatever else he had in mind.

She remembered her quick come-back and smiled. "I've told you not to call me that. I don't want you to buy the airfare; I just want you to leave."

Adam had hunched over and let out a pitiful sigh to her strict order. His eyes shifted upwards in an attempt to give her puppy-dog eyes, but when she noted the movement of his irises as they danced over her half-naked body, his look had the opposite effect that was intended. She had pointed towards the door without saying another word and he sulked towards it. He opened the door and gave her one last sorrowful look and attempted to say something, but she was fast on his heels. She had given him a swift shove and slammed the door behind him.

She remembered hoping that would be the last time she would see him, though at the time, she thought that was wishful thinking on her part. It turns out, other than his annoying phone calls, it really was the last time she laid eyes on him, and she had never been more relieved to be rid of her pussy of an ex-husband. She needed a real man in her life; someone who knew how to take control. She already had a vagina and sure as hell didn't need another one.

*

Lying in bed, her eyes fluttered open and closed as sleep began to take her over.

I plan on banging you six ways to Sunday...

Her eyes popped open when Tucker's words seeped into her mind unbidden. She sighed irritably, turned onto her side, and closed her eyes again.

Why don't you educate me then, Sweetheart?

She refused to open her eyes this time and punched at her pillow trying to fluff it up. When her nethers began to throb, she sat up angrily and stared into the dark. Standing, she paced the pitch black room in a small circle, forcing herself to get her hormones under control.

A good hard fuck is exactly what you need...

She swallowed hard and cursed under her breath when she felt her own wetness dampen her underwear. Pissed off at the effect Tucker was eliciting, despite his being nowhere in sight, she turned quickly to go into the kitchen for a cold beverage. She made it into her living room when she walked straight into an unpacked box, harshly stubbing her toe.

"Fucking, Tucker!" She shrieked.

She bent down, gripped her foot and hopped around only to fall over and crash head-long into another stack of boxes. She thrashed around for a moment, trying to stand and finally gave up. Lying amongst the toppled boxes for several minutes, her breathing gradually slowed. As she stared up at the darkened ceiling, she wondered how ridiculous she must look lying in the lightless room, her tank top up and over one breast, her arms and legs splayed out in an unnatural position, and the crotch of her favorite panties sporting a wet spot the size of Nebraska. Now it wasn't only her pussy that was throbbing - but also her head, lower back and left big toe.

Mustering up all the energy she could, she rolled onto her knees and pushed herself up with both hands as she slid around on the papers and photos strewn around her. She almost lost her footing again but finally managed to stand and slowly back away from the mess.

Flipping on the light in the kitchen, she moved to the refrigerator for a bottle of water. Just as she was opening the door, Tucker's image caught her eye. Damn that shit-eating grin spread across his gorgeous face and those fan-fucking-tastic, brilliant white teeth. She ripped the business card from the fridge causing several small round magnets to skitter across the floor. Tearing it in two, she tossed it into the nearby sink.

She gulped down her water swiftly and turned to go back to bed when she skidded backwards on the magnets lying on the floor, doing an awkward ballet-move gone terribly wrong and landing on her still sore butt from her fall only moments before. She didn't think it was physically possible, but she swore she bounced when she hit the parquet.

"Fuck you, Tucker McGrath!" She yelled again.

That man was proving to be a pain in the ass in more ways than one and she felt that somehow, this was only the beginning.

***

On the other side of town, Tucker lay in his large, king-sized, four-poster bed going over financial figures in his head while daydreaming about the endless possibilities of the elusive tract of land that kept slipping through his fingers. He was in a slightly panicked mode thinking about all the other real estate agents and investors that would soon be descending on the property, all making their bids. He would have to fight them tooth and nail and he knew it wasn't going to be pretty.

Creeping up on him were thoughts of the thorn in his side named Lilliana. Unable to turn off his brain, he sat up and reached for his laptop to do a basic background check on the feisty little girl while he sat in bed. Correction, feisty little *woman.*

Who the hell did she think she was accusing him of not knowing women's needs? He huffed out loud at the thought. He had spent so many years doing nothing but pleasing women, there wasn't a single doubt in his mind that, given the opportunity, he could bring Ms. Norris to her knees with a simple look or command.

While her information was being downloaded, he chuckled softly at her grating yet funny words. *The amount of fucks not given to what he wants.* No, perhaps not *yet.* He would just have to make sure he made his wants very clear to her and that plenty of fucks would indeed be given at a later time.

He read with interest about her upbringing, college and marriage, but found nothing of great value in the information presented. Upon delving further into her background, he found her assets were modest despite having been married to a wealthy man, and he found it surprising that she wasn't interested in at least hearing his offer.

On even further investigation, he found a small article in her hometown newspaper about the scandalous divorce from her philandering husband. Apparently it was the news of the town. Tucker felt a twinge of sympathy for Lilliana when he saw the picture of her distraught face in black and white.

He also grew up in a small town and knew that nothing was secret and confidential in such a closed-off environment. Though, now that he was somewhat well-known in the area, he didn't fare any better for keeping his personal life private. He stared at the picture of her for a few moments, taking note of her plump lips and previously flowing, long hair. She was definitely a looker and quite photogenic, regardless of her hair style or length.

He glanced at the image of her now ex-husband and snorted in disgust. *What a fuck-up.* Tucker knew his type; he had grown up with them his entire young adult life; small-town asshole living off his parent's wealth. Hell, Adam probably hadn't even accomplished anything on his own and was simply surviving off his parent's name and fortune. Having grown up on a farm, Tucker knew the meaning of hard work and there was no greater pride for him than his hard-earned education and self-made success.

He was repulsed that Adam had cheated on Lilliana. Despite his reputation as a playboy, he took his wedding vows very seriously and had never once cheated on either of his two wives, despite being given plenty of opportunities. Some things were just sacred, in his opinion.

He briefly chastised himself for having had sex with the married woman whose husband had pummeled him earlier in the day. If he had known she was married, he never would've slept with her.

He found it odd and disconcerting that that no prenuptial agreement had been signed and still, Lilliana hadn't sought any financial support from Adam Roberts during the divorce proceedings. She must be woman with scruples and values. *Great.* That's just what he needed - a woman who wasn't at all interested in financial gain. He would just have to find another way to entice her.

Satisfied with his search, he laid his head back on his pillow and began to mentally plot out his course of action, both with Lilliana and the 100 acres of pristine land. Tucker began to drift off to sleep with dollar signs in his eyes when Lilliana's pouty mouth flashed past his closed eyelids, along with that perfect heart-shaped ass of hers. He had gotten a look at it, but he didn't see nearly enough of it to satiate his manly needs. He wanted to see all of it - *all of her* - every inch of her curvaceous body in the buff. Most of all, he wanted to see her on her knees, begging to please him and looking contrite for the way she had spoken so unkindly to him. He would show her just how wrong she was for accusing him of not knowing a woman's needs.

Without thinking, his hand snaked down to his crotch and began rubbing his hardening cock. Frustrated with the aching need throbbing between his strong, muscular thighs, he sat up brusquely and made his way to the shower. He set the water to a cool temperature hoping it would stave off his horniness, but it was ineffective. He closed his eyes tightly, rested one hand against the shower wall for support and began to stroke himself slowly as the cool water cascaded down his shoulder blades and back.

You have the most amazing molars...

He gripped his thick shaft tighter and picked up the pace. A deep groan escaped his throat as he leaned into the wall, his face hidden in the crook of his arm.

It just so happens that I admire all of your teeth, but it's your ass I want...

Oh, how he wanted her ass, too; to fuck and punish it like she deserved. He squeezed tighter yet as he sunk his teeth into his bottom lip, his climax building rapidly with images of Lilliana Norris invading his brain.

You just don't know when to stop, do you?

He would prove to her he wouldn't stop until he was satisfied and had his way with her. That mouth, those eyes, those magnificent tits and stunning ass... He grunted, threw his head back and his hot load burst forth. He stroked the remaining bit of his come out, all the while imagining the brown-haired beauty licking at the head of his cock and savoring every last drop his manliness.

Soon... Very soon, he sighed.

CHAPTER 4

A full two weeks had passed since Lilliana had heard from Tucker. She was surprised, frankly, that he hadn't attempted to get in contact with her sooner, and she began to wonder if he had lost all interest in her. What she meant was - her land. *Oh, hell.* Who did she think she was kidding? There was a tiny part of her that had liked that he was interested in bedding her.

Despite his absence, her life was no better for it. The other realtors had slowly started to come out of the woodwork like roaches. They were making their way not only to her home, but to her place of business, and she was being inundated with business cards left on her doorstep and windshield of her Karmann Ghia. Overwhelmed and with no one to talk to, she wished Margo were around more than ever.

Out of curiosity, she had spoken with a land appraiser to see exactly what kind of investment she was sitting on, but mainly to gauge the amount of taxes she was going to be burdened with by owning so much land. She was dazed and shaken when the man called to inform her that that the one-hundred and twelve acres of waterfront property that Margo had gifted her with were worth almost three million dollars. Her stomach churned at the thought of being responsible for such an asset. How would she ever be able to pay the taxes, her student loan, and the mortgage she was still paying on her condo back in Kansas? On her meager salary, and until the sale went through on the condo, it would be near impossible. She briefly contemplated giving up three meals a day just make it happen, but decided that probably wouldn't make a difference anyway.

The gifted land was turning out to be more of a nuisance than a boon. Now her nights were restless, and her stress level was nearing an all-time high. Except for when she had lost her mother and Margo, this was the worst news that had ever been delivered to her. Not even her divorce and the humiliation that came with that compared to the thought of having to give up her family's land.

After her miserable shift at work from worrying about her financial responsibilities to Uncle Sam, she walked out of her office building to see Tucker sitting on the hood of her car. Each time she laid eyes on him, the pull was stronger. She wanted to be annoyed, but the way he was resting casually and looking around, she found it hard to be angry with him. At least he hadn't been hounding her like all the other realtors. He looked handsome in his dark blue business suit that was complemented by her orange car. His jacket was opened, his tie loosened and his slightly long, dark wavy hair was blowing in the light breeze. When she approached, he stood up. The way his slacks hung low on his hips, she found it hard to make eye contact with him. When she did, his eyes lit up and the look of lust on his face woke that dark part of her womanhood that had been locked away for far too long.

"Ms. Norris, it's good to see you again," he squared his shoulders. "You look as charming as ever."

"Thank you. Is there something you want?" She asked, kicking herself for the suggestive question.

"I think you already know what I want," he smiled, his eyes moving over her body slowly. His eyes came to rest on her chest momentarily and then moved to her face, his seductive smile widening as he bit into his bottom lip.

Placing her hands on her hips, she countered, "I'm still not interested in selling my land."

"That's fine. Would you be interested in dinner?"

She was confused at how easily he had swept her comment aside. Her eyes roamed over his face as she tried to assess his unreadable expression. Wasn't he interested in buying her property anymore? She narrowed her eyes and looked him up and down distrustfully. What was this devious man up to?

Without thinking, her eyes paused at the crotch of his pants as she scanned the length of his body.

Ella Dominguez

"*Dinner*, Ms. Norris; let's not get ahead of ourselves."

Lilliana's rounded hazel eyes darted up to Tucker's irises. He was grinning stupidly and her cheeks burned with embarrassment from being caught ogling the moderately-sized package resting between his legs and hanging to the right. She cleared her throat and eyed the parking lot in an attempt to appear uncaring to his comment.

"I'm busy," she remarked nonchalantly.

He chuckled. "No you're not."

Her eyes shot back to his. "And how would you know?"

"I've done my homework and I know you're not seeing anyone."

Homework? Had Tucker done a background check on her? She felt uneasy with his statement and even more uncomfortable with the ravenous look in his eyes.

Offended, she crossed her arms over her chest. "Is that standard protocol for you?"

He gave her a look of not understanding her question.

"Looking up personal information about people and about who they're dating? Is that customary for you to do?"

***

Tucker suddenly realized his fuck-up and sheepishly flashed his teeth. "Ms. Norris," he started in.

She put her hand up in protest. "Just stop. I *might* have been interested in dinner a moment ago, but not anymore. You already know everything there is to know about me, what's the point? Unless you really are just after my land, in which case, I've already told you I'm not selling it."

She moved towards her car door and dug out her keys, but he promptly grabbed them from her hands. He had waited two long weeks to see her again, biding his time impatiently and priming her for his mindfuck, there was no way in hell he was letting her go so easily.

She gasped and her luminous eyes widened, "Give those to me right now!"

31

"Just hear me out. *No*, it's not customary for me to do a background check, but..."

"But *what*?"

"I was interested in finding out more about the woman who seemingly has no interest in money. I'm not often confronted with that kind of person and I was fascinated to find out, as you said, what makes you tick."

His heart beat rapidly, hoping she would buy his almost-lie. It was true that he found her fascinating, but he kept his ultimate motive unspoken.

She lunged towards him and swiped at the keys but he pulled them out of her reach. He wanted to smile at how adorable she looked when she was irritated, and he again felt the urge to tease her, but held his composure. She was proving to be unpredictable and he suspected if he teased her too much, he might end up with busted lip or worse yet, a bruised ego.

"Be reasonable, Ms. Norris. Tell me what it'll take for you to have dinner with me."

Lilliana stepped back and he was relieved to see that she was actually considering his offer.

"I want to read about all your dirty little secrets, too," she said coolly, crossing her arms back over her chest.

Tucker couldn't believe his ears. She wanted a background check on him? Was she fucking serious? He about told her to go to hell until he saw the pout in her lips. Glancing down, he could just make out the shape of her ass through her scrubs, and he gave in. He may have been a businessman, but the keyword there was *man*. For all his professionalism and emotional detachment, he still let his dick do the thinking for him a fair amount of the time, and he was fully aware of it. He couldn't help that he wanted to taste those lips and to feel that fleshy ass grinding up against him.

And more to the point, he wanted that motherfucking acreage.

"Fine," he declared, handing back her keys.

He felt nothing less than sheer delight to see the look of disbelief on her face.

"Well... I can't tonight," she tried to back out.

"Oh, no, you don't. You said dinner was contingent on doing a background check on me, so be it. You're not backing down now, Little Gi... *Lady*," he quickly corrected himself. "Follow me to my office and I'll pull up a file on myself for you to peruse. And by the way, interesting car," he laughed, walking away from her.

Step 1 complete. Her interest was piqued.

***

Lilliana regretted having suggested the background check on Tucker. She wasn't really that interested in reading about his sordid past. *Or was she?* She had already heard more than enough from her coworkers about his womanizing, dick-teasing ways. But she did give her word – sort of. So, reluctantly she followed behind his car to his office.

The entire drive over she pondered what kind of secrets she would read about him. Where had he grown up? Had he committed any fraud or crimes? It wouldn't surprise her – he did have that devilish, deceptive look about him. But that smile... There was just something about his crooked, toothy grin that screamed *fuck me.* No doubt that smile of his had gotten him laid numerous times and was a large part of why he was such a manwhore. That along with his charm and firm body.

When they arrived at the tall, architecturally stunning building in downtown Bridgeport, they parked in the underground garage. Tucker was holding the elevator open with the beginning of a smile on the corners of his mouth, when she climbed into it with him. He touched the button for the twelfth floor and their ascent began with a jump of the elevator. She felt her chest jiggle and peeked up at him to see his eyes resting on her breasts and juvenile grin on his face. *Men never grow up,* she mused. His eyes remained on her the entire time and the silence along with his unrelenting and enigmatic stare was unnerving.

She avoided his gaze, but when she saw his smile widen to her nervousness, she addressed the issue. "Would you please stop giving me *that* smile?" She sniped irritably.

His right eyebrow rose ever so slightly, "What smile is *that*?"

"The *I'm-the-hot-and-irresistible-Tucker-McGrath-fuck-me-now* smile."

As soon as the words left her mouth, she regretted having said them. She needed to remind herself that just because the thought was in her head, it didn't need to be spoken.

Tucker laughed loudly, his deep, throaty voice echoing in the small confines of the elevator.

"Is it working?" He asked in between laughs.

"What?"

"My smile. Do you want to fuck me?"

She huffed and rolled her eyes. "If by *fuck* you mean slap you upside your fat, egotistical head, then yes, I do want to *fuck you*."

His laughter promptly ceased and a muscle flicked angrily in his jaw as he gritted his teeth. His normally lustful eyes conveyed the fury within and he moved in for the kill, pinning her against the wall. "Such attitude, Ms. Norris. And that brazen mouth... It seems to me you're long overdue for a bit of discipline. I think perhaps that round bottom of yours needs to be paddled to a lovely shade of crimson."

Tucker's response startled her and her cheeks brightened again. Despite the panic rioting within her brain, her lower belly warmed and began to throb, and she became outraged at her physical reaction to his threat.

Pressing his body flush against her, he ran the tip of his index finger over her cheek and smiled devilishly. "Yes, that shade exactly."

She stood immobile, both frightened and excited, and she likened the feeling to being a deer caught in a predator's sights. Tucker's eyes were shining brightly as they darted from her mouth to her eyes while he waited for her response. The only sound in the elevator was of both their heavy breathing. The loud ping of the elevator made her jump, but it was a welcome break in the tension. She couldn't get off the elevator fast enough. Pushing past him, she tried to remain cool and unaffected, even though her panties were thoroughly soaked.

Tucker moved past her slowly without another word and led her to a large office space where only security and a few remaining employees were inside. A woman about the same size and age with vibrant red hair met them and looked Lilliana over questioningly. While Tucker walked ahead, Lilliana approached the woman and introduced herself.

"I'm Lilliana Norris, I'm new in town," she offered her hand, relieved to see another person.

The woman politely took it and smiled kindly. "I'm Ariel," she whispered.

Lilliana laughed lightly at her name because it reminded her of the famous Disney movie. The woman immediately picked up on her sense of humor and touched her hair.

"I know. Cliché, right?" She giggled.

"It could be worse," Lilliana grinned.

"True, I could be named Ronnie McDonald or something."

Tucker peeked out of his office door impatiently, "Are you coming, Ms. Norris?"

Ariel shot him a mean look and her soft blue eyes rested on Lilliana. "Be careful with that one," she said sweetly, reaching out and squeezing her hand.

"I will, but thanks for the warning," she told Ariel, wishing she had been forewarned earlier.

Lilliana started to walk away and wondered something. She didn't want to be stepping on anyone's toes with regards to Tucker.

She turned around to face the redhead. "Are you two...?" She hinted.

"Oh, God, *no*, but not because he didn't try. Like the real Ariel, I'm married to my prince charming." Suddenly Ariel looked worried. "I've already said too much. My apologies. But your being new in town and all, I just thought you should know that Mr. McGrath is, well..." She trailed off.

"You're fine. I've heard the rumors. Anyway, I suspect he's only interested in buying my land."

"Yeah, sure he is," Ariel quipped. "And they're not rumors; they're fact."

Tucker again stepped into the doorway of his office. "What are you two discussing out there - the state of world affairs? I don't like waiting," he glowered.

"Three words, Lilliana: Big Bag Wolf," Ariel winked playfully as Lilliana walked away.

When she entered his large office, he eyed her critically, his hands resting on his hips.

"I meant it when I said I don't like waiting. My time is important to me."

"Yeah, yeah, I get it, Mr. Real Estate Mogul. Now where's that file?" She shot back, annoyed with his manner.

He looked aghast that a female would have the nerve to speak to him in such a way and she couldn't help but wonder what kind of power he had over woman that they would put up with his temperamental bossiness. She sure as hell wasn't impressed with it. His looks, yes, but his attitude? Hell no.

"I have to pull it up," he responded tetchily, seating himself at his desk and tapping away at the keyboard.

"You're barking orders and you're not even prepared? Hurry up and wait. Oh, brother," she rolled her eyes, moving to the other side of the room.

"Are you done?" He growled.

The deeply fierce sound of his voice resounded through the room and dazed Lilliana. She had been peering out the large wall of windows, but spun around to look at him. His eyes were narrowed at her and the way he was sitting on the edge of his over-sized, dark brown leather chair, he appeared as if he was ready to spring on her like a large, insatiable animal.

Without a sound they stared at each other for what seemed like minutes, neither of them giving an inch.

When she opened her mouth to say something in rebuttal, he quickly interjected. "Don't test me, Lilliana, and don't mistake tolerance for weakness. That mouth of yours is going to get you in trouble every time. I won't ever disrespect you and I expect the same courtesy in return."

Her mouth snapped closed. *First a threat of a spanking and now this?* No man had ever spoken so strictly to her and she didn't quite know how to react.

"Am I clear?" He asked through a clenched jaw.

"Crystal," she whispered and with that, a smile touched the corners of his lips.

He stood and moved stealthily towards her, his lithe, lean body moving like a wild cat stalking its prey, his eyes never leaving hers. Her fight or flight instinct kicked in and she had the very distinct feeling of running like hell, but like that deer she had thought of earlier, she was caught in Tucker's snare and her legs wouldn't cooperate or move. Her brain was buzzing, her belly fluttering, and her heart pounding uncontrollably in her chest.

Tucker closed in on her, his body so close she could feel his breath on her cheek. His scent invaded her senses, making her thoughts fuzzy and clouded with desire. He reached down and swept an index finger over her forehead, down her cheek and glided it over her lips, the roughness of his skin speaking volumes to his masculinity. Twice now he had touched her, and she craved more. She closed her eyes and swallowed hard, wondering how a man who sat behind a desk all day could have hands like a laborer. Her mouth parted as she panted anxiously pondering what secrets his past held.

"So you want to know my secrets, do you?" He breathed into her ear.

God, *yes*, she wanted to know. If for any other reason, than to know what made him so damned irresistibly devastating.

CHAPTER 5

Like putty in his hands, Tucker scoffed. Despite Lilliana's sarcasm and cheekiness, she was proving to be just as easy as all the rest of the female persuasion he had devoured. All he had to do was blow them off and make them think he wasn't interested, then show them a little bit of attention and voila, he could slip right into her panties at will. He leaned in to tease her with a kiss when she abruptly pulled out of his reach. When her eyes opened, they were on fire. He momentarily thought she had read his mind or maybe he had spoken his thoughts out loud at the heated look on her face.

"That file, Mr. McGrath; I'd like to see it now."

Tucker stood momentarily stunned. His dick was now semi-hard and he felt discomfited in the fact that he hadn't gotten to taste her lips after all. He waved towards the computer and she promptly moved to his desk and seated herself front and center.

He gazed out the windows at the Bridgeport landscape and the dark clouds that were beginning to form over the horizon while he tried to talk his dick down. Perhaps she wasn't as easy a mark as he had thought she would be. When he looked over his shoulder, she was engrossed in what she was reading making him feel even more ill at ease.

He moved behind her and peered over her shoulder to see what exactly she was concentrating on. She was browsing an article about his multiple sexcapades and girlfriends, and his stomach roiled, but she flipped through the pages seemingly not interested in that sort of gossip. She scanned the pages quickly, and nothing seemed to keep her attention until she came to his childhood information.

He leaned down behind her and covertly ghosted his nose through her short hair as she read. He wondered what the hell was so absorbing about his boring upbringing. He would've thought his numerous flings were far for entertaining than his dull and uneventful youth growing up as a farmhand to his father.

He inhaled deeply and was struck with her fragrance. It was obviously a cheaper brand of perfume, but it was charming and hypnotic nonetheless. Oddly, though, the scent vaguely reminded him of home.

"Interesting," she whispered.

What the fuck was so interesting? Tucker didn't like her tone. It was reminiscent of the marriage counselor that he and his second wife had spoken to just before their divorce.

He straightened up, and grumbled, "Are you finished yet?"

"No, not even close," she responded back.

"Well dinner reservations are in twenty minutes, so make it quick."

She spun the chair around to face him, her face only inches away from his crotch. Her eyes widened when she realized her closeness to his cock and she readjusted her chair sideways to avert her eyes away from his groin. Tucker's mouth twitched with amusement.

"You made reservations?"

"Of course, I did."

"How did you know I would accept your invitation?" She asked, petulantly.

"I just knew," it was hard to disguise the confidence in his voice.

She stood and pushed past him toward the door. "This is a bad idea. I'm not sure who you think you're dealing with, but I'm really not interested in being another one of your groupies, despite how pleasant you are to look at."

Tucker chuckled with a dry and cynical sound. When his laughter lingered on a little too long, she glared at him crossly.

"I'm not a rock star, Ms. Norris. I don't have groupies, but I'm glad to hear you find me attractive."

"As if you don't know you're attractive? Whatever. I'll see myself out," she stated with determination as she made her way speedily out the door.

"Ms. Norris..." He said loudly, making her slow her gait. "If you must know, I had *hoped* you would accept my offer of dinner. I made reservations regardless because if you hadn't taken me up on my invitation, I still need to feed myself."

He left out what he was really thinking, which was: if she had rejected him, he would've just called one his *groupies* whom he was positive would've taken him up on his invite.

She had a look of bewilderment on her face, like she wanted to go to dinner with him, but was fighting her own inner demons about it. Tucker thought he knew exactly what to do. He turned off his computer without further ado and walked past her without a look.

"I'll be at The Cantina if you'd like to join me."

***

Tucker moved past Lilliana swiftly, brushing up against her as he passed her. His cologne was delectable and she briefly hemmed and hawed. *Should she or shouldn't she?* She knew by going to dinner with him it would be opening up a can of worms, and there would be no turning back. She watched him until he disappeared on the elevator.

She blinked rapidly, feeling out of sorts. She looked for Ariel, hoping the redhead could shed some light and help her with the tough decision, but she was long gone and the only other person in the large office space was someone cleaning the cubicles.

She decided to take the twelve flights of stairs down to the main level and get her cardio work out of the way. When she reached her car, she started it, revved the engine loudly and made her decision. The last thing she needed in her life was a man telling her what to do, especially a man whose wealth and fooling-around rang all too familiar. And most definitely not a man who enjoyed paddling bottoms.

Back at home, she showered and made herself something to eat. After putting in her Koop Island CD, she reluctantly settled in to finish sorting through the last of Margo's things that would be given to charity.

***

Tucker was growing more irate by the minute as he sat alone in the expensive restaurant waiting for Lilliana. He couldn't believe that she had really stood him up. With all his years of dating, no woman had ever done such a thing to him - *ever*. He shifted uncomfortably in his chair thinking about the numerous women he had stood up. The sudden realization of how they must've felt hit him and he didn't like it. It stung.

He began to mumble obscenities under his breath when a business rival approached his table.

"Dinner alone? That's a first," he snorted sarcastically.

"I figured you do it so often, I might as well give it a try," Tucker shot back.

The man completely ignored his and continued. "So I heard you got your ass handed to you. I guess maybe you shouldn't have messed around with Jensen's wife."

"That prick got lucky and he didn't hand me anything except an expensive dental bill. Did you see his face? I'd like the see the medical bill he got for his cracked jaw. Trust me; he's worse for the wear than I am. Anyway, I didn't know that was Jensen's wife, you fuck. If Jensen had been giving her what she needed at home, she wouldn't have been so eager to suck my dick and you can tell that piece of shit I said that," Tucker hissed back.

The man looked completely offended at his language. He shouldn't have been, Tucker was known for being brutally honest in all things and he very rarely held back. The man looked around fretfully like he was plotting his escape before Tucker ripped into him anymore for bringing up the subject.

"So how's that land deal on the edge of town going," the man asked, trying to change the subject.

"Why? What have you heard?" he asked defensively.

"Just that the new owner was asking around for appraisals."

"I haven't heard that."

The man rolled his eyes. "Just because you haven't heard it, doesn't mean it's not true."

Ella Dominguez

He waved his hand in dismissal. "What the fuck ever, Edwards."

Coming to the conclusion that Lilliana was a no-show, Tucker left The Cantina. He stopped off for a little house warming gift to try and schmooze her with in hopes of getting her guard down. He'd be damned if he was allowing that woman to get away without keeping her word about dinner, though.

***

Just as Lilliana was taping up the final box, a knock on the door startled her. She went to the large window to peer out and was surprised to see Tucker's black Maserati parked out front. She had been so engrossed in what she was doing she hadn't heard his vehicle pull in. She looked at the wall clock which read just after 10:00 p.m. Was Tucker insane showing up so late? She had to work in the morning.

She took a quick glance at herself and realized she was only wearing a sheer white tank top and short shorts. She started to run towards her bedroom to change, but there was another bang on the door, this time louder and more emphatic.

She hesitated, wondering whether or not to let him in when she remembered the austere look on his face when she made him wait before, and she didn't want to upset him like that again. What the hell was she thinking and why on God's green earth should she care if he was upset? She shook her head violently. *To hell with him.*

She threw the door open irritably, ready to read him the riot act, but when both their heated eyes locked, they froze. It was as if they had both been ready for a fight only to be stopped in their tracks by their craving for one another. Tucker's jaw gaped open as his eyes moved over Lilliana's body. She hoped he liked what he saw, because she sure as hell liked what was standing in her doorway. He drew in a slow, steady breath and smiled as his irises darted back up to hers.

43

"Booty shorts? That's an interesting look for you," he commented, quirking an eyebrow at her.

"I was planning on changing but I didn't want you to throw another tantrum about waiting," she countered.

"You haven't seen a real tantrum, yet, my Dear," he pressed past her, unperturbed by her sarcasm.

Tucker's pushiness reminded her of her ex-husband and how forceful he was on their last visit, and she was less than amused. "Excuse me. Did I invite you in?"

He ignored her remark and made his way around the living room, looking casually at the pictures on the mantle and wall.

Suddenly, he offered her an arresting smile and shimmied his hips. "I love this CD. It's one of my favorites. Care for a dance?"

A dance with Tucker was the last thing she wanted and she sure as hell didn't need him bumping those fantastic hips of his all over her.

To her dismay, he continued to sway to the music, his toned body rhythmically moving to the upbeat jazz tune. He gave her a crooked smile and motioned with his index finger to come hither as he mouthed the words to the song *Come to Me.* She squeezed her thighs together for some kind of relief from the throbbing that he was causing between her legs.

She took it back; she wouldn't mind his hips grinding into her after all. Along with that nicely sized package she had eyed earlier. Hot damn that man could move. She couldn't help but wonder if he had the same musicality in bed that he had on the dance floor.

"Hellooo. I'm talking to you," she stated, trying to ignore his taunting.

"I heard you; I just choose not to respond. Anyway, I'm not a vampire, I don't need an invitation into your home to take what I want," he hummed out in a sing-song voice.

Like hell he wasn't a blood sucker, she thought. "Listen here, you smug..."

Tucker spun around rapidly at the tone of Lilliana's voice. His playfulness was gone in a flash and his eyebrows pinched together. He was glaring at her much like he had been in his office. The sharp reprimand he gave her earlier, along with the threat of a red ass, was still ringing in her ears and she promptly shut her mouth.

"It's late and I have to work in the morning," she said more politely, but still very aggravated.

His smile and good humor returned, and he continued dancing around the room. "Regardless."

"Regardless of *what*?" She asked, not knowing what he was getting at.

He glided to the kitchen table, pulled out a chair, and seated himself facing her.

"Regardless of whether or not you and I have to work early, you owe me dinner and I expect you to follow through with it. Seeing as I already ate, I'll settle for dessert."

Now she was the one who stood with her mouth wide open. Was he kidding? And what the hell did he mean by *dessert?*

"Look, I'm not sure what you think is going to happen here, but you really need to leave," she declared.

"And I will, after you've prepared something delightful for me. I hope you can cook, Ms. Norris. I'm in the mood for something sweet," he said resolutely, digging his heels in. He loosened his tie, took his jacket off and draped over the back of the chair, making it very clear that he wasn't going anywhere. "Something fruity and light," he added.

"You're fruity and light in the brains," she mumbled, making her way toward her bedroom.

"What was that you said?" He asked with a raised eyebrow.

"Nothing. If I'm going to cook, I need to change."

"Don't change on account of me. I'm growing quite fond of your choice of attire - booty shorts and all."

"Yeah, I'm sure you are."

45

She kept moving when his voice resonated loudly.

"Ms. Norris, I thought I made my wishes clear. Do. Not. Change."

She turned expecting to see a harsh look on his face, but instead she was greeted with soft brown eyes that danced with mischievousness. It was quite a becoming look for him. So he wanted a show did he? Sure. Why not? She hadn't been made to feel like a woman in so long, she welcomed the challenge.

Let the games begin.

CHAPTER 6

Tucker watched with satisfaction as Lilliana dug out several items from her refrigerator and cupboards. When she bent down to retrieve something from a lower cabinet, he could've sworn she swung her ass his way. She stood slowly, peeked over her shoulder and batted her eyelashes at him.

So she was teasing him.

He couldn't take his eyes off her ass that was fit snuggly into her tight shorts. Her smooth, firm thighs were calling to him and his mind was racing with all sorts of ideas of things he wanted to do that little body. Surely she knew what she was doing to him by wearing something like that. Lilliana swayed her hips again and it occurred to him that she obviously had no idea the danger she was placing herself in by poking the untamed wolf with a stick.

As she began to peel some apples, he moved behind her quietly, brushing up against her purposefully. He happened to glance towards the refrigerator where he spied his business card underneath a small round magnet. He liked that she had kept it and had it prominently displayed, that is, until he found it taped down the center. He held it out questioningly with a light laugh.

She pretended not to see him and simply shrugged her shoulders. "I have no idea how that got there," she commented monotone.

"Riiight," he chuckled. "It looks like you might need a new one. You can't see my amazing tricuspids with this tape in the way."

Lilliana giggled. "It's bicuspids. Anyway, I said you have amazing *molars*, not bicuspids. Molars are in the back of your mouth, just for your information. But now that you mention it, your bicuspids are quite spectacular, as well. It's hard to believe you've never had orthodontia."

"My parents never had enough money for that sort of indulgence," he said softly as he replaced the mended card back on the fridge.

"Mine either, but working for a dental office has it perks. I had braces as an adult."

"A mouth full of metal? Real sexy. Tell me, though, how does one go about giving head with braces on?"

He was genuinely curious, and Lilliana smiled and shook her head at him. "Very carefully."

His eyes widened and he contorted his face. "I should hope so."

He opened the refrigerator and began to snoop around, taking note of her preferences in snacks. Many of the same items that were in his refrigerator were also in hers. Same likes in foods and music? *Interesting*.

She eyed him dubiously. "So in addition to being bossy, you're nosy?"

If she only knew. "I am officious in all things, Ms. Norris; not just in business, but in my private life as well. I'd love nothing more than to show you just how bossy I can be behind closed doors," he flirted.

"I don't need to be given orders, thank you. I've done just fine on my own without having a man lording over me."

Tucker doubted that very much. Lilliana clearly needed to be dominated. Or maybe that was just wishful thinking on his part. "I beg to differ. I think you not only need a man to take charge of you, I think you *want* it, but not just any man... "

"Wow. You're a piece of work," she huffed, keeping her eyes on the apple in her hand as she peeled it slowly.

"You bet your booty-shorts wearing ass I am, and I'm just the piece of work that's going to show you how much you need to be commanded." Standing directly behind her, he breathed on her neck. "For starters, you're doing this all wrong, Lilly. Let me show you how."

***

Lilliana's body stiffened in surprise to the sudden closeness and her breathing quickened. Tucker's voice was low and throaty, and the moisture of his breath tickled the hairs on the back of her neck. She had never allowed anyone to call her Lilly, but the way Tucker said it, gritty and raw, and so damned sexy, she didn't dare deny his use of the nickname.

He removed the small paring knife from her right hand. He gripped his left hand over the top of hers while it held on tightly to the partially peeled apple.

"Forces darling - stop fighting them," he exhaled into her ear, referring to the song playing in the background as he skimmed the blade over the apple bit by bit. Starting at the top of the fruit, he guided her hand in a rotating fashion, leaving a decorative strip of peel when they were finished.

"See how it's done?" He whispered, grinding his hardened dick into her bottom.

Her heart beat wildly in her chest when she felt how much he wanted her. When his thigh brushed her hip, she felt a jolt of electricity and her senses piqued. She hadn't felt a man's touch in so long that it felt foreign to her, but, God, how she had missed it. She closed her eyes for only a moment, fully conscious of where his warm flesh touched her. His large hands were so strong and rough, she wondered what other kinds of magic they could work. When they finished with the first apple, he removed his hand from hers, laid down the knife, and placed his palms on the counter face down.

"Now show me how well you can follow orders. Peel it, Lilly. No mistakes. I want it perfect, just like you."

Tucker's voice was different than before - deeper, more hushed, and authoritarian. Yes, she did want to be under his command, as much as she hated to admit it to herself. She felt far from perfect, but she accepted the compliment and purred with his praise. It had been far too long since a man had spoken so sweetly to her.

Trying to simmer the heat in the room, she attempted to engage him in conversation while her trembling hands peeled the apple. "Tell me, do you get your ass kicked often?"

Tucker laughed softly in her ear. His laugh was deep, warm and rich, and made her pulse skitter. "No, not often," he said, nuzzling his nose into her hair.

"Do you sleep with married women often?"

"So you've heard the rumors," he murmured, undeterred.

"Do you?"

"No, Lilly, I don't sleep with married women often," he answered, moving his hands from the counter to her waist.

"Or do you mean *often enough?*" She prodded.

Squeezing her waist tightly, he responded firmly, "Stop talking, Lilly, and do as you're told."

Her hands shook even more thinking about the things she wanted him to do to her body with those beefy, skilled hands. She pushed her ass back into him and got the response she yearned for: a low growl ending with a sigh. She steadied her hands the best she could to show him that she could follow his instructions.

***

Tucker could hear the gulp of Lilliana's hard swallow. He had only expected something to eat from his visit, but this little layover was turning out far better than he had anticipated. Good music, a beautiful woman with an ass like an onion that could brings tears to his eyes cooking for him and doing what he had instructed her to do. How lucky could one man get?

As she began to peel the fruit just as he had demonstrated, he grabbed her shoulders and sunk his teeth into the soft flesh on the nape of her neck just hard enough to leave a mark without drawing blood. She tasted heavenly, salty, and clean. She let out a high-pitched moan and her hands began quaking.

When she paused, he licked the crook of her ear and said softly, "Continue, Lilly." He liked the shortened version of her name. It suited her better.

Doing as she was told, Lilliana finished and began on another apple. Pleased with how well his new pet was following his directions, he inched his mouth down her spine and slipped her shorts down to her ankles, exposing her bare ass. It was absolutely, fucking, flawless - round and firm and nothing less than glorious.

"Tucker," she said uneasily as she began to turn around.

He gripped her hips firmly, holding her in place so that she couldn't resist him or move.

"Hush, Ms. Norris," he snarled as he bit into her ass cheek. She squealed as he licked and nibbled her other cheek in response.

Just as he began to ease a finger into her pussy, she said more ardently, "Tucker, please."

He slid her shorts back up and spun her around. Her eyebrows were furrowed, but her eyes were languorous.

"There's no need to beg," he teased as he leaned in to kiss her.

He wanted to taste her lips so badly his cock throbbed with an intensity he hadn't felt in ages. Just as his lips touched hers, her hand came up between them and she pushed against his chest, forcing them apart.

"Please, stop," she uttered breathlessly.

It had been so long since a woman had said no to him, Tucker was mildly dazed. He stepped back and scanned her body. It was obvious by her rapid breathing, her clenched thighs, and the fuck-me eyes she was throwing his way that she wanted him, so what was the problem?

As he and Lilliana stood watching each other, the next song on the CD began. "How apropos," he kidded her about the title of the song.

"*Let's elope*? I don't think so. I may be horny but I'm not dense," she huffed.

"Where's your sense of romance?"

"Romance is dead."

His eyebrows knit together and he ran his hands through his hair. "How long do you plan on doing this, Lilly?"

"Doing *what*?" she asked, gripping the counter behind her for support.

"Pretending like you're not attracted to me."

She sighed and shook her head. "I've already admitted that I find you attractive, but that doesn't mean I have to act foolishly and do something I'll regret."

He laughed in response to her statement. "I promise that your experience with me will be enjoyable, not regretful."

"You're so full of yourself, aren't you? I know your type and the last thing I need is to get involved with someone like you."

His cheerfulness was gone in an instant. *What the hell did she mean by that?* "And what *type* is that?"

"Like my ex-husband," she frowned.

Had Lilliana really just compared him to that douchey motherfucker Adam? No. Fucking. Way. He clenched his jaw, straightened up, and glared down at her.

"I'm nothing like that man. I worked hard to get where I am and to earn my own way, never once relying on my parents for help. And I never, *ever*, cheated on my wives. Anyone who says otherwise is a Goddamn liar," he barked.

Suddenly, Lilliana looked remorseful. "I'm sorry. I didn't mean to compare you...," she said in a whisper as her eyes scanned his face for forgiveness.

He wanted to be pissed, but the look of sadness in her eyes touched him. She might never admit it, but Adam had hurt her deeply and her defense mechanism of pushing men away was glaringly apparent.

"Finish making whatever it is you're making. I have something for you in my car. I'll be back."

***

Tucker walked out without saying anything more and Lilliana was left feeling horrible. She swore she would never compare anyone to her useless ex-husband. From what little she had read about Tucker, she knew they were worlds apart in their upbringings. The last thing she had read about him was that he began supporting his parents after their farm went bust. It was a noble thing to do and something her selfish ex-husband wasn't capable of.

Damn Tucker for being so enticing. She wanted him but she knew she was kidding herself to think that being with a man like him would be anything more than just sex. And her heart just wasn't ready for that kind of punishment.

She forced herself to finish her task. She brought out the flour, brown sugar, walnuts, oats and her secret ingredient, mayo. She felt so bad for her remark and by the legitimately hurt look in Tucker's eyes, she hoped her meager apple crisp would make up for her harsh attitude and sharp tongue.

Just as she was placing the dish in the oven to bake, she heard a melodic chiming coming from the porch. She set the timer and went out to see where the tinkering was coming from. When she stepped onto her porch, Tucker was arranging a wind chime he had hung near the porch baluster. It was colorful and appeared to be made of hand-blown glass and brass.

She stood watching while he struggled to hang the decorative chime, stunned at how very attractive he was. Upon closer inspection, she could see the farm boy in him with his strong hands, well-defined biceps and muscular thighs and calves. But it was his smile and eyes that gave away his true upbringing. She had always wanted a home-grown, farm boy to call her own; someone with Midwestern values and charisma. She had given up long ago trying to find that.

After several attempts to get the wind chime just right, he stood back, tilted his head and nodded his approval. He hadn't seen her watching him and when he turned, he blushed, something that Lilliana found charming. Tucker didn't seem like the kind of man that would feel embarrassed about anything.

"I thought it would make a nice house-warming gift."

"You were right; it's beautiful. Thank you," she gushed, walking over and tip-toeing to touch the glass.

"So are you," he replied lustfully.

She looked at him with reservation, unsure how to respond. She was still on her guard with him, uncertain of his intentions.

"You don't expect me to believe you've never been told you're beautiful before," he snorted.

"Yes, I have, but not like that."

"Like *what*? Sincere?"

She raised her eyebrows at him. "Are you being sincere?"

Tucker turned away from her and walked towards the front door, seemingly upset by her question. "Please don't question my intentions and motivations, Ms. Norris."

She moved past him and into the house. "I've learned to question everything and everyone, Mr. McGrath, and if you have a hidden agenda, it would serve you well to find someone else's emotions to play with."

***

The steadfastness in Lilliana's voice reminded Tucker of his mother, and so did the stern look she was giving him. He managed a small, tentative smile in return, remembering her kind spirit, but unwavering staunchness. He missed his family and had the sudden urge to visit home. He hadn't been back to his old stomping grounds in almost five years. He glanced over at the chime guiltily. The gift didn't come from his heart and a wave of shame washed over him for his deceitful plans. It wasn't how he was raised and his parents would be appalled at his actions all in the name of the almighty dollar. Especially considering that the land he was standing on had been family owned for almost a century.

When he stepped inside the house, a sweet fruity scent filled his nose and it, too, reminded him of home. He closed his eyes and was taken back to when he was a child. He loved living on the farm and the solitude and peace it provided him with. He inhaled deeply once more before pushing all sentimental feelings aside. He didn't get to where he was by being wishy-washy and schmaltzy, and he'd be damned if a stubborn woman from the Midwest was going to bring him to his knees. If anyone was going to be on their knees, it was going to be the tenacious little tease named Lilliana. He wanted that fucking land and he vowed it would be his.

"I'll take that dessert to go," he said brusquely.

As she removed the pan from the oven, her eyes darted towards him and sparkled with confusion and irritation. "To go?"

"Yes, it's already late enough and as you mentioned, we both need to be up early for work."

Lilliana glowered. "This isn't drive-through service, Chucklenuts. You don't get to show up, bark an order, and then leave. You made me make this damned apple crisp and you're going to sit down and enjoy it properly." Her voice was velvet-edged, yet strong and unyielding.

He couldn't help but grin stupidly at her. "Chucklenuts?"

"You heard me. Now get that fine ass over here and sit down."

"If you think my ass is so fine, then why won't you let me plant my lips on you? I've been denied twice now, Lilly. *Twice*. I want that mouth and I'm not a man who takes no for an answer without a fight."

She quieted for a moment as if pondering his statement and chewed on the corner of her lip nervously. "Alright, you can have a kiss, but *only* a kiss. Deal?"

So be it. If it was to be *only a kiss*, he would make it a kiss she'd never forget. He wasn't going to miss out on the opportunity to finally feel her mouth on his and he moved quickly before she changed her mind.

He grabbed her hand and jerked her over to him as he sat in a chair at the table. Tucker pulled Lilliana into his lap and gripped her face forcefully with one hand and fisted her hair with the other, yanking her head back so he had complete access to the wet depths of her mouth. He lunged toward her but then slowed his movements at the last moment, his lips only centimeters away from hers.

"I will see you on your knees, Lilliana Norris. I promise you, that," he breathed into her parted mouth.

Her cheeks flushed and he knew he had hit a sweet spot with her. Yes, she would be on her knees and begging for his touch, and the land would be his. He just had to play his cards right and be patient with her.

He moved his mouth over hers, devouring its softness. Her lips parted and she leaned in to meet his kiss. He pushed his tongue gently past her lips, taking his time and enjoying their slow mouth fuck. Gliding his tongue over her teeth and the roof of her mouth, she shivered to his touch. *God damn, she tasted good*. He pulled back slightly and kissed the corner of her mouth tenderly, only to grip her face more firmly and ravage her mouth completely. His kiss was urgent and exploratory as their tongues twisted and twirled together, the smacking wet sounds filling the kitchen. Lilliana's hands moved around his shoulders and neck, and she gripped him aggressively and buried her tongue even deeper inside his mouth as she bit and nibbled his bottom lip. Her mouth moved to his cheek and then down to his neck where she sucked viciously.

"Tucker," she sighed in his ear as she ground her ass down into his rock hard cock.

When her tongue began to make small circles in the shell of his ear, he lost complete control of himself. He stood, picked her up and dropped her onto the table with a loud thud. Yanking her tank top up over her breasts, he dove into her bare tits with immediacy. He sucked and plucked at her puckered pink nipples with his teeth and she fisted his hair, guiding his head up to her mouth.

"A kiss, Tucker. *Only* a kiss," she mewled.

"I want more," he groaned into her mouth.

"Please, only a kiss," she whispered.

Tucker stood and when he saw the frightened look in her eyes, he reminded himself to be patient with her. If he was to win her over, he must be more patient than he had ever been in his life. Hesitantly, he backed away from her, his hard-on pressing uncomfortably tight into his slacks.

"Okay, Lilly. Only a kiss. *For now.*"

CHAPTER 7

As Lilliana lay on the table with her breasts exposed, they both watched each other, Tucker's expression unreadable. She wanted to jump up and cover herself, but the way he was staring at her, she didn't want the moment to end. His eyes moved endlessly over her body, heating her from the inside out. Finally, he offered his hand in assistance and helped her up. Gently, he righted the tank top that he had damn near ripped off her body.

She tried to straighten it gracefully while he seated himself and continued to gawk at her. His intense gaze was maddening. Was he going to blink or just continue to stare bug-eyed at her? She blinked her eyes rapidly in a sympathetic response to his lack of doing so.

Moving to the dessert, she began to slice into it, thankful for the distance between them when he was suddenly upon her again, guiding her hand while she cut into the apple crisp. His movements were slow and deliberate, his mouth so close to her neck it was only hairbreadths away from her soft flesh. She couldn't take his tortuous teasing anymore.

"I want you, Lilly, and I don't like waiting. It will serve *you* well not to forget that," he said sternly.

"I don't think I could forget it if I tried."

"I'm glad to hear that," he said with a smile that resonated through his manly voice.

Seated at the table, Lilliana kept her eyes fixated on Tucker's mouth while he ate. It had only been on her body moments ago, her under-used nipples to be exact, and she wished she hadn't told him to stop. She wanted more too; however, she feared the kind of intimacy that he sought from her. She didn't yet fully trust him, but it had been a long nineteen lonely months since she had a man's hands on her body or throbbing cock between her legs. While she thought of all the ways she wanted him to take her, she watched him devour her desert as if he hadn't had a home-cooked meal in ages.

"This is excellent, Lilliana. Really, it's just *amazing*. I haven't had home-cooking in a very long time," he said, answering her unspoken question. "So you can cook. What else can you do with those hands?" He winked suggestively.

"I can shuck corn faster than anyone I know," she replied, immediately wanting to retract her lame admission when he burst out laughing.

"Fuck! That's a riot! You are a red-neck!" He bellowed.

She stood and swiftly flicked the back of his neck. "Who's the red-neck now?" She pouted, grabbing his unfinished plate along with hers and taking them to the dishwasher.

"Hey, I'm not done with that!"

"Yes, you are."

"Oh, boo hoo. I'm a red-neck, too. I just hide it better. Now give that delightful sustenance back to me, *right now*," he emphasized with a silly smirk on his face.

As she placed it back in front of him, he reached around and smacked her ass harshly, the loud slap echoing in the large kitchen. She dropped the plate down onto the table and looked aghast. She rubbed her bottom and a ridiculous grin spread over her face and her panties dampened. Tucker paid no attention to her and inhaled the last few bites and then licked his index finger as he slid it around on the plate to get every last crumb. An image of him licking his fingers post foreplay popped into her mind, and she blushed at her sinful thoughts.

"Fucking, delicious," he mumbled.

Oh, she had something delicious and juicy for him right between her legs. Still stunned that he had actually spanked her, she inwardly rolled her eyes at herself. *Get a grip, Lil,* she reprimanded herself. Her horniness was starting to cloud her judgment and she damned well knew it.

Watching Tucker practically lick the plate, she found it cliché, but she had learned early on that the way to a man's heart really was through his stomach; that and his pants.

When she looked at the clock on the microwave, she was horrified to see it was almost midnight. She had to be up in five short hours.

"Yes, I know, it's late. I'll see myself out," he declared, standing and heading toward the entrance.

As he opened the door, she stood next to him and held the door open for him. He eyed her neck and grinned devilishly. "Have fun trying to explain that."

She had no idea what he was talking about and she was too tired to try and figure out his man-code. He fingered her chin just before turning away, tilting her head back.

"You really are beautiful," he kissed the end of her nose, then her lips.

The touch of his mouth was a delicious sensation and she craved more, but his eyebrows pulled together as if struggling with something.

When he gently pulled away from her, she responded, "And you really do have a fine ass."

"I know," he said cockily, walking away from her. "Ciao, Pet," he waved from behind.

Her heart thudded in her chest to his term of endearment and the memory of his lips pressing against her bosom. She was beginning to think being Tucker's pet might not be such a bad thing. He sped away, his back wheels spinning out and kicking up a whirlwind of dust and pebbles. A gust of wind blew past her and the wind chime tinkled tunefully, reminding her that Tucker McGrath had been there.

She seated herself on the bench swing. Other than the sound of the crickets chirping and the gentle breeze, only her breathing could be heard. It was serene and the smell of freshly cut grass was enlivening. It brought back fond memories of her childhood when she and her mother would visit Margo, and how she would play in the fields under her mom's watchful eyes. Lilliana hated the thought of having to give up the land that her Auntie had fought so hard to keep and that her ancestors had owned for a century. *But the taxes...* She dreaded the thought. There had to be another way. She prayed there would be another way.

Morning came too quickly, and she barely had enough time to brush her teeth and hair. She almost rear-ended an expensive sports car in her mad dash to be on time. As soon as she made it into her office and past the front desk, she heard several giggles.

"Nice going, Lilliana. Is that from *Tucker McGrath*?" Dana oozed curiosity.

"What?" Lilliana was puzzled by her remark and the sudden interest in her private life.

Dana motioned toward her neck but Lilliana couldn't see what she was referring to. She made a beeline to the restroom and cranked her head to the side to see a fresh, red bite mark on the nape of her neck. She gasped and tried to rub it as if it were going to magically disappear like chalk on a blackboard. Still tender, she winced. *Fucking, Tucker!* How the hell was she going to explain that? Tucker's statement came back to her and now she knew what he was referring to. She tried not to smile, but the country-boy grin plastered on his face when she mentioned her corn-shucking skills flashed in her mind. She began to giggle when Dana came into the restroom.

"It was Tucker, wasn't it?"

"How..." Lilliana started to ask.

"Jordana saw him waiting on your car yesterday. OMG, Lilliana! Did you sleep with him?" She asked excitedly, gripping Lilliana's shoulders.

"Good Lord, Dana, I just met the man. *No,* I didn't sleep with him."

"So he was just marking his territory? Where else did he *mark* you?" Dana laughed, poking her butt.

Lilliana rubbed her bottom thinking about Tucker's teeth sinking into her cheek and the smack on her bottom. Now that Dana mentioned it, the idea didn't sound out of line with the way he got all alpha male on her. She felt lucky he had simply bit and spanked her as opposed to pissing down her leg.

"He just got a little playful," she rebutted. "Now, seriously, I don't want to talk about this."

When lunchtime arrived several hours later, Dana came barreling into her small office, waggling her eyebrows up and down. "Tucker is here! He's asking for you, and he has something, too."

Lilliana tried to hide her enthusiasm, but it was almost impossible. She had been thinking about him off and on all day, and about that *kiss*. It had been difficult trying to concentrate on cleanings and cavities when all that kept popping into her mind was Tucker's suggestive remarks, his low growly voice, and hot breath on her neck and body.

She ran her hand through her short hair and pinched her cheeks for color. She rushed to the lobby but then thought it better to slow her pace so she didn't appear too desperate. Pausing in the hallway, she watched as Tucker paced the lobby. He had a tin can in his hand and she wondered what kind of gift he had gotten her.

Dana came around the corner so fast, she bumped right into her. "What are you waiting for, go get him," she shrieked as she pushed Lilliana forward and into the lobby.

Dana made such a ruckus, several pairs of eyes zoomed in on her, including Tucker's. His infectious grin and the sheer brilliance of his naturally perfect teeth made her want to fling herself onto his solid, semi-muscular body and into his arms. When he pushed his hair from his eyes and bit his bottom lip, it was all she could do not cream her scrubs.

Maintain your composure, she reminded herself, unsure if she could do such a simple thing. She closed her eyes and, miraculously, pulled herself together.

"Hey Lilly, it's good to see you again. I was hoping we could grab a quick lunch. Are you available?" He asked as his eyes examined her body.

"I think so..."

"Yes, she's *available*," Dana said with a giggle.

Lilliana shot her a shut-the-fuck-up look and Dana slunk away like a puppy with its tail between its legs. "I was just trying to help," she muttered.

Tucker did the most polite thing and grabbed her hand as he led her out into the parking lot. The warmth of his brawny hand was a welcome, sweet gesture. Perhaps romance wasn't dead after all, and maybe she had been all wrong about him. Perhaps he really was a good guy.

At his car, he opened the door for her and helped her in. She had never been treated so lady-like. Adam certainly was never this polite or chivalrous. She watched Tucker move around the front of the car, his eyes never leaving hers. After he climbed into the driver's seat, he leaned over and buckled her in and paused with his mouth right next to her ear.

"I've been thinking about you all day, Pet, and those amazing lips and tits. I see I left my calling card on you," he breathed, reaching his hand around and touching the tender love nibble on the back of her neck. He gripped her tightly and pulled her into his mouth, his tongue slipping past her lips. She moaned from the pain and he inhaled, sucking the breath from her as she sunk her teeth into his long, thick tongue.

He tasted so good she didn't want him to stop. She would've been content to spend her whole lunch break sucking face with the gorgeous Tucker McGrath hovering over her and his hands all over her body.

Ending their slow, deep kiss, he replied, "I couldn't sleep so I made something for you."

He sat back and handed her a tin container that had a Christmas scene on the lid. She opened it to find homemade biscuits. She laughed a little not understanding its meaning, but was still touched by his gesture.

***

"They're my mother's recipe," Tucker lied.

When he saw the genuine elation on Lilliana's bright and eager face, he stared forward and out the window, unable to make eye contact with her. It was too easy to get lost in the way she looked at him. That feeling of guilt was burgeoning in his belly again and he swallowed hard. The fluffy biscuits were no more his mother's recipe than a frozen Hungry-Man dinner. He had stopped off at a 24-hour food mart after leaving her place the previous night and bought some instant dough. At the time, he was tickled with himself for thinking so quickly on his feet, but now... Now he just felt like shit when he saw Lilliana bite into one of them and how happy she was.

"Oh, Tucker, they're delicious. Thank you. I... " She trailed off. Her eyes roved over her face and rested on his mouth. "I think I had you pegged all wrong."

Feeling deeply uncomfortable with the look in her eyes, he reached for his phone and touched the screen. "I received a text message about something important. I have to leave," he said clipped. Feeling like a complete asshole, he just wanted to get the fuck away from her.

Confusion settled on her face. "I didn't even hear it notify you."

"I have it on vibrate," he lied again.

"Okay," she answered sadly, opening the vehicle door, obviously disappointed.

Tucker couldn't make up his mind. He wanted Lilliana's acreage so badly he pushed his guilt to the very back of his subconscious and pressed forward with his plan. "No, wait. Fuck work. Let's do lunch."

"Are you sure?"

"Yes, let's do this," he said decisively, speaking more about his plan than about lunch.

Once at the restaurant, Lilliana was proving to be a hard nut to crack. He kept trying to engage her in conversation by asking personal questions, but she kept redirecting those questions back to him. She was delectable in her Mediterranean blue scrubs with a floral print top, and he was itching to get her out of them. Why couldn't she just be easy, peasy, nice and sleazy like all the rest of his flings? And why the fuck did she have to be so damned adorable?

"What are you thinking about?" Her face brimmed with curiosity.

He decided to be honest for a change. "Getting you out of those scrubs and burying my cock deep inside you for hours," he responded frankly.

Her eyes rounded and she coughed on a mouthful of water. Once she got her voice back, she reprimanded him. "You just proved that romance is truly dead. I don't know if you're aware, but you can be honest without being blunt."

Tucker moved his shoulders in a shrug of indifference. "Where's the fun in that? Anyway, romance isn't dead, it's just overrated. There's something to be said about being filthy and talking dirty. You should try it sometime. It's quite liberating," he quirked an eyebrow at her.

She leaned toward him, exhaling with disapproval. "And you kiss your mother with that dirty talking mouth?"

A faint satisfied smile flashed across his mouth. "Occasionally. Try it, Lilly. Say: *I like being fucked hard, Tucker.* Say it."

She shook her head *no* but the smile on her face gave away her liking to his orneriness.

"I never figured you for a prude, Lilliana Norris."

She suddenly looked offended. "I am *not* a prude!" She whisper yelled, sitting forward on the edge of her seat.

Amused with her reaction, he continued to tease her. "Then say it. Better yet, say: *fuck me in the ass, Tucker. I like it when you go deep.*" Knowing full well she wouldn't give in, he was bound and determined to embarrass her and get a rise out of her. She narrowed her eyes but remained silent. When he laughed, his tone had a sharp edge. "I fucking knew it. P-R-U-D-E," he stressed.

She smiled sweetly in return, leaned back in her seat comfortably and licked her lips. Confused by Lilliana's reaction, he suddenly worried about what he may have provoked the fiery brunette to do.

Closing her eyes, she sighed softly and moaned out, "Oh, Tucker... Fuck me in the ass. Give it to me deep. Don't make me wait until later, you dick-tease."

His eyes nearly popped out of his head and it was his turn to cough on his beverage. He scanned the room to see several pairs of bulged eyeballs staring at him and Lilliana.

"Take me now, Tucker!" She continued, groaning louder.

He reached over the table and gripped her hand. "Okay, okay!" He howled with laughter.

She immediately opened her eyes and sipped on her water, not showing an ounce of humiliation.

He continued to laugh while he held his stomach. "I didn't say you had to go on about it," he told her when he finally caught his breath.

"I thought I'd improvise a little. You're right, it is liberating. Shall I have another go at it?" She batted her eyelashes.

"Fuck no! Tell me, though, do you really like being fucked in the ass?" He grinned.

Her eyes narrowed again and she crossed her arms, "You're pushing your luck. Now say it."

"Say *what*?" He asked.

"You, Lilliana Norris, are no prude. Come on, say it."

"I'll do no such thing."

"I did what you asked. Say it!" She exclaimed, irritated that he wouldn't retract his statement.

Tucker showed no signs of giving in. "I won't. Not until you really prove otherwise," he winked.

She met his unwavering eyes without flinching. "Whatever. Then I stand by my assertion that you're a dick-tease."

"I never tease, Lilly, and I always follow through with my plans."

If only she knew just how true his statement was, she'd go running for high ground and never look back. Wondering how to bring up the subject of her land without being obvious, he tiptoed around the subject and then finally asked, "So what are your plans with Margo's property?"

He called her Aunt by name to make his question more personal, and it worked wonders. She initially looked defensive, but when he appeared nonchalant, she let her defenses down and he inwardly sighed. His plan might just work after all.

"I'm not sure yet. The taxes are going to be exorbitant. I've been thinking about maybe donating some of it for charity purposes, like an animal haven or something, just to cover the taxes."

Tucker wanted to stand, slam his fist on the table and scream. *Charity? Fucking charity?* She was sitting on a motherfucking goldmine and she was considering *giving* her land away? He clenched his jaw and kept his eyes downcast for fear that his disbelief and rage would be easily read on his face.

"I see," he mumbled softly.

"You think that's a bad idea?"

Tucker looked up to see Lilliana's eyes scanning his face earnestly. His mind was in over-drive. There were so many ways he could play her. He could manipulate her into thinking anything he wanted; including that charity was completely illogical.

"I think charity is a viable option. You just need to remember that once you've given any portion of your land away, it's gone forever. No matter what good intentions you may have, a charity foundation can do whatever they want with the land and later sell it for profit."

She looked distressed. "I guess I never thought of that."

"What kind of taxes are we talking about? Have you had your land appraised?"

"Yes, just last week."

Shit, Edwards was right. She was seriously considering keeping the land. He hadn't expected that answer and he was briefly at a loss for words.

"The appraiser assessed it at just under three million dollars."

He snorted sarcastically. Apparently whomever she had talked to must be in cahoots with another realtor. Suddenly, felt protective of Lilliana. He may be trying to take advantage of her, but he sure as hell didn't want anyone else trying to fuck her over.

"No, Pet, that man is dead wrong. If your land was raw it would be worth three million dollars, but it's not. Raw land means natural property that has no sewers, electricity, streets, buildings, water or telephone service, etcetera. Your land is developed, albeit developed for farming purposes. Double that assessment and that's something more in line to what it's worth."

Lilliana suddenly looked ill. "Oh, God, I'm going to be sick," she whimpered, jumping up from the table and running toward the restroom.

Tucker stood in response, feeling unwell himself. She was so naïve. She really did need his help and advice. He cursed himself for his greediness. Here Lilliana was trying to do the right thing by considering charity and he was manipulating her, along with some other asshole.

He stepped outside to get a breath of fresh air and dialed his parent's phone number. He needed to hear their voices and be reminded where he came from.

"Yep," his mother answered.

"Ma," he whispered.

"Dad, it's Tuck!" She yelled out of the mouthpiece. "Sweetie, it's good to hear your voice. Is everything okay? You don't sound well."

His mother had an uncanny ability reading his emotions. "I'm fine. I just wanted to hear your voice. How's Pops?"

"The same, old and grumpy. Like you," she laughed heartily.

"I am not grumpy," he grumbled and then chuckled at the sound of his own cantankerous voice. He really was turning out to be a crabby old cuss just like his father.

"So why the call? Have you started seeing someone?" His mother asked wistfully.

"Of course not. I'm just working on a tough deal."

"Oh? Something big?"

"Potentially. If things work out, I could retire early with a deal like this. I'm just stressing about the... " He couldn't think of how to word his deceitful plan. "Circumstances."

"Well, Tuck, I know how competitive you can be, but try to remember, it's only money honey and retirement isn't everything it's cut out to be. Don't make yourself sick over it, Son. Just be honest and hard-working and everything will work out. I know you don't want to hear it, but you win some, you lose some."

No, Tucker didn't want to hear the same old speech he'd heard his entire childhood. His parent's *only-money-honey* attitude is what got them into the predicament of losing their farm. If not for him, they'd be without a pot to piss in. He sighed irritably and shook his head wondering why the hell he had called.

"Dad says he loves you and to take care, and bring whoever it is you're *not* seeing over so we can meet her. Oh, and call your brother. I think Mason is up to no good."

He couldn't help but laugh at his mom's keen sense. After hanging up, he lingered outside, enjoying the crisp fall air. He felt a tap on his shoulder and turned to see Lilliana looking irate and still green around the gills.

"I should get back to work. I'm not feeling so hot and I've lost my appetite."

"Is this because of what I said about the assessment?"

She nodded, turning her face away from him. "I have no idea what to do. People are calling me day and night, my lawn and porch have been littered with business cards, I can't even eat lunch with you without being accosted by someone wanting my property and warning me about... And now I find out that the appraiser lied to me and I'll never *ever* be able to afford the taxes. It's too much. Margo never would have wanted me to go through this. She worked so hard to keep the land that she and my mother grew up on."

She let out the most pitiful sob and it tore at Tucker's heart.

"Someone approached you just now?" He asked, puffing his chest out protectively. "Listen, Lilly, everything will be okay. I promise," he whispered, pulling her into his arms.

She abruptly jerked away. "No, it won't. You're just like all the rest of those vultures after my land. You, with your devil's smile and body built for sin. I know what you want from me: one-hundred and twelve acres and my panties in your trophy case. I'm not stupid, Tucker McGrath. You think you can win me over with your steamy verbosity and by pushing my buttons because you know I long for a man's touch and authority. But I've been to this dog and pony show before, and I won't be made a fool of again. My land isn't for sale and neither am I!"

Lilliana's harsh unprompted words jarred Tucker's cool exterior. Was he that easy to read? Had he lost his touch? She stood glaring at him, waiting for his response, but he had none to offer. She was right - he was just like the rest. No - he was *worse*. He wasn't only trying to get her land, but inside her mind and body, knowing full well he was only using her to get his way. What could he do?

Just keep up with the lie at all costs.

This deal could set him up for the rest of his life and he wasn't about to let his feelings get in the way of that.

When he stood silently defenseless, she turned away and walked to his car. He wasn't far behind her and when he entered, she was putting her seat-belt on. He tried to assist her, but she batted his hands away.

"I've got this," she snapped.

The awkward silence in the car was deafening. He kept replaying her words over and over. What exactly had Lilliana been warned about and by whom?

Frustrated with her ostracizing him, he tried to prompt her. "I don't know what you were told about me and by whom, but I have a lot of enemies who would say just about anything to hurt my reputation. Including lies."

"Good, honest people don't make enemies, Tucker, and someone who has a lot of enemies usually has them for a reason. I, for one, am not going to end up like the rest of the people you've stepped on to get what you want."

Again, he was defenseless. He hated that she could see right through him. More than that, he despised the fact that she was right.

Stopping in front of the main entrance to the dental office, he started to say something but she was out the door before he could even get a word in.

Back in his office, he was having a difficult time concentrating. He was on an emotional roller-coaster thinking about the land deal and about what Lilliana had accused him of. Her sad and defensive eyes flashed in his mind.

Who the hell had approached her at the restaurant and gave her pause about him?

He called the restaurant and spoke with his waiter who divulged the name. He had suspected maybe it was Edwards, but to his surprise, it was Darren Schumacher; the man who had once been his business partner and confidant.

He promptly dialed Darren's cell phone number. As soon as his voice came on the other end, Tucker ripped into him. "What the fuck did you tell Lilliana Norris?"

"Nice of you to call, McG."

Tucker waited impatiently on the other end, about ready to blow a gasket. "What did you tell her?" He repeated.

"Who again? Oh, the brunette that owns Margo's land? Nothing that wasn't true. I just thought someone should warn her about your conniving ways."

"You asshole, this deal is mine. Do you fucking understand me? You stay away!"

"From the land or the girl?" Darren asked condescendingly.

"Both, you prick."

"So you think you can have that land, that sweet little slice of pie and eat her too?"

"You bet your ass I'm taking both and nothing, I mean *nothing,* is going to get in my way," Tucker growled in a murderous voice.

"Like the Newsom deal?"

Tucker was seething mad that Darren would even bring up the dreaded Newsom deal. It was still a point of contention, and the memories of losing out on that deal were still fresh and raw.

"How many people are you going to step on to get what you want, McG? How many people have to suffer because of your greediness?"

"Fuck you, Schumacher. You won that deal, so what are you bitching about?"

"Everything's a contest with you, isn't it? I only *won* that deal because I was honest and the Newsom's were sick of your bullshit. It's amazing how a little honesty goes a long way. You may want to try it sometime. Do you even know how to be truthful anymore? I remember a time when you did. You and me. Remember? We were going to take on the world, *honestly.*"

Tucker quickly hung up the phone. He didn't want to be reminded of his past and how things had ended badly with Darren. They were once best friends and had even gone to college together. He missed Darren and their closeness. He even missed Darren's cheesy, infectious sense of humor, and yes, his sincerity, too. Tucker was also known for his honesty, but it was his brutal honesty that set him apart, and it wasn't necessarily a good trait and he knew that.

Trying to figure out how to make up for Darren's big mouth, he decided it was best to let Lilliana cool down before he approached her again.

*

During their time-out, Tucker was hit with inspiration and instructed his assistant to call any and all local and outlying animal shelters. Lilliana and how much they seemed to have in common kept seeping into his thoughts, day and night. He was determined to keep their venture *business only* but the corn-shucking, brown-haired beauty had somehow managed to get under his skin.

By day four of not having any contact with Lilliana, he was itching to get in contact with her. He even felt the creepy urge to drive past her house to see if he could spy a look at her. He talked himself out of it, knowing full well it was a disgusting thing to do let alone think about, but no woman had ever caused such chaos with his emotions and impeded his ability to think logically.

At the end of a long painful week, he finally heard back from several shelters and mustered up the courage to venture out to her place again for a little butt-kissing session.

Before he even got out of his car, Lilliana was on him, pointing toward the road. "Off my property!"

"Just hear me out."

"No, thanks. I was warned twice about you from two people who seem genuinely sincere, and I'm not waiting for lightening to strike me down in order for me to open my eyes about you."

Two? Tucker wondered who the first was when he remembered Lilliana's overly long conversation with his secretary. No doubt it was her after the way she had rebuffed his advances before he knew she, too, was married.

"Just let me show you I'm not like the rest, Lilly," he responded calmly. "I want to take you somewhere."

"Yeah, I'm sure, right to bed so you can royally fuck me," she said with glossy, enraged eyes.

Tucker couldn't help but smile at her sharp come back. She was more temperamental than any woman he had ever encountered, and he had come across far too many females to even recollect.

"There's an animal shelter in the next county over that's actively looking to lease land for their outreach animal program. I thought maybe you could go and speak with them."

CHAPTER 8

Lilliana wanted to believe Tucker, but there was something nagging at her about him, and the man who had approached her in the restaurant put a seed of doubt in her mind about Tucker's motives. She had the same troublesome feeling about her ex, but instead of listening to her gut instincts, she ended up with an STD, a divorce, and a small-town scandal. She promised herself she would be more vigilant this time, despite Tucker's smooth ways and warm caress, and in spite of the fact that his smile had been invading her dreams since she last saw him.

She thought she had seen the last of him the week previously and that he wouldn't show his face again, but she knew that was wishful thinking. If everyone was to be believed, he would stop at nothing until he had gotten her to sign over the deed to her land. She hated to admit it, but seeing him again was almost a relief. Even if he was smug as hell and untrustworthy, he was pretty to look at and she knew he was attracted to her, so there was at least that.

Feeling embarrassed at her outburst, she wiped her eyes of the angry tears that threatened to burst forth and avoided Tucker's gaze.

"Let me lock up the house," she replied, finally giving in.

It wouldn't hurt to at least speak with the animal shelter and she swore to herself that she would keep her guard up and her eyes open at all times around him.

After grabbing a light jacket and locking the house, she settled into the passenger seat when Tucker proceeded to buckle her seatbelt like he had before. It was a peculiar gesture that no man had ever done before, let alone twice in a weeks' time. Still leaning over her, his large thumb swept away a stray tear in the corner of her eye as he watched her mouth keenly.

"I'm a big girl, I can buckle myself in," she told him, even though she relished the close physical contact from the man she neither trusted nor cared for.

Ella Dominguez

"I have no doubt that you can, but I enjoy doing this and knowing that I'm the reason that you're safe."

She found his response self-gratifying yet strangely endearing. He paused near her lips and leaned in as if he was going to kiss her when she put a stop to it.

"You're taking a lot for granted. I haven't even decided whether or not I like you."

His eyes darted from her eyes to her mouth and back. "Oh, you like me," he responded a little too confidently.

His self-confidence both annoyed and turned her on, something she was having a difficult time coming to terms with. "Drive, McGrath," she stated coldly, turning her face to the window.

He sighed and revved the engine loudly. "I don't know what you think you're accomplishing by being so damned defiant. I've already told you that you've got me all wrong. However, if you insist on making me wait, I'll respect that."

Lilliana almost wavered, but something in Tucker's voice alluded to deception and she wasn't about to let it go. "Then prove me wrong," she stated clipped, glaring at him through narrowed eyes.

His eyebrows raised and he pushed his chest out as if accepting her challenge. "I will and then you *will* be on your knees for me," he said softly through gritted teeth.

She had the sudden urge to slap him upside his narcissistic head, and she just about did until he began chuckling. It started out lightly but quickly built into a full rolling boil.

She was beside herself and couldn't help hide the irritation in her voice. "What the hell is funny?"

"You! Holy, fucking, Devil Woman, if looks could kill I'd be dead and castrated on the spot. Damn, Lilly, you really need to keep that shit in check before you hurt someone. Or yourself!"

She wasn't sure exactly why her irritation was so entertaining but his statement reminded her of her mother, Kate. As a child and teenager, Lilliana had been grounded on more than one occasion for the harsh looks she had thrown her mother's way.

"You're lucky I'm a somewhat reasonable woman."

"I think you're overestimating yourself, Pet. And you're lucky I'm feeling generous and *somewhat* patient or else I'd simply take what I want," he countered.

Had Tucker just threatened her *again*? His countenance remained stoic and she didn't know how to interpret his remark. "And what exactly is it that you want, McGrath?"

Readying herself for all hell to break loose, she sat forward in her seat and turned to face him. His eyes stayed on the road, but the corners of his mouth rose in a sarcastic grin.

"I've already made it very clear what I want. I don't particularly enjoy repeating myself so you'll just have to jog your memory to last week's encounter."

She found his statement so ridiculous, she began to mumble under her breath. "Take what you want," she snorted along with a few expletives. "I'll give you a foot up your..."

"Zip it, Lilly. Seriously, I'm doing my best here to remain gentlemanly but you're treading on thin ice."

She couldn't believe his gall. "Unbelievable. *Seriously*, I don't think you know the first thing about being gentlemanly. I'm not sure what kind of women you're used to dealing with, but you don't get to *take what you want* with me. You're haughtiness goes beyond anything I've ever experienced and right at this moment, I could care less about discussing my land with an animal shelter. Just turn this stupid, over-priced car around and drive me home!"

***

Tucker slammed on the breaks, locking up both their seat-belts as he skidded onto the gravel shoulder. To say Lilliana was treading on thin ice was the understatement of the century. She had broken through that ice and they were both about to drown in the frigid cold water. He flung his car door open, jumped out, and threw his hands in the air as he spewed out a long line of obscenities that reached the celestial heavens.

Ella Dominguez

He wanted this deal more than he had ever wanted anything else, but he wasn't sure he could withstand the fork-tongued brunette any longer. Damn her for being so unmanageable, inflexible and fucking beguiling. He hated that he was so attracted to her and that they had so much in common. More to the point, he despised that she had gotten under his skin and peeled away the layers of his cool exterior.

When he was finally able to calm his raging temper, he leaned over the hood of his car, his hands resting on the hot metal and his head downcast. He peered up through his long bangs to see Lilliana watching him wide-eyed and motionless. He stood, turned and sat on the hood, trying to catch his breath. He hadn't lost his temper like that since before he left his parent's home. He had always prided himself in his cold detachment and aloofness, but this woman... What the fuck was she doing to him? Hearing the passenger door close softly, he turned to see Lilliana moving toward him warily.

"Tucker, I'm sorry. I know I can be... Difficult. I get my temper from father. Or so my mother said. I wouldn't really know. Anyway..." She shook her head as if getting side-tracked.

He watched her inquisitively. She could be quite a charming little thing when she was repentant. She was so charming, in fact, the image of her unblemished, bee-stung lips trying to form the words to make him less irate made the thought of burying himself in her pop into his mind again.

She kept her eyes to the ground as she stuttered out something incoherent and kicked at the rocks underneath her feet, bringing up dust. She reached up to tuck a strand of hair behind her ear when he reached out and pulled her to him.

"Difficult isn't the word I would use to describe you," he whispered. "Cheeky, insolent and imprudent are far more accurate a description."

When she opened her mouth to speak, he rapidly forced his mouth onto hers, holding her firmly by her waist with one hand and the back of her neck with the other. His unyielding grasp on her didn't allow her to resist, even though she tried. She placed her palms on his chest and tried to push him away but he forbade it. He was going to show her that, *yes*, he could take what he wanted and right now, what he wanted more than anything was to shut her the hell up.

***

When Lilliana realized her efforts were futile, her body sagged in his arms. She accepted Tucker's tongue in her mouth. God, it felt just as good as it did the first time they kissed. She couldn't deny that she wanted this man in all his conceitedness and untrustworthiness. She wanted desperately to believe that he was different and that everyone else was lying about him. Her voice of reason was screaming at her to run the other way, but his controlling hands felt so amazing on her and his mouth... That sweet, soft, delicious mouth of his... Christ, how she wanted it roaming over every inch of her body. Anyway, how could she resist him when he wouldn't allow it? At that moment, she was his captive in every sense of the word and she basked in it.

Tucker's mouth ghosted her jaw line where he licked tenderly, then glided over to her ear where he delivered another soothing lick. She rested her hands on his thighs and tilted her head to the side, permitting him access to her neck.

"That's it, Pet, give in. It'll make things so much easier," he murmured as he bit gently into her flesh, sucking ferociously and bringing the blood to the surface of her delicate tissue.

Reality slapped her in the face and she reluctantly backed away when she felt his grip loosen. "Easier for whom?" She asked, cringing at the desperation and hurt in her voice.

His lips parted and his eyebrows furrowed, but only a long sigh could be heard.

CHAPTER 9

Easier for Tucker, of course. Lilliana's poignant, terrified eyes spoke volumes, and as she waited for his answer, he contemplated backing out of his whole nasty plan. *Early retirement*, he kept repeating over and over in his head. Despite the nagging feeling of guilt beginning to overwhelm him, he slid off the car and drew near her, telling himself: *move forward, break her spirit, and win at all costs.* Without answering her question, he smiled down at her, took her hand and led her back to the car.

He got what he wanted and the rest of the drive was silent. However, now faced with the quietness, he longed for Lilliana's vicious tongue.

"So you think my car is stupid and overpriced?" He prodded her, but she simply shrugged as she continued to look out the passenger-side window. "And what was that about my arrogance?" He poked, still attempting to elicit a response from her. Still, she remained hushed. It was driving him crazy on a level he had never experienced. He just wanted her to give him that fiery attitude back, no matter how infuriating it could be. "Where was it you were planning on putting your foot?" He tried one last time.

She finally looked at him with confusion flitting across her face. "Are you trying to pick a fight with me?"

"No, Pet, I just wanted to hear your voice," He spoke honestly for a change.

Unsettled, she asked, "What is it that you want to hear from me?"

"Tell me about your father," The request came out before he could stop himself. He wasn't even sure why he asked. He didn't really want to know *or did he?*

"I thought you knew everything about me," sarcasm laced her words.

"I was just trying to make pleasant conversation."

"A discussion about a man I never knew would be anything but. Next question?" Crossing her arms over her chest, Lilliana sat glaring frigidly at him after her clipped response.

She was one tough little lady to break. At a loss for words, he sat staring forward, unable to think of anything else to ask. He had obviously hit a sore spot with her and decided it best to back off considering how tenuous their situation was. Without thinking, he started babbling on and on about his childhood. He didn't even know why he was doing it, other than to fill the awkward silence and to cut through the tension.

"I grew up on a farm and used to help my father," he started out. "We never had a lot of money and their finances were always fragile. I remember thinking: *when I grow up, I'm going to make enough money so that I never have to worry about where my next meal is coming from and I can support my family.* That's part and parcel why I got into real estate. When my parents lost their land to the greedy sons-of-bitches who whored it out to build an apartment complex on it, I knew instantly where my fortune was to be made."

"So you decided to take advantage of people's unfortunate circumstances and whore out their land yourself? That seems a little backwards. I'd think you'd want to help those who were in your parent's situation," she came back with.

He swallowed hard. He had said too much in his quest to kill the silence. *And what the hell did she know anyway?* "I just meant that I knew there was a market for buying up land."

Her eyes bore through him. "I know what you meant, but it still seems backwards."

His irritation bubbled to the surface. "Maybe to someone who knows nothing about realty it does, but I can tell you no one ever made a red cent helping the *unfortunate*," he snapped back.

"It's only money, Tucker," she voice was steady and uncompromising. "And some things in life are more important than the size of your wallet. I find it hard to believe that your parents didn't instill that value in you, or are you just ignoring your upbringing?" He could feel her glaring at him. "And just because I'm not *into* realty doesn't mean I don't understand the fundamentals of business and buying and selling for profit. I'm not some dim-witted, red-neck like you'd believe me to be. I have a formal education, too, or have you forgotten? My expertise just happens to be teeth, not land values and foreclosures."

Tucker felt chastened by Lilliana's reproof. *Yes*, his parents had instilled that value into him. And, *yes*, he willingly chose to ignore it. He bristled under her unnerving stare but refused to make eye contact. If there was anything he hated, it was his mistakes being blatantly pointed out to him.

***

Lilliana wondered if battle of the words and verbal sparring would always be commonplace with Tucker. Would the threat of an all out war be just over the horizon when dealing with him? She sighed thinking about the man he was the week before; all alpha dominant and sexy as hell. He was so beautiful to look at, but he was without a doubt, pure sex appeal and charm deceptively wrapped up in one big, muscular, pompous package.

After a long silent half hour, they arrived at a moderate sized animal hospital and shelter where he led her in and made introductions. She was impressed at how well-spoken and well-behaved he could be under the right circumstances.

The woman in charge, Aubrey, began chatting her up about the shelter and their plight to find land. She was older and looked to be about Margo's age. She even had the same grey-hair as her Auntie. She was touched at the joy in the woman's words about the work that she obviously loved. It was infectious, not only for her but quite noticeably for Tucker as well as evidenced by the grin on his face.

Lilliana noted that Aubrey glanced at her neck several times. She looked at Tucker questioningly only to see a boyish, crooked grin spread across his face. She could only imagine what other kind of *calling card* he had left behind.

Heading out back of the large building that housed all sorts of animals from domestic to exotic, she was pleased to see a small stable with horses. Though she had never owned one herself, she had grown up around them. She remembered the days when Margo had several of them on her land, and riding them endlessly during her summer vacations in Connecticut. God, how she missed those carefree days.

Without hesitation and showing no fear of the large beasts, Tucker moved up next to one and pet its long nose as if it was commonplace. As comfortable as he appeared, it made her wonder if he, too, had grown up around them. He continued to stroke the horse and run his fingers through its mane as he conversed excitedly to Aubrey. Lilliana became fixated with his casual sensual movements. He really was a specimen to behold. She wouldn't mind if was petting her as well and raking his fingers through her hair.

Tucker glanced over at her and did a double-take when he caught her longingly gazing at him. Playfully, he winked and bit his lower lip, sending her hormones into overdrive. *He was such a player.*

Aubrey obviously felt the sparks pass between the two because she suggested they take a few of the horses for a short stroll and then made a hasty retreat inside the building, leaving them alone.

"Did you hear that, Lilly? They're looking for land to house these beautiful creatures."

She had been so engrossed in her naughty thoughts she hadn't heard a word Tucker and Aubrey were saying.

"Mmm-hmm," she answered, gliding her hand over the steed's back.

"Do you like horses? You seem at ease with them," he asked.

"Yes, I grew up around them. How about you?"

"Me too. Before my parent's lost their farm, we had several work horses. I loved riding them when I was young," he stated pensively as if thinking back.

"It's hard to believe that Tucker McGrath, real estate mogul and playboy extraordinaire is one and the same to the Tucker McGrath who grew up helping his father on a farm," she declared as she walked around and poked him in the ribs.

His eyes reflected astonishment. "Is it really that hard to believe?"

Batting her eyelashes animatedly, she quipped, "Maybe to the untrained eye, but being as I'm a dim-witted, red-neck, I can sniff out my own kind."

"I never suggested you were dim-witted. The red-neck part, yes, but never dim-witted," he joked, tugging her cropped hair. "And are you suggesting I'm dim-witted?"

"I never suggest," she grinned.

"You don't know when to stop talking, do you?" A sigh and a shake of his head made Lilliana smile.

"Why don't you make me?" She dared him, hoping he would shut her up the way he had twice before: with his tongue firmly planted in her mouth.

One of his eyebrows went up and the corners of his lips curled upwards, "How about a ride?"

"Excuse me?" She perked up as her mind began spinning in all kinds of salacious directions.

"Horseback, Lilly. Let's not get ahead of ourselves," he belted out a laugh. "You're not even sure you like me, remember?" He commented sarcastically, obviously reading her thoughts. "I'm haughty, arrogant, and…"

"Dim-witted," she finished his sentence.

He simply nodded without answering and gave her a smile that sent her pulses racing. The undeniable gleam in his eyes made her wonder if he was somehow keeping a tally of all the times she was being unruly.

He reached a hand out to her. "Do you need a lift?"

"No, I've got this."Without delay, she gripped the reins of the saddle, put her foot in the stirrup and pulled herself onto the back of the mare in one fluid motion. She was proud of her own poise considering she hadn't ridden in over ten years. She looked over to Tucker, hopeful he was impressed with her gracefulness as well. His slack-jaw and wide, lusty eyes gave away his awe of her, and she smiled conceitedly. "Do *you* need a lift?"

He chuckled and shook his head. "No, I've got this, too."

Tucker moved with such agility and velocity, she had to focus on not drooling a puddle of saliva onto the poor beast's back. His biceps bulged through his shirt when he pulled himself up and swung his leg over the horse. She had expected him to saddle another mare, but instead he was now sitting directly behind her. Their bodies were so close that they seemed to meld into one. Taking the reins from her hands, he gently tugged on them, making the stallion whinny and jerk its head back.

"Whoa, there, girl," he cooed soothingly.

His authoritative voice, the feel of his solid body pressed against her, and the control he radiated was so intense, she feared she would burst into flames from internal combustion.

He ghosted his lips next to her ear. "Are you ready, Pet?"

Before she could answer, he yanked on the leather straps and they were moving in a slow trot, their bodies bouncing in unison. She began to pant as the horse's trot broke out into a brisk jog. He circled the horse around the stable and then out into a small open field. With every click of his tongue as he guided the stallion and tugged on the reins, she became wetter and more excited. She wondered if he had any idea how damned tempting he was at that moment.

"How does it feel to have so much power between your legs, Lilly, and to be sitting atop a creature that has so much strength?"

Every word spoken from Tucker's mouth was deliberately suggestive and oozed sexual overtones. It utterly exasperating.

"It feels like home."

***

Lilliana just couldn't hold back from giving back a bit of sarcasm any chance she got. For that reason, and a few others, she was proving to be the most frustrating, vexing yet evocative undertaking Tucker had ever been burdened with. He had originally wanted to break her spirit, however, it was her spirit that was proving to be her most appealing quality.

In all his sexual years and the many women he had been with, none of them had proven to be such a challenge. Most women had just given themselves over without a second thought and the majority of them far too quickly. He had taken pleasure in their easiness and lack of reticence at the time, but he was enjoying chasing Lilliana even more. With their bodies in such close proximity, the wind blowing over them as they rode around the field, and the beautiful sunset just starting to peak - he forgot his goal.

He slowed the horse to a stop and let go of one of the reins so he could wrap an arm around her waist. Cuddling into her neck, he ground himself up against her ass and thrust upwards, making her gasp out.

"Are you really dry humping me on the back of this horse?"

Leave it to Lilly and her ever-running mouth to ruin the moment. "What? You've never heard of horseback humping?"

She giggled, "No, but I can't imagine it's any fun for the horse. The poor thing has already had a rough life; we don't need to traumatize it anymore. We can save that sort of thing for later."

Later? He was actually shocked. "So now you like me?" He thrust upward again.

"*Let's not get ahead of ourselves*, we're only talking about humping," she mocked and rolled her eyes.

A wave of frustration crashed against him. He could deal with her quick-wit, but he was growing intolerant of her taunting. When she pushed her rear-end back against his rapidly growing hardness, he seized the moment.

With the speed of an oncoming derailed freight train and before she could react, he dropped the reins and snuck the hand that was around her waist, under her shirt. He tugged her bra down below her breast and clutched it firmly. With his other hand, he reached over her arm and chest, effectively pinning it down, and wrapped his long fingers gently around her throat, guiding her head back onto his chest so he could see her face.

"Don't mock me, Lilly," he whispered into her ear, caressing her neck tenderly with his fingertips.

"Tucker," she whimpered, clearly surprised by his quick reaction. She tried to buck away from him, but the precarious and vulnerable position he had her in, left her helpless.

"I'm all for fun and games and witty banter when it's appropriate, but *do not* mock me. And you sure as hell better *never* tease me if you don't plan on following through with your actions. Am. I. Clear?" His voice, though commanding and urgent, was a low, sensual sound.

When she hesitated with her response, he clutched her breast tighter, making her mewl.

"This is the part where you say, *yes, Sir*," he exhaled and a deep, guttural growl escaped his throat.

"Yes, Sir," She panted out in short breaths, with her eyes tightly shut.

The hard-on in his pants was raging and painful. When he caught scent of Lilliana's arousal, he growled deeply again, but this time it was the primeval rumble of a ravenous wolf aching to be satiated by the only thing that could slake his thirst – *Lilly.*

Her body trembled beneath his steady grip, her fear and excitement pulsating through his core. He had truly never wanted to plunge into the depths of a woman more than he had right at that moment. He wanted nothing else but to fill her mouth with his cock and to fuck the mockery right out of it and make her surrender completely to him. *And he would.*

As he held onto the dark-haired tart hell-bent on making his life difficult, and whom he could physically overpower if he chose, he no longer gave a shit about the one-hundred and twelve acres and his early retirement. He wanted *Lilliana;* her trust, her heart, her body and mind, and most of all – *her absolute submission.* He didn't even know why. He knew what love felt like and that wasn't the emotion coursing through his veins. It wasn't even just lust anymore. It was something else - something he had never felt before, something primal and *necessary.*

There was a craving within him to take care of this woman who had been hurt and lied to; a yearning to make her feel whole again; to get to know her completely and to get past her insolence. *And to learn her perversions.* He vowed to himself to teach Lilliana the ecstasy that could be had by allowing him to dominate her. He wanted to rebuild her spirit, to make her his own and to give her the authority she said she longed for. He didn't know if it would be possible to do all those things with the walls she had built up, along with his own defenses, but he was sure as hell going to try.

As for the land, he would deal with that issue later; *after* he had made Lilliana his pet.

CHAPTER 10

Easing his grip around her throat and bosom, Tucker rolled Lilliana's stiffened nipple through his fingers and skimmed his tongue over the curve of her exposed neck. Her body reacted instinctively. She moaned and ground her ass back into him, but then immediately tried to pull away when she realized what she had done. She thrashed momentarily and elbowed his ribs harshly, cursing him under her breath. But he held his ground. She was seething mad at herself for allowing him to handle her the way he did and pissed beyond comprehension at her arousal of his actions.

There was an edge to his voice as he purred and tugged her back to him. "Stop resisting me, Lilly. This thing between us is inescapable."

Yes, it seemed this thing, or *non-thing*, between them was unavoidable and his statement spoke to some hidden part of her soul. No longer able to deny him, she allowed him to cradle her against his chest. She should've jumped ship at that point and she damned well knew it, but no one had ever taken control of her the way Tucker just had and it felt good. *Too good*. More than that, it felt *right*. His touch was powerful and overwhelming; passionate and devastating.

When his hot hands loosened their hold, coldness settled on her skin where his infernal hands had been, and she felt naked and alone without his contact. He took the reins once more and she leaned back into him for his warmth, half expecting rejection.

Instead, he cooed in her ear, his breath searing and his voice unwavering, "My Pet."

God, yes, she wanted to be his pet; the consequences be damned to hell and her own fears and everyone else's warnings be damned for eternity. She was in control of her own destiny. Come what may, right or wrong, good or bad - she was no longer going to deny herself the pleasure of Tucker McGrath.

Back at the stable, he dismounted first and then lifted her off the mare. When her feet hit the ground she felt weightless and her legs wobbly and unsure.

He touched her chin tenderly and lifted her face to his. "I'm strict and often times unyielding, but rarely harsh. But you..." He trailed off, his eyes darkening to near black as they scanned her face. "You make me feel like an untamed, wild creature; feral, rabid and unpredictable."

"You don't ever have to explain yourself to me, Tucker," she tried to soothe the ache in his eyes.

His eyes dilated widely and his mouth twitched into his signature devilish, country-boy grin. "I want you, Lilliana Norris; not your land. Just. *You.*"

His eyes were burning so brightly, she had no choice but to believe him. Her mouth was unbearably dry, but she managed to squeak out what she had been denying for days, maybe even weeks. "I want you, too."

The next few moments were a blur for Lilliana. She was still on an emotional high from her horseback encounter with Tucker. She could still feel his possessive fingers seductively wrapped around her neck, and her lower belly throbbed with an intensity like she had never felt before. They walked in silence back to his car where he helped her in. She waited before buckling herself, wanting him to do it for her. Without hesitation, he reached over and secured her.

"I like that you do this," she admitted.

"I'm glad you like it. But I should warn you: I have an affinity for belts," he lifted a mysterious eyebrow. Without further elaborating, he continued, "Do you work tomorrow?"

The implication sent waves of excitement through her and there was no way she was letting a statement like that go without further explanation. "What else do you have an affinity for?"

"A great many things. Beautiful, intelligent women; cooking, bondage, traveling..."

The way he threw out the word *bondage* nonchalantly piqued her curiosity. What kind of kink was this man into? And was he purposely trying to be vague? *Of course he was – he was, after all, Tucker McGrath: Man of Mystery.*

"When you say…"

He summarily cut her off, "All in good time. Now answer my question, please."

"Yes, I have several appointments," she answered, flustered and disappointed she couldn't spend the following day with him and learn more of his likenesses. She inwardly shook her head at herself. Her feelings for this man had nothing to do with reason or logic, and everything to do with raw sexual attraction.

"What about tonight? I'm free the rest of the night," she suggested.

"Lilly of the Valley, one-hundred and twelve acres Lilly," his mouth curved with affection, "I have business to attend to this evening. After your appointments tomorrow I'll be waiting for you. Make whatever arrangements are necessary, but I want you the rest of tomorrow night and the weekend. Make it happen."

"Tucker the Feral and Rabid, Tucker the Irresistible… I have responsibilities."

"I want this to work with you, so I'm going to make my rules very simple: I command. You obey. *Always*. Am I clear?" He stated more firmly and without a hint of ambiguity.

Entranced by his compelling intensity, she whispered, "Crystal."

With Tucker still hovering over her, she reached her hand up between them and touched the mouth that she knew was going to be her downfall. He took her finger into his mouth and bit the tip of it, an evil grin splaying over his faultless, rugged and scruffy face.

"I can't wait to see you on your knees and show you that I *do* comprehend your desires," he said softly.

His nearness made her senses spin. She licked her lips, delighting in the fact that he recalled their first conversation.

He continued to grin at her before finally putting the car into drive.

The journey back to her house was quick, but he kept his hand on her upper thigh the entire ride, squeezing it occasionally.

When he parked in front of her door to drop her off, she started to get out without saying a word, but he latched on to her wrist. "Lilly," he said seductively, "I also have an affinity for fine asses and you, my Pet, have one of the best I've ever had the pleasure of sinking my teeth into." He paused and his eyes sparkled fiercely. "Oh, and licking pussy. I love that, too. *Immensely.* Have a great night and I'll be waiting for you after work tomorrow. Ciao, Pet."

With a wink and a wave, he sped away, leaving her standing immobile and watching as his car flew down her long driveway. *Licking pussy...* Mmm. Yes. But, *one of* the best asses? How many asses had he bitten? Suddenly his beautiful bicuspids and eyeteeth took on the mental image of a wolf's fangs. What the hell was she getting herself into? Damn that man. He really did know just how to get her juices flowing.

***

Tucker drove away with his eyes on the rear-view mirror. He was finally going to have Lilly, but he still had to wait another fucking day. First, he had business to take care of in the form of dealing with all the realtors vying for a shot at her land. He would just have to put the word out that it was no longer available as a *deal* was in the works and he would be buying it in the near future. It was only a mild lie at best and it would get the *vultures,* as Lilliana called them, to back off for now and allow him time to concentrate on her. He figured once he had her where he really wanted her, under his complete control, he could then convince her to sell the land to him or at least advise her on what to do with it.

When he had spoken his simple rules, she seemed very amenable. It had opened the door for things to come and he hoped there was a little less fight in her than before.

91

He spent several hours at home in his office sending out multiple emails and then finally making several calls about her land. Everything seemed to be finally falling into place and he couldn't help but feel pleased with himself.

After showering, he lay in bed thinking about all the events since meeting Lilliana.

Early retirement seeped into his thoughts again, but it was soon overcast by his memory of how she felt in his arms and under his control. *Later,* he reminded himself. He just wanted to focus on her for now; not work.

For so long, he had yearned for a woman whom he could command completely, but his search had yielded nothing. All of the women he had been with were either lacking in skill or enthusiasm. Or worse yet, both. It was frustrating how they were all willing to spread their legs for him, but too timid to consider the kind of kink he had suggested. Whenever he mentioned any form of *punishment,* he either got a look of horror or disgust. He hoped Lilliana wouldn't turn out to be another unsuccessful endeavor. It seemed to him that because they had so much in common, surely they would be a better fit for each other.

He thought he had her figured out. He had believed that all along, yet, at every turn, she was proving him wrong. But the way she responded to him on the elevator; the way her eyes watched his mouth and the way her body responded to his touch on the horse... He could sense how much she had been turned on; he could feel how much she wanted him. Was he wrong? Was he deluding himself? Jesus, he hoped not.

Wanting to reassure himself that he wasn't making everything up in his head, he picked up his phone. It was late, but he was hopeful that Lilliana was still awake.

McG: You awake?

Lilliana: I am now. Don't u ever rest?

McG: No rest for the wicked, they say.

Lilliana: Is that a warning?

McG: More like an assertion.

Lilliana: Go to sleep.

McG: Too much on my mind.

Lilliana: Should I ask?

McG: I wish you would. ;)

Lilliana: Are u trying to sext with me? Ewww.

McG: Ewww? WTF? LOl

Lilliana: In shock over here. Tucker McGruth, real estate mogul and playboy extraordinaire just LOL'd after attempting to sext with me. What next? Zombies? Aliens? The apocalypse?

McG: More like ACOCKALYPSE because my dick is so powerful it can end worlds.

*Lilliana: *rolling eyes**

McG: And stop with the playboy title. I simply enjoy the company of beautiful women and (.)(.) and (_Y_) That's tits & ass to the untrained eye. :D

Lilliana: Your knowledge of texting symbols and lingo frightens me. I'm seeing u in a whole new light.

McG: I'm a deep and multifaceted individual with many layers that you can't begin to comprehend :P

Lilliana: Funny. By deep do u mean shallow and by multifaceted do u mean daft?

McG: Don't make me go all rabid on you again. BRB gotta piss.

Lilliana: TMI. And I rather liked rabid Tucker. ;)

Tucker laid his phone down while he did his business. From the bedroom, he could hear his phone chirping at a constant rate. He never was fond of being rushed. At *anything.* When he finally climbed back into bed, there were numerous responses that made him genuinely *laugh out loud.*

Lilliana: U ok over there? How long does a piss take?

Lilliana: Hellooo? Should I call out the paramedics?

Lilliana: Did u drown in a sea of yellow?

McG: Fucking A you're impatient. No, I didn't drown. Can't a man urinate without being harassed?

Lilliana: ME impatient?! You= black pot. Me=black kettle. Get the picture?

McG: Funny. So you like me rabid, huh? Good because you bring out the animal in me.

McG: Q: What are you afraid of?

Lilliana: A: Hairy spiders and massively furry chests that resemble ewoks. Ewww. Please tell me you don't have one.

McG: EWOKS? As in Star Wars? Ewww. And no, my chest is rock hard and smoooooth as butter baby.

Lilliana: Again *rolling eyes*. And don't u judge me! Those movies ROCK!! What r u afraid of?

McG: Nothing. I'm bad ass and fearless. :D

Lilliana: You're probably afraid of snakes and scream and cry like a little girl when u see one. Am I right or am I right?

McG: Not even close. I kill those MF'ers in my sleep. I grew up on a farm, remember? You'll be the one screaming and crying with excitement when you see my snake ;)

Lilliana: Ugh. I'm not biting. G'night.

McG: Boo. You suck. And anyway, I'm not into biting. MUCH.

Lilliana: Liar. My ass and neck are proof. And YES, I suck gooood.

McG: Tease. A: Bushy prehistoric looking veggies frighten me.

Lilliana: Veggies? WTH are we talking about here?

McG: Fucking auto correct. VAGINAS! Bushy vaginas put the fear of God in me. Seriously, if you've got one, groom that shit unless you want to see a grown alpha male curl into the fetal position and cry. It won't be pretty. Just sayin'

Lilliana: BWAHAHA! Where did bad ass, fearless, rabid Tucker go? Who are you and what have you done with him?

McG: Who's judging now? FACT: A monstrously shaggy bobo will bring even the most vicious, sadistic dominant to his knees.

Lilliana: I get it. No ewok pussy. And did you say BOBO? What are you 5 years old? Wait... SADIST?

McG: Don't spaz. I'm no sadist. Though, I do enjoy paddling for disobedience. I've been keeping u tally, and you, my Pet, have one coming after your numerous verbal offenses. Correction: SEVERAL coming.

He smiled thinking about doing exactly that. His phone sat silent and he wondered if he had completely freaked Lilliana out. He shifted uncomfortably in bed when no reply came for several long minutes. Perhaps this was going to be another failed attempt at finding someone would obey his every command and take his discipline after all.

McG: Does your silence mean no to paddling?

His phone remained quiet still, prompting him to dial her number. On the second ring she picked up.

"Talk to me."

"Sorry. I know you warned me before about doing that sort of thing," her soft voice was edged with nervousness, "but I didn't realize you were serious. It's just a shock reading it."

"You didn't answer my question."

The sound of her moistening her lips could be heard through the phone. "I've never been spanked, but that doesn't mean I'm unenthusiastic or opposed to the idea of it."

A warmth settled deep in his stomach and his blood buzzed. So she was up for a spanking. What other things could he experiment with her? "A spanking doesn't always mean punishment, so keep that in mind. It can also be for pleasure. Do you know anything about bondage and discipline, Lilly?" He threw out the gauntlet.

"Are you talking about BDSM?" Her question surprised him.

"Yes and no."

Curiosity brimmed in her voice. "Are you into that sort of thing?"

"Yes and no. I'm not into the S&M aspect; just bondage and discipline."

"Were your wives into that, too?"

He laughed. "Not really. I didn't even realize I was *into it* until my second marriage. When I proposed the idea to her she played along, but wasn't really fully invested in the seriousness of it to the degree that I was. I have yet to find a woman who's completely compatible with me on that level."

Her voice was barely a whisper. "Seriousness?"

"The lifestyle isn't a hobby. At least not for me, though I'm sure for some people it is. Look, maybe you should read up on it tomorrow and we can discuss it later. It's late and I don't want to scare you away. Hell, I just got you."

Her confidence was back in a flash. "You don't have me yet, Tucker."

He could just imagine her hazel eyes narrowed in that sexy, disobedient way, and the look of rebellion on her adorable face. "Soon enough, I will. I have my sights set on you, Lilly, and I always get what I want. *Always.*"

"Always? Interesting," she seemed to be talking to herself. "I'm tired. It's been a helluva crazy, horny day. Good night, McG," she yawned.

"Good night, Pet. I'll be dreaming of you on your knees."

After ending their phone call, he lay in bed for several minutes with an idiotic grin plastered on his face. Something about Lilliana brought out both his animalistic nature and his playful side. He had truly never laughed the way he did with her or let his guard down to such a degree. He had also never lost his cool around any other woman the way he had with her. It was worrisome to him, yet, it was a strangely freeing feeling to be able to be himself and not hold back.

Thinking about how he had initially lied to her, he inwardly chastised himself. *What if she ever found out? Could she forgive him?* He doubted it. He would just have to make sure that she only knew of his intentions post horseback humping.

Horseback humping. He chuckled at that memory as well.

He didn't know where this thing with Lilliana would take him or how long it would last, but he was glad to have found another playmate to keep him busy in the interim, and possibly even one who would actually be up for his brand of kinkiness.

It was just after midnight when he made a note in his phone planner to call his jeweler for the usual order before deciding to finally call it a night. Docking his phone, he rolled over.

Several minutes later his phone chirped again.

Lilliana: Almost forgot — what's this about my ass being ONE of the best? How many asses have you bitten, you freak?

He laughed out loud yet again. When he realized she was lying in bed thinking about him and their encounter at the animal shelter, his cock hardened.

McG: Countless asses, but yours is in a league of its own.

Lilliana: So what's a girl gotta do to have THE BEST ass in your book?

McG: Throw some glitter on that plumpness and shake that money maker!

Lilliana: Sorry I asked. I earn my money the old fashioned way — by working. :P

McG: FYI prostitution is the oldest known profession.

Lilliana: Ewww.

McG: Ciao, Pet. ;)

CHAPTER 11

Lilliana slept soundly and woke energized, yet uneasy. She still had serious reservations about Tucker, however, her arousal and curiosity of him outweighed any apprehension she was feeling. The yearning to feel his strong, rough hands on her body again and to get lost in his deep brown eyes was a potent distraction to her inner warnings. The longing to dive into his soul, search its depths and learn his secrets, fears and desires was overpowering. His casualness the previous night was nothing less than enthralling and it was nice to see another side to him other than his usual arrogance.

Bondage and discipline. The idea excited her, but to what end? She had no idea what that sort of *lifestyle* entailed and whether or not she would even like it. She remembered what Tucker had suggested and decided that during her lunch break, she would do a bit of research into the subject.

Arriving to work early, she was once again met by Dana's squeals. "A hickie from Kenickie!"

"Buggers, Dana, be quiet," she scolded. "I tried to cover it. Can you really see it?"

"Only close up," she rolled her eyes. "It's a good thing your patients don't sit right next to you under a bright light or anything," she laughed sarcastically. "So are you two an item or what? Have you seen him naked? Does he have amazing pecks?"

"No, no, and I don't know yet. Now, go work or something," she gently pushed Dana out of the way.

Lilliana's morning was tedious. All she wanted was to see Tucker's roguish eyes gleaming with lust and the glow of his smile again. During a short break between patients her phone beeped. She smiled like a groupie fan girling when she saw who the message was from.

McG: I find myself feeling jealous that you're peering into the mouths of other men. Are their molars as amazing as mine?

Lilliana: Not nearly.

McG: That's because my molars are outta this fuckin' world. Are you ready for tonight? I have big plans for you ;)

Her mouth suddenly became dry. *Big plans*? She hoped those plans didn't include a spanking. Not yet anyway.

Lilliana: I'm askeered O.o

McG: Nothing to be afraid of. I simply plan on showing you that I know my way around a woman's body.

She liked the sounds of that. Despite what she had told him, she never really doubted he knew how to please a female. She, on the other hand, had serious misgivings about her own abilities to satisfy a man like Tucker McGrath, and she began to wonder how she would compare to his other conquests. Undoubtedly, he had vast experience with all sorts of sophisticated, exotic women who had rocked his world, and she was merely a small-town girl who had been with a handful of men in her lifetime.

Adam's philandering had left her feeling so self-conscious about her sexual skills, or lack thereof, she began to hem and haw about going through with Tucker's *big plans*. She sat back, staring at the screen trying to think of a way to get out of it.

Hating how Adam had left her questioning herself, she stood and moved to the window to gather her thoughts.

She had grown up the only child to her mother and without a paternal figure in her life. But she had never missed it. Her mother filled that void and so did her auntie Margo. She was raised to be strong and confident, and to believe in herself. Starting at a very young age, she had been reassured over and over that she was nothing less than bright and beautiful. Never once during her youth did she ever doubt herself.

Until Adam.

He made her feel as if she couldn't satisfy a man and he proved it when he slept around with half the damned pussy-bearing population of their small town.

When she had started college immediately after her divorce, Adam said her plans were laughable and that there was no point in a girl like her getting an education. He further advised her that all she was good for was to cook and clean - not to think or act or do.

Despite all that, she reminded herself that she had proven Adam wrong by leaving his ass, finishing dental hygiene school, and making her own way without his help.

Why else would a man like Tucker McGrath be interested in her if he didn't find her attractive? He had point-blank told her that his interests were beautiful, intelligent women and that she was in his sights.

Fuck Adam.

She pushed her shoulders back and grabbed her phone.

Lilliana: I look forward to your big plans. BTW, I'll be groomed so as to not cause any curling into the fetal position. :D

McG: Are you making fun of me?

Lilliana: I'm poking fun, not making fun.

McG: There will plenty of POKING fun tonight. ;) Colleagues waiting, ciao for now, Pet ;)

Her next appointment was spent daydreaming while attempting to make friendly talk with the patient. It was difficult as all of her thoughts were on the upcoming weekend.

During her lunch hour, she stayed in her office and ate while she Googled bondage and discipline. She was shocked at some of what she found, even a little frightened. But overall, she was pleasantly surprised at what she read. Yes, it was kinky and a bit old fashioned, but the idea of it seemed intriguing.

Several questions came to mind, though. Like did Tucker have set rules he wanted followed? If so, what kinds of things would he demand from her? She liked the idea of knowing exactly what she could expect from him and what was expected of her, so long as his demands weren't too outrageous or dangerous.

Perhaps if she and Adam had set boundaries like that, they wouldn't have ended up divorced. She belted out an ironic laugh at her ridiculous assumption. That man didn't know how to keep his word, signed contract or not, and boundaries meant nothing to him.

She recalled what Tucker had said about her verbal offenses. She had always had a smart mouth and if anything was going to get her into trouble; it would be her inability to keep herself from speaking what she was thinking.

*

Lilliana's schedule had a sudden cancellation and she couldn't have been happier to leave early to prepare herself for the weekend. First, she made a stop at the mall to pick up something sexy to wear.

Excitement coursed through her veins. She hadn't had a first date in so long she had nearly forgotten how much fun it could be. As well as nerve-wracking. Two new outfits later and a stop at the lingerie store, she made her way out of the mall when she ran into the same man who had accosted her at the restaurant the week before.

"Ms. Norris," he smiled.

She stood silently scanning him, praying he wasn't going to give her another warning about the man she was about to spend the weekend doing unspeakably naughty things with.

"I'm glad to hear you've made a decision about your land. I sincerely hope everything works out for you. By the way, my name is Darren Schumacher. Tucker and I go way back. Welcome to Bridgeport," he waved as he continued on his way.

A decision about her land? She was bewildered by Darren's statement. She stood watching him and contemplated chasing him down so he could further elaborate, but her phone buzzed.

McG: One more hour and counting. If I were the kind of man who counted, which I am not. I don't count and I don't wait. I simply bide my time impatiently.

Lilliana suddenly felt panicked. *Only one more hour?* She had spent too much time shopping and now she was rushed to get ready. She quickly texted Tucker back.

Lilliana: Yes, I remember, u don't wait. No time for chit chat. I have a bobo that needs to be shaved.
McG: I'll never be accused of getting in the way of a clean-shaven juice box :D Ciao, Pet.

She laughed loudly. It was no wonder he had his way with so many women. With his dreamy smile, hard body, and wicked sense of humor – what female could resist?

She raced home trying to put her nervous energy aside.

Once home, she showered and shaved quicker then she knew was possible and even managed to do a fine job without nicking her precious *bobo*, aka *juice box*. She dressed in the silk and lace matching bra and panties set and sheer India-green, halter dress that she bought, and smoothed her thick hair with a bit of mousse. Next, she packed an overnight bag with all the necessities and a change of clothing.

As she was packing the last item, a little something fun she had picked up, her nerves started to take over. Was she really going through with this? *Yes, she was.* Was she crazy for considering sleeping with Tucker? *Without a doubt.* Were all the warnings about him true? *Probably.* Was Tucker going to be another man who would simply use her and break her heart? *Possibly.* Could she stand another heart break? *No, she couldn't.*

She sank onto her bed and stared at her knotted hands as they shook.

It was just a weekend of fun. *Right?* That's all Tucker and she were planning, not a lifetime together, she tried to remind herself as her hands continued to quake.

She stood and wobbled over to the full-length mirror and took a long look at herself. She hadn't felt attractive in years. Adam had always loved her long mane, but when she found out about his many marital transgressions, she had cut it off, feeling the need to start afresh and wanting nothing to remind her of the son-of-a-bitch who had shit on her heart.

Gazing in the mirror, the image staring back at her filled her heart with self-assurance. She smiled at her reflection. She wasn't the most beautiful woman ever, but she was pretty. Nor was she the most intelligent brainiac ever, but she was smart. And most certainly, she *was* worthy of a man like Tucker McGrath.

A loud knock on the door made her jump, and her head began to swim. Getting ready to show off her best assets, she pushed her chest out and licked her teeth. She moved unhurriedly to the door, wanting to keep Tucker waiting just a bit longer until she gave herself to him.

Opening the door slowly, he had his hand raised in midair about to knock again. He froze when he saw her and his look of absolute desire was so crushing, she feared she would melt at his feet. His tawny-golden brown hair was a fantastic mess and his cocoa eyes were smoldering. A slow, furtive smile trembled over her lips and he rewarded her with a smile of his own.

He wanted her. *He really wanted her.*

***

Standing before Tucker was the most Goddamn beautiful creature he had ever laid his eyes on. The color of Lilliana's dress brought out her brightly shining hazel eyes, and her smile was so completely genuine, he felt as if he had been punched in the stomach by some otherworldly force.

Christ, her body.

His eyes roamed over her figure, resting on her heaving chest. The fabric of her frock was just sheer enough that he could make out the white lace of her bra. When he realized his hand was still hovering in midair, he dropped it to his side and tried to restore his poise.

Unable to fight back the urge to touch her, he ghosted his fingertips over the curve of her waist as he moved his hand upward, skimming her nipple. He feared what the feisty Midwesterner would do to his inappropriate gesture, but to his absolute joy, she pushed her breast into his hand.

"You're absolutely stunning, Lilliana Norris," he said softly, leaning down so their lips brushed.

"You're pretty spectacular yourself, Tucker McGrath," she breathed into his mouth.

When their lips touched, his dick hardened. He squeezed her tit and reached a hand around her waist to pull her roughly, almost violently, to him, almost lifting her off her feet. He slid his tongue into her mouth, savoring the minty flavor. She in turn responded by fisting his hair and nibbling his tongue.

"I've wanted you from the first moment I laid eyes on you," he sheepishly admitted.

"I wish I could say the same," she pulled back slightly, "but you were so damned arrogant, all I wanted to do was kick your..."

He smashed his mouth over hers before she could ruin the moment. When he came up for air, a found a smile the size of her home state, Kansas, spread across her face.

He glanced quickly at her shoes. "You may want to bring some flats for what I have planned. Oh, and bring some music that you like."

He could barely contain his enthusiasm. He had originally planned on taking Lilliana on a helicopter ride and aerial tour of all the land he acquired and sold during his twelve years of being in real estate. It was something he did with every woman on their first date and it was a proven trick for getting into their panties. However, he knew braggadocio wasn't the key to impressing Lilliana. Actually, it would probably have the opposite effect he was hoping for. After thinking a little longer and harder, he decided on something more entertaining and original.

She looked questioningly at him, but promptly complied and walked into her bedroom. During her brief absence, he browsed through her music and picked a few CD's out. He was impressed with her music selection and found it both fascinating and unsettling that their tastes were so similar.

When she came back out with a different pair of shoes in her hand, she smiled at the music he had chosen. While she sorted through her albums, Tucker took the time to study her more closely, noting her three best features: graceful, feminine, and charismatic.

But that mouth... It was her only flaw that he could find. Still, it was part of what made her so damned charming. She wasn't afraid to lay it on the line and say what she was thinking, much like himself.

Lilliana brushed up against him to move past him and her clean, floral scent assaulted his senses. It was then that he realized what it was about her perfume that reminded him of his youth. She smelled of lilac - the very flower that grew wild and in abundance in the backyard of his childhood home. He inhaled deeply and closed his eyes as a primitive growl started in his throat, low and deep. When he opened his eyes, she looked unnerved by the sudden change in his demeanor.

"Pet..." He called out to her.

She backed away and he couldn't help but smirk at the alarm on her face. In the blink of an eye, he reached out and snatched her wrist and yanked her close. Wrapping his fingers in her hair, he pulled her head back. Her hands came up and gripped his biceps as he licked the length of her neck up to her chin. Gently bit into her chin and nibbled his way up to the corner of her mouth where he placed a delicate kiss.

He leaned back to stare down at her. Her eyes were closed, her lips parted with tooth paste-scented breaths fluttering past his mouth, and she had a look of pure bliss. He wanted her and he wasn't going to wait until later. He was sick and tired of waiting. This woman had driven him to the point of no return and there was going to be no more fucking waiting. His dick throbbed in his pants as he thought about tearing her clothes off and fucking her passionately and without restraint. Or better yet, *with* restraints.

"I want to taste you," he grunted as he slicked his tongue across her mouth, dipping it between her lips.

Her hands tightened around his arms, and she sucked his tongue in that brief moment it was in her mouth. He swept her up into his arms and carried her toward the direction of her bedroom. Her eyes reflected nervous apprehension, but only her soft panting could be heard.

Once in her room, he kicked the door closed behind him and tossed her onto the bed roughly. She attempted to sit up, but he grabbed her ankles and pulled her to the edge of the bed. When he did, her dress hiked up over her ass, exposing her smooth thighs and silk-covered pussy. He tugged at her panties, almost ripping them before sliding them into his pants pocket.

Lilliana didn't disappoint. She laid back and pulled her dress up higher, exposing her smooth labia and flat tummy.

He stood at the foot of bed, glaring down at her. "You're taking a lot for granted," he repeated the sarcastic response she had given him not so long ago.

Her eyebrows pinched together in bewilderment.

He bent down and grasped her ankles again, and in one swift motion he flipped her onto her belly bringing her bare ass front and center. She must've sensed what was coming because she tried to crawl away, but he gripped her waist and held onto her firmly. There was no way in hell he was letting her get away when her perfect ass was within reach and in sore need of discipline.

"I meant it when I said you had a spanking coming for all the sass you've given me."

"Tucker, wait..." She squeaked out.

"I'm done waiting for you."

He grabbed a hold of her wrists and pinned them behind her back. Leaning on top of her, he whispered into her ear, "I demand your respect, Lilly."

"Please... I've never... Please don't hurt me," she answered softly.

He promptly eased his grip on her wrists and gently kissed her ear when he heard the fear in her voice. "I would never hurt you. This is simply to teach you that I won't put up with your smart mouth and to show you that I always carry through with my plan of action."

Lilliana's breathing became ragged but she said nothing more. Had she resisted any further or said *no,* he would've backed down. He waited, giving her time to mull over his words. Would she balk like all the rest or would she take his punishment? He hoped for the latter.

When she remained silent, he spoke from his heart, "You need this as much as I do."

With his final declaration, she nodded, sending a tidal wave of exhilaration flooding through him. With her consent given, he knelt between her legs, nudged them open further with his knee and brought his hand down onto her ass. For all his talk about discipline and paddling, he had actually only spanked a woman a handful of times, and he had never felt so alive than he did at that moment.

Lilliana shrieked and pulled her wrists out of his grip. She clawed at the bed and tried to twist her body, but his grasp was too strong. He smacked her one more time on the other cheek with equal vigor, the loud slapping sound reverberating off the walls. He wanted to give her more, but he knew he was pushing his luck.

His heart was pounding so loudly in his ears he could've sworn she could hear it, too. When she twisted and arched her body to get free, he released her. She promptly jumped up and backed herself up against her headboard.

He stood and backed away from her, allowing them both time to process what had just happened. She was breathless, panting, her eyes as wide as the moon and he didn't know whether to laugh out loud or jizz in his pants from her reaction.

"Are you okay?" He asked calmly. She ground her teeth and narrowed her eyes, but to his utter astonishment, she didn't say a word, and he didn't know if that was a good thing or a bad thing. "Lilly, are. You. Okay?" He repeated more emphatically.

She blinked rapidly, and her eyes examined his body. "If by okay you mean pissed, flustered and turned on; then, *yes,* I'm okay."

A slow smile spread across his face. She was something else. Her mouth never failed to both irritate and entertain him. "Good. Now get over here so I can taste you," he pointed at the foot of the bed.

She opened her mouth and he was positive it was to give him more of her brand of sarcasm. "Before you speak, I should warn you: my palm is still itching to give you more."

***

Still shocked from her spanking, Lilliana's mouth snapped closed and she swallowed hard. Her ass was throbbing along with her pussy, and she was having a difficult time making sense of her emotions. Pissed was an understatement, flustered didn't quite nail it, and turned on? *No,* it was more like raging horny.

The look on Tucker's face was unyielding, and his usual playful umber eyes were now pitch black and merciless. Rabid Tucker was now in her presence, and she feared what kind of reprisal she might face if she didn't learn to temper her tongue.

He had hit the nail on the head when he said she needed his discipline. But how could he have known? She had always wanted someone to see her for who she really was and what she truly desired - to be controlled and put in her place. However, she had never spoken those desires for fear of what people might think. *Yes, she needed this, but how could she let go of who she was on the outside to let out what she wanted on the inside?*

When she didn't heed his command, he became visibly incensed. "I once told you I always get what I want. Are you going to make me prove that?"

Though his tone was fearsome, she was quickly becoming annoyed. "Again with the *I always get what I want?* Maybe it's high-time someone gives you a challenge," she retorted.

He clenched his jaw and she knew she had pushed his buttons, and not the right ones.

"You've been nothing but a challenge. Let's get something straight; I'm all for a strong, smart, independent woman outside the bedroom. In fact, I encourage it. But behind closed doors, I want your submission. I crave it. I *need* it. So *do not* try to top me or act bratty seeking out discipline thinking it's cute, because it's not. It's a deal-breaker is what it is."

Lilliana thought long and hard before she responded. There was no *deal* yet. She thought all that lie ahead was a weekend of naughtiness. *But this?*

"Total submission comes with trust and..." She paused thoughtfully. "I don't fully trust you yet. I want you, yes, there's no denying that. But to give myself over the way you want... So soon?"

He stepped back from the bed and blinked several times. "I'm not a patient man, but you're right. I can't expect insta-trust. It'll take time for that, but I'm optimistic we can get to that point. I hope you are, too."

He removed her panties from his pocket and laid them on the bed. "Put yourself back together. Hopefully you're still interested in going through with this weekend because I think you'll enjoy what I have planned."

Placing her hands on her hips and kneeling upright on the bed, she asked, "Another spanking?"

He shook his head and chuckled. "Why? Is that what you want?"

Her eyes widened. God, *no*, she didn't want another paddling. Well, *maybe* she did. "Perhaps, but not one because I've misbehaved."

Tucker's eyes brightened and he gave her a lop-sided grin. Damn. His smile was like the icing on the cake, the cherry on the pie, the lube on the dildo. She shifted on the bed and felt the dampness between her legs. She looked down at her panties and realized she was still naked from the waist down underneath her dress.

It had been eons since a man's mouth had been on her severely neglected nethers, and she said a silent prayer that he still wanted to taste her. She also hoped he was as good at tonguing vag as he was at wielding his arrogance. She lifted her dress up over her thighs and rested her bottom on her heels trying to entice him.

"I thought you wanted a taste?"

His eyes darkened once again. "Are you goading me, Ms. Norris?"

"More like imploring," she whispered, running her hands up her thighs and skimming her fingers through her slit.

Tucker stalked toward her. "There's nothing more rewarding than a stunning beauty begging to have her pussy licked," he slicked his tongue over his lips. "That is what you want, isn't it?" When he reached the foot of the bed, he ran his hand over his visibly stiff shaft and lifted an eyebrow at her.

Like an eager puppy, she wagged her head and practically panted out her response, "Not to put too fine a point on it, but... Yes."

He bit his bottom lip and his eyes flicked from her eyes to her pussy, and back. "I'd be more than happy to oblige. But not until you say *please*."

She sat silently considering his compliment and request. Her libido willed her mouth to move, but her pride stood in the way of what she wanted.

"It's easy, Lilly. Say: *please, Tucker, shove your tongue into my cunt. Make me scream for more. Tongue fuck me.* Say it."

There was an inherent look of orneriness on Tucker's face when he spoke and his eyes revealed his enjoyment in all things perverse. When he licked his lips again as he waited for her answer, she was surprised she didn't see a forked-tongue like that of a serpent or demon come out of his mouth.

Her mouth opened, but nothing came out. His dirty talk had her pussy on the spin cycle and had rendered her speechless. No one had ever said such deliciously vile things to her. Why did everything with him have to be so damned grueling? *And again with the haughtiness?* If she wasn't in need of a stiff dick so badly, she'd shove something of her own up *his ass.*

Tucker's ass. She salivated thinking about his firm rear-end. She wondered what else of his was firm, besides the obvious hard-on pressed tightly into the dark, expensive jeans that clung to his hips seductively. She really did want his tongue shoved deep in her pussy, along with his hard cock. She had screamed for him to ass fuck her at the restaurant kiddingly, but sitting there in front of him, exposed, it was different.

"I thought you said you weren't a sadist," she pouted.

He threw his head back and laughed. In a desperate attempt to resist his captivating smile, she blinked several times and shook her head trying to make sense of her jumbled thoughts. Cripes, that smile did it to her every damned time. She was beginning to suspect he knew it, too.

When his laughter died down, his smile faded to a mere smirk. "I thought I made my rules very clear. I command; you obey. Or have you forgotten?"

"I haven't forgotten," she was able to feebly remark.

"Apparently you have as you seem to be having a difficult time following a simple command, Lilly. Maybe we should just go."

He turned to walk out of the room and her words came frantically spilling out of her. "Please, Tucker, I want your mouth on me," she begged, throwing her pride out the window.

Facing her, a smile ruffled his mouth. "That's not what I told you say, but it's close enough."

***

Lilliana perked up, and Tucker showed her mercy. Luckily for the both of them, she had called his bluff. Moving to the edge of the bed, he motioned for her to lie in front of him as he knelt over her. He took in every detail of the parts of her body that were bared to him, wondering if she had any idea how spectacular she really was. She didn't come off as the kind of woman who knew what kind of cards she was holding, and as far as he was concerned, she was holding a royal flush.

He ran his hands over the tops of her thighs and hiked her dress up to her breasts so he could see more of her. Her skin was the color of ivory lace, soft and unblemished. Every other aspect of her was spot on from slightly curvy hips, small waist and full breasts, and a soft tummy. She was a bona fide woman in every way. He reached his hands up to caress her tits, enjoying the fact that they were real, just like every part of her.

"Please, Tucker," she whined when he took too long giving her what she wanted.

The way her mouth moved and formed his name drove him insane. By guiding her hand to his dick, he was giving them both what they wanted.

"Every time you say my name, I feel it right here," he pressed her palm against the outline of his shaft. "Every. Single. Fucking. Time."

Her glassy, sleepy eyes watched his mouth pensively. With her free hand, she touched her glistening entrance and slipped a finger inside. "And this is where I feel your smile."

If only she knew his smile was reserved only for her, and it wasn't something he shared with just anyone... He never had, but something about her drew it out of him and he felt comfortable being playful with her. Perhaps it was her genuineness. Or maybe it was the way she didn't put up with his shit. Whatever it was, he was glad to know she appreciated it and that it spoke to her sexuality.

He let go of her hand and gripped the other, pulling it to his mouth. He sucked the digit that was just inside of her, closing his eyes and savoring her sweet, salty, uniquely Lilly essence. He leaned down and licked each of her thighs, then her labia, gliding his tongue up the length of her, slowly and deliberately prolonging his tortuous teasing. She bucked her hips upwards in response, but he backed off and smiled down at her.

"All in good time, Pet."

She gripped his shoulders and dug her nails in, sending painful jolts of electricity up his spine. When she lowered herself back onto the bed, he spread her open and blew warm air up and down her opening to her clit. He was aching to be inside of her, but he wanted to enjoy the vision before him. He sucked and nibbled her pink pearl and slipped two fingers inside of her. She mewled and ground herself into his palm.

The way her body was responding to his touch, his head began to buzz with arousal and exhilaration. Overcome with passion, he began to finger her while his tongue flicked her clit. She squealed and writhed, thrashing her bottom and swinging her hips. Her reaction had him wondering if she had ever experienced the pleasure of release from a G-spot orgasm.

He was about to find out.

He tugged ferociously until he felt the familiar swell and sound of fullness. Her eyes widened and she promptly tried to crawl backwards away from him.

"Tucker, I'm going to pee!"

He laughed softly. Apparently she was going to experience her first G-spot orgasm with him.

"Let it happen, Lilly."

She shook her head violently and continued to try and escape his fingers, but her gripped her hips and pulled her back. "Don't fight it," he stated more sternly, fingering her relentlessly.

Her hands grasped the sheets beneath them and tugged. With her eyes tightly closed, she moaned, grunted, and spasmed as a stream of her come flowed from her body in short spurts. The picture before him was so arousing, he grunted too, unable to take his eyes off of her.

"Fuck…" He breathed out.

***

Lilliana lay on the bed, her body still contracting in a way it had never done before. She swore she saw the heavens open up and a beam of light shine down on her soaking pussy while angels sang their praises.

Tucker reached out to touch her but she wasn't ready for more stimulation just yet. "No, wait. Please don't touch me," she murmured.

His face creased into a sudden smile and he slapped her crotch cruelly, making her shriek out and convulse again as a few more drops of come trickled out.

"What the hell was that?" She asked when she was finally able to speak.

"Sweet nectar from the forbidden fruit, Baby!" He declared proudly.

"Did you really just call my come *sweet nectar*?" She laughed, embarrassed.

"Hell yes, I did. That was so fucking hot. So I take it you've never orgasmed like that before?"

She sat up and backed away from the massive wet spot on her bed. That was definitely not like any orgasm she had ever experienced before. She shook her head and Tucker beamed with joy.

"Say it: you're a God, Tucker McGrath; a G-spot orgasm God. Say it, Woman!"

"Is that what it was? I thought the G-spot was an urban legend."

"Don't change the subject. I want to hear how amazing I am," he puffed his chest out. "Now do as you're told."

"Oh, brother. Fine," she rolled her eyes. "But only because I think I may have just met the actual Deity. You, Tucker McGrath, are a G-spot orgasm God. Are you happy?" She asked unenthusiastically.

He waggled his eyebrows up and down, "I'll be happier when you're screaming my name."

Helping her off the bed, he hauled her into his arms and kissed her with purpose. Her body softened and her brain went blank. The heat he was putting off was staggering. All she could think about was that his mouth was just on her. It was the sort of thing most people took for granted, but not her. She missed a man's touch and was thankful that he found her attractive enough to engage in such an intimate act with her.

"Thank you for that," she said quietly, trying to convey her gratitude.

"Anytime. I plan on making you forget all about that cheating SOB who hurt you, Lilly," he breathed into her mouth as he pulled away.

His unwelcome words took her by complete surprise and she suddenly felt like running in the opposite direction. She wasn't looking for someone to help her forget anything or to try and fix her. Tucker really was an arrogant piece of work. What did he think she was - *broken*?

"Let's not get ahead of ourselves. It was only one orgasm, Tucker," she stated clipped, pushing past him.

"I can also help you work through that fear of letting go if you let me. But first you have to drop that wall of cynicism you've built up," he countered as he abruptly spun her around to face him.

"You're making me seriously reconsider this weekend, so can we go before I completely change my mind?"

He narrowed his eyes and she regretted having spoken so harshly when all he was just trying to do was be kind. She also couldn't help but wonder if she was going to end up with a red bottom again.

An angry muscle twitched in his jaw. "Yes, we can go. But I'm only going to say this once: restrain that mouth of yours."

She sighed. Damn it to hell. He was right and she knew it. "I'll do my best," she answered honestly, because at that point, that's all she could offer.

One side of his mouth lifted in a half-smile. "That wasn't so hard, now was it? Anyway, that goo-gasm was the best motherfucking one you ever had, so some respect for my mad oral-fingering skills is in order."

"Ugh. Your terminology is so immature. Seriously, Tucker? *Goo-gasm?*"

He stared at her and then burst out into laughter. "Would you prefer sexplosion? Or happy sneeze?"

She poked him in his firm abs and couldn't help but giggle. This man went from alpha male to juvenile teen at the drop of a hat. It was both exasperating and endearing.

After the fantastic orgasm he had given her, she felt the urge to repay him. Reaching down, she ran her fingers along the outline of the bulge in his pants. Arousal and thrill surged through her when he closed his eyes and thrust himself into her hand. Eagerness to please him overcame her, and she dropped to her knees.

Slowly unbuttoning his pants, she pulled on the waistband of his boxers and jeans. She had to remind herself to slow down, but it had been too long since she had her hands on a man and she was anxious to have him in her mouth. Closing her eyes, she inhaled slowly and deeply. She felt dizzy and drugged from his clean, fresh-water scent. Without further delay, she yanked his pants down around his ankles, revealing the naked lower-half of his body. Her eyes wandered over his muscular thighs and calves, firm and toned belly, and pleasure trail leading to the ultimate prize.

Faced with his pulsating and stiff manhood, she could only stare at it in awe. It wasn't the largest dick she had ever seen but it was far from the smallest. It was like Goldilocks' porridge – *just right.*

She scratched her nails into the soft furry patch below his navel, and tugged the immaculately manscaped hair that framed his thick shaft. "Did you trim this yourself or does a man of your wealth and stature pay someone to keep this shipshape?"

He left her question unanswered and quirked an eyebrow at her. "Are you going to just stare at it or are you going to do something with it?"

"I thought I'd bask in its glory for just a few moments longer," she smiled as a bit of drool pooled in the corners of her half-open mouth. "Ain't nothing like the real thing, Baby," she whispered, having missed the warm, pink, hard, pleasure-inducing piece of man-meat.

"I'm all for you basking in the gloriousness of my dick, but I'm itching to learn what kind of oral skills you have."

"You're so romantic," she rolled her eyes.

"Is this romantic enough for you?" He asked, contracting his abdominal muscles and making his dick jump and slap her cheek.

"What a dreamy talent you have," she grinned, delighting in the bouncing of his cock.

"Now open wide and show me," he stated sternly, grabbing a handful of her hair in the process.

When their gazes met, his cocoa-colored eyes dilated widely and his jaw clenched. Playful Tucker had left the building and she was now facing rabid, no-more-fucking-around-Tucker.

Keeping her eyes on him, she leaned forward and kissed the head of his dick lightly. Next, she stroked the length of him and slicked her tongue up his cock slowly, starting at the base. When she reached the tip, she flicked her tongue firmly against the soft crown. He hissed his enjoyment and his mouth parted as his harsh breathing quickened.

Wetting her lips, she tilted her head to the side and ran them along the extent of his thickness down to his sack where she delivered several small sucks and nibbles. Her hand came up and she squeezed his shaft tightly, twisting her hand up and down.

His grip in her tresses tightened. "Suck it," he instructed.

Pushing her mouth over his slick head and engulfing the entirety of his hardness, she began the enjoyable task of pleasuring him. When he pushed down on her head, she heard herself gag and she pushed away from him, her eyes tearing up. He attempted to push her head lower onto his erection again, and his body trembled as her mouth caressed his strained cock. Even though he was gentler than before, she still continued to wretch every time his lengthy rigidness hit the back of her throat. She grinned up at him awkwardly, ashamed of her lack of expertise.

A sympathetic smile touched his mouth and he winked. "No worries. That sort of skill comes with practice and I intend to give you plenty of it until you get it right."

His kindness and patience with her urged her forward and she bobbed her head up and down as she gripped him firmly between her lips and fingers. She sucked at his head eagerly, wanting to prove that despite her lack of deepthroating skills, she could still push him all the way.

"Damn, Lilly, that greedy little mouth of yours is going to make me come..." He whispered out with a slow rush of air.

He began to thrust into her mouth more rapidly and grunt as his finish neared. His legs began to shake and she could tell by the subtle change in his breathing that he was close. He rose on his tiptoes and she looked up to see his head thrown back, his mouth parted and his eyes shut tightly.

"Here it comes," he warned her, resting both his hands on her shoulders.

A sudden splash of hot, salty come filled her mouth and she swallowed quickly. With Tucker still in her mouth, she continued to glide her hand along his dick, milking out every last bit of his precious gift. A small drop of come dribbled from her mouth and she swiftly wiped her chin and grinned up at him proudly.

She stood, pulling his pants and boxers up and buttoning them for him. She then put her panties back on and turned to see Tucker quietly resting against her bedroom door watching her.

"I told you I would see you on your knees."

CHAPTER 12

Lilliana was more attractive on her knees than Tucker ever could've imagined. The best part of all was that he hadn't even asked or expected her oral reciprocation. As she moved toward him, she gave him a bashful smile. She truly was a beauty to behold when she was in submissive mode. Or at least her version of acquiescent.

He led her to the car and helped her in, his excitement bubbling to the surface once again. He couldn't decide whether or not to go through with his plans of taking her for a dance lesson or to just take her back to his place and fuck her senseless. He wanted inside her so badly he could scarcely breathe or concentrate the entire drive. She sat silently looking out the passenger window and he wondered what was going on inside that overactive brain of hers.

He reached a hand out and slid it up her dress, skimming his fingertips along the inside of her thigh and crease of her pussy. He wanted another taste. Pushing his fingers past her panties and into her, she leaned her head back and turned to face him. Her eyes were languid and needy as they watched his mouth. He withdrew his fingers and sucked her juices off them.

"You're insatiable," she smirked.

He flashed his teeth at her. "You have no idea."

And she really didn't. He could go for hours. And he planned on it, too. He had yet to find a woman who had the kind of stamina he did and he prayed Lilliana could keep up with him. She definitely could keep up with him when it came to warring with words, so he had high hopes for his feisty new mistress.

"So where are we going?" She gazed back out the window

"Dance lessons."

She sat up straight and her eyes lit up. "Like ballroom dancing?"

"Swing dancing. The music you were listening to the other night really put me in the mood and I'd love to feel that sweet little body of yours moving in time with mine."

"I've never taken dance lessons. Have you?"

"No, but I've always wanted to. I've just never found anyone I wanted to try it with."

"Ahh, shucks. Thanks, McG," she batted her lashes playfully. "I knew you had it bad for me."

"Let's not get ahead of ourselves, it's just a dance lesson," he mocked.

"First a BJ, then dance lessons, next starry eyes, and BAM, you're at my beck and call, boning me day and night," she giggled.

He liked mischievous Lilliana and hell, maybe she was right. "You can only hope," he grinned back at her.

Parking the car, they made their way to a small brick building in downtown Bridgeport. A few people were milling around out front, several of whom he knew from past business ventures.

To his horror, a former girlfriend spotted him. If that's what you wanted to call her. She was more like a short-term playmate than a girlfriend. Nonetheless, it was awkward. Of course, he only had himself to blame for having had such a bevy of females and it was inevitable that he would run into them on occasion and at the most inopportune times.

He tried to guide Lilliana away but Bethany quickly approached them. Lilliana was friendly as usual and introduced herself. The two engaged in a brief conversation while he avoided Bethany's gaze. He just wanted her to go the fuck away before Lilliana became aware of who she was.

"Tucker and I go way back," Bethany hinted.

He immediately shot her a nasty look.

Lilliana was quick and it was obvious she sensed his discomfort and irritation. Her eyes flicked between Bethany and him. "That's twice in one day I've heard that."

Twice? Tucker's stomach roiled.

He gripped Lilliana's upper arm and addressed Bethany brusquely. "Good night, Beth," he stated clipped, giving her a cold, hard stare.

Just as he expected, Bethany backed down. She was one of the few who had allowed him to punish her and she knew well what he was capable of. When he faced Lilliana, she had a bewildered look on her face but said nothing.

Inside the dance studio, several couples were already gliding around the dance floor when an instructor approached them and directed them to wait with the others. He felt odd and out of place, but Lilliana held onto his hand, putting him at ease. The teacher informed them both that the nice thing about swing dancing was that if they were good at it, they would look fabulous and if they were terrible, they would still look like they were having fun.

He always considered himself to be a good dancer, and he felt he had a fairly good sense of rhythm. It was good because once the lesson started, Lilliana proved to be quite a challenging partner. Her movements were awkward and out of sync with his, but still – they laughed and he was having a fantastic time. When she harshly stepped on his foot, he took the lead. He desperately hoped she would allow it because he wasn't sure his feet could withstand anymore abuse.

"I'm so bad at this," she apologized sweetly.

"Just relax, let go of your inhibitions and let me guide you."

Her body softened in his arms, but she held on firmly. It was at that point that their bodies became one. Slowly, their movements matched each other and he held her close, dipping and spinning her. It sounded corny, but it was magical. He chuckled at the cheesy thought and she looked up at him puzzled by his expression.

"What's so amusing?"

"This whole situation. Here you are in my arms like there's not a care in the world, and a week ago I wanted to shove my foot up your ass for being so damned exasperating and frustrating."

"Me? Again, pot calling the kettle black," she huffed.

"How's your ass feeling?" He reminded her.

Her face flushed. "A little sore, but fine."

"How about your ego?" He grinned broadly.

"I don't have an ego. You hold all the cards in that department."

Just then, a song from one of their chosen CD's came over the loud speakers, Urban Cone, *Searching for Silence.*

He pulled her closer. "You have great taste in music, Lilly."

"I have great taste in many things."

"I have no doubt about that. You are, after all, with me."

"You really are a piece of work," she shook her head.

The remainder of their lesson went far too quickly for Tucker's taste. He hadn't laughed with a woman the way he did with Lilliana since... He couldn't recall. The fact was; he hadn't had that much fun in years. He was enjoying himself so much, he almost forgot about his long term goal - Lilliana's land.

Almost.

On their drive to his place, he reminded himself that achieving his goal was neither here nor there and he simply wanted to enjoy his time with Lilly, however long or short that duration might be.

"I'm having a wonderful time, Tucker."

When she cut into his thoughts, the look on her face stirred something inside of him. He felt it deep down and not just in his dick. It was more than lust, and it was disquieting. Stopped at a red light, he faced her. Her eyes were burning fiercely and he could feel her attraction for him. He could even smell it on her, like an animal putting off potent pheromones.

"Dinner at my place?" He asked.

"Yes, please."

Lilliana was an ever-changing mystery. He hoped she was submissive though he doubted it by her stubborn actions.

However, every now and then, a small flicker of that trait he craved for shone through.

Pulling up to his large home, her eyes widened and she let out a burst of laughter. "Are you trying to compensate for something?"

His eyebrows rose in deep surprise. "You've seen my dick, I don't need to compensate for anything."

She scanned the expansive yard and immaculate landscaping. "It's beautiful but... Why on Earth so *big*? It's just you."

Irritated at being reminded that he was alone, he didn't feel like explaining that he had bought the house with his second wife in hopes of having a large family and kids to fill the home with. When that didn't work out, he just didn't have the heart to sell it.

"I bought it when I had bigger plans for my future."

He hadn't meant for his answer to be snotty, but he didn't particularly enjoy being put on the spot and having to explain his life decisions. He had never planned for his life to be spent going from one failed relationship to another; it just turned out that way. Having given up on love a long time ago, he was content experiencing different women and experimenting with them.

When he glanced in Lilliana's direction, he caught her watching him. Reaching over, she laid her hand on his thigh as he parked the car, and she let the subject go.

Inside, he led her to the kitchen where she seated herself at the large island.

"What's for dinner?"

"A little something-something," He waggled his eyebrows suggestively. He was in the mood to show off his culinary skills.

"Are you sure you know how to use all that fancy equipment?" She asked when he pulled out several skillets and utensils.

"Woman, please. I'm not only a God in the bedroom, but a force to be reckoned with in the kitchen and business world.

I'm what people refer to as *the whole package*," he winked and chuckled at his arrogance.

"If by force you mean vexing and wearisome, then you most *definitely* are a force."

He briefly flashed a grin before clearing his throat and giving her his best fearsome expression. "That mouth of yours is going to buy you a time-out."

"Time-out? What am I, a three-year-old?"

He smiled widely. He would let her in on the little joke later.

***

Watching Tucker glide around the enormous kitchen effortlessly was mesmerizing. He unbuttoned the top of his shirt, folded his sleeves up and untucked it from his pants, then laid his jacket across a chair. Reaching into his suit pocket, he pulled out her Greg Laswell CD and placed it into his stereo. *Come Back Down* fired up and while the music played, he poured them each a glass of red wine.

He raised his glass, "Here's to fine women, fantastic fucking, and fabulous food."

Lilliana lifted her glass in response, "And to arrogant yet orally gifted, goo-gasm giving alpha males!"

He bowed his head in appreciation then gulped down a big swig of wine.

Without saying anything more, he set his wine down and began his preparation of dinner. First, he sliced the vegetables and sautéed them, taking care not to overcook them. He reached over to a massive spice and herb rack and pulled down several things. Next, he was in the refrigerator getting meat, a large assortment of other vegetables, and a bottle of cooking sherry.

She wanted to engage him in conversation, but he was so totally focused that she didn't want to break his concentration. Mentally, she caressed his qualities and found herself studying his profile. The way his body moved was the sexiest damned thing she had seen in ages. The ambiance of his large chef's dream kitchen, the music playing in the background, and the smell of the food was intoxicating. She basked in the moment and time seemed to slow down. On occasion he would glance up at her with lusty eyes, don his crooked grin, and poke a finger into his mouth to taste it. It was hard to believe the man standing before her was the same man who was an egotistical ass just days before.

When a new song would start that he seemed to enjoy, he would hum along with it and sway his hips. This went on for nearly thirty minutes as she sat silently hypnotized by him.

Lowering the volume of the music, he reached into a drawer and pulled out a kitchen towel. The devilish grin on his face as he stalked toward her made her wonder what he had planned. She didn't have to wonder for very long. He moved behind her and slipped the cloth over her eyes, tying it tightly and shielding all light from her vision. Her hands moved to the fabric and touched it, but she said nothing.

"Let's play a little game," he whispered into her ear from behind.

The stool she was sitting on spun around and she could hear his movements as he moved around the kitchen. It was maddening not knowing what he had up his sleeve. When she opened her mouth to speak, he swiftly cut her off.

"Shhh… No speaking. Place your hands in your lap and don't move," he instructed from across the kitchen.

Doing as she was told, she closed her mouth and laid her hands across her thighs as she kicked her shoes off. She had never played a game like this before. She had never been blind-folded before, either. All of her previous lovers were strictly vanilla, and being blind-folded was sure as hell too kinky for Adam. She smiled. Being without her vision didn't seem that kinky at all really; just a bit naughty and new.

Without her sight, all of her other senses came to life. The music seemed to become louder, the soothing notes of *Landline* filling her ears. She could smell Tucker as he moved close, and almost feel his warmth and eyes on her though she couldn't see him. A savory aroma filled her nostrils, although she couldn't place what it was.

"Can you tell me what this is? For every item you get right, I'll give you an orgasm in return," he whispered as he touched something wet to her lips.

Her nerves prickled with anticipation. She wanted all the orgasms she could get from him. She opened her mouth and he pushed something round into it. It was firm and smooth, about the size of a large grape or olive. The taste was heavenly and nothing she had tasted before. She bit down slowly and the food in question popped and a gush of juice filled her mouth. It was a cherry tomato, but the herbs coating it gave it a whole new flavor.

"Tomato," she mumbled out, chewing on the vegetable. "With something else," she continued.

"Saffron," he laughed richly.

"It's so delicious. More, please?" She asked, wiping the corner of her mouth.

She could hear a plate being placed on the island behind her, and the sound of Tucker's jeans as they swooshed with his movements. Warmness glided over her mouth and she opened it and leaned forward, but he pulled away. He was teasing her. She sat back and waited. Again, she felt the heat of the food and inhaled deeply. It was salty with a hint of spice. She poked her tongue out quickly to get a taste and he laughed as if sincerely amused.

"I forgot how impatient you are."

"Give it to me," she demanded politely.

"Oh, I'll give it to you, Pet," he growled. "Open wide."

She opened her mouth like a hungry bird and he laid a thin strip of meat onto her tongue. She rolled it around in her mouth before sinking her teeth into it. It was tender, lean beef with a spicy kick. The slight tang of blood on the rare meat turned her stomach slightly. She liked her meat well-done, but she pushed back her inhibitions and focused on the herbs and spices.

"Beef, medium-rare with a kind of pepper, but not quite. It's something like pepper. And lemon."

"You have a good palate. It's braised veal with cardamom and lemon preserves. And that's two orgasms for you."

She smiled and licked her lips. She had only eaten veal twice before. It wasn't her favorite, but it was soon becoming a special treat given the circumstances.

Tucker reached for the plate again and she could hear the clink of the plate as he laid it back down on the counter. "If you get the next one right, I'll be surprised."

She sat up and squared her shoulders. She liked a challenge. "Double or nothing?"

He snorted, "You're feeling bold, aren't you?"

She grinned but prayed she would get the answer right.

His finger swept across her lips. She opened her mouth and sat patiently waiting. He dipped his finger in, allowing her to suck it. She had to concentrate on the flavor and not the fact that his digit was in her mouth but it was an impossible task when he began to pull it out only to push it back in, over and over, mimicking the motion of his cock in her mouth. Her core temperature began to rise with his seductive movements.

"Tell me what it is," he stated with a hint of laughter in his voice.

"You're making this difficult. One more taste, please?"

"Okay, but only because I'm feeling generous."

His finger could be heard squeaking across the porcelain as he picked up more of the sweet and salty liquid. He slipped his finger back into her mouth, his thumb this time. Again, he pushed it in and pulled it out, teasing her.

"God damn, that's sexy as fuck," he whispered.

As turned on as she was, she tried to detect the flavors floating around in her mouth. She knew the bitter flavor, but she couldn't name it. She thought and thought, the seconds ticking by slowly.

"Time is running out, Lilly."

"Just one more taste, please?" She begged.

His breathing quickened. "I do love the begging."

One last time, he poked his finger into her mouth. That taste, what was it? Something familiar along with the salty taste of Tucker's skin.

"Coriander!"

He tore off her blindfold, the bright overhead lights making her squint. Her eyes immediately found his and his burning gaze held her still.

"Close, but no cookie," he shook his head. "It's ginger."

Heartbroken, .she sighed loudly and pouted. Leaping off the stool, she stalked around the kitchen in her bare feet, irritated with herself. What the hell was she thinking by doubling down like that? Damn it to hell.

Suddenly Tucker was on her, backing her up to a blank spot on the wall. He pinned her arms high above her head, holding on tightly to her wrists. His mouth was on her throat and his other hand up her dress, pushing her panties to the side and clutching her pussy.

At the end of the CD, the music stopped and the only sound in the room was of the sizzling vegetables and their frantic breathing. He pushed her legs apart with one foot as he buried his fingers completely inside of her, making her squeal out.

She was in heaven as he forced himself on her, pressing her body to the wall and taking complete control of her. Her thoughts were bleary, her blood humming through her veins, and her mouth unbearably dry.

He sucked at her neck so ferociously, the painful sensation brought tears to her eyes, but she allowed his passionate kiss and pleaded for more. "Don't stop," she mewled out.

He let go of her wrists and lifted her off her feet by her waist. With her legs wrapped around him and her arms around his neck, their mouths smashed onto one another's. He wobbled over to the island again and plopped her down onto it as he tore her panties off, shredding the fabric. It, too, was painful and her eyes welled up again from the sudden harshness.

He dug into his back pocket and pulled out a condom, and with the ease of a man who had clearly done it a thousand times before, he had it on in a matter of seconds. Pushing her legs open as far as they would go, he sunk into her, slowly pushing the head of his cock past her velvety, glistening folds.

He hiked her dress up and over her breasts as his hand outlined the roundness of her breast, then tugged the lacy cup of her bra down underneath her tits, revealing them completely. He buried his face in them, his tongue caressing her sensitive, swollen nipples. Unhurriedly, he began to sink into her little by little. Unaccustomed the kind of manly intrusion she was being faced with, she resisted the initial penetration and clenched down unintentionally.

"Fuck, Lilly. When was the last time you were with a man?" He moaned out as he looked up into her eyes. Her cheeks brightened and his movements stilled. "Relax, Pet."

She slowed her breathing and arched upwards against his rigid shaft. He smiled and began to push further into her. Straightening up, he pulled her to the edge of the counter and dove deeper and deeper into her. As his hands explored her soft flesh, she focused on his movements, trying to predict his next move. His eyes flicked from her pussy to her mouth to her eyes, and back. She writhed beneath him and gasped when a jolt of electricity shot through her lower abdomen.

Lowering himself onto her, his eyes became languid. "That's it... Right there..." he grunted as if talking to himself.

The look on his face was entrancing and his tormented groan was a thrilling invitation. She reached up and gripped his face and pulled herself up to suck on his perfect lips. With his palms resting on the counter, their tongues danced inside each other's mouths as his cock twitched inside of her.

A timer buzzed and he pulled away without warning, leaving her sitting on the edge of the island with her legs dangling, her dress around her waist, and her pussy dripping wet. Tucker held onto his pants as he stirred the vegetables, his stiff dick pointed skyward. He replaced the pan lid and reset the timer as if nothing had happened, and walked back and plunged right back into her pussy.

She was so close to coming, her body screamed for release. Her pussy muscles began to contract at a rapid rate when he swiftly pulled out and glared at her.

"No coming. That was the deal, remember?"

She lay gape-jawed, panting and with her chest heaving. He couldn't be serious. *Could he?* "But, Tucker," she started in.

"Shush," he barked as he gripped the back of her neck and pulled her into his mouth.

Again, he shoved his cock in her and began to drive into her over and over, pushing her to the edge. Just as she felt the warm chill of an orgasm building, he grunted loudly and his movements ceased. He had come and now she was left without release. Gently, he pulled out of her and slipped off the condom. As he tied the end of it and tossed it into the kitchen trash, she lay back on the counter, catching her breath.

She turned her head to the side and watched as he bent down and picked up the condom wrapper and tossed it away. He proceeded to wash his hands and stir the vegetables once more before addressing her.

"The bathroom is that way. Get cleaned up for dinner," he instructed nonchalantly and pointed toward the door. Sitting up, she stared him down. One of his eyebrows went up and he let out a short, breathy laugh. "Again with the evil-eye?"

"Better you get my evil eye than my sharp tongue."

He stepped back and placed his hands on his hips. "Oh, really? Better for whom? You or me? You shouldn't have made a bet like that if you didn't plan on keeping it."

She didn't need to be reminded of her ridiculous decision. When she huffed under her breath, he rubbed his palms together signaling what was to come if she kept up her attitude. Quickly, she hopped off the island to find the restroom before her motor mouth got her into trouble.

Now pantyless and thoroughly fucked, she was a complete mess. She eyed her makeup and hair and did the best she could to make herself presentable.

Making her way back to the kitchen, Tucker had the food plated and was heading toward the dining room. She followed and was astounded to see a massive table with an opulent but absurdly huge chandelier hanging overhead. The room was stunning with lush velvet and leather furnishings and a fireplace with a hand carved mantel at the far end of the immense room. The smell of expensive wood lingered in the air and she couldn't get over the sheer size and magnificence of his home. Yes, it was beautiful but it was way too overstated. He was a farm boy from Iowa for fuck's sake.

As he began to set the plates down she stated her request. "Can we eat in the kitchen? The island will do just fine. It's cozier in there."

He nodded perfunctorily and turned back towards the kitchen.

As they ate, he sat quietly. The food was delicious and the fact that he had cooked it made it all the more enjoyable. He really was the whole package. Albeit, an annoying, orgasm-depriving package.

"Why so quiet?" She asked.

"No reason," he shrugged.

His expression revealed nothing and the way he had suddenly become distant, she began to worry that she had overstayed her welcome. They had both gotten what they wanted, so maybe it was time for her to leave.

"If you're uncomfortable with my being here, perhaps I should leave." Her voice was soft and a little uncomfortable.

He creased his forehead as he laid his fork down. "I thought you were staying the night. Wasn't that your plan?"

"Was it?"

"You brought an overnight bag with you."

Shit. She had just assumed that was the plan without discussing it with him. She mentally kicked herself as she sat staring at her plate while trying to think of a way to get out of sounding like a jerk.

"I apologize for assuming that. I have a tendency to jump to conclusions."

He snorted and nodded in agreement. "I've noticed."

Her cheeks flushed miserably. Oh, hell. She got some dick, that's all that mattered. She picked up her plate and moved toward the dishwasher.

When she rose, Tucker shot her a penetrating look. "What are you doing?"

"Cleaning up."

"I see that, but why?"

Quickly, she rinsed her plate and placed it in the dishwasher. "Where I come from, we clean up after ourselves."

Just as she reached for her jacket and purse, he stood and sighed with exasperation. "I thought we decided you were staying the night."

"We didn't decide that. Anyway, it's late," she took a step toward the door.

He let out a long audible breath and placed his hands on his hips. "Oh, Christ. Are we going to do this awkward dance? Look, I want you to stay, but if you want to leave, I respect that."

Slowly, she turned to face him and stared at him a moment as she tried to gauge his expression. "You're the most confusing man I've ever met. You want my land... You don't want my land. You don't like that I assumed I would stay... Now you want me to stay."

All of a sudden, he looked affronted and nervous; however, she had no idea why. Come to think of it, her statement reminded her of the man at the mall.

What was his name? Derrick? Darold? *Darren.*

***

"Darren approached me at the mall today. He said something about my making decision about my land, and that you two were old friends."

Tucker didn't know how to respond. The unprompted comment about Lilliana's land had him feeling uncomfortable. More than that - *uneasy*. No, he wasn't interested in her land. *At the moment*. And why the fuck had Darren approached her again? He didn't want to lie to her anymore, but now this?

"Yes, we went to college together," he responded without answering her question directly.

Her eyes brimmed with confusion. "Do you know what he was talking about?"

He cleared his plate and loaded it in the dishwasher as he tried to formulate his answer. "I put the word out that you weren't selling it." He had told the truth, even if it was only a half-truth.

"Thank you," she said softly.

When he faced her, the grateful look on her face delivered a mental kick to his balls. "Sure," he shrugged her off, not wanting to think about his shitty actions.

"I bought you something at the mall today," she grinned, her face beaming impishly.

"Oh?" He responded with incredulousness. He was the one usually handing out the gifts. What could Lilliana possibly have gotten him on her meager income?

"Well, it's actually for the both of us," she smiled. "It's in my overnight bag."

He lifted a brow. "So you're staying then?"

She wavered back and forth before finally responding precisely the way he was hoping she would. "Yes."

He was glad to hear it. He hated the waiting game of dating. He was a grown man and she was an adult, and he just wanted to dispense with the fake pleasantries and get down to business like they had earlier. Hell, yes, an uninhibited, passionate, and willing Lilly in his bed is exactly what he wanted more of.

"So what is it that you bought?" He hoped it was some sexy lingerie or maybe something kinky.

"Right here in the kitchen?"

"Where would you prefer?"

Her pink blush turned to crimson. "The bedroom."

Very nice. He was hoping to hear that, too.

After getting her bag from his car, they made their way to his large bedroom. When they entered, she looked it over carefully and then gave him the same laugh she had when she first laid eyes on his home.

While she disappeared into the master bathroom, he slipped his pants and shirt off. He docked his phone, cued some music overhead, and laid back. He could hardly wait to be inside of her again. He also couldn't wait to show her the time-out room.

How would she react to it? Would she run? Would she submit? Would she…

His thoughts were interrupted when she came out, laughing at herself. She had on a black lace tank top and nothing else. He loved her unabashed comfortableness with her own body. She wasn't shy and she didn't pretend to be. There was nothing more irritating than having a beautiful woman in his bedroom only to have her suddenly act as if she was virginal or demure. He cherished a confidently alluring woman. That was not to say that he liked an easy woman. Quite the opposite. An over-aggressive woman was more of a turn off than was a prude, in his opinion. But Lilliana seemed to walk that fine line between being at ease with her sexuality without being too assertive and flashy. He was, after all, a dominant male and he wanted to be the one calling the shots when it came to sex.

"This is a perfect song," she giggled when she heard *Bamboleo* by Gipsy Kings.

She began gyrating her booty around in time with the music as she inched closer to him. He grinned stupidly as he watched her version of a strip tease. She was a terrible dancer and her rhythm was completely off, but she was cute as hell. She laughed louder as she moved next to the bed making him wonder what the hell was so funny. She turned her back to him, backed her ass up and lifted the lace, revealing her plump, glittered ass.

He sat up, kneeled on the bed, and howled with laughter as he held his stomach. God damn, Lilly knew how to entertain! Her sense of humor was quickly jumping to the top of his favorite things about her. He bounced up and down on the bed like a sex-depraved lunatic at a strip club, clapping his hands as she continued to shimmy her ass to the beat, her bottom jiggling with each shake.

"Shake that money maker!" He hollered.

To his absolute joy, she pushed her ass out further and reached around and slapped it, sending rainbow-colored, sparkling flakes flying everywhere. Just before the song ended, she leaped onto the bed with him, pushed him onto his back and pinned his arms beneath her knees.

"Say my ass is the best one!"

***

Lilliana's pussy was only inches away from Tucker's face. Their laughter slowly died down and his smile turned into something more sinister. She lifted the lace up, revealing herself to him.

"I'm waiting."

He lifted a sexy eyebrow at her. "Are you attempting to top me, Lilliana Norris?"

She had to think quickly. "Sitting *on top* of you does not equate to *topping* you."

He was quick and before she realized what had happened, she was beneath him, his strong, hot body suffocating her. His smell was exhilarating. When he shifted, she could feel his hard cock against her thigh.

"I'm still waiting," she whispered, undeterred by the slickness between her legs.

He glided a finger down her cheek and across her lips, the rough tip of his digit igniting a fire within her belly. He was trying to manipulate her like he had undoubtedly done to countless women, but she wouldn't allow it. She had embarrassed herself for him and she wanted to hear the words from his beautiful mouth.

"Say it, Tucker," she pleaded.

"Beg for it, my beautiful, little Pet," he leaned down and licked the crook of her ear.

"I did what you asked. Are you a man of your word or not?"

His eyes narrowed to mere slits. "Most of the time."

There was a hidden message in his statement, although she had no clue what that message was. "I still don't trust you, but I want to. Give me a reason to."

His eyes became fixed on her mouth, and she could feel his heart begin to beat rapidly in his chest as he lay on top of her. The internal struggle in his eyes was clearly visible, but he finally gave her what she asked for.

"Your ass is the best I've ever bitten," he stated in a low, composed voice.

CHAPTER 13

Lilliana woke sometime after a short nap. She rolled over, her body still covered in sweat from the sex she and Tucker had before finally falling asleep. Her body ached, her pussy was sore from the pounding it had received, and her jaw creaked and throbbed from sucking him off again. He had finally allowed her to come and her pussy was still vibrating from the massive orgasm she had.

Sitting up on one elbow, she blinked several times trying to adjust to the darkness of the room. When her eyes finally came into focus, Tucker's glistening silhouette practically glowed in the dark. She had been surprised to see his upper arms covered in tattoos when she had come into the bedroom to shimmy her ass for him, and it was just another thing that fascinated her about him.

Dusting a finger over the family crest on his upper arm, he stirred and shifted from his side to his stomach. He was absolutely flawless. His muscular thighs and ass reflected the moon filtering through the large window, and she couldn't resist reaching down and squeezing a cheek just to convince herself that he was real. Having only caught a glimpse of the tattoo between his shoulder blades during the heat of the moment, she could now inspect it closer. She traced the ambigram tattoo of the word *family* in gothic print, gliding her index finger along the large, bold etched letters in raven black ink. There was nothing sexier to her than an inked body beneath a business suit. She leaned down and kissed his back, the taste of his salty skin stirring in her nethers.

The urge to urinate suddenly hit her and she trotted quietly to the restroom. It was tastefully laid out, but was gigantic and over-the-top just like everything else in the house. As she relieved her bladder, she eyed the in-floor whirlpool tub and open shower stall encased by stone walls. There was no denying Tucker had good taste when it came to decorating, even if it was extravagant.

When she was finished, she stood at the mirror and opened a drawer, curious what kind of personal items a man like Tucker McGrath kept in his restroom. There was nothing of note in the first two cabinets other than the standard fare of hair products, cologne, and an electric shaver. She dabbed a bit of the aftershave onto her wrists and neck, and smiled. She loved the smell of a man lingering on her.

When she opened the bottom drawer, she came face to face with a photo of a strawberry blonde-haired woman staring back at her. The female was stunning with her long hair, straight white teeth, and modelesque figure. She flipped the picture over where it read *Aubrey 2011, Venice*. She looked back into where she had found the image and found two more pictures. One was of a brunette with medium-length, wavy hair and haunting blue eyes. She was young, probably in her mid-twenties or so. On the back was written *Sarah 2008, Paris*. The last photo looked much older than the other two and featured a gorgeous, golden-haired girl who looked very young, late teens to early twenties, with sad brown eyes. The name scrawled on the back: *Gwen 1999, Iowa*.

Lilliana was struck with what she was looking at; his ex-wives and ex-fiancé. She suddenly felt like a nosy bitch for snooping, and hurriedly put the photos back into the drawer and closed it. For a man who got around, it was strange that he kept these images so close to him. Was it possible that he had a bit of a romantic side that he was hiding? It shouldn't surprise her considering his upbringing. Most country boys that she knew had a rough exterior with a soft inner core. But Tucker was no longer a country boy as evidenced by his surroundings, home and attitude. She glanced one more time around the bathroom and shook her head.

When she snuck back into bed, he rolled over and opened his eyes. "You're beautiful," he whispered, reaching out and running his fingers through her hair.

His eyes shone brightly in the pale light of the moon and she moved closer to peck his lips. The pain of missing a man's touch, smell, and warmth hit her like a ton of bricks. She had suppressed it for so long, but lying next to Tucker only reminded her how alone she really was. She turned away from him, trying to get her emotions under control and remind herself that it was just a weekend of fun, then back to the real world.

Unable to fall back to sleep, she dressed in her lace tank top and panties, and tiptoed around his large home, getting turned around several times in the darkness. It seemed like she walked forever from one end to the other. She counted eight bedrooms in all and six restrooms. That's a whole lot of toilets. How much could one person piss anyway? Though, now that she thought about it, Tucker could be quite a shithead, so maybe that's why he had so many turd receptacles.

As stunning as his home was, she found it to be cold and sterile with all the standard issue paintings on the walls and expensive décor. What it was lacking was personal items. There were no family photos to be seen anywhere. How could a man who had the word *family* etched into his skin have no images of that family he loved so much hanging from his walls?

She found what was clearly his office and though it was lovely, it was just as impersonal as the rest of the house. The only upside was that it had the distinct scent of him in it. She inhaled deeply and hugged herself. Hot damn, she loved the scent of masculinity.

***

Tucker had awoken to find himself alone in his bed. Lilliana's perfume was still lingering in the room and glitter was strewn everywhere and shimmering in the moonlight. He knew she couldn't have gotten too far considering her clothes and bag were still in his room, so he went out looking for her.

Several minutes later he found her wandering around his home. The hallway was almost pitch-black when he came up behind her and took her by surprise. "What are you doing up at this hour and at this end of the house?"

"Taking a tour of the McGrath Estate," she responded looking around the lightless room she had entered.

He reached over and flipped on a light, and she snorted when faced with the expansive room and luxurious furnishings.

"What's so funny?"

"You. This house."

No one had ever complained about his home before. "You don't like my home?" He couldn't help but sound offended when he responded.

She looked around the room and nodded. "Of course I like it; it's gorgeous. I've only seen this kind of extravagance in magazines."

"My home is hardly extravagant," he huffed, though he supposed in her eyes it might seem that way.

She motioned with her head toward the gold-leaf, Italian billiards table and lavish chandelier hanging overhead, and raised her eyebrows accusingly.

He looked around the room and was finally forced to admit, "Okay, that might be a little superfluous."

"A little?" She wrinkled her nose. "Do you even play pool?"

He hadn't purchased the damn billiards table to play on it; he had bought it because it looked good in the large room and because it was a great place to fuck. Seeing legs spread wide on the black baize fabric or a firm ass bent over the hand-painted rails made it well worth the investment. Hell, he didn't know anyone who owned a table that actually used it for its designed purpose.

He gave her his best condescending grin and fake upper class accent. "The pool, my Dear, is out back. It's where us highfalutin folk dip our toes while we sip on mimosas. This here..." He waved to the table, "Is called a *billiards table*."

"Potāto, potàto," she puckered her mouth. "So do you play or not?"

"As a matter of public knowledge, I do indeed play, Madam," he raised his nose in an exaggerated snooty gesture. "Am I any good at it?" He started to laugh. "No," he silently mouthed and shook his head.

Lilliana gripped her chest and staggered backwards. "Oh. My. God. Did Tucker McGrath just admit he's not good at something?"

"Zip it, Woman."

A hint of amusement sparkled in her eyes. "Tell me: why does a single man with no children need a 10,000 square foot house?"

"If you want to get technical, it's only 8,000 square feet," he winked. "And if I'm not spending my hard-earned money on living extravagantly, then what?"

"Making memories? Traveling? Charity?"

"Charity?" He asked sarcastically. "Since when did you become a humanitarian?"

"I'm not. I just can't figure out why you need all this," she nodded her head toward the room.

"No one *needs* a house this big, silly girl,"

"Who are you calling silly? You're the one living in a castle. All this place needs is a moat with a draw-bridge and a few dragons in the front yard to complete your look. I mean, seriously, why do you have a place like this? To prove something?"

He shrugged his shoulders and chuckled at her remark. He did like to think of himself as country royalty. However, his intentions with owning a house this size wasn't to make people believe he was a Goddamn king.

"Everyone knows you're successful, brilliant, and commanding, Tucker. Everyone respects you. You don't need a big house to prove that."

Do they? He wondered. Yes, people respected his ability to get things done and make money for everyone, but did they really *respect* him?

"Not a lot of people like me, Lilly."

"Well whose fault is that? You want respect and reverence, and you demand it. I've seen it firsthand. You can't expect to treat people the way you do and make besties along the way. It just doesn't work like that." She squeezed his shoulders. "But I'm not telling you anything you don't already know, am I?"

He exchanged a smile with her and shook his head. Her honesty was something he was still getting accustomed to. "No, you're not."

Her eyes became unfocused and she stepped back. There was clearly something she wanted to ask him.

"What's on your mind?" He prompted her.

"What did you do to make that woman outside the dance studio so afraid of you?" She asked with an expression of deep concern.

Did she really want to know? He had been holding back his true perversions for fear of scaring her away, but there was no time like the present to make his intentions clear. "Unspeakable things," he answered.

Her eyes rounded. "If by unspeakable you mean..."

He covered her mouth with his index finger. "By *unspeakable,* I mean I'd rather not go into the details out of respect for her. Come with me. I want to show you something."

Nervous apprehension settled in his gut when he led her by the hand to a room on the east wing. Entering the smallest room of the house, he turned the light on.

"This is the time-out room."

Her jaw gaped and her eyes scanned the select few pieces of equipment furnishing the space. He was expecting the worst - a slap across the face, a blood-curdling scream, *something*.

"Why didn't you show me this room before?" She asked, placing her hands on her hips and facing him. He stood silent, not really knowing the answer to her question. "Do you really like doing this sort of thing?" She waved to the equipment.

"That, I do."

"So, is this what you meant by *unspeakable*?"

"Yes."

She raised her eyebrows and moved to the wooden bed that contained a whipping cross on one end, a bed with a neck and wrist yoke, a cage on the bottom, and an assortment of suspension points and padding. "If you're embarrassed about your sexual preferences, then why do you do it?"

His blinked in surprise. "I'm not embarrassed about this. Is that what you think?"

"Why else would you keep it from me?"

He had no real excuse except to say that he didn't want to freak her out. "Because I'm discreet."

She moved to the small wooden horse that's designed purpose was for spanking, and ran her hand along the leather seat. The gears in her head were turning; that much was clear to see. He admired her driving intelligence and wished he could be inside her head for just one minute. Next she moved to the only other piece of equipment in the room - a sex swing that hung from the ceiling in a corner - and seated herself in it.

"So you're not freaked out?"

Her gaze simmered as her eyes raked over his body. "Does it look like I'm freaked out?"

No, it didn't. In fact, it looked like she was intrigued. When her eyes moved around the room once again, they stopped on a wall of ropes and belts. Her eyebrows pinched together.

"I told you that I have an affinity for bondage," he responded before she could speak.

"You also told me you're not a sadist."

He couldn't resist a smile. "I'm not. The things in this room are for disciplining purposes and pleasure, not pain. Though to a certain degree, pleasure can be derived from pain."

Her eyes darted back to his. "Did you use all this stuff on your girlfriends?"

"Some of them. Every woman was different. Some liked it. Most didn't. The majority ran, but some stayed and played. Which are you going to be?"

Lilliana planted her feet on the floor to stop the swing from swaying, and glared at him defiantly. "I haven't decided yet."

"You say that as if the final decision is only yours to make, Lilly."

Her expression was thoughtful and she paused before sitting up straighter. "What is the purpose of a room like this, Tucker? No more innuendos and man-speak. I want to know right now, what you *really* want from me."

He took a moment before responding, forming his words carefully. If it was the honest truth she wanted, then he was going to give it to her. She may not like it, but it was better for him to find out sooner rather than later if she was going to fulfill his needs.

"I want to control you and make you submit. I'm asking you to give into my will within these boundaries. In this room, in my bedroom - give in to me in all ways. When you do, pleasures untold await the both of us. Are you brave enough to do that?"

Her hands tightened around the nylon straps and her eyes rested on her feet. "I want to be brave enough, but submission is a scary concept."

"Submission isn't a concept; it's a living, breathing thing. Domination is, too, and it's both frightening and electrifying when someone gives you control over their mind and body. It's also a great responsibility and not one I take lightly."

She simply raised her eyebrows in acknowledgement as she chewed on the corner of her lip. He moved to the stereo and loaded a song from his iPod, and adjusted the volume while giving her time to think about what he had just told her. He glanced over his shoulder to see her watching his movements cautiously. He liked to keep her guessing.

"You know... I have yet to be with a woman who has allowed me to do all the things I want with them in this room," he walked around her slowly.

Despite what kind of confident aura she tried to put off and her closed expression, he smelled her fear and arousal, and sensed her vulnerability. He skimmed the tip of his index finger over her upper arms and shoulders while he continued to circle around her. His erection was building, but he tried to contain his urge to dominate her and appear cool and collected.

She leaned back in the swing and held onto the straps above her head. "Is that a challenge?"

He stilled and took in the image before him. *Fucking A, Lilliana was stunning.* "I'm simply stating a fact. Do with that knowledge what you will."

She spread her legs and slipped her heels into the stirrups with such poise, he could've sworn she had done this sort of thing before. *So much for maintaining his cool.*

"Just when I think I have you figured out, you reveal another kinky layer to me. What else are you holding back, Tucker McGrath?"

He moved to the head of the swing. Staring at her upside down, a devious smile curves his lips. "I told you I'm a deeply complex individual with many layers."

"If by complex you mean..."

He gripped the straps firmly and adjusted them swiftly, dropping her head down below her body and cutting her smart-ass statement short as she gasped out. "Stop talking, Lilly. This room is for accepting my will, not for exerting your own. Am I clear?" He leaned down and ghosted her mouth with his lips.

Her eyes widened and gleamed lustily at him as she panted out her response, "Crystal."

He hoped this was the beginning of a good thing; a *really* good thing. He had already found himself wanting more and more of Lilliana, and if she submitted to him the way he wanted, he feared he would never be able to get enough of her. Ever.

***

"Good. Now open wide for me," Tucker ordered.

He peeled his t-shirt off, slipped his sweat pants down his hips and let them pool at his feet, revealing his hard-on and the perfect V of his pelvic muscle. The room was unlike anything Lilliana had ever seen before. She had read about rooms like the one she was in, but it was the thing myths were made of. She couldn't believe that men like Tucker really existed; men who liked to dominate women and exert their power over them. There was a mystique about it, a certain appeal that she couldn't put her finger on. He truly was multifaceted.

Everything about him captivated her; from his choice of music to the foods he ate; to his fashion choices. But that was all superficial. It was the things that went much deeper that truly enthralled her; his kindness and sense of humor, his love for his family... And now this room. She was awestruck that he had built a room to sexually please women, not to hurt them.

She let the music of Bastille, *Pompeii* wash over her and opened her mouth, ready to gratify him in whatever way he wanted. She wasn't sure if she could submit totally, but she wanted to. More to the point, she wanted Tucker to make her submit and to control her, and to do with what he wanted.

He guided his hard shaft into her mouth and pushed deep. Just as predicted, she gagged. *Damn she hated when she did that.* She closed her eyes tightly, concentrated and opened her throat. His breathing became louder every time he pushed into her mouth. When she felt his hand around her neck as he pushed to the back of her throat, her lower belly throbbed with such intensity, she was sure she was going to come simply from his possessive touch.

Just when he pulled out of her mouth, she felt the momentum of the swing spin her around. He reached into the top drawer of a tallboy dresser that was just within reach and retrieved a condom. In the blink of an eye he was inside of her. She opened her eyes to see him in between her legs, thrusting rapidly into her. His eyes were focused on her mouth, only occasionally flicking to her pussy. As he slicked his lips, his eyes rolled back in his head.

"Yes, my Pet. That's it, right there," he mumbled softly as his pace slowed and he swiveled his hips.

His skilled movements were breathtaking to watch. He was so devastatingly handsome it was physically painful, making her chest ache. The way he fucked with such passion and concentration, it was like watching a master sculptor at work. His hand moved to her clit and she let out a small moan as he pressed his thumb down firmly.

"Louder, Lilly. This room was built for your screams."

He adjusted and tilted the swing at an even sharper angle, causing his cock to hit her G-spot forcefully. Her concentration was broken and she held on for dear life, feeling as if she was going to slip out of the swing.

"You won't fall. Stop holding back and give in," he cooed.

Entrusting herself with Tucker, she let herself go. His hands were all over her body, roaming, pinching, squeezing, and owning her completely. The blood rushed to her head and when he hit that delicious spot over and over, she soared to new heights. A cool chill crept up her belly and she felt the sudden jerk of the swing as he yanked the head of the swing up. His hand was around her neck again, controlling, yet tender, and there it was - the flowing wetness. She screamed out his name and clawed at his arm as his fingers gently released her.

He continued to thrust into her, his powerful thighs and abdomen contracting with every forceful push. As she floated in and out of some other worldly place, he grunted loudly, pulled out and snapped his condom off and allowed his hot come to cover her belly and chest.

Lifting her out of the swing, he staggered with her in his arms back to his bedroom where they both collapsed and fell into a deep slumber.

***

The following morning Tucker woke early and before Lilliana He hadn't planned on her staying the night but when he had seen her overnight bag, he had resigned to the fact and now, watching her sleep, he was glad she had stayed. He hadn't had a woman stay the whole night since his ex-fiancé had moved out. There were plenty of spare rooms for his overnight guests, but things had gotten so heated the previous night, he didn't have the heart or strength to send her to sleep anywhere else. Even though he hadn't initially wanted her to stay the entire night, he enjoyed having someone else in the house and it was a nice change from his usual solitary morning routine.

He decided to let her sleep in and rummaged through her overnight bag, picking out the outfit she had brought along and laid it out for her.

He decided to cook breakfast, the entire time his mind replaying the episode in the swing and the look on Lilliana's face when confronted with his true sexual proclivities. As he was finishing up, she came into the room, freshly showered and looking spectacular.

"Good morning," she smiled sheepishly.

"Yes, it is. How are you feeling?" He winked over his shoulder.

"I hurt everywhere. And I mean *everywhere*."

"I'm glad to hear that. You've been out of practice."

"Unfortunately, that's the stark truth."

He liked the fact she hadn't been with a man in a good while. His dick began to harden at the thought of how snug a fit she was for his cock. He plated the omelets he made and turned to set them on the island when he saw her standing with her bag and purse in hand.

"Leaving so soon? I was hoping for some more time-out."

"That's sounds nice, but I really should go," she nodded gloomily.

He sighed. "Breakfast first."

She set down her bag and seated herself.

"You're a fantastic cook, Mr. McGrath," she stated, shoveling a forkful of egg into her mouth.

"Thank you."

She began to choke and gulped down a swig of water. "Holy shit. Did you just say thank you? Wow. Was that painful for you? Did you break anything doing that?"

His eyes widened. He thought she had genuinely been choking, but instead she was giving him unadulterated sass.

"It's not too early for a spanking," he stated firmly. She quickly quieted down and continued to eat. Tucker pretended to choke as well, mocking Lilliana. "Holy fuck. Did you just suppress your sarcasm? Wow. Was that painful for you?" He laughed.

She glared at him and crinkled her nose. "It was very painful."

"Not as painful as my hand across your glittered ass would be. By the way, there's pixie dust and sparkles all over my damned bedroom and master bathroom now, not to mention in my bed. It looks like there's been a fairy orgy in there. It was all up my ass and in my dick fur, and I had a hell of a time getting it off in the shower."

"Good to hear. Every time the light hits a spot of it, you'll be reminded of the best ass you ever sunk your amazing teeth into," she grinned.

Tucker truly enjoyed their back and forth banter. As Lilliana was nearing the end of her breakfast, he was trying to come up with ways to get her to stick around a little longer. She grabbed her belongings and moved toward the door, and he followed behind.

Not wanting their weekend together to end so soon, he took his time driving through town, giving her a small tour of the business district. He wanted her for as long as he could have her and before he knew it, they had been driving for hours.

"How about a helicopter ride and a late lunch?" He suggested. He figured it would at least keep them busy for another few hours.

She eyed him dubiously. "Why do I get the impression you've done that sort of thing before with other women? You schmooze them with a sweet ass aerial ride and then ride them hard later?"

He sat silent but grinned from ear to ear. Her ability to read him was astounding. He winked and licked his lips teasingly. "It does sound tempting, doesn't it?"

She shook her head disapprovingly. "You're such a player."

"Don't hate the player, hate the game, Sugar Lips."

"Ugh. I'm suddenly feeling nauseous. How about we just go back to my place and I make us some lunch, and give you a tour of my meager digs?"

***

Tucker smiled mercurially. "Gee, why didn't I think of that?"

Lilliana had the feeling that he had been stalling all morning in taking her home. She didn't mind. After their little fuckfest the night before, she wasn't eager say goodbye to him quite yet. She was still thinking about the time-out room. It was such a strangely soothing place to be with its dark blue walls and the smell of leather and oil. Of course, she hadn't been disciplined there yet so perhaps the room would take on whole other aura once that happened.

What the hell was she thinking? She couldn't believe she was seriously considering allowing Tucker to do those kinds of things to her. She was reminded of the fear in Bethany's eyes when he had spoken to her. Or was it respect and awe? Or maybe a combination of all of the above? Already she was more careful about the things she said around him for fear of his hand across her bottom, and she barely knew him.

Once at her home, she gave him the grand tour of her acreage. It was a beautiful fall day, cool with a light breeze and the skies were bright and blue. The leaves were just starting to turn a rusty red and amber, and the normally green grass was now a dark-golden yellow. Fall was Lilliana's favorite time of the year. It brought back fond memories of football season, pumpkin carving, and warm sweatshirts wrapped around shoulders while stargazing.

Tucker looked at home as they walked in silence through an overgrown calico-bush field. He plucked one and chewed on the end and she wondered what he was contemplating. She could see his imagination going into overdrive behind seductive eyes and it was hard to mistake the money signs reflected back in them. After he was so adamant about her land, how could he just blow it off so easily? Perhaps he hadn't. Maybe this was all a part of his grand scheme. Her stomach turned at the thought. *Had she fallen into his trap?*

She stepped back and watched Tucker cautiously as she tried to discern his expression. *Yes*, he was definitely sizing up her property.

"It's still not for sale. And neither am I," she blurted out before she could filter her thoughts. He spun around to face her. He appeared offended, but what was more disconcerting was that he looked guilty. "Just so we're clear: neither I nor my land will ever have a price tag on it."

She turned without giving him a chance to respond. Frankly, she didn't care what he had to say. She walked quickly back to her house and several minutes later he entered her home. She began to dig several items out of her cupboards to make them something to eat when Tucker gripped her waist from behind. The feeling was reminiscent of their first sexual encounter together. She expected an apology or denial, but instead she received a nip on the back of her neck, and a hard cock pressed into her lower back.

"To hell with lunch. All I want is to fuck that sassy mouth of yours and to see you on your knees again," Tucker growled in her ear.

She tried to ignore him, but he spun her around harshly and pushed down on her shoulders, forcing her to her knees.

She slapped his hands away. She liked pleasing him, but on her own damned terms. Tucker unzipped his pants and slid his cock out, but she glared at him and refused to acknowledge the massive hard-on only three inches from her face

"Do it," he whispered.

She remained silent and sat back on her haunches, her gaze never once leaving his.

"Do. It." His mouth twitched with agitation, but she didn't budge.

"Do you want to be punished? Is this your way of trying to elicit a response of that kind out of me?"

"You don't own me, Tucker McGrath, and I haven't signed anything yet stating that you can do whatever the hell you want to me. You wanted me on my knees and that's where I'm at. If you want something else, then you can ask nicely." She swallowed hard. A show-down of the wills of epic proportions was taking place and it wasn't lost on her. "Do you know how to do that or would you like me to demonstrate? Like this: *please, Lilliana, suck my cock. Make me come.* Say it."

Tucker's agitated response came quick. "I once told you that I won't be topped and I meant it. I'm not playing games with you. Either you provide me with what I need and submit to me, or I'll find someone who will."

She promptly stood and walked towards her door and opened it. She'd be damned if she was going to allow Tucker to threaten her. Her heart sank because she truly wanted him in a way she couldn't explain. Maybe it was his bad boy outer shell that masked the country boy within, or quite possibly she liked the fact that he couldn't be tamed and demanded her surrender. Whatever the case may be, she wasn't going to be walked on again, especially when she couldn't trust him as far as she could throw his supercilious ass. It all came down to the fucking land and the fact that he hadn't denied still wanting it. *Of course he still wanted it*, she screamed at herself.

Lilliana couldn't bring herself to look into his angry eyes as she stood in the doorway because she knew it would break her heart. His statement from the previous night about wanting her submission had resonated with her. *God, how she wanted Tucker and his discipline...* And that room... She wanted to experience more of it, but not like this. Not when all he wanted her for was to satisfy his needs. *What about her needs? What about what she wanted?*

"Then find someone else," she said defiantly.

Tucker's zipper could be heard and a rush of air passed her as he walked through the doorway. Turned away from her, he stopped a mere few inches away from her, his breathing ragged. She stood immobile as did Tucker while they both internally struggled with what to do next. After a long pause, he turned to face her and fingered her chin. She feared what she would see staring back at her – anger, hatred, disgust. When their eyes met, his confusion was easily readable.

"Fucking, stubborn, woman," he said barely audible.

His perfect mouth was calling her; *kiss me*, it begged. Her insolence wavered and she leaned forward, unable to control her bodily response to Tucker's touch. She closed her eyes, fearful that he would reject her and walk away. She braced herself for the worst but felt his warm lips brush against hers. He parted his mouth and she breathed in his hot breath, and then he was gone. A cool gust of wind blew past her and the wind chime tinkled against its urging, reminding her that Tucker had been there, but was no longer present. She left her eyes closed as his engine revved loudly and he sped away.

She finally mustered up the strength to open her eyes and sulked back into her house, alone. So that was it; one passion-filled night with the one and only Tucker McGrath. He had spoken of pleasures untold, control and submission, and now she would never experience any it. She sighed, disappointed in herself for not having given Tucker what he wanted, but damn if that man wasn't aggravating as hell.

Her one night with him was amazing and she was grateful for his opening her eyes about what she really wanted - to submit. Though she couldn't help but wonder - would she ever be able to do it?

CHAPTER 14

Tucker couldn't believe the scene that had just played out. He kept his foot firmly planted on the pedal as his car rocketed down Lilliana's driveway. He had never been more wrong about a woman in his life. Every time he thought he had her figured out, she threw him a new curveball and each time it caught him squarely in the diaphragm, knocking the wind out of him.

He suddenly wished he had never laid eyes on her and her fucking land. She had read him like a book and if he had just denied still wanting it, he would be getting his cock sucked right about then. He detested himself and his greed. He wasn't always like this. His competitiveness was a mainstay since childhood, but the greed... Where the hell did that come from? He didn't need the money and he knew he was kidding himself for thinking the land would set him up for life. Hell, he could retire now if he wanted.

But his pride, that was a whole other matter. He was not going to be topped by Lilliana or any other woman. No way in hell. Who the fuck did she think she was dealing with - her little pussy of an ex-husband Adam?

Adam.

That bastard cheated and lied to Lilliana and hurt her in ways he would never understand. He had told her that he would try and make her forget about Adam if she allowed and then he proceeded to say something shitty like he'll find someone else?

He pulled off the side of the road to try and contain his rage and disappointment in the whole fucking Lilliana Norris situation. She was maddening, mouthy and alluring, and everything he never knew he wanted. The previous night was so incredible and he thought it was only the beginning of things to come. *Should he go back*? He wanted to, but his fucking ego...

With his head in his hands, his phone beeped.

Lilliana: I enjoyed last night. I'm sorry things ended the way they did. I hope we can remain amicable.

What the fuck? Did he just get friended? *Fuck. No.*

Tucker turned his car around and sped back to Lilliana's place. In a matter of minutes he was back on her doorstep, banging on the door.

This was such bullshit.

When she opened the door, her cheeks flushed and she looked utterly shocked.

"Did you really just try to friend-zone me?" He barked.

"I... No... I just wanted to convey my gratitude for last night."

He laughed sarcastically. "Gratitude? By trying to tell me *let's just be friends?* I'm fucking thirty-seven years old. I don't do the friend thing. Next you'll be telling me, *it's not you, it's me.*"

Her surprise turned to annoyance in the blink of an eye. "Fine, I guess we won't remain amicable then. What the hell is your problem anyway, Tucker? Why did you come back here? Just to chew my ass? And just to clarify: it's not me, it's *you.*"

He couldn't help but smile. *Chew her ass?* More like bite it. God damn, that ass of hers was tempting. Her eyes scanned his face and came to rest on his mouth. In the same amount of time it took her to become annoyed, she was now clearly turned on. It was his smile, he reminded himself. It was his secret weapon against the fiery brunette. He widened his grin and flashed his teeth.

Lilliana shook her head. "No. Absolutely not. I have reconciled the fact that you and I are finished. Done. Over with. One night of passion is all we get."

"In the seven minutes that I was gone you decided all that? Give me a fucking break. Tell me, is one night with me all you really want?" He paused, allowing her to stew on his statement. "There's no need for a spoken answer because I'm willing to bet your wet pussy is all the proof I need to make my point."

Lilliana's eyes widened. "Here we go again with your overconfidence."

"Tell me I'm wrong," he demanded.

Just like she could read him, he could read her and what was written all over her stunning little body was *fuck me now, Tucker.*

She folded her arms across her chest and scanned the floor. "You said you would find someone else to provide your needs. So what are you waiting for?"

Oh, shit. *That.* Tucker sighed. "I won't be topped," he answered, not really addressing the issue.

"I wasn't trying to do that, but this whole land thing just has me put off about you. I know you still want it so don't try to deny it."

"Fine, then, I won't. I'm a businessman, Lilliana. I can't help that the entrepreneur in me is always running in the background. It's who I am."

She was still clearly hurt and he knew he would have to swallow his pride a little and try and make amends. He hated it, but if meant giving Lilliana peace of mind, then so be it. "As for finding someone else... You're the only one in my sights at the moment."

She raised her head to look him eye-to-eye. "At the moment?"

Shit, that came out all wrong, too. "I mean... Ah, hell." He stopped before he put his foot in his mouth any further. "Lilly..."

She put her hand up and covered his mouth. "Stop. I'm not looking for any kind of commitment either. *For the moment* is just fine with me. But you seriously need to learn to say please and that's not because I'm *topping* you, it's because it's just good manners. And I'd imagine it would make your mother proud."

He lifted an eyebrow at her. He liked to see Lilliana's walls come down. He doubted she was truly attempting to top him, though he still had doubts about her ability to be submissive.

"I like you're controlling side, I really do, but... you... you're so damned... Ugh. You frustrate the hell out of me."

He smiled. That wasn't the first time a woman had spoken those words to him. Yes, he imagined his dominance would be difficult to come to grips with for someone as headstrong as Lilly, just as her stubbornness was not easy for him to get past. But he couldn't deny his attraction for her – unreasonableness and all.

"So what do you want to do?" He asked.

Lilliana's cheeks pinked up and she blinked long and hard. "At the risk of sounding desperate and unladylike, what I really want is for you to bang me six ways to Sunday like you promised you would do the first time you came here. I want a good, hard fuck like the one you gave me last night, twice. I want you and that amazing dick to make me forget about the fact that you want my land and that we're completely wrong for each other."

His cock immediately hardened. Yes, her request was more than a bit unladylike, but he could care less. She was being completely honest – no insinuations, no games, no overtones... Just *real*. As for being wrong for each other – that was most likely true, but they were both being up front with each other and there were no allusions or pretenses.

He wanted her and she wanted him *for the moment*, and that was good enough – *for now*.

Tucker grabbed Lilliana around the waist and hoisted her up into his arms. A good, hard fuck was precisely what he intended to give her. She wrapped her arms around his neck as he staggered into her home and kicked the door closed behind him. He pressed his mouth to her warm lips, and stumbled into her bedroom where they both frantically tore at each other's clothes. Jeans and underwear flew every which way in a flurry of movement of limbs intertwining and grasping onto any part they could latch onto.

He heaved her onto the bed and reached back down and fumbled through his pants pocket for a condom. He feared he had run out but sighed with relief when he found the last one. If this thing with Lilliana was going to be somewhat regular, he needed to get this whole birth control thing under control and speak with her about it, and the sooner, the better.

He ripped the foil open with his teeth and slid the wet skin over his rigid shaft while he kept his eyes on her. Her eyes became fixated on his cock and widened with anticipation. It was a mesmeric look for her and he paced his movements, wanting to enjoy the look of expectancy on her face.

"A good, hard fuck, huh?" He whispered. Lilliana's pupils darted up to his with a spirited toss of her head and she nodded. "Are you sure you can handle that?"

She licked her lips and her chest heaved with her heavy breathing. "Yes, I can handle it. Please…" She whimpered.

He reached for his jeans again, pulled the belt from its loops, and her look of anticipation turned to trepidation.

"On your stomach, hands behind your back," he ordered. Lilliana sat frozen and unblinking. "Why the hesitation?" He knelt on the bed in between her legs.

"I'm not ready for that."

"I see. So you're okay with sucking my dick and swallowing my come, but being bound is off limits?" He asked incredulously.

She rolled her eyes. "I guess when you put it like that… But can we save that sort of thing for later? When I'm more comfortable?"

He ran the leather through his hand, stopping at the buckle. His fingers skimmed the cold metal while he mulled over her request. Now was as good a time as any to find out what Lilliana was made of and if they were going to be compatible. His dick twitched as if reminding him that it was now or never and to get on with it. He came to the conclusion that the way to earn her trust was to allow a little leeway, especially considering how fragile things were at that point.

"I'm not much for concession, but I am willing to compromise if it means you'll start to trust me. Hands in front of you, wrists crossed. You still have a semblance of control that way. And... You'll still look fucking magnificent bound in my leather."

She cocked her head and blinked several times before finally nodding in agreement. She laid back and crossed her wrists low on her belly.

He moved quickly before she had a chance to balk. He looped the belt several times around her wrists and tucked the buckle neatly inside the binding. When his gaze met Lilliana's, she looked like a frightened animal, her breathing ragged and harsh, and her eyes wide and glassy.

"Damn, Tucker. The way you handle that belt... Your speed and agility ... I get the feeling you've done this sort of thing before. Frequently."

He threw his head back and laughed. *If she only knew.* Though in realty, he wished he had done it more often than he had been allowed.

She shook her head, "Okay, you need to seriously lose the sinister pervert laugh because you're freaking me out."

***

The look on Tucker's face was the sexiest thing Lilliana had ever seen staring back at her, but that laugh... It sent shivers down her spine and into her ass crack – something that was new to her. She didn't know it was possible to get goose bumps in her butt, but there they were, inching up into her pussy. It was a strangely annoying and delightful feeling.

She giggled when the tingling sensation crept up her labia, making her once smooth pussy now stubbly.

He stiffened as though she had struck him and gritted his teeth. "You think I'm funny?"

She swallowed hard. His statement reminded her of one of her favorite movies, *Goodfellas*, and what happened to the poor idiot who had laughed at Tommy Devito. Her laughter promptly died down, fearing that she would end up in the trunk of Tucker's Maserati, bound and gagged.

"No, it's just that you gave me the willies in my muffin and now I have cactopus."

Tucker's eyes widened and laughter floated up from his throat. The sound was marvelous and catching.

"Shit, Lilly, this is supposed to be sexy-time. You're lying here bound in front of me and looking like a hot as hell little sex kitten and I can't even keep a straight face with you!"

She grinned at him, and a part of her reveled in his openness with her. She absolutely adored his laugh and was thrilled to bring it out of him.

He took a deep breath, closed his eyes and settled himself. When he opened his eyes again, She knew playtime was over.

"Now... Back to business," he growled.

Grabbing the belt, he positioned her hands above her head and flipped her onto her belly. He bent her over the edge of the bed, holding onto the leather securely, pinning her hands high and forcing her face down.

"Just like the song: Face down, ass up... That's the way I like to fuck..."

Lilliana tried to comment about the song, but only her muffled voice could be heard. Barely able to catch her breath, she turned her face to the side. The urge to speak was ever present, however, she held her tongue and waited for Tucker's invasion. When it finally came without warning, it was hard and deep, and a cry of surprise broke from her lips. She clenched down and ground her body into the bed, trying to escape his forceful penetration, but there was nowhere for her to go.

He drove into her repeatedly, unrelenting and severe, his breathing louder with each thrust. Her eyes began to water as he hit her cervix time and time again. She had asked for a hard fuck and Tucker was giving her exactly that. Unable to stop herself, she began to moan out loudly, panting and gasping for air as he lay waste to her defenses.

"Yes, that's it, Pet... Louder," he grunted.

She complied and screamed out. He felt so damned good, his cock inside of her felt intense – the heat of his core radiating inside the walls of her pussy. His slicked shaft worked in and out and an impending orgasm built quickly. She became mindful of where his hot flesh touched her and she felt the tingle of his thigh brushing her hip. She pushed her ass back into Tucker's pelvis, meeting his thrusts bravely.

The palm of his hand was felt on her lower back as he pushed her down into the bed, reminding her to submit to his brutally passionate fucking. Inch by slow inch, he snaked his hand over to her hip and squeezed unsympathetically as he leaned down onto her and sunk his teeth into her shoulder blade.

His breath was warm and damp against her ear as he whispered, "My sweet, docile, Lilly..."

Lilliana had never been called something so unassuming yet sensual, and her body softened to his words.

"Yes, that's it... Give into me. Let go of yourself," he continued to purr against her ear as he plunged deeper and more powerfully into her.

Her whimpers and heartbeat became so thunderous in her own ears, all other sounds were drowned out. He tilted his pelvis and began to hit that spot that was all consuming. She closed her eyes, bit and tore at the bed sheets below her and fisted her hands trying to find some kind of relief from the sweet torture that Tucker was forcing upon her.

"Give it to me, Lilly," he nibbled on her collar bone.

She drifted away for only a brief moment as the wave of an orgasm washed over her body. It started low in her belly and then hit her like a tidal wave – smashing her against the rocks as her body convulsed and twitched violently.

"Ahh, Tucker!" She screamed out.

The entire lower half of her body was intensely sensitive, but he was merciless as he continued to delve into her, seeking out his own release. She whined and attempted to remain as still as possible as she tried to rein in the spasming of her body. The way he held her hands above her head and the sound of his voice was overpowering all of her logic. She wanted him so much; more of him, all of him. She wanted to be fucked like this on a daily basis until her body couldn't take anymore. It had been far too long since a man had taken control of her and even at that, no one had done it quite the way Tucker was doing it.

She had always associated sex with love and began fighting her own inner demons as she screamed inside her head – *no!* She didn't want love. She didn't need love. She just needed *this*. She shook her head trying to fight the next oncoming orgasm that was edging closer.

Tucker's voice was low and deep as he spoke to himself. "Right there..."

She felt the distinct pulsing of his cock as his movements became frenzied. He gyrated and swiveled his hips as he slid himself all the way out only to force his dick into her time and time again. He hit her G-spot unexpectedly and there it was – another wave of ecstasy. It came so suddenly that she didn't have time to prepare herself, and she jerked against Tucker and shrieked so loudly that her voice cracked as she choked on her own unintelligible words.

Sweet heavenly stars above, it was like being taken to another place. She was drenched in her and Tucker's sweat as it dripped off of his face onto her back. Suddenly, he stilled, cursed and came. Collapsing onto her back, he smashed her into the bed and rendered her helpless and unable to move under his muscular weight.

"Damn, Lilly," he chuckled softly, rolling off of her and finally letting go of her belted wrists.

She rolled onto her back. Every muscle in her body burned and ached, and it took every last bit of energy just to bring her arms down in front of her. Turning her head, her eyes met Tucker's.

Reaching over, he touched the tip of her nose. "Have you always been this docile in the bedroom?"

"As much as I'd like to be, I don't consider myself docile or submissive."

"In the real world you're not, but behind closed doors... You, my little Pet, are proving to be quite compliant. As for wanting to be submissive - you can be whatever it is you set your mind to. Some women are born submissive, some are taught to be, and others are somewhere in between."

There was truth in his statement. She had always felt that despite her stubbornness and strong will, there was a desire to be submissive to her man in the bedroom, though no one had ever given her the opportunity. She had tried her best to please Adam by being accommodating, not only in the bedroom but in everyday life, but he ended up just walking all over her. She guessed she was in the category of somewhere in between, and she wanted Tucker to help her reveal that side of herself.

She held up her bound wrists. "Have you done this sort of thing a lot?"

"I've done it, just not near as much as I would've liked. Not every woman is as open minded as you and certainly not every woman I've proposed binding has agreed to it. You did quite well your first time out."

She smiled proudly. Yes, she did do quite well and Tucker hadn't done too badly himself. She had feared he would take complete advantage of the situation but he hadn't. He had conducted himself both gentlemanly and animal-like, and it was a heady and mesmerizing combination.

He sat up and unbound her wrists. The imprint that was left on her skin was both exquisite and fascinating. Even artistic in a way. She traced the outline of the impression around her wrist with a finger.

"It's beautiful isn't it?" Tucker asked, kissing the inside of her wrist.

She nodded and gave him a smile of pure bliss. Yes, it was - just like Tucker.

CHAPTER 15

Tucker and Lilliana sat quietly eating the light dinner she had cooked. The fresh corn pulled from the small garden her aunt had left behind and the baked chicken was like a taste of home. They were both showered and clean, and seated across from one another as One Republic, *If I Lose Myself* played in the background. He found himself comfortable in his surroundings; the small, cozy house with family photos adorning the walls, the smell of home cooking, and the faint scent of wild flowers and grass blowing in from the open window. The ambiance and the sun low on the horizon felt nostalgic as Lilliana babbled on and on about everything and nothing at all. Her voice was soft and feminine, pleasant and almost sing-song, and Tucker appraised her with intense interest.

Once again, he found himself missing his family and the conversations that would ensue every night a suppertime. A visit sounded like it might be in order and he made a mental note to check his upcoming schedule.

His eyes wandered to her wrists which still showed signs of his belt. When his eyes rested on her green and brown flecked pupils, she was grinning at him as she watched his mouth. He hadn't even realized he was smiling. It was strange how she seemed to have that effect on him. When he reminded himself of how Lilliana thought they were all wrong for each other, he promptly suppressed his joy. *But were they really?* Their backgrounds were so similar, their upbringing and values...

No - their values weren't the same. Maybe a long time ago they were, but they clearly had different ideas of what was important to them now. For Tucker - money and career; for Lilliana - family and honesty. His throat tightened when he thought about her being all alone in the world. And about his deception. Both her mother and aunt were gone, and she knew nothing about her father. All she had was what they had left her – the acreage and her fond memories of them.

It was at that very moment he realized he couldn't and wouldn't take that away from her - not ever. Fuck the land; fuck the money. He would just have to find another real estate project to concentrate on. As for Lilly, she had his full attention, regardless if things were going to last or not. Her joy was so sincere and captivating, he could do nothing else but accept her for everything she was - willful, trying, often times infuriating, and completely loveable.

Uncomfortable with the emotions that Lilliana's home and smile were evoking, he scanned the tabletop and picked at a loose thread on the tablecloth. He didn't need another failed attempt at a relationship and Lilliana had made it abundantly clear that she wasn't interested in any kind of commitment.

Sex - that's all this was, he told himself.

He stood and began cleaning his and Lilliana's plates when she slid up next to him to the dishes that he quickly washed by hand. The way they moved in unison together, it was as if they had done it for a lifetime.

"I should go," he abruptly stated.

She shot him a despondent look. "So soon, Tuck?"

His eyes widened and his jaw gaped. No one but his family ever called him that. He didn't allow it. But the way Lilliana said it like it was common place had him struggling to find words. *Should he correct her?*

"Lilly..." He swallowed.

"Please don't go. Today was so wonderful. Well, most of it, anyway. Does it have to end so soon? Can't we go back to your place for some time-out?" She grinned widely, waggling her eyebrows up and down.

Yes, some time-out is exactly what he needed to get his mind off his sappy feelings, but he knew she was referring to getting down and dirty. Her fingers crept up his chest as he stood silently watching her.

Locking her fingers behind his neck, Lilliana tiptoed up to his lips and brushed her mouth against his. "Please, Tuck?"

The hunger burning in her eyes spoke of untold desires. Brusquely, he grabbed her and planted his lips firmly onto hers. He wanted to satiate those desires and stoke the fire blazing within her with his power and control. He wanted her, he couldn't deny it or himself, and he most definitely wasn't going to deny Lilliana when she was being so meek. Hell, who knew how long it would last before her obstinacy returned.

"Yes, of course, Pet. Anything you want."

***

The only *anything* Lilliana wanted at that moment was Tucker's arms around her. She felt dizzy with arousal as her heart beat rapidly.

She swiftly packed a change of clothes while he browsed through her unmentionables.

He plucked out a pair of pink panties and bra. "These," he stated placing them on the bed. He returned to her drawer and grabbed two more sets. "Oh, and these, too."

Next, he moved to her closet and dug out several pair of jeans and button-down, dress shirts and laid them out for her. *How long did he think she was staying at his place?* She just nodded complacently and added them to the growing pile.

With her house locked up, she found Tucker standing on the porch gazing at the darkening skyline and out into the open fields. He was at it again and it troubled her. She peered into his eyes, fearful that she might see dollar signs again, however, she was relieved when instead she saw a look of peacefulness on his face.

Her land had the same effect on her, as well. She felt at home on her family's land, like Margo and her mother were somehow watching over her. She hoped they were. Moving next to Tucker, she and slipped her arm into his and leaned her head against his bicep.

"I love this place. I can really feel my mom and Margo here. I swear I can sometimes even hear their voices carry with the wind. It's the sound of two happy little girls playing in the calico field."

He stared down at her and blinked long and hard. "I wish I could've gotten to know your aunt a little better."

"You met her?" She smiled up at Tucker.

His eyes widened with exaggeration. "Oh, yes, I met her."

"Ha! I bet she busted your balls!"

"She sure as hell did. Damn, she was a feisty thing. She wanted nothing to do with me. Sound familiar?"

Her eyes welled up and tears threatened to break free. She missed the closeness of her aunt and mother so much, it was painful. She would've loved to have gotten their collective opinion about Tucker, though she knew Margo would've told her to kick his ass and run the other way. She let out a small choked laugh as she fought back the tears.

"What is it?" Tucker hugged her close.

"Nothing. I was just thinking about what Margo would've told me about you."

"What's that?"

"To run like hell," she giggled.

She was only half-kidding, but Tucker's eyebrows knit together. She hadn't meant to offend him or hurt his feelings, though she clearly had.

"Deep down, I'm really not a bad guy," he whispered.

"Oh, Tuck, I didn't mean that. I know you're not. You're just, you know, a haughty piece of work."

His sexy grin returned. "You mean hottie," he spelled out the word phonetically, "And not condescending, right?"

"No, I meant condescending. Haughty and naughty, that's all you, Pretty Boy."

He shook his head in kidding dismay. "That mouth, I swear it'll be the end of me."

She hoped it would be the end of his arrogance, anyway.

During the drive to Tucker's place, Lilliana's phone rang. She recognized the tone as being that of Adam's. She had been avoiding him for weeks. On their last conversation, she had tried to make it undeniably clear that his calls were unwelcome. Yet, there he was, again, phoning. She glanced nervously at Tucker and put her phone back in her coat pocket.

"Aren't you going to answer that?" He asked curiously.

"No."

He narrowed his eyes and creased his forehead. "Why, is it your boyfriend or something?"

"Or something. You already know I don't have a boyfriend from that ridiculous background check you did on me. Anyway, it's no one important and it can wait."

Luckily Tucker was satisfied with her answer because she didn't particularly feel liking having to explain her situation with her ex. She detested that he wouldn't leave her the hell alone. She had moved half a country away from him and still that good-for-nothing, shit stain was intruding on her life.

She looked out the window at the picturesque view of the countryside as they headed into town. Fall was in full bloom and the Connecticut landscape was breathtaking. She had always adored Bridgeport during her visits, but now, living there, she truly felt like this was the place she wanted to call home – for good. She prayed everything would work out and that the small amount of money she had inherited from her aunt, and the sale of her condo, would cover the taxes for at least the first year.

"What are you stewing on over there?" Tucker prodded.

"Money. Taxes. My ex."

"I see. Well, everything will work out. As for your ex…"

Lilliana hadn't even realized she had mentioned Adam.

"He lost out on a good thing with you. Dumb fucker. I can't help but feel a little sorry for him. You're quite a catch, Lilliana Norris, and I'm one lucky SOB to have gotten you on your knees."

Her heart did a flip flop. Tucker's statement knocked the wind out of her and she suddenly felt short of breath. He had no idea the feelings he stirred within her. She reminded herself that his enticing words had undoubtedly been told to numerous females.

Not wanting to reveal how much his words really meant to her, she kept her gaze steadily focused out the window when she responded, "Thanks."

She closed her eyes for only a moment and drifted off. A bump in the road woke her up, reminding her that her body was sore and achy. Tucker had given it to her good two days in a row and her poor undersexed body wasn't adapted to such use. Getting out of his car at his house, she did a big stretch. She wanted more of Tucker's brand of sexy time, but she was exhausted. He walked over, put his arm around her waist and kissed the top of her head.

"I'm feeling it too. How about a nap before time-out?"

"That sounds fantastic."

***

Lilliana woke several hours later, hot, sweaty and uncomfortable. She was lying in Tucker's bed in only a tank top, and their limbs were a tangled mess of body parts. He was lying in only boxer shorts and deep asleep, and putting off some fierce heat. She pushed his arm off her chest and was able to pull herself out from underneath him without waking him. She leaned down and ghosted her mouth over his ear and kissed it gently. She sat back and traced the outline of brightly colored burning heart tattoo on his bicep and kissed it, too, and then made double time getting to his bathroom.

On her way back out, she glanced at her phone on the granite counter of his restroom, noting the time was much later than she had thought. Just as she picked it up, it rang out Adam's ringtone, startling her. It was loud and she feared it would wake Tucker.

Damn, Adam. Why the hell was he calling after 2:00 in the morning? Was he drunk or just a complete inconsiderate idiot? She already knew the answer to her own question and rolled her eyes.

She fumbled with the phone, trying to answer it before it rang out again. "What the hell, Adam?" She whisper yelled into the phone.

"So you are alive."

"Yes, I am. It's two in the mother-friggin' morning!"

"Watch your tone, Lil. I'm not in the mood. I've been trying to call you for weeks. I have half a mind to get on a plane and go out there to see what the fuck is so important that you can't pick up your Goddamn phone."

Who the hell did Adam think he was talking to? Did he suddenly grow balls or what? He hadn't spoken so harshly to her since they were married — back when he was sticking his useless dick into anything with a pussy. She bit her lip trying to restrain her anger and stop herself from screaming at Adam. She didn't owe him an explanation, but the last thing she needed was for him to show up and muck everything up with her and Tucker.

"So?" Adam barked.

"So, *what*?"

"So why the fuck haven't you returned my calls or picked up your phone?"

"Because I didn't want to talk to you and the last time I checked, we're still divorced and I don't have to answer to you."

He huffed, "Try again."

She didn't respond. The tone of Adam's voice was unfamiliar. He was usually just whiny and annoying. "Get a clue, Adam. I don't owe you anything. Stop. Calling. Me."

"Nope. Not gonna happen, Babe."

She cursed under her breath. She absolutely hated when Adam called her *Babe*. It disgusted her beyond reason. "God damn you, Adam. I thought moving three-thousand miles away from your worthless ass would keep you at bay."

"Wrong again. You should be used to that by now, though, right? You were always fucking wrong about me. If anything, your moving away has made me think about you more."

"That's the most truthful statement you've ever spoken to me. I believed you enough to marry you and you did nothing but lie and cheat. How wrong I was to think that you could ever be trusted."

"This again? How many times do we have to rehash this shit? I cheated, so what? If you had kept me happy it never would've happened, so get over it."

She would not allow herself to be put down by Adam, but she knew the conversation was pointless and going nowhere, and she wasn't going to argue any further with him. "Why the hell did you call anyway?"

"To tell you it's time to come home. Vacation is over. Sell that land and do what you need to do, and get your ass back here. Your friends miss you and I want you back."

Unbelievable. What an utterly moronic statement. She laughed loudly – the kind of lunatic laugh that only Adam could induce. "You just told me I couldn't keep you happy and now you want me back? Wow. Just. Fucking. *Wow*," she retorted in cold sarcasm.

"Now you know what I need and want, and you'll do better next time. Won't you?"

Lilliana was flabbergasted. "*I'll do better next time?* Oh, my, God, Adam. Seriously, you're going to make me vomit... In my mouth no less because you're so sickening. And then I'm going to piss down my own leg because you're so laughable. Piss and vomit, Adam, those are the bodily functions you elicit from me. I am never, and I honestly mean *never* going to have you again. Ever. Never, fucking, ever. Are you writing this down? Do you want me to send it to you in a memo or email, or would you prefer I come over there and shove that statement right up your pisshole?" She spat out the words impatiently.

She was feeling good about her verbal assault until Adam began his vocal backlash.

"Listen here, you little bitch. No one leaves me! No one! I allowed the divorce because I know how motherfucking stubborn you are. I played the waiting game, but I'm done with it. I have a fucking reputation and people are starting to talk about how you fucked me over!"

"I fucked you over? And you *allowed* it? Are you listening to yourself?" She shrieked back.

"Get your ass back here, Lilliana, or I swear to God, I'll come out there and drag your ass..."

She held the phone away from her ear. She didn't want to hear anymore and she was tempted to hang up, but knew Adam would only call right back.

Adam was still yelling about her not returning his calls and dragging her ass back to Kansas when she heard Tucker's whispered voice in her ear.

"Hang up the phone, Pet."

She hadn't even heard him approach. Her hands trembled from embarrassment and anger, and she just wanted to end the call and hide. When she didn't immediately comply with Tucker's order, he gently took the phone from her hand and hit the end button. When she turned to face him, she felt relieved he had taken the initiative to cut Adam off. He powered the phone down and casually laid it back on the counter.

"I want all of your attention and your ass back in my bed *now*," he said with quiet emphasis.

She nodded fervently and moved quickly, but not fast enough. His hand caught her bare cheek with a harsh slap making her yelp and jump. She ran to his bedroom and sat waiting for him on her knees on the bed, anxious energy coursing through her veins. When he came into the bedroom, he smiled at her, his eyes dancing with lust and filling her with a kind of longing she had never felt before.

"Stunning," he spoke in a broken whisper, his voice echoing her own sentiments about him.

Tucker held his hand out and helped her lay back on the bed. When he slid in next to her, he pulled her onto his chest. His voice was calm and steady, and exactly what she needed after the distressing conversation with Adam.

"Are you okay?"

He must've heard what was going on and she suddenly felt reserved. She didn't particularly enjoy talking about Adam and her past marriage woes. "Yes, I'm fine."

"Do you still have feelings for him?"

Lilliana leaned her head back and gazed into Tucker's eyes and shook her head, trying to reassure him. "Oh, I have feelings for him alright, just not the sentimental kind and there sure as hell isn't any love lost for him."

He lifted one side of his mouth in a crooked smile, but raised his eyebrows at her in disbelief. "Then why are you still in contact with him?"

"I'm not in contact with him; he's in contact with me."

"Why haven't you put a stop to that?" He asked, pushing her off his chest and lying next to her.

"I've tried. I've even gone as far as changing my phone number twice, but he's... Relentless."

He clenched his mouth into a tight line and some indefinable emotion flickered in his eyes. "Perhaps someone should have a talk with him about that."

"And that someone is going to be you? That'll go over well. The last thing you need is anymore damage to your pristine smile."

His lips twitched with the need to smile. "What makes you think it would come to that? Why can't two reasonable, grown men have an adult conversation?"

"It depends on the two men in question. You and Adam, reasonable? Not so much."

"I can be levelheaded when necessary," he countered defensively.

"Maybe you can, but Adam doesn't like being told what to do."

With a hint of censure in his tone, Tucker responded. "Most men don't, Lilly. That's where the power of persuasion comes into play and as you know, I can be very convincing, especially when it comes to what belongs to me. Also, my amazing molars would be just fine. His on the other hand — those are the ones you need to worry about."

Lilliana's body shuddered at the staunch look in his eyes. *She belonged to him.* But then again, she thought she belonged to Adam. How wrong she had been. She sighed miserably thinking about her failed marriage.

Before she could stop herself, her feelings came out. "Love is such a sham." Tucker looked taken aback and sat up on one elbow to face her. "It's not only blind, but deaf and dumb. And it sure as hell doesn't conquer all. Why do people tell little girls that? Why don't they just put a kibosh on the whole fairy tale with a happy ending BS and tell them that life is unfair and love sucks."

"Because it doesn't suck. Shit, Lilly, why such a bleak outlook? No, love doesn't always conquer all, but when it's real, it feels so fucking good — no matter how fleeting it may be."

Now it was her turn to be taken aback. This coming from the man whose name was synonymous with being a man-whore? It didn't make any sense.

"Why so bleak? Because the man I promised forever to ripped my heart out and stomped on it. He took an oath to be faithful and he whored himself out right under my nose. The whole damned town knew about it, my supposed best-friends knew about it, and no one cared enough about me to let me in on the little joke. *Oh, poor little Lilliana. Look at her, she can't keep her man satisfied so he gets it somewhere else.* What a joke. I did my best to keep Adam pleased and he still dicked every hole he could get into," she said softly.

Tucker touched her face, soothing her irritation as he ran his index finger over her lips. "How did you find out?"

"When my gynecologist informed I had Chlamydia. Isn't that nice? That douche nozzle was sleeping around and not using a condom, and then coming home and spreading his filth. That man is nothing but a disgusting puddle of enema juice."

"You certainly have a way with words, Pet."

His smile and laugh made her giggle in response, but her joy quickly died down. "When everything was said and done, it turns out he slept with almost a dozen women in the short span of our four year marriage. So you of all people should understand why I don't buy into falling in love."

Tucker furrowed his eyebrows at her. "Why *me* of all people?"

"Because you've been divorced twice," she stated plainly.

"Just because I'm not looking for love and I've given up on it doesn't mean I don't believe in it. Or miss it. The grand scheme for my life never included divorce. I was young when I married for the first time, and my career goals and education were more important than my love life. In retrospect, I didn't fight hard enough for my first marriage, and I fought too hard to make something out of nothing with my second," he stared into her eyes. "I'm a firm believer in true love, Lilly. I've found it twice. I thought I found it with my almost third wife, but it turns out I wasn't in love with her so much as I was with the idea of love and having my own family. It turns out she was infatuated with the prospect of living the kind of lifestyle she had always wanted."

"I'm sorry to hear that," she responded sadly.

His focus drifted off onto something in the background, his eyebrows pinched together. "Some people will lie to try and get whatever they want. My fiancé, she... She lied about..." He sighed. "She wasn't who she pretended to be."

Her heart hurt for him. She couldn't imagine only being wanted for money and popularity, and not knowing who was real or phony.

He lay on his back, his hands clasped behind his head. "I'm no saint and I've told my share of lies, but some things are sacred. You know?"

She didn't understand what Tucker was trying to say, but she sat, listening and wondering what lies he had told. *Had he lied to her?*

"Like marriage," he clarified. "I know you've heard all sorts of shit about me, but I'm no cheater."

"So it's okay to lie but not cheat? How does that work? I was under the impression the two went hand in hand." His mouth popped open and he looked astounded at her statement. "Don't ever lie to me, Tucker. I mean it. That for me is a deal breaker. I've been hurt by lies; sometimes I think irreparably. I know we're not, you know... Serious or anything, but I won't ever lie to you. It's not who I am."

He swallowed hard and looked away and out the window on the far wall.

Feeling Tucker withdraw, she tried to draw him back out. She hadn't meant for the conversation to get so intense. She also hadn't intended to reveal so much about herself or expected him to divulge such personal information.

"I'm sorry that your fiancé lied to you."

He breathed heavy and let out a loud sigh. "It's funny, but I remember when I was young and my parents struggled for money, all I ever wanted was to be wealthy enough to have anything and any woman I ever wanted. Now that I have the kind of wealth I've always dreamed of, I'm not interested in the women that come along with this lifestyle. They're without a doubt attractive, and accommodating in more ways than you can imagine, but rarely genuine. I miss the small-town girl that doesn't pretend to be anything other than what she is."

The room was unnervingly quiet for several long seconds as she pondered his words. "Don't worry, I'm not looking for love, either," she whispered, breaking the silence.

Tucker looked disconcerted. He sat up again and turned to her with a stern look on his face as if wanting to say something more. Slowly his face relaxed, and he put the matter aside with sudden good humor. "I'm not asking you to fall in love with me, but unadulterated lust and infatuation would be nice."

Seeing the amusement in his eyes and the flash of his teeth, she laughed. There was something warm and captivating in his brand of humor. She smiled naughtily. "Unadulterated lust? Yes, I think I can be of service to you in that regard."

"I have no doubt that you can," he winked.

She changed the subject. "Are you still in contact with your ex's?"

"No. I'm not interested in being friends with my ex's and I don't believe in dwelling on the past. There's a bit of advice in that statement you may want to consider."

"I'm not friends with Adam. Trust me, that man is as useful as a tape worm and as appealing as a raging case of syphilis."

Tucker chuckled and shook his head.

"Adam is..."

He put a hand up to her mouth. "I don't want to hear that man's name again. The only name I want you saying when you're in my bed is mine, in which ever form you choose. For example: Oh, God, Tucker or Master Tucker. I'd even settle for Sir or King Tucker. Better yet, you can call me Tucker, tongue wielding expert and God of cunnilingus and love making."

Lilliana laughed and fell onto her back.

"What's so funny? You think I'm joking?" He poked his finger into her belly button and swirled it around. "By the way, if I ever hear that shithead speak to you that harshly again, I'm thrusting my fist down his throat and tearing his vocal cords out, and that's no joke."

Her lower belly throbbed at the intense look in Tucker's eyes. She hoped it would never come to that, but damn would she love to see Tucker wail on Adam. She leaned in and kissed the corner of his mouth. "I didn't know you could be so chivalrous."

"I told you I'm a multifaceted man with many layers. Chivalrous and bad to the bone are just a few of those layers."

"Bad ass with a boner. Bad to the boner," she joked.

Tucker rolled his eyes.

"I really like the word *boner*. It's so descriptive and fun," she continued. "We should try to use it as often as possible in everyday situations," she quipped. "Let me start: I'd really like your boner in my bobo. If you would be so kind to place your boner in my moist, delicious muffin, I would greatly appreciate it," she laughed.

He face palmed and grunted. "You're not as funny as you think you are."

Like hell she wasn't. She had grown up an only child and learned very early on to entertain herself, and there was no one who could make her laugh harder than herself.

"You know, I really am the fastest person I know at shucking corn," she stated to which it was Tucker's turn to chuckle heartily. "No, really - I won first prize at the county state fair in 2000."

His eyes widened with humor. "No, shit? How many entries were there?"

"You'd ask something like that, wouldn't you, Mr. Competitive? Eight entries."

"Impressive," he tilted and nodded his head in a deep gesture.

"That was the same year I was runner up for Ms. Cloud County," she declared proudly.

"Shit, I'm banging a genuine Cloud County beauty queen! That was a good year for you," he grinned.

"Runner up beauty queen," she clarified. "The first-place winner was well-deserved. She played the flute beautifully for her talent. I heard years later that it was her skin-flute talents that really got her the crown," she chortled.

"Nice. What was your talent?"

Lilliana's cheeks blushed with embarrassment and she shook her head in disapproval.

"You brought it up, now disclose," Tucker ordered.

"I could balance books on my head while doing various chores. It was so silly."

"Show me!"

"Uh... No."

Ella Dominguez

"Do as you're told, Woman!" He pushed her off the bed. "Entertain me!" He clapped his hands as if he was the king and she was the jester.

She looked around the room and pulled a few hardbacks of various sizes off his large shelf. Holding up a thick book, she raised her eyebrows sarcastically as she peered over her shoulder. "*The History of Western Philosophy?* How existential of you." A twinkle of humor crossed her face as she rolled her eyes.

"Layers, Baby; kinky and philosophical layers as you can see by my copy of *She Comes First: The Thinking Man's Guide to Pleasuring a Woman,*" he flashed a smug grin at her.

She scanned the bookshelf and found the copy of the aforementioned book and pulled it out. *Holy shit.* It actually looked like it had been read — more than once. The spine was cracked and worn, and there were even a few dog-eared pages. Her eyes darted back to the shelf and she saw a plethora of other paperbacks on sexuality, female orgasms and ejaculation, and several titles that included loving sex, oral sex and slow sex.

Lilliana stood dumbstruck. This man seriously knew his stuff. And hers, too. Hell, he probably knew more about making her body hum than she did.

Tucker donned his cheesiest smile and waggled his eyebrows. "Feel free to borrow any books from my vast library."

"I'd like to learn more about you, but I don't see any books about arrogance in this *vast* collection."

He lifted an eyebrow at her but his smile widened. "It might do you well to read the title *Punished into Submission.*"

Shocked at all the smut, she asked, "I don't think so. So you read erotica?"

"When the occasion calls for it. I'm a lonely man. Erotica satiates my needs."

"You, lonely? I doubt that. In between all your women, when do you find time to read?"

181

He summarily changed the subject. "Are we going to talk books all night or are you going to show me this so-called talent of yours?"

She grabbed two more hard covers to prove her talent wasn't *so-called*. His eyes rounded when he saw how many books she was holding. She winked and grabbed one more, totaling five in all. Tucker sat up in bed, his deep chestnut eyes dancing with humor.

"What'll you give me if I can serve you a beer with these books on my head?"

"Anything you want," he licked his lips. "But I'd be even more impressed if you could suck me off with those books on your head."

She wondered, *could she do it*? She did enjoy a challenge. If doing it meant seeing that magnificent smile of Tucker's, she sure as hell was going to do her best.

"*Anything* I want?"

Dipping his head slightly, he nodded.

She bit her bottom lip. "I intend on holding you to your word."

Tucker beamed and swung his legs off the edge of the bed and spread them wide. Grabbing a pillow, he tossed it on the floor between his feet making her heart pound madly at his sweet gesture.

She knelt on the pillow and slowly placed the books on her head, one by one, while holding absolutely still. It had been years since she had attempted this action and she was unsure if she would be successful. She bent forward slightly to get the books to sit better on her head and then gingerly placed the last book on top. They teetered and she held her breath until they steadied.

Looking up at Tucker, the grin on his face was one like she had never seen on any man alive. It was pure, unadulterated joy. She fought the overwhelming urge to throw the books to the side and lunge herself at him and focused all her lust on giving him what he had asked for.

She gripped his shaft in one hand and rested her other on his lower belly in the soft hair below his navel for support, and slowly began to stroke him into hardness while keeping her movements paced and unhurried. He hissed through his teeth and his smile faded into something else – desire. His eyes fluttered opened and closed until he became completely hard. Bit by bit, she lowered her head until her mouth met the head of his dick. She licked casually, but was quickly becoming aroused herself. She took him into her mouth and sped up her efforts, but when she did so, the books began to wobble. With his cock still in her mouth, she stilled until the books settled and little by little, she began to move up and down his dick again. The salty taste of his pre-come filled her mouth and she moaned, wanting more. She squeezed her hand around him tighter when he suddenly came undone.

He grabbed the books from her head and threw them to the floor violently and gripped her head as he pushed it down onto his cock, forcing her to take all of him to the back of her throat. She gagged loudly and she pushed away from him. His hips thrust upwards as he forced her to swallow him again, fucking her mouth with such fervor, she thought she would implode. Tucker grunted loudly every time he pushed into her mouth and only a few short minutes later, she felt the bitter taste of his come hit the back of her throat. Again, she wretched noisily but swallowed quickly. She really hated that she had such a weak gag reflex, but was happy Tucker was still pleased nonetheless.

He fell backwards onto the bed, his breathing heavy and his hands fisted in his hair. "Damn, Lilly. I had no idea you were so gifted." He laughed, moving onto his side to face her. "You're quite talented at the skin-flute as well, though there are a few things we need to touch up on," he said breathlessly.

"A girl can learn a lot from porn," she batted her eyelashes as she reached over and gulped down the bottle of water on the nightstand.

His eyes widened. "You watch porn?"

"On occasion. I'm a lonely woman in my sexual prime and I have needs. You read erotica and I watch porn. It's a trade-off. Feel free to borrow any of my DVD's from my vast collection."

"Sounds like a good trade-off, but hopefully I can help you out with your needs. So tell me: what other kinds of things have you learned from watching porn?" He asked suggestively, sliding toward her and pulling her nipple to a point before engulfing it in his mouth.

"Besides the finer points of dick licking, I've learned that screaming *'your cock is so big'* to the high heavens while playing bouncy time on a gigantic wiener is not charming no matter how attractive you are."

"In your opinion. I think it's hot as hell. I'd love to see you screaming while playing bouncy time on my dick right now."

Tucker reached into the nightstand and pulled out a condom. Lying back, he spread his legs wide and propped himself up on a pillow, stroking himself into complete hardness as he waited for her.

How could he get so hard so quickly after having just come? She was amazed at the stamina he possessed.

"Ride it, Pet," he stated when she didn't move fast enough.

"You're so impatient," she told him, sitting on top of him and helping him with the rubber.

"Hush, Woman, and do as you're told."

He licked his fingertips and slicked her pussy, then held his cock steady for her to climb onto. She positioned his pelvis between her thighs and slowly sank down onto his rigidness. Throwing her head back, a small whimper escaped her mouth. He reached up and gripped her waist. His touch was firm and persuasive and invited more. Pulling her down slowly, her lips met the base of his shaft, completely sheathing his dick inside her.

"That's it, Lilly," he groaned, his eyes unblinking, piercing and demanding.

She brought herself up and down rhythmically, her body tingling from the contact. Tucker met her thrust for thrust. When he guided his thumb to her clit and began to circle it and press down firmly, a fire in her lower belly to burn fiercely.

"So damned beautiful," he grunted as he tilted his pelvis to hit her G-spot.

The sensation was still new to her and she quivered with an ache that felt both good and painful. He raised his upper body and pulled her close by her waist while keeping his thumb firmly planted on her swollen nub. Snaking his other hand around the back of her neck, he squeezed tightly causing her to gasp out from the strength of his touch. His thrusts came faster and more powerful. The wet sound of her pussy filled the large dark room and her body began to respond to his demands.

"Soak me," he ordered as he claimed her lips and crushed her to him, stifling her scream.

A literal gush of wetness released and her body began to spasm uncontrollably.

When Tucker freed her mouth from his, her impassioned words spilled out as her trembling limbs clung to him, "Oh, God, Tucker! Master Tucker! Sir Tucker! King Tucker, thumb wielding expert and God of G-spot manipulation and love making!"

Tucker's laughter rang out hysterically as he held onto Lilliana. He continued to laugh until his cock softened and jiggled inside of her, and she became a limp mess in his arms.

CHAPTER 16

Lilliana was floating on a cloud high above Connecticut, looking down at Margo's land. The once lush green fields were no more and all that could be seen were strangers in hardhats building tall complexes and laying down pavement as far as her eyes could see. Bulldozers and cranes were scattered where the calico fields had once been and the home where her mother and auntie had lived was a pile of rubble. She screamed for them to stop, but her voice was stifled by the distance between them and the misty fog in the air.

"My sweet, Lilly..."

She felt Tucker's warm hands on her body as he gently shook her while she fought her way through the cobwebs of her nightmare. Her eyes fluttered open and his thumb swept away a hot tear that rolled down her cheek.

"My family's land," she whimpered with more tears trembling on her eyelids. "I don't want to sell it. But the taxes... Oh, God. It's the only thing I have left of my family. It's all I have left."

His arms encompassed her. "No, Lilly, that land is yours to keep. I'll make sure nothing happens to it."

She pressed her open lips to his. They were warm and sweet, and soothed her anxiety. With the nightmare still fresh in her mind, there was a dreamy intimacy to their kiss. Comforted by his presence, she fell immediately back to sleep.

When she awoke again, she could hear men's voices in the distance. She slipped on a tight fitting tee and some panties, and followed the sounds of men's chattering. There was soft laughter and the scent of masculinity as she got closer to the kitchen.

She stood in the entrance to see Tucker hugging another man and talking animatedly. She turned to walk out and put something more appropriate on when she caught his eye. He furrowed his eyebrows disapprovingly at her, making the stranger turn to face her as well.

"Well hello, there," he greeted her with a warm smile.

Lilliana blushed. "I'll be right back," she attempted to leave.

"Don't leave on account of me. Come sit with us. I'm Mason McGrath. And you are...?"

Her eyes lit up. It was Tucker's brother. My God, the resemblance was uncanny. He looked like a younger version of Tucker, only slightly shorter. Their facial features were similar – right down to the small dimple in their cheeks. His hair was a mess of ash-blond waves, and he was just as handsome and solid as Tucker. He also had a keen sense of style like Tucker.

She suddenly became unaware of her attire and reached a hand out to Mason. "I'm Lillia..."

Tucker immediately cut in. "This is just a friend."

Mason shot him a critical look and waved aside his hesitation. "Please forgive my brother's rudeness. You were saying?"

Irked by Tucker's abrupt cool aloofness towards her, Lilliana didn't feel so friendly anymore. "Lilliana," she whispered, dropping her hand to her side.

"A friend," Tucker emphasized with a decisive tone to his voice.

"We've established that," Mason puckered his mouth at him.

There was something about Mason that she couldn't quite put her finger on. Perhaps it was his mannerisms and the way he stood. He had a barely noticeable hint of femininity about him when the realization hit her that he was gay. *Was Tucker embarrassed about that*? Was that his reason for being so frosty and obviously not wanting to introduce them to each other? Her annoyance increased when Tucker still refused to acquaint them.

Mason chimed in, "My brother's been out of the country life for too long, so you'll just have to excuse his poor attitude. I on the other hand, am still familiar with the customs and values that I grew up with and would love to have a chat with you, Lilliana."

She smiled with satisfaction at Mason's ribbing.

"Where are you from?" He asked, seating himself at the island.

"Kansas. I just moved here a few months ago."

"How lovely. Do you like it here? How did you meet Tucker?"

Mason's questions came spilling out and Tucker became visibly irritated, but it didn't stop her from responding. "I love it here. My family is originally from these parts. I met Tucker..."

"Where are you staying, Mason?" Tucker interrupted.

He winked at her before rolling his eyes at Tucker's persistent impoliteness. "The usual."

"I won't have it. Bring your things over, you're staying here."

"Okay, then, Mr. Bossy Pants," Mason laughed, deep and husky.

Lilliana giggled and anger lit Tucker's eyes. "Lilliana was just leaving."

She winced at his words and expression, and Tucker ran his hand through his hair and sighed heavily when he saw the look of hurt on her face.

"Yes, I was. It was nice meeting you," she spoke with quiet firmness.

Like a true gentleman, Mason stood and took her hand into his own, placing a gentle kiss on the top of it. "Likewise, Dear. I hope we can get better acquainted another time when Crabby Panties isn't around," he nodded his head toward his brother.

She smiled but promptly left the kitchen with a heaviness in her chest. Their short time together had been so amazing, but Tucker's attitude toward her had left her with a feeling of emptiness that was unwelcome.

She packed her bag quickly and made her way to Tucker's front gate and waited by his car, taking in the chilly morning air. She leaned against his vehicle and set her bag down, and shook her head at herself regretfully. Romance truly was dead as far as she was concerned. She had sorely wanted to spend the rest of the afternoon with Tucker in his time-out room, but that clearly wasn't going to happen. Just as she heard Mason's car leave, her phone rang out.

"Where are you?" Tucker asked, a hint of panic in his voice.

"Waiting by your car. I'm ready to leave."

He hung up and only a few seconds later met her by the car. "You don't have to leave right this minute."

"No, it's fine. I'm already packed."

He stood before her, silent, the tension increasing by the second. "If that's what you want," he dismissed her with the wave of a hand.

No, that's what *he* wanted, but she maintained her curtness to hide her true disappointment in the way he had treated her.

He loaded her bag and buckled her in per his usual protocol, and their journey back to her place began. It was quite apparent that he was taking the long route which confused her even more. If he wanted her gone so badly, why the slow ride back?

"Is your brother gay?" She asked, trying to break the uncomfortable and awkward silence.

"Yes. How did you know?"

"I have a good sense for that sort of thing, I guess."

"Hell," he huffed, "I didn't know until he told me."

"Are you embarrassed about it?"

Tucker jerked his head around to glare coldly at her. "Fuck no. I love my brother and I'm proud of his accomplishments. I could give a shit less what his sexual preferences are," he said in a severe, raw tone.

Perturbed, she crossed her arms and pointedly looked away. "So then it's me you're embarrassed of," she countered trying to keep her fragile control in check.

Just then they came to rest at a stop light. "Don't be ridiculous. You're beautiful, intelligent and strong. Why the hell would I be embarrassed of you? I just don't need Mason running back to my family and blabbing to everyone that I've met a woman..." His voice softened, losing its steely edge. "Especially considering we've just met and we don't know where this thing between us is going."

He had made a valid point and she couldn't argue. But his actions still stung. She had only wanted to be introduced, not doted on and fawned over.

As she sat motionless staring out the window, Tucker huffed. "If I had known you were going to be so dramatic about it, I would've just introduced you."

There was no drama as far as she was concerned. "I'm glad you didn't introduce us. Your actions let me know where you stand." She tried to remain collected, but her voice rose an octave making him turn his head to face her.

"Where is it that you think I stand when it comes to you?" His eyes clung to her, analyzing her reaction to his question as he waited for her response.

"The same place I stand. This thing could've gone either way, but I'm glad to know early on that you aren't serious about me. It saves me a lot of heartache in the long run," she replied with light bitterness.

Without looking directly at Tucker, Lilliana could see him shake his head. The ten minutes it took to get back to her place were agonizingly hushed. When they arrived at the main road to her driveway, she instructed him to stop.

"Just drop off me here. I could use the fresh air." She jumped out of the car and retrieved her bag from the rear seat. Turning to walk the distance back to her doorstep, she heard the passenger window slide down.

"Lilly," he yelled to her.

She turned and bent down in the window.

"I want to see you again."

"Oh, you will. You have a follow-up appointment on Wednesday at 10:00 a.m. See you then."

***

Stubborn. Fucking. Woman.

Lilliana turned and walked away with her bag over her shoulder swinging in time with her hips. Tucker watched until she reached the landing of her porch and turned his car around to head back into town. *So that was it?* He neglected to introduce her to his brother and now it was over? What was the big fucking deal?

He recalled her tear-filled dream and the promise he had made to her and her soft lulling voice drifted in and out of his thoughts as drove home. He was serious about her, in as much as he could be. Hell, she was the one who said they were wrong for each other. Why then should either of them agonize over the loss of something that never was? Not only was she obstinate but fucking indecisive. He chuckled to himself. As unique as she was, she could also be a typical woman.

Dialing Mason's number, it rang several times before going to voice mail. His visit was unprompted but a welcome surprise. Apparently his mother had phoned Mason to tell him about their conversation and her concerns for Tucker's emotional well-being. Undoubtedly she had also mentioned her suspicions about his seeing someone.

Back at his home, Tucker made his bed. He picked up the pillow Lilliana had slept on and brought it to his nose. Her perfume was still lingering on it and his driving need to be with her stirred within him. *Was it really over?* He hadn't even gotten to fully experiment with her limits yet or do the things he wanted with her.

Having a difficult time coming to the realization that he may never get to do those things, he denied the truth of the situation to himself. She craved his touch as much as he did hers so surely she would call him, wanting more of his masterful seduction.

Just then, his phone rang out. He smiled smugly to himself, convinced that it was Lilliana calling, wanting to see him again. The smile of satisfaction quickly disappeared when he reached for his phone only to see his brother's name displayed across the screen.

"What's for dinner, Tuck?" Mason laughed into the phone.

***

Nightfall came and Mason was settled into one of the guest suites. Dinner and conversation had been pleasurable and Tucker had forgotten all about Lilliana's abrupt departure from his life. Thankfully, Mason hadn't prodded him about her and he was left with only the memory of their passion-filled weekend sans drama.

As he lay in bed reading over financials and browsing the land for sale ads online, Lilliana kept seeping into his thoughts. His phone beeped signaling a text message and, again, he smiled to himself. *Right on cue*, he thought.

He picked up the phone and was once more disappointed to see it wasn't Lilly contacting him. Instead it was a standard issue message from his jeweler that the item he had ordered was in, only reminding him that his brief fling with the spirited brunette was over.

Although, if he was honest with himself, it had felt like more than a *fling*. Their intimate and witty expressions towards each other and banter were exciting and new. Her familiarity with the kinds of music he liked, their similarities in upbringings and their sarcastic exchanges were something he doubted he could find in anyone else.

He slept uncomfortably that night. He guessed it might have something to do with the fact that Lilliana's scent was still on the bed sheets and pillowcase. Waking at three in the morning, he tossed the pillow to the floor, hoping to stop dreaming about the beautiful and frustrating woman that was haunting his dreams. It didn't help. She still continually made appearances in every single one of his dreams.

Monday morning rolled around and his crabbiness was apparent to everyone in the work office, and they all avoided him. He continually checked his phone for some kind of life, but the only thing happening on it was work related. Lilliana wasn't going to call and he damned well knew it. She was too headstrong and stubborn for that. He had hurt her feelings by being frigid with her in front of Mason and he was now kicking himself for it.

He had introduced women to his family that he cared for less than Lilliana, so what the hell was his problem? He just didn't want to see the disappointment in his parent's eyes when he *again* told them that things hadn't worked out and the barrage of questions that would follow.

Exasperated with thinking about her and what could've been, he swallowed his pride and texted her.

McG: What time did you say my appointment was on Wednesday?

Seriously. Fucking. Lame. And he knew it. He rolled his eyes at his stupid attempt at trying to strike up a conversation with Lilliana.

Lilliana: 10.

Her message was curt and to the point. What else did he expect after the way he had treated her?

McG: Can I get in any sooner? I have a busy schedule this week.

Again, fucking lame.

Lilliana: Not sure. You have to call the receptionist desk and ask. Do you need the number?

McG: No. I have it. Can you check for me?

Lilliana: Yes. BRB.

He sat impatiently waiting for her next response. Tomorrow would be good. Now would be better but he knew they closed their offices shortly.

Lilliana: The soonest is tomorrow at 3:00 pm. Your hygienist will be Sue Ellen.

Tucker's heart sank. Had he upset her so badly that she was going to completely blow him off now?

McG: 4:15 PM: Why not you?
Lilliana: The sale of my condo back in KS suddenly fell through. :(I have to go back and deal with paperwork pronto. I leave tomorrow afternoon. I'm less than thrilled. Sue Ellen is good. And cute. You two should hit it off.

He wasn't interested in Sue Ellen, whoever the fuck she was, regardless of whether or not she was cute.

He immediately instructed Ariel to look into the sale of Lilliana's condo to see what the hell was going on. Sales didn't just *suddenly* fall through. There were usually mitigating factors involved and always a little forewarning.

Adam. Tucker gritted his teeth thinking about the way he had spoken to Lilliana on the phone and his threat that could be heard in the next room. He suspected her ex may have had something to do with the loss of the sale and there was no way in heaven or hell he was allowing Lilliana to be in the same state, let alone the same city as Adam.

McG: Thanks, but I don't need help in the dating dept.
Lilliana: No. U don't. U do just fine on your own. Ciao, pet.
Her cold response threw him off balance. He shuffled his phone between his hands before typing his response.
McG: You stole my line.
Lilliana: No worries. I won't be using it ever again. Gotta go home and pack. Goodbye.

Goodbye. Tucker didn't like the way the word just hung there on the screen of his phone, mocking and reminding him of how he fucked things up with Lilliana.

He called Ariel into his office to get things settled swiftly. When all was said and done, there would be no need for Lilliana to make a trip to Kansas – now or ever again.

CHAPTER 17

Lilliana stared at the last message she sent Tucker. *Goodbye.* She hated that word. It was so final, but that's what she had intended it to be. She wanted him, but she knew he was wrong for her. She had known that all along. From the very first moment she laid eyes on his perfect smile, every fiber in her body warned her against him. But, damn if he wasn't sex personified. He was even sweet on occasion and tender, just like when he had calmed her nightmare and held her in his arms. His strong body had felt so good pressed against her; his mouth and that delectably, alluring grin of his... And that room with all the sexy equipment...

She bit her bottom lip harshly and the pain brought her back to reality. She had a tendency to romanticize things and she wasn't going to allow herself to do it this time. Tucker hadn't wanted to introduce her to his brother and it was a rude awakening as to how he really felt about her. Sure, he found her attractive and wanted to have his way her in his time-out room. So what? Was that all she was good for – a fuck? No, she deserved better than that. And truth be told, she wanted more. How much more, she hadn't decided yet, but she wanted more than to just be someone's jump off.

Once she got home, she packed slowly. She dreaded being back in Cloud County because she knew Adam would be sniffing around and making trouble. She also dreaded her busy morning at work followed by a long flight. Not hungry, she forced herself to eat a light snack and go to bed early.

Lying in bed, she stared up at the black ceiling thinking about the strange wooden bed that was in Tucker's time-out room. She closed her eyes and envisioned herself shackled to the cross at the end, her hands high above her head and bound, and her legs spread wide with her ankles cuffed at each corner. What kinds of things would Tucker have done to her? Hurt her? She didn't believe he was the kind of man to do that.

Just as sleep was about to find her, the sound of her phone woke her.

McG: You left your CDs at my house.
Lilliana: U woke me to tell me that?
McG: You were sleeping at this hour? What are you – 80?
Lilliana: Some days I feel like it. I have a busy day tomorrow or have u forgotten?
McG: No. So, do you want me to bring them by?

She rubbed her eyes. Was Tucker deliberately trying to make things more difficult for her?

Lilliana: No. U can drop them off at the office tomorrow when u have your appt. G'night.
McG: Lilly... my Pet...

She sighed and blinked with bafflement as she waited for his next response. Impatient and tired, she messaged him back.

Lilliana: I'm not doing this with u. Not now. Not ever. G'night.
McG: 8:51 PM: I was just going to tell you that I've cancelled your flight to KS and got you a refund. The paperwork for your condo is being over-nighted and should be here by early afternoon. I'd be happy to go over the conditions of the sale with you sometime. Let me know if you're interested in utilizing my expertise in these matters. Free of charge, of course. You're welcome and goodnight.

She stared at the message with dazed exasperation. How did he manage it? She supposed it was because of his infinite knowledge regarding real estate laws and such. Whatever the case may be, she was grateful for not having to deal with it or Adam.

Her dreams that night were more pleasant than the previous night, and she woke early. At work, she managed to rearrange the schedule so that she would be the one to see Tucker's fine set of molars that late afternoon.

When lunchtime arrived, she received a message from him and her mouth curved into a smile thinking about his efforts to help her. He really could be kind.

McG: The paperwork on your condo arrived. IMO, you're not asking near enough for it so it may be a blessing in disguise that the sale fell through. We should discuss this more in person.

Yes, in person sounded nice, however, she didn't need the temptation. She moistened her lips nervously as she replied.

Lilliana: Why didn't u have the papers sent directly to me?
McG: I took it upon myself to look them over first.
Lilliana: Haughty as ever.
McG: Correction, Ms. Norris: a HOTTY as ever. ;)
Lilliana: BTW, thank u for your help with this matter.
McG: My motives were somewhat selfish so there's no thanks necessary.
Lilliana: How so?
McG: Do I have to spell it out?
Lilliana: Apparently.
McG: I don't want you seeing Adam.

She hesitated, torn by conflicting emotions. Why should Tucker care? Hell, she wasn't good enough to meet his family, what did it matter if she saw Adam or not?

Lilliana: Adam wasn't the issue at hand and not the reason I was going. My condo was.
McG: You're naïve if you don't think those two issues are one and the same.

A knot rose in her throat. She sure as shit wasn't naïve, but it never occurred to her that Adam would go to such measures just to see her. The more she thought about it, the more livid she became.

Lilliana: Thank u for bringing it to my attention.

Fuck. Adam.

With the last few minutes of her lunch break, she walked outside and dialed Adam's number. He no sooner answered when she ripped into him.

"You manipulative son-of-a-bitch! What gives you the right to fuck with my life? That money was going to help me keep Margo's land!"

"Watch your language, Babe," Adam ground out between his teeth.

His contemptuous tone and use of the repulsive term *Babe* sparked fury in her.

"I swear to Christ, Adam, if you had anything to do with the loss of the sale..."

"You'll *what?* Cry for mommy and Auntie Margo to come and rescue you like they always did? You've got no one except for me now, so you'd better lower your voice and start showing me some motherfucking respect."

She spoke in a tear-smothered voice, "I hate you, Adam, and I'll never have you again. N-E-V-E-R. I'd rather be struck down with vaginal leprosy than to be subjected to your lies and bullshit. Don't you ever fucking call me again or so help me, I'll press charges on your ass for harassment."

She hit the end call button and rigidly held her tears at bay. How could Adam bring up something so cruel like being alone and without the love and support of her family?

Just then Dana came out into the parking lot and placed a hand on her shoulder.

"You okay, Hun?" She asked softly.

"No, I'm not. My ex may have just cost me my land," she sniffed.

"Oh, Lil, I'm so sorry. What can I do to help?"

There wasn't anything Dana could do, but her sad eyes and pitiful attempt at a smile warmed her heart. She needed a friend, especially now, and she welcomed Dana's comfort. Dana wrapped her arms around her shoulders and held her close.

Pulling away, Dana's eyes lit up. "Do you want me to kick him in the junk for you? Because I will, Lil."

She managed a smile and with the determination that was instilled into her, she grimly went about the rest of her day, counting down the minutes until she could see Tucker's handsome face and sensual smile.

Always punctual, he showed up five minutes early to his appointment. She watched as he seated himself in the long dental chair. His self-confidence and ruggedness was deliciously appealing. As usual, he was dressed immaculately in a tailored, dark-gray suit with black oxfords. He made himself comfortable, loosened his tie and unfastened the top button of his shirt, and as he did so, the smell of his tantalizing after-shave wafted past her nose.

His naked, sculptured and tattooed body flashed in her mind and her pussy softly whispered its longing for him. She needed to seriously pull herself together because Tucker had an eerie way of reading her body language and no doubt he would sense how turned on she was. Maybe sending Sue Ellen in to deal with him wasn't such a bad idea after all.

Reminding herself about the way he had dismissed her in front of Mason, she turned to leave before Tucker saw her. Still out of sorts from smelling his cologne and imagining him nude, she ran into the edge of the wall, making a loud ruckus. He turned his head and when their eyes met, they exchanged a courteous, simultaneous smile.

"I was hoping I would see you," he greeted her.

She cleared her throat and pulled up a chair directly in front of him without saying anything. She flipped on the bright overhead light and slowly reclined his chair back as she studied him. Her mouth hung open in awe at his attractiveness even under such harsh lighting. His eyes fixed on her expression and the corners of his mouth lifted in an unspoken invitation.

"Relax and lay back, please," she instructed, trying to remain professional.

A muscle quivered in his jaw and his right eyebrow went up a fraction. "I'm usually the one saying that."

In an attempt to prove to herself and Tucker that she was immune to his sexual innuendos, she did her best to keep her expression blank while maintaining an even, unconcerned tone when she spoke her next command. However, as soon as the statement, "Open wide," left her mouth, the unwelcome blush of embarrassment crept onto her cheeks.

"That, too," a lascivious grin spread over his face. "But you already know that, don't you?"

Fumbling with a bite block, Tucker seemed to enjoy her struggle to recapture her composure. As she brought the bite block to his lips, he skimmed his fingers lightly over her bare forearm. Her eyes darted to his and she pulled her arm away.

"Would you like me to get Sue Ellen to finish this exam?" She threatened, the uncertainty of her statement making her voice harsher than she had intended.

His mouth formed into a hard, thin line as he cautiously regarded her. When he finally opened his mouth, she slipped the bite block in and got right back to business.

"Your gums seem to be healing quite nicely. Are you having any issues with pain?" She asked, poking around inside his mouth with a dental mirror.

"Nuh-huh" He mumbled.

"Damn, Tuck... Your teeth are so beau..." She snapped her mouth closed when she realized what revealing statement was about to come spilling out.

"Yeth? You were thaying?" He crookedly smiled.

Abruptly, she stood. "Dr. York will be right in."

Before she could make her getaway, he reached out and gripped her wrist tightly and yanked her back to him. With his other hand, he pulled out the bite block.

"It seems I've forgotten your CD's. I'll just have to bring them by your place later." The expression in his toffee-brown eyes seemed to plead for something inexplicable.

She pinched her eyebrows together, "For not wanting anything to do with me, you sure are making a lot of effort to see me."

A perplexed look flickered in his eyes. "I never said I didn't want anything to do with you."

"I won't be your jump off or booty call, Tucker."

He shook his head and his mouth twisted into a wry smile. Just as he was about to speak, Dr. York entered the room and she was able to escape whatever wrath Tucker was about to unleash on her.

After her last appointment and as she was leaving, her phone chirped.

McG: You never answered me about bringing your CD's over to your place.

She sat defiantly not responding and the entire drive home fighting the urge to call Tucker and tear into him for making her act petulantly and immaturely. She was thirty-two years old and she found her actions more like that of a teenager. It was maddening as hell. Everything about him made her lose all self-control and act illogically. She reckoned it must be her lack of sex and hormonal overload that was clouding her brain. What else could it be? *Love?* She snorted out loud and rolled her eyes. No, it most definitely was *not* love. Lust and love of dick, yes, but *love* – absolutely, without a doubt, no.

Back at home, She showered and made dinner. She was glad Tucker hadn't texted her any further, though on a certain level she had hoped to speak to him one last time. She tried to do some online window shopping to take her mind off of

Adam's horrible actions and Tucker's chilly sentiments in front of Mason before eventually falling asleep on the couch.

Hot hands on her body, her arms and face; fingers laced through her hair; warm, soft lips brushing against her mouth. Her dream was a pleasant and one she didn't want to awaken from just yet.

"Tucker…" She whispered, knowing his familiar touch without seeing his face.

"Yes, Pet, I'm here."

His voice was quiet and soothing, but all too real. She pried her eyes open to see the face she had been dreaming about kneeling next to her, only inches away from her. She froze, her mind incapable of understanding the serene yet needy look in his eyes.

"How did you get in?" She whispered.

"You left the door unlocked. You really need to be more careful with that."

His eyes scanned her face while his fingers curved under her chin and fluttered to her neck. As soon as his long fingers touched the warmth of her flesh, she felt safe.

She squared her shoulders and her body stiffened. "Why are you here?"

"Stop being so Goddamn willful," his voice was uncompromising yet soft. "I want you. How many ways do I have to say it?"

Her body sank back into the couch as she picked at an imaginary fleck of dirt on his shirt to avoid his stern gaze. His firm touch brought her chin up and a shiver of wanting ran through her at the desirous flame burning in his eyes.

"I shouldn't have been so shitty to you in front of my brother. I just didn't want to have to explain things to my parents if things don't work out."

Tucker's words were heartfelt. Remembering how she had once told him he didn't need to explain his actions, she was touched that he had anyway. The heat his body was emanating was overwhelming and she felt the sudden urge to push her fingers into his thick hair and pull his mouth near to hers. Her heart hammered in her ears as his lips inched closer. When his mouth covered hers and he thrust his searching tongue past her lips, she moaned her approval.

He pulled away gently only to recapture her mouth again, more demanding than before. His lips seared a path down her neck to her shoulders as he continued to explore her body with his mouth. He tore and fumbled with her tank top, revealing her full breasts. His tongue teased the tightened pink buds of her nipples as he rolled them through his teeth, pulling them to a point while his hands roamed her body for pleasure points. Impatiently, he forced a hand into her sweat pants and past her panties. Digging his fingers into her wet pussy, his tongue flicked down her ribs to her stomach.

"So wet..." He whispered against her navel.

His fingers moved in and out at a slow pace, each thrust deeper than the one before. He tilted his head and his eyes rested on the movement of his hand as he tried to lift the fabric of her pants to see her mound. She lifted herself on her elbows to watch the show, too.

He raised his head and smiled up at her. "Do you have any idea how beautiful you are, Lilly?"

No, she didn't, but she took delight in the fact that Tucker believed she was and that was enough for her. He removed his hand and brought his fingers to her lips and slicked them across her mouth. She glided her tongue over her lips, tasting her own salty juices. His gaze dropped from her eyes to her mouth, and he offered her a sudden, heart-stopping smile before claiming her mouth once more. His tongue darted in and out of her mouth, relentlessly teasing her as his large, strong hands tortured her body with their slow caresses. There was a tingling that started in her toes and worked its way up to the pit of her belly where it settled and throbbed. Aching for him to crawl inside her body, she dug her fingers into his shoulders to relay her unspoken message.

"Do you want me, Lilly?" He breathed into her open and panting mouth.

She couldn't stop the needy and desperate words from pouring out of her. "Yes, yes… God, yes."

He lifted an eyebrow at her. "Do you still think we're wrong for each other?"

"Absolutely. Without a doubt. But I still want you," she moaned.

"You're wrong and I'm done playing games with you. I want you – *all of you*. I'm taking you home and fucking you the way you were meant to be fucked, and prove to you once and for all that you and I are right for each other."

Her heart jolted and her pulse pounded in her veins. Unable to think straight, she shook her head and fisted her hair trying to clear her thoughts. Tucker's arrogance was vexing but she knew there was no point in denying what she absolutely couldn't get enough of – his touch.

***

Tucker stood, his stiff dick begging to be freed from his pants. He hauled Lilliana off the couch and into his arms. With her still unpacked bag in tow, he led her to his car.

The drive to his house was uncomfortable due to his hard-on and he shifted every few seconds trying to readjust himself. His gaze kept returning to Lilliana's body again and again as she leaned her seat back and watched him lustfully. Her green-flecked eyes bore into him in silent expectation of what was about to take place. Her aura radiated pure sex appeal and it was drawing him like a magnet. Her hands wandered over her own body, over her breasts, caressing her thighs and running her palms over her stomach as if she was powerless to resist her own touch.

"That's it, play with yourself, Lilly. Prime that pussy for me," he ordered.

She snuck a hand into her sweat pants and began to finger herself, her eyes traveling over His face and searching his eyes for approval as her shallow breaths fluttered past her lips. He moved his free hand under her tank top and massaged a breast; pinching her nipple and making her mewl and hiss.

He was having a difficult time concentrating as his eyes fixed on the movement of her hand inside her pants. When they came to rest at a stop light, he crept his hand lower into her panties and over her own hand, guiding her movements. The light turned green and a horn blared behind them, prompting them to move along. When he pulled his hand out, she whined, her eyes imploring him to hurry. Beside himself, he was ready to crawl right out of his skin in his rush to get her into his time-out room. He wanted her bound, wet and ready for his taking.

Lilliana must've sensed his thoughts because she swiftly unbuckled her seat belt and buried her face in his neck as she reached her arms around his shoulders. "You drive me insane, Tucker McGrath. Damn you for being so irresistible."

He laughed under his breath and groaned when she slipped her tongue into the shell of his ear and nipped on his lobe. His hands squeaked tightly over the leather steering wheel as her mouth roamed over his neck and she sunk her teeth into his salty flesh.

"Mmm, Tucker..." She moaned.

Her hand gripped his cock through his pants, making him lose focus and swerve the car dangerously near the center line. She then proceeded to unzip his slacks and thrust her hand inside to jack him off. The fierce kneading of his cock sent currents of desire throughout his body and blurring his vision. Again the Maserati veered off, this time towards the shoulder, forcing him to pull her hand out of his pants.

"We're almost there. I don't want to end up injured on the side of the road with a raging hard-on. Fuck, the papers would love to print that."

She giggled and smoothed her mussed hair. "I know I would."

Only a few minutes later they arrived at his home and Tucker and Lilliana practically fell over each other to get inside, leaving her bag to be dealt with later. He fumbled with his keys, too anxious to steady his hands. She took them from him and unlocked the door, eager to get inside.

She glanced up at Tucker and smiled guiltily. "I'm not topping you, I'm just helping you out."

He puckered his lips and fought back the smile that was threatening to break free.

Once inside, he made his wishes clear. "Wait for me in the time-out room; naked, on your knees."

He had to prepare himself mentally before he could deal with Lilliana. Keyed up, he feared his extreme arousal would lead to a quick ending to their encounter. He wanted to enjoy her for as long as he could hold out and he knew by keeping her waiting, it would make both their experiences all the more intense.

After stripping down in his bedroom, he put on a plush black robe, and retrieved some condoms from his nightstand. He made his way to Lilliana, opening the door slowly. To his absolute astonishment, she had done exactly as she was told. Standing in the open doorway, he watched her as she waited on her knees. She hadn't seen him and her eyes were roving around the room, taking everything in.

Opening his robe, he stepped inside and closed the door as he dimmed the lights. Lilliana's eyes met his, but slowly and seductively her gaze moved downward to his cock. Something intense flared in her pupils as they darted back to his. She wanted him and he could feel her longing as it filled the room and encircled his body.

Moving directly in front of her, he touched the top of her head and spoke his praises. "You look so good on your knees in this room Lilly; even more beautiful than I ever could have imagined. It's as if you've belonged here your entire life – at my feet and waiting for my command."

"I like being on my knees for you, Tuck. No..." She shook her head. "I *love* being on my knees for you," she stated purposefully seductive.

"I know you do, Pet, and I love to see you there."

Tipping her head back, she peered at his face and smiled the kind of smile that told him she was content, satisfied, and happy to be under his rule. He held his hand out and she placed hers into his. He tugged on it, standing her upright and nodding towards the cross. Her eyes widened and her breathing became ragged and shallow.

"No worries, Pet, baby steps," he reassured her, trying to put her at ease. He wanted her to enjoy their time together without fear and to accept the things that would bring her ecstasy and pleasure.

He backed her up to the large wood structure and tapped the inside of her ankle with his foot, widening her step. He bent down in front of her while keeping his eyes locked onto hers and gently shackled her ankles loosely. His heart was beating unevenly in his chest as he moved up her body. A ripple of excitement passed over him when he saw the fascination in her eyes as he neared her mouth. He leaned in and placed a delicate kiss on the corner of her mouth as his hands skimmed down her arms to her wrists and slowly brought her hands above her head. His mouth ghosted her neck and without looking, he slipped her hands into the leather cuffs that were already latched. They were far too loose to be effective, however, he wanted Lilliana to feel safe and with them being unrestricting, she could slip them out at any point if she so desired. It would have to do for now until she became more comfortable with her surroundings, and gave herself over to him completely.

Meeting her gaze again, he spoke calmly to her. "You can say stop at any point and this will all end."

Her brows pinched together and a flicker of despondency shone in her eyes. "Even us?"

Tucker felt a certain degree sadness to her response. Is that what she thought? That if she didn't give into him he would end things? He studied her terrified eyes and ran his index finger over her mouth. "No. If you want me to simply make love to you, I will, and it won't mean the end of us."

"But that's not what you want, is it?"

He smiled. "It's not the only thing I want. But I want you."

In an instant, her body relaxed, her breathing slowed, and her face took on a brightness that was vibrant and enthusiastic. "Then let's find out if I'm going to like this or not, shall we?" She whispered.

Lilliana's invitation was hard to resist. He wanted to make damn sure she was going to experience everything he had to offer, and make it so she would never want another man's touch ever again.

"Challenge accepted," his voice broke with huskiness. "I'm going to take you like you've never been taken before, Pet. I'm going to leave you unable to think and vulnerable, and open to accept my will. I'm going to ravage you and make it impossible for any other man to satisfy you the way I will. I'm going to make you feel things that no other man has and you'll want no other after I'm done with you. I know you think I'm being arrogant, and perhaps I am, but I fully intend to keep my word without a care for how challenging that statement may be, no matter how long it will take. This will be no small undertaking because of the walls you've built up, but I promise you, Lilly, before the night is through: I. Will. Ruin. You."

CHAPTER 18

The prolonged anticipation of being in the small room alone with Tucker was almost unbearable, and Lilliana squirmed uncomfortably against the wooden cross. *Ruined...* It was a powerful word. Is that what she truly wanted him to do to her? His stare was bold and confident as he assessed her frankly, his gaze raking over her face and dropping from her eyes to her mouth to her breasts as he took in every needy and tingling inch of her. *Hell, yes, she wanted Tucker to wreck her.* It was as if he had unlocked some deep, dark part of her soul that she didn't know existed as she stood waiting for him to do whatever it was he wanted with her body.

He moved to the wall of belts and pulled down a short-length, black flogger. The handle was braided decoratively and the leather looked soft, supple, and had the appearance of being worn. He looped the end of the handle over his wrist and swung it in small circles as he stalked toward her. The air around him crackled with sexual electricity, and when he spoke, her heart lurched into her throat and her breath left her.

"Whatever shall I do with you, Lilliana Norris? You've been such a naughty girl," his eyes caught the reflection of the dim overhead light and sparkled. "Perhaps now I should teach you how to hold that sharp tongue of yours. Would you like that?"

Her mouth became parched and she could barely speak, and her body suddenly felt heavy and warm. Slowly, she nodded.

"Say it, Lilly. Say you've been a bad girl and deserve to be punished."

Tucker's brown eyes became pitch black and a shiver ran down her spine. Her heartbeat throbbed in her ears and her eyes were riveted to his mouth. *Who the hell was this man?* It certainly wasn't the same Tucker she had been with the previous weekend. Yes, he had the same confident aura and alluring authority, but the Tucker standing before her now was his deliciously wicked and frighteningly naughty doppelganger.

"I'm waiting, Pet, and you know how I feel about that. Don't you?" His voice dropped an octave.

"Yes, Tuck. I've been a very naughty girl," she was finally able to say in a fragile and timid whisper.

He lifted his right brow at her mischievously. "And?"

Was he really going to make her say it? He glided over to her and swished the flogger lightly over the tops of her thighs. Even though there was no pain involved, his motion startled her and her body jerked.

His voice was low, thick and uncompromising when he spoke his command. "Say. It."

Recovering from her unwarranted panic, she answered almost inaudibly, "I deserve to be punished."

Tucker seemed to intuit her anxiety and gave her a smile that warmed her insides, and was she knew at that moment that he wasn't going to hurt her.

"I'm not a violent man nor am I sadist, Lilly, and I'll never punish you in anger, so put your mind at ease," he dipped his thumb into her mouth. "You'll only experience your first time once, so relax and soak up all the sensations you're about to feel."

Lilliana tried to rein in her nervous energy but it was a futile effort. She was too tense. The bindings on her wrists were so loose-fitting that her hands kept slipping out due to the dampness of her sweat. It had been a polite and welcome gesture that Tucker had allowed them to be that way, but they were proving ineffective and she wanted to experience true restraint.

Just as he began to load some music on the stereo, she made her simple request. "Tuck?"

He turned his head, looking over his shoulder at her. "Can you tighten these, please?"

Facing her, his mouth parted and his eyes flared, and she knew she had spoken exactly what he wanted to hear. Approaching her slowly and deliberately, he adjusted the leather cuffs to a comfortable yet snug fit. His breath fluttered past her cheek as his hands moved skillfully and quickly.

Stepping back, he inspected his handiwork. "That's much better and more suited for a disobedient little thing such as yourself. Now there's nowhere for you to run, is there?" He winked waywardly.

Her eyes rounded, her pulse skittered, and she suddenly felt like Little Red Riding Hood who had been tricked by the Big Bag Wolf.

She closed her eyes and let the sounds of Ellie Goulding, *Lights,* penetrate her senses and drown out the sounds of her own heart beat thumping in her ears. She began to drift when the sudden sting of leather seared across her belly. Unprepared and surprised, she shrieked. Her eyes popped open and she looked down at her belly expecting to see blood spewing in all directions, but was pleased to see only faint pink stripes. The skin warmed and tingled, and moved down to her groin.

"That was for accusing me of wanting you for only a booty call." One side of his mouth lifted in a roguish smile. "These next swats are just for pleasure."

He brought the flogger up again and began a barrage of light flicks on her upper thighs, reddening her flesh. She twisted and churned her body against the wood as she tried to adjust to the mildly uncomfortable heat emanating from her upper legs. Her arousal was piquing and her breathing and heart rate sped up with each of his lashings.

"Deep breaths, Lilly; slow it down. Listen to the sound of your heart beating and try and focus on something, like my eyes or mouth. Watch them," Tucker instructed.

Lilliana did exactly as she was told and when she did, it was as if time grinded to a halt as she immersed herself in the scene. The leather flashed over her body – her stomach, thighs and breasts, over and over. After several minutes a strange sensation she was unfamiliar with wrapped itself around her like a warm blanket, and her body felt weightless and as if she was floating on a cloud.

He dropped the flogger to the floor and began to massage and knead her breasts as he kissed and sucked at her neck, bringing the blood to the surface. Her flesh was over-sensitized and she writhed uncomfortably against Tucker's assuage.

Suddenly her arousal turned to icy fear as she teetered on the edge of losing control. Tucker's smell, contact and nearness were overpowering all her senses as she drifted in and out of reality. She didn't know what was happening to her. She wanted more of his touch, more of the fire he was kindling within her, and more of the thunderous wanting he had awakened within her... But her breathing became erratic and her pulse slammed in her veins as panic twisted itself around her heart. The invisible cloud that she had been floating on faded and her mind and body went into freefall.

"I'm falling!" She cried loudly as she wrenched against the leather cuffs, trying to free herself.

Tucker's fingers laced with hers and he smashed her with the weight of his body against the cross. "I'll catch you, Lilly," he calmly breathed into her ear. "Let yourself go. Let it all go and fly, Pet... Fly..."

Two of his fingers slid into her wet depths and leisurely eased in and out. Her mind struggled with what was happening to her, but she drank in the comfort of his closeness. He paused to slide on a condom before returning to her mouth to dip his tongue inside and whisper his adoration of every inch of her body.

He began assaulting her pussy again more fervently with his shaft, and the warm feeling of an orgasm began to fill her lower belly. He intertwined his fingers with hers again and he ground into her. His breath was hot and ragged as he leaned into her ear. A glistening layer of sweat slicked both their bodies as they fucked intensely, and Lilliana licked the crook of his ear, wanting to taste his salty skin. Her whimpering cries sounded foreign in her ears, and after only a few minutes, all her blood surged to her pussy as hot and cold chills signaled her release. She unconsciously arched into Tucker as her body began to explode with fiery sensations.

"Can you feel how right we are for each other, Lilly?"

She thrashed her head in denial. *No, she wouldn't admit it.* Not to Tucker and not to herself.

"Stop denying this thing between us," he whispered low and deep into her ear. "It's real; it's tangible and undeniable. We belong together."

He mercilessly thrust into her depths trying to force an admission out of her.

"No," she choked out.

"You're bound and at my mercy, and still you're fucking obstinate. What am I going to do with you, Lilliana?" He growled.

He pulled out of her and knelt in front of her. Thrusting his fingers into her, he relentlessly began to finger her swollen G-spot. She shouted random words and instinctively bucked her hips. Smothering her clit with his mouth, Tucker sucked at it viciously and rolled it between his teeth. She began to float up above herself as her body heated to an unbearable temperature and she screamed, ear-piercingly loud.

"Say my name," he demanded. "Scream it for the neighbors to hear. Tell the world how right we are for each other," his voice was muffled against her pussy.

"Tuck...er!" Her voice cracked as her body shuddered against his embrace and she came, soaking the front of his chest. She closed her eyes and flew high up and far away to some other place.

Standing, he buried his cock deep inside of her. His rhythm increased briefly before he suddenly stilled, grunted, and clasped her hands tightly as he, too, came.

A deep sigh of elation escaped her lips, and her body went limp and began its descent. Tucker had broken through her walls and left her bare and defenseless, but still... She had never felt so free. She soared to an even greater height than she had before, and to a place that she never knew existed.

He had kept his word: He had *ruined* her - utterly and totally. No other man would suffice and she both adored and hated him for it.

What if things didn't work out? Then what?

The effects of Tucker's gentle savagery had left her an emotional mess as her body shook uncontrollably. Now, wondering if this thing with him would last was too much of a strain on her fragile psyche. It sent her over the edge and she broke down completely, crying, sobbing and wailing as the tears streamed down her flushed cheeks.

He unshackled her and lifted her into his arms, holding her so closely he squeezed the breath out her. "Let it all out, Lilly," he whispered in her ear.

She had no choice to but let it all out. Everything Adam had ever done to her and the way he made her feel self-conscious and defensive was erased by Tucker's strong hands and overpowering touch. He made it all go away. She knew that if Tucker broke her heart, too, she would never recover.

"Don't leave me," she stammered out, trying to stifle her cries.

***

Lilliana was still coming down from her post-sex high and Tucker knew she didn't realize what she was saying. Still, at that moment, his heart beat only for her. He was too emotion-filled to reply back, so he simply carried her the distance back to his bedroom. She hid her face in his neck as her cries slowly died down. His legs were weak and shaky, and he just wanted to lie next to her and hold her near to him, but he managed to get to the restroom to retrieve some wet washcloths to clean them both up. When he returned to her, she was propped up against his headboard with her knees pulled up to her chest.

"I'm sorry I said that," she stated softly with only her eyes peering out at him.

He gently wiped her tear streaked cheeks clean. Next, he pushed her legs apart and cleaned in between her legs. When he was finished, he laid her back down and pulled the comforter up over her, and finally addressed her.

"That kind of intense bonding brings out the sort of feelings we normally hide, so don't ever be sorry for what you say in that room. I like it when your walls come down; it shows me who you really are."

Lilliana was pensive and quiet for several minutes. Her eyes drifted off and she stared at the overhead lights before eventually speaking. Her voice was soft and delicate, and her eyes came into sharp focus on his face.

"That was some powerful shit. Like mind and pussy-numbing, fuckilepsy inducing, reproductive organ-exploding powerful. You really are some kind of flogger wielding sex God."

And just like that, unfiltered, witty and sarcastic Lilly was back. Tucker stared a moment before bursting into a peal of laughter. "I'm glad to hear you enjoyed yourself. Speaking of reproductive organs... We need to get you on the pill. I detest condoms; they rob me of my mojo."

Lilliana's smile faded and she chewed the corner of her lip fretfully. "I'm already on birth control."

"Why didn't you tell me?"

She sat up and threw the comforter to the side as she climbed out of bed. "You didn't ask. Anyway, condoms do more than prevent pregnancy," she replied as she unsteadily rose from bed.

Her curtness caught him off guard and he couldn't help but feel defensive. "I'm aware of that, but I'm not sleeping with anyone else."

She rocked impatiently from foot to foot, clearly needing to use the restroom. "Even if you were, it's not like you would admit it," she countered before making a beeline to the restroom, still obviously in a weakened state by her unsteady gait.

He spread out in bed and tucked his hands behind his head. He recalled what happened to Lilliana when Adam cheated on her, and her fear of contracting an STD. But he wasn't Adam and as far as he was concerned, Lilliana was *it* and there weren't going to be any other women in his life in the foreseeable future.

When she returned, she put on one of his t-shirts and slid in next to him.

"I'm not Adam," he glared down at her.

"I never said you were." Her tone was flat and her stare was blank.

"Good, then we can be done with the condom use."

Fear, stark and undeniable, gleamed in her eyes. She rose up on one elbow and her eyebrows knit together. "No, we can't."

His voice was quiet but revealed an undertone of displeasure. "I don't have any STD's and I'm not going to cheat on you, Lilly. When I'm with a woman, I'm monogamous to her."

Her mouth curved into an even deeper frown. "Nothing personal, but I've heard all that before. I'm tired. You used and abused me and I need to rest." She rolled over and irritably fluffed her pillow.

Put off with her attitude, he lay next to her, staring at her with incredulousness. "So what you're telling me is that you don't trust me and our relationship will be perpetually doomed to using condoms?"

She sighed loudly and she shot him a beleaguered look over her shoulder. "I trusted you enough to let you tie me up. *Twice*. Isn't that enough? Do we really have to talk about this right now? I'm so tired. Please..."

He wasn't about to give up so easily but he was exhausted as well. His thoughts were a mixture of frustration and speculation as to what he could do to put her mind at ease about his fidelity. Just as his eyes closed, inspiration hit him and he reached over for his phone to leave a voice mail at his physician's office. If it was proof Lilliana wanted about his truthfulness, then it would be hard and tangible proof she would get.

CHAPTER 19

Lilliana woke early, feeling slightly panicked. Her sleep was so deep and her dreams felt so real, she had forgotten where she was. Once again, she woke hot and uncomfortable, and with Tucker's limbs wrapped around her like an electric blanket. The sun was on the horizon and the time was just before 7:00 a.m. Peeling her sweaty body away from him, she placed a kiss on his cheek. After searching his pockets, she found the keys to his vehicle and retrieved her bag. She showered hurriedly and when the water hit her still sensitized skin, the night's previous activities flooded her mind.

She dried off and looked over her body in the large mirror, but was surprised to see no evidence of the flogging he had submitted her to. He was good; maybe too, good. She splashed some of his cologne on her breasts and dabbed a bit behind her ears and on her wrists, wanting to smell Tucker all day long. She hadn't brought any scrubs along, but the clinic kept several spare pairs in case of blood spills or splashes, so she would just have to change when she arrived at work. Not having any of her other feminine necessities, she borrowed Tucker's toothbrush and deodorant. It felt intimate and even a bit forbidden to be using his personal items, however, she had no other choice.

Just prior to leaving, she woke Tucker. She knew he didn't usually get to work until closer to 9:00 a.m. so he still had plenty of time to get ready.

"Wakey, wakey, Flogger Boy," she whispered playfully in his ear.

He stirred and moaned, and a smile touched his face. His eyes danced with arousal when she came into focus. "You smell like me," he grinned.

"As much as you admire yourself; that must really turn you on."

He pulled her down into bed with him and buried his face in her neck. "That mouth, Lilly. It makes me want to do bad,

bad things," he spoke muted against her flesh. "You brushed your teeth, too. With what?" He asked.

"Your toothbrush," she blushed.

"I like that something of mine was in your mouth this early. Now, how about you suck me off before breakfast?"

She pushed away from him reluctantly. "As much as I'd like to, I can't or I'll be late for work."

"Fuck work. My dick needs attention. Now suck it, Woman."

He grabbed the top of her head and attempted to push her down to his groin. Slapping his hand away, she laughed at his aggressive neediness. "Don't be a dick nugget, I have responsibilities. Your peter will get sucked tonight. I promise."

"Hmmph," he pouted and stared at her with rounded eyes. "So how do you plan on getting to work exactly?"

"I'll call a cab."

Looking offended, he sat straight up. "Absolutely not. You can drive my Lexus. The keys are by the front door in the side table."

"Does it go really fast?" She asked with a glimmer in her eyes.

"Uh... Yeah. Why?"

"Just askin'," she kidded.

"Don't get all kamikaze in it. Speed limits are there for a reason," he crabbed.

Moving toward the door, she couldn't resist another peek at Tucker. When she paused to gaze at him optimistically, the corners of his mouth curled upwards. There was something lazily seductive in his look as he propped himself up on one elbow. Maybe they were right for each other. Then again, it was probably more likely that he was completely wrong for her, regardless of how good in the sack he was. Whatever the case may be, she knew she was ensnared in his sensual trap and there was no escaping it.

"Are you sure you don't want to stay and play for a little bit? I have a new tawse that needs breaking in," his dark eyes reflected a twinkle of hope.

Her eyes clouded with visions of the previous night. *God, yes, she wanted to stay and play*, but work... She shook her head sadly. "I really can't," she sighed, unable to hide the disappointment in her voice.

"Then, ciao for now, Pet," he winked. "And drive safely. *At the speed limit*."

She drove the stunning and no doubt expensive Lexus IS-F to work, fearful of damaging it. The leather seats were supple and hugged her body as if they were made specifically for her. Even the striking color was appealing – Ultrasonic Blue Mica. She had read it on the paperwork in the glove compartment when she did a quick inspection of it. The vehicle was such a delight to drive, she wondered why Tucker didn't drive it more often.

Her day at work was tedious and the only thing she could focus on was the intense throbbing in her crotch and the occasional sparks of heat from her tender belly, thighs and breasts. They only served as a reminder of how Tucker had marked his territory and the lusty things spoken to her.

During a routine cleaning, she inadvertently spoke her thoughts to patient. "Can you feel how right we are for each other?" She whispered.

A puzzled expression crossed the patient's face and she tried to quickly think of a way to get out of the inappropriate remark she had made. "I'm using a new piece of equipment and just commenting on how much I really like it," she giggled nervously.

Luckily, the patient seemed satisfied with her answer and she kept moving right along.

During her lunch break, she dug out her phone to give Tucker a piece of her mind for making her a hot and bothered mess.

Lilliana: Thanks. I can't even concentrate because of you.

McG: Then my evil plan worked. Is thinking about my B===D in your ({}) making you wet? That's a penis in a vagina to the untrained eye ;)

Lilliana: If by wet you mean frustrated, then yes, I'm 'wet.' BTW - your knowledge of perverse texting symbols is just terrific, Tucker.

McG: Fresh sushi?

She stared at the phone, confused and offended by his response. What the hell was he insinuating? That she smelled fishy?

Lilliana: WTF? Comparing my pussy to fresh tuna isn't going to get your dick sucked tonight.

She was about to send her response when he appeared in the doorway of her office, holding two plastic containers.

"How about lunch, Doll Face?" He grinned.

She smiled humbly and immediately hit the backspace button to erase her snappish message. He was dressed casually in dark jeans and a white button down shirt underneath a black suit coat. His shirt was unbuttoned at the top and he was wearing the same belt he had bound her with the first time at her home. Her cheeks flushed thinking about the encounter, and when her eyes met his, he had an intense but undisclosed expression as if he had read her thoughts.

"Let's not get ahead of ourselves, Lilly. It's only lunch," he mocked, running the tip of his index finger over the smooth silver buckle. "But maybe later I can accommodate you."

"Did you go to work dressed like that?" she asked, completely ignoring his remark and pulling out a chair for him to sit.

"No, I haven't been to work yet. I'll go in for a few hours when I'm done here. I had a matter that needed handled," he responded with hooded eyes.

She watched him impassively, unsure what he was referring to, but let it go. She didn't know Tucker well, but she knew him well enough to realize if he wanted her to know what he was talking about, he would just come out and say it.

As they ate, the conversation was light and playful, and she felt a slow burn flow through her veins at Tucker's upbeat mood. Dana kept peeking in and trying to see what was going on and Lilliana guessed, to also get a good look at Tucker.

When she saw the young receptionist lingering around her doorway pretending to be doing something, she finally invited her in.

"Dana, get in here, please."

She came shuffling in like a school girl with a crush. Her cheeks brightened and she batted her eyelashes at Tucker. Lilliana began to smile when Dana's eyes nervously scanned her shoes.

She introduced them and Tucker reached a hand out to Dana in a polite gesture.

"It's nice to meet you," Dana stammered. "I've read a lot about you. You built and sold the apartment complex that I live in. Also, the house that my mom and dad live in was once owned by your company."

Tucker smiled and nodded, and glanced at Lilliana diffidently and winked. She guessed he must get be confronted with that sort of behavior a lot. Dana was adorable and the most genuine person she had ever met, and Lilliana didn't feel an ounce of jealousy or animosity towards her. She was a good seven years Lilliana's junior, but they still shared a connection and she wasn't about to let the girl's little harmless crush on Tucker get in the way of that.

When Dana finally excused herself, Tucker turned his attention back to her. "That was cute," he shook his head.

"Yes, it was. I think she has a crush on you," she laughed.

The heavy lashes that shrouded his eyes flew up in surprise. "And you're okay with that?"

"Sure. It's just a crush; like the kind a young girl has on a rock star or celebrity. It's nothing to get yourself in a tizzy over."

"I'm not in a tizzy. She's not my type. Anyway, who can blame her?"

He seemed very pleased with himself and she rolled her eyes. "Your ego is absurd."

He threw his head back and laughed. "You're the one who called me a rock star... Twice!"

"No, I didn't call you a rock star, I compared you to one. I also simply stated that Dana's crush was juvenile in nature."

"Around these parts, I am a fucking rock star, Baby!" He continued to hoot joyously.

He stood and pulled her into his lap and unabashedly planted a kiss on her lips. His eyes were humorous and tender as he stared at her. She never figured him for the type for public displays of affection, but she drank it up and arched into the curves of his body.

"You want me so bad. Admit we're right for each other," his eyes darkened with need.

"I'll do no such thing."

"Why do you persist with being so Goddamn mulish? This little body of yours was built for me and only me. Say it," he demanded.

"Your arrogance is impossible to deal with sometimes."

He drew his brows together but the hidden smile on his mouth was undeniable. "That's not what I told you to say. Are you going to make me brighten your ass cheeks right here in your office, in broad daylight and in full view of your coworkers?"

For an instant, his glare sharpened and she thought he might really go through with his threat. She tried to stand, but Tucker held onto her tightly.

"You've read too many books. You can't *punish me into submission*, Tucker McGrath."

"I can sure as hell try," he retorted with a significant lifting of his eyebrows.

Her eyes widened and then narrowed. She opened her mouth to say something sarcastic, but decided against it.

When she snapped her mouth closed, Tucker's lips curved into a devious smile. "See, you're learning already."

Irked by his pomposity, she opened her mouth again to really let him have it, but Dana walked in.

"You're just in time, Dana," Tucker glanced sideways at her. "I was just about to paddle Ms. Norris' ass."

Lilliana gaped, shocked at his admission. Dana and Tucker exchanged a subtle look of amusement, and Lilliana squirmed to get free from him.

"Why? What did she do?" Dana asked, only making matters worse.

"I didn't do anything. Cripes, Dana, you're supposed to be on my side," Lilliana's voice rose in surprise.

"I am on your side, but people don't get paddled for nothing."

She shot Dana a horrified look and decided that Dana's wide-eyed innocence was merely a smoke screen.

"Ha! A woman wise beyond her years!" Tucker bellowed before finally freeing her from his grip.

Just as she stood, his hand caught her bottom swiftly, making her yelp out noisily and jump.

Dana shook her head in sympathy. "I don't know what you did, but if I were you, I wouldn't do it again."

He smirked and the candidness in his eyes beckoned to her. "Words of advice from a very intelligent woman, Lilly." He moved to the door while she rubbed her cheek briskly, trying to ease the sting of his palm. "I'll see you at my place tonight. I hope you're feeling healthy enough for another time-out."

"I need to stop off at my place and pick up some womanly essentials. Like a toothbrush and pit stick."

He rolled his eyes. "Such refined language, Ms. Norris. Fine. I'll see you later. Ciao, Pet."

The rest of the day went by blissfully quick with thoughts of Tucker overpowering her brain. It felt good to have someone in her life. She had accepted the possibility that she might never meet another man whom she trusted; however, Tucker was proving to be one tough nut to crack. Although she denied it to him, she knew on some level, they were meant to be together. Even if it was just for a brief moment in time, she vowed to enjoy him for as long as she was allowed.

With her head so far in the clouds, she hardly remembered the drive home. She was so lost in her thoughts, she hadn't even noticed the rental car at the far end of her driveway until she stepped foot out of Tucker's car.

"You must've hit the lottery when Margo died if you can afford a car like that."

The familiar voice prickled at her nerves.

Fucking. Adam.

She was barely able to withhold her gasp of upset when she saw him on her porch swing, casually relaxed, and his long legs leisurely stretched out in front of him.

"What the fuck..." The alarm of seeing Adam caused the words to wedge in her throat.

"It's good to see you, too, Babe," he glowered, his sparkling green eyes giving away his pleasure in her utter shock.

Lilliana was breathless with rage and there was no hiding the unbridled anger in her voice when she spoke. "It's not my car. Now get the hell off my land."

Adam's head tilted and he laughed with easy boldness. "That's some kind of shitty greeting. What happened to your Midwestern values? You used to be so gentle and obliging. Shit, it wasn't that long ago you were eager to wrap that pretty little mouth of yours around my dick."

He seemed to find some kind of perverse pleasure in bringing up their past, but she was undeterred by his disgusting words. "A hell of a lot of good that did me. My *obliging* attitude got me a cheating husband who gave me the clap."

He waved aside her remark and looked out in the distant field and long driveway as if seeing something. "Again with that?"

"I was serious about pressing charges," she grumbled.

"You threatened to press charges if I called, so here I am in person," his eyes shot back to hers. "You brought this all on yourself. I gave you plenty of time to get your ass back home. Now I'm here to make it happen."

"My home is here! Get your dick out of here, Adam. I mean it. I'm not going back to Kansas. *Ever.* How dare you come here and..."

He stood and pointed a finger in her direction. "I'm sensing aggression," he chuckled derisively as he cut her statement short.

All she could hear was the sound of her pulse beating loudly in her ears. She had seriously heard enough of Adam's bullshit. "You're going to sense my foot up your ass in about thirty seconds if you don't get the hell..." Her voice broke off midsentence when she heard a car door close behind her.

She spun around to see Tucker moving towards her with his head downcast and fully dilated pupils firmly fixed on Adam. She stared wordlessly at him, her heart pounding in her chest. As he stalked closer to her, she was stunned by his cool appraisal of Adam. He glided next to her and wrapped a possessive arm around her waist and pulled her next to him.

His action sent her brain spinning for fear of what was about to go down. Her stomach churned with anxiety and her eyes darted over to Adam. He was no longer sitting, but standing on the last step of the landing and making his way rapidly to her and Tucker. She tried to slip out of Tucker's grip, but he held her steadfastly.

"Who the fuck are you?" Adam demanded as he eyed Tucker.

"Her boyfriend. Not that it's any of your Goddamn business." There was defiance in Tucker's tone as well as a not-so-subtle challenge when he answered.

Lilliana's emotions veered from trepidation to tenseness to arousal, and back.

Adam's nostrils flared and his eyes blazed with anger, but he laughed mockingly and gave her a hostile glare. "It didn't take you long to spread your legs for someone new, did it?"

She felt Tucker's body stiffen in response to Adam's vehemence and she winced from his hateful words.

225

"Only two years," she countered, making her point that she was no floozy.

Adam waved towards the Lexus. "So, what? You suck his cock and he lets you drive his car? Is that how this shit works?" His eyes narrowed but a condescending smile curved his mouth upward. "I guess things haven't changed all that much for you, have they?"

Lilliana's breath burned in her throat and her cheeks brightened with embarrassment. Adam loved humiliating her. He always had. And he had always held his money and material possessions over her head. But he was wrong. She did the things she did for him, including suck his dick, because she loved him and not for any other reason.

"You must not have gotten any good head in your life for that kind of trade off," Adam laughed acidly as his glared at Tucker.

Unwelcome memories of how Adam used to talk openly about her lack of oral skills to their friends and acquaintances flashed in her mind and suddenly, she didn't feel so bold anymore. Her ex-husband knew too much about her and her composure started to crack like a shell under his barbed and hurtful insults. She just wanted him to be gone and to hide in Tucker's arms.

***

Lilliana's voice had shifted from bold to a hushed whisper. "Shut up, Adam."

Tucker felt her physically withdraw and he tucked her further into his body for protection. Seeing her uneasy and fearful was motherfucking gut wrenching. He knew her to be strong, spirited and brave, and he'd be damned if he would allow anyone to take away her most prized attributes, most especially not the piece of shit standing in front of him.

Tucker sized him up in a matter of seconds: military length, dark-blonde hair, eyes the color of moss, just over six feet tall and with a physique of someone who had too much time on his hands and worked out frequently.

"I've had plenty of head in my life and Lilliana ranks up there with the best. It's too bad you'll never get to experience that again with her," Tucker answered casually as if unaffected.

Adam merely stared back, tongue-tied. His cheeks flushed before he responded. "Who says I won't?" He gritted his teeth.

Tucker took in a steady deep breath. Lilly's ex was pushing his limits and his equanimity was wearing thin. "I say," he snarled.

When Adam realized he wasn't going to back down, he took a step back and snorted his dismissal of Lilliana. "You want her? Have her. She's not worth the trouble. Hell, she's not even a good lay."

Tucker's broad-sculptured face twisted in anger. "You obviously didn't have the talent or skills to bring out her best qualities because as far as I'm concerned, she's the fuck of a lifetime."

Adam sputtered and bristled with indignation as though he had been slapped across the face. He turned to walk away, only to abruptly lunge at Tucker, fists drawn. Before he had a chance to react, Lilliana threw herself in between them and took the brunt of Adam's fist squarely in the eye.

She shrieked like a banshee protecting its child and clawed and scratched at Adam's face. "You fucking prick!"

Tucker pushed her off of Adam who was holding his hands up in front of his face protectively. As soon as Adam's hands lowered, he took one swing, landing it firmly in his smug mouth, brining him to his knees. Adam spat out a mouthful of blood on the gravel road and attempted to stand.

"Stay down," Tucker growled with his hands fisted at his sides, ready to deliver more of his brand of punishment.

He was livid. When he glanced at Lilliana and saw her eye already in the process of swelling, he leaned down and struck Adam once more in the eye as revenge.

"You had perfection and you screwed it away. Now get your lying, cheating ass out of here before I bury you somewhere on this one-hundred acres of land and make sure you're never heard from again," he replied with such contempt that it forbade any further argument.

Adam's face paled with terror as he picked himself up and scurried to his rental. The car's engine whined loudly as it spun tires and kicked up dust in his rush to leave.

He watched Adam's car until it turned on the main highway then faced Lilliana with a stern look on his face. "Why the hell did you step in?"

***

Tucker's voice was quiet, yet held an undertone of irritation and Lilliana couldn't figure out why he was so angry with her.

"He was going to hit you," her answer came out defensively.

"I don't need you to fight my fights, Lilliana."

Tucker's curtness and the silent curses he mouthed under his breath tore at her heart. "I just didn't want him to hurt you," her throat tightened.

"So instead he hurt you. I don't need that kind of guilt. Fuck, look what he did to your eye!"

He gripped her wrist and dragged her inside the house where he led her to the kitchen table. While he disappeared to find the first-aid kit, she patted her eye and winced from the pain. Her vision was already beginning to dim slightly from the swelling and she dreaded what it looked like. When he reappeared, he looked her over and shook his head in disappointment and annoyance.

"If you weren't such a mess, I'd paddle your ass for that little stunt."

"If it'll make you feel better, then do it," she sighed, giving a resigned shrug.

He pulled up a chair in front of her and fingered her chin. "I may be arrogant, but I'm not a complete asshole. Spanking you when you're already hurt would never make me feel better."

"*May be* arrogant?" She puckered her mouth sarcastically.

"Close your eye and your mouth and let me try and fix what that piece of shit did to you."

Tucker wasn't in the mood to jest, so Lilliana did as she was told and allowed him to care for her. His touch was gentle and reassuring as he dabbed antiseptic on it. When she winced, he blew cool air on it while holding her head steady. His expression was grim as he continued to clean her wound and apply a cold pack to it.

Sinking into the chair and tipping it back onto two legs, he eyed her quizzically. "What did you ever see in that man?"

Her face flushed with humiliation. She stood, straightened herself and cleared her throat. Moving to the kitchen window she peered out at the beautiful countryscape. "He promised to love me. He promised me forever."

She hunched over the sink and felt a terrible sense of bitterness toward Adam. And men in general. They were all liars. *All of them*. Turning abruptly, she faced Tucker with renewed doubt about his intentions.

"You should leave now," she snapped as anguish almost overcame her control.

Tucker's eyes flashed confusion and he hesitated, measuring her for a moment. Crossing his arms over his chest, he shook his head. His face was full of strength, shining with determination. "You'd like that, wouldn't you? Then it would make it easy for you to say goodbye to me."

Annoyed at the transparency of her feelings, she could only glare back at him. Yes, it would make it easier for her to be done with him and to say goodbye. She didn't want another heart break or any more false promises and lies.

"I've already said it twice and I'll say it only one more time: I'm not Adam. I'm not going anywhere and I'm sure as hell not going to make it easy for you to say goodbye to me."

She fisted her hands and closed her eyes in exasperation, her mind a crazy mixture of hope and fear. With her eyes still closed, Tucker's arms suddenly crushed her and his mouth was on her ear.

"Let it go, Lilly."

***

Tucker reached into his pocket and pulled out the necklace that he had picked up at his jeweler's. Lilliana's eyes widened and she sputtered, but he quickly fastened it around her neck.

A look of apprehension washed over her face when she spoke in a small, frightened voice. "You hardly know me."

He tried to resist the urge to smile, but couldn't keep it from creeping onto his face. "I've fucked you, licked you, bound you, flogged you, and spanked you. Jesus, Lilly, how much more do you want to get to know each other?"

She smiled back and shook her head in concurrence. Touching the necklace, she brought it up and her brown and green-flecked eyes scanned it.

"It's beautiful, Tucker. Thank you," she gushed. "So, are you really my... You know... What you said to Adam."

His grin widened. He shrugged and feigned ignorance just so he could hear her say the B word. "Yes, I definitely think you're the fuck of a lifetime."

She blinked long and hard and puckered her mouth. "Not that. You know... The other thing."

"Perfection? Skilled at giving head? Yes and yes," he nodded his head.

He moved toward the refrigerator and opened it to grab a snack when Lilliana quickly latched onto his arm.

"Tuck... Come on. Don't torture me. Say it again."

He rolled his eyes and chuckled. "*Boyfriend*. There. I said it and I meant it."

She smiled impishly, but he wasn't content to leave it at that. "Lilliana has a boyfriend! Hoo wee, doggy!" He poked her in the ribs and did a jig around the kitchen like a full-blown red-neck slapping his knee. "This here little filly has a real, bona fide sweetheart!"

"You're impossible! And there's nothing sweet about you, Tucker McGrath!"

He swung her around by the arm and framed her face in his large hands. They both stilled and their smiles faded into something passionate. His heart thudded in his chest and there was a tingling in the pit of his stomach at the way she was gazing back at him longingly. He really would kill that son-of-a-bitch if he ever laid another hand on Lilly. She belonged to him now. *Only him.* He kissed her bruised eye tenderly and trailed his mouth down her cheek to her mouth.

Powerless to resist the perilous and burning ache in his heart, he whispered against her lips, "Mine."

CHAPTER 20

Tucker and Lilliana had fallen asleep far too early. She had suckered him into watching Star Wars: A New Hope as repayment for the BJ with the books atop her head the previous weekend. He had promised *anything* in return and she took full advantage of it. She inwardly laughed at the look of horror on his face when she slipped the movie in the DVD player, and his exaggerated moans and face palming every time a cheesy line would be spoken. She had tried to make the experience a little easier for him by suggesting she play Princess Lay Me Orgasma to his Obi-Wank-His-Knobby. Tucker was only slightly amused and stated he was all for role play, just not her brand of geeky role-play. Her last ditch effort was to keep pointing out accidental sexual quotes from the movie, like, "Look at the size of that thing!" and "Luke, at that speed, do you think you'll be able to pull out in time?" But he was still a no-go.

Before the end of the movie, they had both drifted off to sleep without so much as the dick licking that she had promised him. She was disappointed, but the emotional stress of the throw-down with Adam had taken its toll on the both of them, and after they dragged themselves to her bed and stripped down, they collapsed into an exhausted mess and slept deeply the entire night.

The following morning, she woke him early so he could drive himself home and change for work. Before leaving, he placed another delicate kiss on her swollen eyelid, and reprimanded her yet again for her overzealousness in trying to protect him.

At work, everyone looked horrified at the site of her eye. Dana most of all, was completely enraged.

"That rotten, handsome, son-of-a-bitch! He said he was only going to spank you not beat the living daylights out of you! I don't care how much money that douchetard has, I'll kick a new hole in his ass for doing that to you!"

Lilliana laughed hysterically and Dana's face contorted into an expression of utter bewilderment.

"Tucker didn't do this, my ex-husband did. He showed up at my place last night. I jumped in between him and Tucker and got socked in the eye."

"Why the hell did you go and do something like that? Tucker can take care of himself, you ding-bat!"

She rolled her eyes. It seemed Tucker and Dana had the same mentality about a great many things.

"You're going to press charges, right?" Dana squeezed her shoulder.

"No, but I should. Even Tucker is urging me to do it. If I do, it'll just mean I'll have to see him again and that's the last thing I want. If he ever calls or shows up again, though, I'll definitely call the police."

Dana's eyes narrowed and she placed her hands on her hips. "Promise?"

"Yes, yes. I won't put up with his shit anymore."

Just then, Dana's eyes caught the glint of the diamond and sapphire-encrusted padlock around Lilliana's neck.

"Ooh," she admired with large glassy eyes. "So it's serious then?"

Lilliana shrugged, still unable to admit the reality of Tucker's committal gesture. "I guess so. It was very thoughtful of him to get it for me."

"Thoughtful? I would say it was more than that. That boy has it bad for you, Lil."

She waved Dana away, not wanting to talk anymore about it or the fact that she, too, had it bad for Tucker.

She had hoped he would show up for another unscheduled lunch visit, but there was no such luck. She did, however, receive several teasing text messages making her day go by quicker.

McG: All work and no play makes Tucker a cranky boy.
Lilliana: What are you suggesting?

McG: I never suggest. ;)

Lilliana: Then how about u draw me a picture?

McG: Sounds like fun, but stick figures fucking won't quite relay my need for release accurately. Save the date: next Thursday, company party at the Grand Hyatt ballroom. Lots of schmoozing and boozing.

Elation filled her as she daydreamed about being on his arm at some hoity-toity event.

McG: BTW, I have something of great importance to give to you.

Lilliana: Don't tease! Tell me!

McG: You have to see it. Don't say I never did anything for you. FYI: you owe me. BIG TIME. Ciao, Pet ;)

Great importance? It sounded so ominous. She hated being led on and she detested surprises.

Struck with good fortune, her last appointment rescheduled and she was free to leave early. She had driven Tucker's car again and was looking forward to the drive home. If she ever came into a large sum of money, she vowed to buy herself the very same make and model, albeit a more feminine hue.

When she arrived home, she texted him of her early arrival, and decided to harvest the last of the fruits and vegetables in Margo's garden in order to can them. An early frost was predicted and she didn't want to lose of any of the precious foods that her Auntie had worked so diligently planting.

Donning her scruffiest jeans and a sweatshirt, she went to work in the garden. She worked hard for nearly an hour, plucking and pulling up every last bit of sustenance she could find and placing them in a large basket.

With the last item ravaged from the dirt, she sank onto her knees and hid her face in her hands. A sob escaped her throat thinking about the finality of it all; Margo's death, the harvest season ending, and the reality that she may have to sell her land. She pushed her chin up and stared defiantly into the sun that was low on the horizon. The wind blew past her and the scent of violets and wild bergamot filled her nostrils, and she could swear she heard the joyful laughter of her mother and Margo flutter past her ears. Anguish ripped through her heart, and she wrapped her arms around herself trying to stop her wretched shaking from her unrestrained cries.

Why did they have to be taken at such young ages? They were both good and decent people. *Why?* Who would she share her accomplishments with? Her hopes and fears? Bereft and desolate, she rocked herself.

Her cries were so loud she didn't hear Tucker sneak up on her.

"My sweet, Lilly of the Valley," he cooed into her ear, cocooning her in his arms.

She attempted to stifle her cries, mortified of her breakdown in front of him. She didn't want to appear weak, but, God, how she desperately needed his touch. She turned and clung to him, burying her dirt smudged-face into the lapels of his jacket.

"I miss them so much," she wept.

"I know you do. Death is unfair and cruel, Pet."

He stood and lifted her into his arms, and carried her back into the house. Setting her down on the couch, he peeled her dirty pants and sweatshirt off and set them in a pile. Next, he retrieved a washcloth and cleaned her face, being careful near her still swollen eye. She was so touched by his actions she began to cry again, thinking about her mother's and Aunt's kind words and touches.

Tucker led her to the bathroom where he ran her a hot bath while she sat on the lidded toilet stool. She watched him intently as he ran his fingers through the water, testing its temperature frequently. When it was full enough and loaded with foamy bubbles, he slipped her panties and bra off and helped her in. She lay back and let the hot water soak into her bones and ease her sadness. With her eyes closed, his hands roamed over her body, washing her, fondling her and calming her. His rough touch was oddly soft and caressing, and made her heart hammer against her ribs.

She opened her eyes to see Tucker's gaze imploring her for something unspoken.

"Join me?" She beseeched.

He nodded and his look was so electrifying, it sent a tremor through her. She watched as he began to unhurriedly undress himself. Her eyes fixed on the movement of his hands as they casually removed his black leather belt. His fingers skimmed the buckle seductively and her eyes darted up to his. He winked and smiled in acknowledgement of her desires, then continued removing the remainder of his clothes. When he was standing beautifully naked, she drank in the magnificent image before her.

"You're so beautiful, Tuck. Like, pussy-quivering, make-me-wanna-fingerbang-myself beautiful."

HE dipped a foot into the water and a rush of pink stained his cheeks as he laughed. "You're not too bad yourself."

"Black eye and all?" She batted her eyes.

His smile faded and he blinked rapidly. Her injury was still an area of contention and she quickly changed the subject when she saw the joy leave his face.

He backed his body up between her legs in the small bathtub, and she wrapped her arms around his shoulders and tucked her feet under his thighs.

"Thank you for this and for your kind words. I'm sorry to be so needy."

Tucker turned his head sideways and peered into her eyes. "I need to be needed, Lilly, just like you need to be wanted. We complete each other."

She smiled. *Existential, indeed.* She squeezed his shoulders and kissed his ear. "Wow. That was deep."

He softly chuckled, his body shaking just enough to make the water slosh in the tub and splash over the edges. "Not as deep as I'm going to be when I'm inside you later tonight."

"Perv," she giggled.

"Prude," he countered.

***

Watching Lilliana make dinner was comforting somehow. Tucker wasn't the kind of man who believed women belonged in the kitchen barefoot and pregnant, but it was nice seeing her take control of her surroundings and cook like a goddess. He helped her shuck the last of the fresh corn and laughed when Lilliana couldn't resist turning it into a competition. She beamed with pride when she out-shucked him by two full ears of corn.

After her emotional breakdown and dinner-making fun, he had forgotten all about what he had intended on showing her. He retrieved the piece of paper from his car and presented it to her.

Looking at it questioningly, she took it into her hands. "What is it?"

"Proof that I'm no liar." Her cheeks colored under the heat of his gaze and her eyes quickly scanned the letter of sexual cleanliness. "STD free, Pet. Are you satisfied now?"

"This is what the surprise was?" She asked calmly.

"Yes. So?"

"What do you want to hear from me?" She asked with no emotion in her voice.

"That you trust me now and we don't have to use condoms. That was the whole point, wasn't it?"

She laid the letter on the counter and pushed past him, making her way out the back door. He stood defeated for a moment as Lilliana stepped out onto the back deck without answering him.

When he met her outside, he grabbed her by the shoulders. Awkwardly, she cleared her throat, then bit her lip and looked away. "I didn't ask you to do that."

He dropped his hands to his side, stepped back from her and searched her eyes for something, but they were unreadable. *Had he misread this situation completely wrong?* He thought Lilliana wanted proof.

"No, you didn't, and if you had, I probably wouldn't have done it. I did it because I want you to trust me."

"A piece of paper isn't going to make me trust you, Tucker. You are. Your actions, words and… I wish you hadn't gone through the effort," she sounded displeased.

"Well, what's done is done. I'm a problem solver and I figured the way to get you to believe me about not having any STD's was to prove it to you."

He was exasperated with Lilly. He didn't know what the hell she wanted from one minute to the next. "You run so hot and cold, I never know how to please you."

Raw hurt sparkled in her eyes. "That's not true, is it?"

"That's how I feel. You're up, then down, then up again. You want me, you don't want me. You trust me to tie you up, but you don't trust me enough to believe that I'm not going to cheat on you or that I don't have any STD's. I'm not a fucking mind-reader. Yes, I can read your body well enough… But your mind? Christ Almighty, Lilly. Give a man a break." He threw his hands up in the air and walked back into the kitchen to check on the simmering pasta.

His emotions were all over the place, and he was annoyed that he allowed Lilliana to do that to him. He stirred the pasta tetchily when he felt her arms around his waist and her cheek pressed to his spine.

"I'm sorry, Tuck. I don't mean to be so difficult. Maybe it's my hormones or something. Or maybe it's just that you make me feel so many different things. Happy, irritated, angry, irritated, horny, irritated, giddy…"

He turned and stared at her. "Let me guess… Irritated?"

"Did I mention irritated?" She smiled.

"A few times. All I have to say to that is: welcome to my world."

Both of their moods lightened and as she prepared their dinner plates, he assisted her, and nothing more was mentioned about the STD test.

When Lilliana had apologized for being difficult, it reminded him of her earlier comment about her father and not knowing him.

"So what happened to your dad?" He cautiously asked.

Her eye shot up at him and she blinked several times while she chewed her food.

She swallowed, wiped her mouth and answered. "I have no idea. I never met him. He left my mother when he found out she was pregnant. They were both very young. I guess he wasn't ready for the responsibility and he gave up all rights for me."

Tucker couldn't help but feel angry at her father. *What a selfish bastard.* He had the chance at a family and he threw it away. More than that, he missed out on getting to know a beautiful person. He furrowed his eyebrows but kept his thoughts to himself.

"I'm not angry about it, Tucker. I don't know him. My mother never talked badly about him. In fact, she said she held no animosity toward him because of the wonderful gift of motherhood that he gave her."

He smiled. "You're mother must've been an amazing person."

"She was. I never missed having a dad. Really. Margo and my mom were my family, and I grew up feeling loved and wanted."

She tried to smile but her eyes filled with tears. She sniffed and dabbed the corners of her eyes with her napkin, and continued as if nothing had happened.

While they finished eating supper, his longing for his family grew by the minute. He missed them immensely and didn't want to put off a visit to them any longer.

"I've decided to pay my family a visit this weekend," he told her in between bites.

"That'll be nice for you. When will you get back?"

"*We*, Lilly. *We'll* leave tomorrow evening and get back Sunday night."

Lilliana laid her fork down slowly and her mouth parted in confusion. "And you accused me of running hot and cold? Just last weekend you didn't want to introduce me to your brother and now you want me to meet your whole family?"

"I changed my mind. I'm allowed to do that," a bold grin graced his face.

"Ooh, nooo," she drew the words out and shook her head insolently. "I'm not meeting them out of some sense of shame you feel at how shitty you acted last weekend." she

"Yes, what I did was shitty, but that's not why I'm taking you. I'm taking you because I feel differently about you now."

Unflinchingly, she met his gaze. "Differently?" She asked in a silky voice.

"You heard me. I'm your *boyfriend*, remember? Isn't it only appropriate that you meet my parents?"

It was true that he felt differently about Lilliana, but that wasn't the only reason he wanted to take her to meet his family. It was to put their minds at ease that he wasn't going to be alone his whole life, and to give Lilliana a little piece of serenity, knowing how much she missed her mother and aunt.

"I suppose," she huffed. "But we'd better stop off and get plenty of Preparation-H for the trip."

He gasped in disgusted shock at her honesty. "Why? What the hell's wrong with your asshole?"

"You. You're a major pain in it."

CHAPTER 21

The flight to Iowa City was comfortable and Lilliana wondered why she had ever flown any other way than First Class. Though, she did feel a bit sorry for the poor chumps sitting in coach while she was being served champagne and getting a neck massage.

"A girl could get used to this, Tuck. You've really spoiled me," she whispered wistfully.

"First Class is quite becoming of you, my little red-neck," he winked.

She pursed her lips in fake irritation. She was thirty-thousand feet in the air, high above the ground and her heart was somewhere out there floating on a silvery, fluffy cloud. She hadn't been this happy in years. Even before things got really bad with Adam, they weren't this good. He neglected her half the time and when he was home, his mind was somewhere else. Most likely on where his next piece of ass would come from.

She readjusted herself in the soft seat. Her bottom was still tender from the playful yet intense spanking Tucker had delivered the previous night after her pain in the ass remark. But the fucking that came after was nice. No bondage; just plain, old-fashioned sex on a stick. With a condom, of course. She had insisted on it but feared Tucker would hold out if he didn't get his way. True to man form, she licked his dick just enough to change his mind and helped him slip it on.

She turned her body toward him and leaned her seat back to gaze at him. "Tell me about your family. I should probably know some deets before I actually meet them."

He nodded and took a big gulp of his gin and tonic. "You've met Mason and already know his *big secret*," his rounded his eyes in faux exaggeration. "He's a year older than you and an architect at a firm in St. Paul, Minnesota. He wanted to stay close to home without being in Iowa, so that's where he ended up after college. He's a creative genius and as

241

stubborn as a mule. He wouldn't let me pay for his college and was set on earning his own way. I respect him for that. He's won all sorts of accolades for his work. So many, in fact, I've lost count of them all. I'm proud as hell of him. He designed my house. You know, the big, extravagant one that you like making fun of?" He lifted an eyebrow at her. "I'll have to let him know what you think of his talents."

"You'll do no such thing!" She punched him in the arm before summarily changing the subject. "When did you find out about the *big secret*?"

He shook his head. "About five years ago. I still can't believe he waited to so long to tell me. I think maybe sometimes he tried to hint at it, but I was too involved in my own life and drama to hear what he was trying to say. I never suspected it, either. He was bullied in high school to a certain degree, but he would never tell me why or allow me to go and kick some ass for him."

She was mesmerized and touched by the obvious adoration Tucker had for Mason. There was a burning in his eyes when he talked about Mason, and it was heartwarming.

"When did he tell your parents?"

"About a year after he told me." He picked up his drink and sipped on it slowly, his eyes wandering to some far off place.

"How did that go?"

He focused on her again and the corners of his mouth curved upwards. "Just as well as you can imagine. Small town values and mentality – that's my folks. My dad took it the hardest. He said some pretty awful things to Mason and then just tried to blow it off like it was no big deal. He still thinks it's just a phase Mason is going through and that he'll outgrow it someday."

He rolled his eyes and poked at the ice in his glass and placed a cube into his mouth. She sat waiting to hear the rest while he swirled the ice around in his mouth.

As he started to crunch down onto the cube, he continued. "My mom thinks if she prays hard enough, God will change his ways and Mason will miraculously start liking pussy." He let out a short breathy laugh. "She holds out hope for his heterosexuality, so don't be surprised if she asks if you know any women you could set him up with."

She grinned and snuck an ice cube from Tucker's glass and sucked on it. "Raising two McGrath boys; I can't imagine what that was like for your mom."

His brows went up. "Two? There are three of us, Pet. My youngest brother is twenty-nine."

Lilliana laughed and choked on the ice. "That woman must have the patience of a saint!"

"Most of the time she did, but we definitely knew how to push her buttons. Gavin is the baby of the family. In every sense," he rolled his eyes. "My parents let him get away with way more than they ever allowed me and Mason. I guess their old age has mellowed them a bit. He's in his last year of residency at University of Alabama. Thankfully. I'll be glad when he can pay his own damned bills. That boy is a spend thrift of epic proportions."

"So he's the bright one in the family, huh?" She quipped.

"We're all bright, but Gavin is by far the dimmest of us three," He belted out a sarcastic laugh. "No... Not really. He's just a pain in my ass. I actually had to put a limit on his credit card when he was in his early twenties. At first, I thought he had a gambling problem, but it turns out he just likes the ladies and strip clubs. He finally pulled his head out of his ass when he was twenty-three and applied to medical school. I was shocked as shit that he got accepted."

Lilliana poked Tucker in the ribs. "He likes the ladies, huh? I guess he gets that from you."

"He likes *all* women. I, on the other hand, am more selective about the females whom I choose to spend my time with."

She felt a sense of pride to his statement. "Then I guess I should count myself lucky on some level."

"Yes, you should. You're special, Lilly. One of the proud. One of the choice few whom I've graced with my..."

It was Lilliana's turn to roll her eyes. "Here he comes... Mr. Haughty. I get it, Tuck."

The remainder of the flight was dull and Tucker worked on his laptop most of the time. Only occasionally would he throw her a tidbit of information about his past that he thought might be important for her to know. Like the fact that he grew up in Estherville, Iowa, on a small farm, but later moved his parents to Iowa City when their ranch went bust. Apparently his folks didn't like big city life so he moved them to the more reasonably sized city of Cedar Rapids.

His parents were retired thanks to his generous help, however, his mother insisted on working part-time at a retail store and his father was a carpenter on the side just to keep his idle hands busy.

Lilliana had fallen asleep for only a short time when she felt the tires hit the tarmac. Her eyes flew open and nervous energy suddenly coursed through her. She was really meeting Tucker's parents. *This was some kind of milestone, right*? It meant they were serious, *right*? She smiled at him in silent gratitude for having invited her. She missed the closeness of a family and it was a thoughtful gesture on his part to allow her to experience the love of his kin. She began fidgeting with edge of her skirt anxiously when he took her hand into his.

"It's no big deal, Lilly,"

She sat back, momentarily rebuffed and puzzled by his abrupt change in mood. His tone was nonchalant and so casual, it made her think maybe she was making more out of the meeting than necessary. She looked up at Tucker and his face was blank and emotionless.

Deflated, her smile faded.

***

Tucker watched the hopeful glint in Lilliana's eyes turn to dejection. He hadn't meant to be so chilly, but her meeting his parents really wasn't anything to get wound up about.

When they were finally on the road to Cedar Rapids in the rental car, she drifted in and out of sleep. He welcomed the silence as it gave him time to think about everything that had happened with her.

As much as he was looking forward to seeing his family, he was almost dreading it.

First the questions would come. *Are you serious about Lilliana, Tuck? Is she the one, Tuck? Do you love her, Tuck?* How the hell was he going to answer those questions without lying? Yes, he was serious about her, but he didn't love her and he had no idea how long this thing with her would last. What else could he say? They had incredible sex together? She let him tie her up and do depraved things to her? Shit, his mother would slap him upside his head if she knew of his proclivities.

Then the assumptions would come. *So you're going to marry this one, Tuck? You're going to have a family with this one, Tuck?* He just wanted to take this thing one day at a time and let things happen at a natural pace. If it worked out, *great*; if not, well... He wasn't ready to think about that just yet because he really did care for Lilliana on more than just a sexual level.

He reached over and squeezed her thigh to waken her. When she roused and her exquisite eyes focused in on him, a myriad of confused thoughts and feelings assailed him.

God, she was so beautiful in so many ways. She was strong and brave. She challenged his way of thinking. She even forced him to let go of his austere persona. Everything about her was absolutely right for him.

His accusation of her running hot and cold slapped him across the face, because that's how he felt when he was around her; *hot and cold*. Though more hot than cold, if he was completely honest with himself. He gave her a crooked smile to convey his feelings, but her only response was to blink several times.

Without a hint of happiness in her voice or on her face, she spoke. "I'll do my best not to lead your parents on for you, Tucker."

A stab of guilt penetrated his chest for having told her it was no big deal to meet his parents. It *was* a big deal and he damned well knew it. Her sad eyes turned away from him and scanned the small acreage that he had purchased for his parents.

"It's gorgeous here. I've never been to Iowa. It reminds me a great deal of Kansas, only not as hilly." By the tone and inflection of her voice, he could tell she was trying to be polite without revealing anything. "You're such a kind man to have bought this for them. I don't care what anyone says about you, Tucker McGrath; you're an okay guy."

He threw his head back and laughed. Damn if Lilly didn't know how to bring out the best in him. "Well, gee, thanks. You're okay, yourself. A firecracker between the sheets and a ticking time bomb in the streets."

Her face lit up and he was glad to see her joy return. "Do you think I can put that little tagline on my resume?"

"*Resume*? Why? Do you plan on going somewhere?"

She shrugged her shoulders and picked at a piece of lint on her skirt. "You never know. If I can't pay my taxes, I may just have to go where the wind takes me. I've always thought South Carolina sounded nice. Or Florida, somewhere near the beach."

He slowed the vehicle to a near stop and stared at Lilliana. *Was she serious*? He suddenly felt like he had been punched in the stomach and the wind had been knocked out of him. Only moments ago he simply wanted to take things one day at a time, but now, the thought of losing her made him confront a reality he wasn't ready to face.

***

"Shit, Lilly, I wish you would stop worrying about those damned taxes. Everything will be fine." Lilliana inwardly rolled her eyes. That was easy for Tucker to say, he didn't have a care in the world when it came to finances. "I can always pay them for you..."

She jerked her head to the side, shocked at what was coming out of his mouth and blurted out, "Don't!"

He slowed the car to a complete stop and faced her while regarding her carefully.

"I don't want or need your money, Tucker." Her voice started out strong, but ended in a feeble whisper as she quickly became confused by her emotions. "I appreciate your offer. I really do. But I can handle my own financial affairs without the help of a man."

What she left out was that she didn't ever want to owe a man for his monetary assistance. Adam flashed in her mind and how he had always held his money over her head like some kind of prize that he would threaten to take away if she didn't do exactly what he wanted or act exactly how he expected her to. She knew Tucker all of five minutes and there was no way in heaven or hell that she was going to owe him. Shit, for all she knew, he was still interested in her land. *Then what*? If she didn't repay him he could take over her property and do with it what he wanted?

She shook her head at her terrible thoughts. Tucker had been honest with her about his intentions with her land and she felt guilty for assuming the worst of him.

He sat quietly watching her, his brows pinched together as he chewed on his bottom lip.

"I'm sorry, Tuck. I just don't want money to come between us."

He leaned over and tilted his head toward her. "I would never allow that to happen."

"Good. Let's not talk about that ever again," she sighed with relief.

Tucker drove the short distance up the long drive and after only a few minutes they reached the circular drive of his parent's expansive two-story house. Before they stepped foot from the car, his mother was outside, waving, and smiling.

Lilliana beamed in response and waved back, and as soon as she exited the car, his mother was on her, hugging her, and looking her over closely.

"Oh, Tuck, this one's a pretty little thing. Look at you!" She held her by the shoulders. "You're so damned cute! But that eye! Who did this to you?" She frowned.

Lilliana felt her face burn bright red and she glanced at Tucker who was smiling crookedly at her. "I had a run in with my ex-husband."

His mother looked to Tucker. "I hope you took care of that SOB!"

He puffed his chest out proudly. "Hell yes, I did. He won't be bothering Lilly again." He disappeared behind the car to gather their luggage while his mother took inventory of her.

"Good boy. Well, I can already see you're different than the usual women Tucker brings home. You have real boobs!"

Tucker's head popped out from behind the trunk lid, his eyes wide and his mouth hanging open in shock. "Nice, mom!"

Lilliana did her own inspection of Tucker's mom: toned body with large breasts, about 5'7", firm, soft hands, bobbed shoulder-length, gray-brown hair, and a warm, genuine laugh that reminded her of her own mother. Her face showed lines consistent with her age of late fifties, but there was no denying she was beautiful.

"I'm Charlene, but you can call me Char," she winked.

Tucker looked so much like his mother it was strangely odd. They shared the same lips and nose, the same color and shape of eyes, and even the same quirky signature wink. When she looked up, Tucker's father was ambling slowly towards her. His stare was critical as his eyes moved over her body.

Lilliana was accustomed to dealing with old farmers and she suppressed her smile and approached him bravely. "Nice to meet you, Sir. I'm Lilliana Norris of Concordia, Kansas. But my family is originally from Connecticut," she stated with certainty as she thrust her hand at him.

Tucker's father's eyebrows went up and Lilliana could swear she saw the faint hint of a smile in his eyes. He was a handsome man with longish, wavy silver hair, a craggy face, and he was just as tall and solid as Tucker. Despite his rough exterior, his gray eyes were friendly and shined brightly.

He took her outreached hand between his two large, stony palms. "Nice to meet you. I'm Gregory McGrath. Concordia, you say? Where is that? Cloud County?"

Lilliana smiled and nodded.

"Yes, I know the place. I had an aunt and uncle from right near there in Clay County. I used to visit them often. Remember them, Char?" Gregory lifted his head to Charlene.

Charlene nodded in acknowledgement, but was too busy doting over Tucker to pay any attention to Gregory.

As soon as Lilliana walked into the McGrath residence, she felt at home. The smell of something savory lingered in the air and every wall was covered in pictures. The wooden mantle held trophies of every sort and Lilliana made her way over to them. She loved the feel of a lived in home with all its quaintness and familiarity. Two trophies belonged to Tucker from eons ago, one for agriculture and one for athletics. Lilliana ran her fingers over the old painted gold statue and smiled. Her eyes wandered around the immaculate home and rested on several family photo collages. Tucker had always been handsome, just like his younger brothers.

Tucker was speaking excitedly about work and other nonsense, but Lilliana was too caught up in all the family mementos to pay any attention. Charlene laughed and it rang so familiar in her ears that it took her by surprise. She spun on her heel and her breath caught in her throat.

No, she wasn't going to break down. Not today; not here. She swallowed her pain and turned away from the McGrath family to gather her composure.

"Are you alright, Lilly?" Tucker was behind her with his arms around her shoulders and whispering sweetly in her ear.

"Yes. You have a beautiful family. You're so lucky, Tucker. I hope you never take them for granted."

He turned her around by her shoulders and skimmed his fingers under her chin. He opened his mouth to say something, but his mother was on them, dragging them to the kitchen to try and feed them.

He chuckled at her and rolled his eyes. "That's my mom. My brothers and I have an ongoing bet to see how long it'll take until she tries to feed us from the moment we step into the house. What was that? Five minutes? That might just be a new record for her."

"I heard that!" Char sniped. "Your brothers should be here a little later. It was like pulling teeth to get Gavin to agree to come. I think he's afraid you'll give him a hard time about his little fiasco at Tuscaloosa Memorial."

Tucker looked visibly annoyed and shook his head. "He should be afraid. His dick is going to get him into hot water and kicked out of his medical program."

"Tucker G. McGrath, watch your language," his mom snarled.

"It's true and you know it. I'm just not afraid to say something to him. You both allowed him to rule the roost in this house and now he doesn't know his own limits. Everyone knows the Golden Rule in business is to never sleep with your coworkers. Back me up, Lilly." He looked to her for support.

Caught off guard by he and Charlene's pointed stares, she shrugged her shoulders. Not wanting to get in the middle of a family disagreement, she tried to turn away but his mother's voice made her spin back around.

"Come on, girl. You have an opinion. Spit it out," Charlene glared at her.

Clearing her throat, she did as his mother told her. "Well, although I rarely agree with Tucker," she gave him a half-smile before readdressing his mother once again, "and find he's often times brash and frankly ridiculous and arrogant, I think he's right this time. No pussy at work sounds like a good rule of thumb to follow."

Ella Dominguez

Tucker's body stiffened in surprise, his mouth hung open, and his eyes were as round as saucers. When she glanced sideways at Charlene, her eyes were just as wide as Tucker's and her mouth gaped open even wider, though Lilliana didn't know why. She said to state her opinion, so she did. Sheepishly, she grinned at the both of them, and looked to Gregory who had an enormous smile spread across his face.

"Hot damn, I think you found yourself a keeper, Tuck!" Gregory bellowed as he strode across the room to her. Wrapping an arm around her, he slapped her on the back brusquely, "Yes, I think this one will do just fine."

Mentally, she kicked herself for her big mouth and wondered if her ass wouldn't pay for her remark later. Gregory dragged her to the kitchen and began chatting her ear off, and she looked back at Tucker apologetically who was still reeling from her honest, though brazen, statement. She had said she wouldn't lead his parents on and now her father was obviously thoroughly impressed with her. From that moment on, she decided to keep her mouth firmly closed and try her best to be a fly on the wall for the remainder of the visit.

Several hours later both Gavin and Mason arrived and the house became a bubbling cauldron of laughter and love. Lilliana hung back and watched in awe. Tucker waited only a few minutes before thoroughly ripping into Gavin. He proceeded to preach about the rules of engagement when it came to women and work, and about keeping his dick in his pants. That conversation then led to her statement, which Gregory was all too excited to tell them about.

When he finished with the story, they all quieted down and their eyes converged on her.

Mason was the first to greet her. She reached a hand out, but he pulled her close and hugged her tightly.

"Oh, Sugar, that eye. You poor thing. I hear Tucker really walloped him good, though. Anyway, now we can have a real conversation. I have *so* much to tell you about Tucker. Don't

251

let him fool you, he's not as aloof and innocent as he pretends," he waggled his brows up and down.

She let out a short laugh. She was well aware that Tucker was not innocent and she had a few stories of her own she could tell them, however, she decided to let them keep their ideas of who they thought Tucker really was. She looked over Mason's shoulder and smiled slyly at Tucker, and she was rewarded for her silence with a seductive lick of his lips and a wink.

"Lilly, Darling, do you know of anyone you might be able to set Mason up with?" Charlene called over Mason's shoulder.

His mouth puckered into a frown and he rolled his eyes exaggeratedly at Lilliana.

"Yes, I think so. The dentist I work for is single," Lilliana replied. Charlene's eyes widened with hope. She looked back to Mason who looked confused and even a little hurt. "Dr. York is a wonderful man, Mason. Maybe I can introduce you two sometime," she smiled knowingly at him.

Tucker coughed and chuckled, and Mason's grin was so large it practically crowded everyone out of the room. Charlene huffed and went back to talking Tucker's ear off.

"Lilly from Kansas, you're officially the shiz," Mason gushed.

Gavin eventually made his way over and to her surprise, he was soft-spoken and shy. He was young and attractive with layered, short, light-brown hair, and with the same body type as Tucker and Mason; tall with a strong, muscular physique. All his other attributes were like his father, including his piercing gray eyes. As for his smile, she had no doubt it had melted many a heart. He offered a polite hand but only made eye contact when she spoke directly to him.

Lilliana was confused. This was the man who couldn't keep his dick in his pants? *Go-figure*. It's always the quiet ones you had to watch out for. If he was at all like Tucker, then he had charm and charisma in spades.

She was inexplicably able to keep her sarcasm in check the rest of the evening. Tucker kept a firm hand on her at all times. He massaged circles on her back during dinner, and squeezed her thigh possessively during post-supper discussions. When they all eventually moved outside to the back deck, she kept her eyes glued to his mouth, and dreamed of being crushed in his arms. The half-moon was shining vibrantly, the wind was blowing gently, and Tucker's eyes sparkled in the lunar light.

More than once she was caught ogling him and she did her best to hide her obvious embarrassment. He, too, kept glancing at her time and time again, and she couldn't help but feel hopeful for their future. It must have been the atmosphere and her surroundings, but for a change, she allowed herself to daydream.

Settling into the spare bedroom that was clearly designated for Tucker, she looked over all the ribbons of awards and trophies scattered around the room. There was a corkboard with high-school photos and she laughed loudly at his dated hairstyle.

"I was hot, wasn't I?" He chuckled from behind her as he stripped down to his boxers and dug into his suitcase.

"Absolutely. It's amazing how good looking all the McGrath men are. You're all blessed with amazing genes. Your mother, too. She's so pretty."

"I'll be sure to tell her you said that," he stated proudly.

"So tell me, what does the G stand for in your name?"

He smirked and flashed his teeth. "Girthy."

Not amused, she stared blankly back at him. "I'm serious."

"Yeah, seriously; *I'm girthy*. Want me to remind you?" He asked, gripping his cock through his underwear.

"Never mind," she gave up, turning her back to retrieve her pajamas from her bag.

"It stands for Garrett." His voice deepened and became husky. "So, tell me..." He repeated her words. "How's your ass feeling?"

She whirled around to see his usually brown eyes now pitch-black. "I didn't mean what I said earlier... I was just... I..." She stammered.

She smiled evilly. "Yes, you did. And I think that little remark deserves punishment. If I'm going to be accused of being brash, then I should live up to that," he pulled a hand out from behind his back.

"Where the hell did that come from?" She gasped when she saw a large wooden paddle in his hand.

"I brought it just in case I might need it."

Startled at the sheer size of it, she countered breathlessly, "Were you hoping to use that on me here?"

His face lit up. "Honestly, yes, but not for punishment."

She took a quick look at the paddle and turned away. Without Tucker instructing her on what to do, she leaned her upper body over the edge of the bed, her chest resting on the plush, comforter. Her breathing became shallow and rapid in response to what he was about to do, or rather, what she was *allowing* Tucker to do. If she hadn't felt so guilty about what she said, she would've put up a fight, but she had to admit to herself that, yes, she was deserving of some sort discipline for her wayward mouth.

When she attempted to tuck her arms beneath her for support, he chimed in. "Hands behind your back, Lilly. Wrists locked."

She was amazed at how authoritative his voice could sound and the sheer control he exuded when placed in the position of punisher. He truly was a man with many layers.

Doing as she was told, she moved her hands to her lower back and her heart beat began to beat uncontrollably.

Why was she allowing this? Why did Tucker need this? Why did she need this? What if his parents heard her?

When Tucker raised the paddle, she flinched, her body tensing up.

"Wider, pet," he whispered, pushing her feet apart.

She buried her face in the down blanket and stifled a whimper. She was afraid, though she knew Tucker would never hurt her irreparably. His rough skin was felt on the small of her back, his caress hot and savage as he ghosted his fingers up and down her spine.

"It's essential that you understand you need to control your mouth. I value your opinion, Lilly, I really do, but I demand respect."

His voice was otherworldly and resolute. She should've run, but it was too late. She was in too deep and she knew it. She had accepted Tucker knowing full well his perversions. Still, she trusted him. More than that, she *needed* him, and he deserved the same respect that he gave to her.

Just before bringing the oak down onto her left cheek, he warned her, "Prepare yourself; this is going to smart."

One solid whack later, she buried her face in the bedding to muffle her shriek. She didn't want to embarrass herself or Tucker any further by allowing his parents to hear their private moment. He swatted her backside a total of six times, alternating between cheeks and the crease of her thigh. She suspected he was being lenient on her, but she was grateful.

When all was said and done, Tucker hauled her into his arms and kissed her face. "You're so beautiful, Lilly. I'm so lucky to have found you."

Snuggling into his embrace, she felt whole, and except for the hot tingling on her ass, the punishment was already forgotten. She stretched out on the bed, her bottom blazing and sending embers of arousal throughout her body. Tucker had marked her body and now she wanted to feel his hands and mouth on her. He seemed to intuit her desires as he crawled on top of her, crushing her with the weight of his body.

"Just so you know, I didn't bring any condoms on this trip," he quirked an eyebrow at her.

Her heated libido was aching with a sense of urgency to be filled by Tucker far too much to really care, but she tried to put up a good front. "Then we'd better go to the store and get some."

His toffee-spoked eyes narrowed with mischievousness, then roamed over her body. He reached his hand underneath her nightshirt and plucked at the tight bud of her nipple, sending shock waves of pleasure throughout her lower belly.

"This town closes down at 10:00 p.m."

She sighed miserably, trying to hide her overwhelming arousal. "I guess tonight's going to be a long night without sex."

He didn't miss a beat. His eyes cooled and he jumped off the bed. "Yes, I guess it will be. I have some work accounts to go over so I'll just utilize my time that way," he replied nonchalantly, reaching for his laptop.

She wanted cock. More to the point, she wanted Tucker's cock. "Tucker McGrath, get your ass over here!" She snapped.

He tilted his head and showed no reaction. "Not until you grovel."

Her mouth dropped open. "Grovel? *For what*?"

With his brows set in a straight line, he placed his hands on his hips. "For making me jerk off in a cup to prove I'm STD free and then still demand I use a condom."

She leaned forward and batted her eyelashes at him animatedly. "Aw! You spunked in a cup for me? How romantic!"

A flash of humor crossed his face, but the burning in his eyes when she got down on all fours and crawled to him was undeniable.

"Let loose the juice? Impregnated the air?" She continued. "Bopped your bologna?"

Obviously having a difficult time refraining from smiling, he bit his bottom lip and dropped his hands to his side. Walking her fingers up his legs to his thighs, her face was only inches from his crotch. He ran his hands through his hair as if frustrated, but gave her a conspiratorial smile.

"Your knowledge of terms for jacking off frightens me. I'm seeing you in a whole new light," he kidded.

She pressed her palm over his hardening dick and rubbed against it.

"Did you jizsturbate in a Dixie cup or a Red Solo cup?"

"Neither," he breathed out deeply, clearly turned on.

She continued to bat her eyelashes at playfully at him. "Did you think of me when you did it?"

He closed his eyes and slicked his tongue over his top lip. "I looked at a porno mag."

Her movements ceased. "Hmph."

Opening his eyes, he tried to suppress a laugh. "Is this your version of groveling?"

Rebelliously, she stood and walked back toward the bed. "I don't grovel."

"You'll accept my punishment, but you won't grovel?" He asked with astonishment. "Yeah. That makes perfect sense."

"That's completely different. I'd rather be submitted to having my face dry-humped than to grovel," she spoke boldly.

He stifled and choked on a laugh. "If that's how you want it."

Without warning, he pushed her onto the bed, straddled her, and gripped her head as if ready to dry-hump her face.

She shrieked with laughter and slapped his hands away. "Okay! Stop!"

Pinned beneath him, he tore away her panties and shed his boxers. She suddenly became aware that they were in Tucker's parent's home and she felt a bit guilty that they were about to engage in unprotected sex under their roof.

"Tuck," she whispered. "Maybe we shouldn't do this in your parent's house. What if they hear us?"

"Ooh, how wicked would that be?" His eyes lit up as he rested the head of his cock on her pussy. "I guess we'll just have to be extra quiet, won't we? Like we're having secret, naughty, unprotected, covert sex."

He slipped a finger into her wet folds and she let out a quiet whimper.

"That's it, Pet. Stay real quiet like that while I pound this pussy for all it's worth. Think you can do that?" He smiled with a devious look in his eyes.

She nodded but she wasn't sure she could follow through with his wishes. Sliding his finger in and out of her as he primed her, he stroked his shaft with his other hand. She spread her legs wider as he shifted his body weight.

She couldn't help but feel apprehensive about their not using protection. Yes, he was STD free, but still, having that kind of intercourse was so incredibly intimate. Lilliana ran her palms over her belly and held onto the tops of her thighs in anticipation of Tucker's penetration. Tucker's hand skimmed her hip, took her hand and guided it to his cock, allowing her to be the one to direct it to her pussy. Tucker's dick throbbed and pulsed his need to be in her, and her fingers prickled with sensation to the warmth Tucker was putting off. His eyes dilated widely as she slowly brought the head of his rigidness to her entrance. He readjusted his body once more and slowly breached her opening. The pleasure was pure and explosive.

No, she couldn't feel the difference without the condom, but she knew there was, and her mind allowed an even deeper ecstasy because of it.

***

A bright flare of desire filled Lilliana's eyes as her body curved and thrust against Tucker. *God damn, she was stunning*. He watched hypnotized as she bit her fisted hand to stay as silent as possible. He grinded into her passionately and his hardness seemed to electrify all of her senses. The heat of her supple flesh as his hands roved her breasts and thighs was intoxicating. The soft sounds of their heavy breathing filled his ears as did the wet sounds, and their skin on skin slapping against each other.

Wanting to see her squirm, he pressed his thumb firmly against her clit and zealously rubbed it. She thrashed her head back and forth, and he couldn't help but smile at her frenzied movements to back away from the intense fiery sensations he was sending throughout her body. She tilted her pelvis and a spark of heat hit the head of his dick, making him grunt loudly. Lilliana's eyes popped open and she grinned, delighting in his attempt at keeping quiet.

She tipped her pelvis upward again and he about came undone, making him growl and swallow his outcry of pleasure.

"I love to hear how much you want me..." Lilliana muttered quietly.

That voice, her body, those eyes and mouth... His eyes scanned every inch of the body which was now his to do with what he pleased.

Pulling out, he stood at the end of the bed and yanked Lilly into the standing doggy-style position. With one of her legs resting on the edge of the bed, he plunged into her. He licked a finger and gently pressed it against the tight puckered hole of her anus and gently rubbed it. She seemed to enjoy it. Wanting every part of her, his plan was to prime her tight ass before penetration. Gently poking his finger into her opening, Lilliana's entire body clamped down and she let out a smothered shriek. He could sense her discomfort so he withdrew it and squeezed her hips.

"We'll get there eventually, Pet."

She peeked over her shoulder and smiled her appreciation for his waiting. She dropped her head and pushed back against his hips, and a whimper escaped her throat. He wanted to explore her depths so he drove into her, wanting to hear her cries of desire.

Placing his palm on the small of her back, he could feel the heat of her body course down the entire length of his torso and down to his toes. Momentarily, he drifted to some other place when, without warning, Lilliana pushed her ass upwards and hit that magical spot causing him come deep inside of her. He stilled while his cock pulsed and twitched violently as her pussy clutched him tightly.

Still in a hardened state, he continued to drive into her until her breaths came out in long, surrendering moans. She collapsed onto the bed face down and he fell onto the bed next to her. His body shivered with chill and fatigue, and his abdominal muscles ached from the strain. Reaching over to the nightstand where his mother had placed fresh towels for the both of them, he gently cleaned her. Spooned up behind Lilliana, her breathing deepened and her soft curves molded to the contours of his lean body.

Just as his eyes closed, she whispered, "I like secret sex. And I still stand by my assertion that you're brash and ridiculously arrogant at times."

He shook his head and sighed heavily, then chuckled. There were no amount of spankings that would ever stop Lilliana's audacious mouth, and he was okay with that.

CHAPTER 22

Tucker woke with Lilliana's arm splayed over his chest and her face buried in his ribs. The sun was shining brightly into the window and lit her body magnificently. A layer of sweat was covering her body and he glided his index finger down her spine and licked it. She tasted divine, salty and sweet.

With raging morning wood and a rumbling stomach, he leaned into her ear. "I'll scissor-fuck you if you get me something to eat."

Her mouth curled into a broad grin and her eyes flickered open. "Sexual favors for trips to the fridge?" She yawned.

He nodded. "How about it?"

She sat up on one elbow with a look of confusion passing over her features. "I thought only two girls could scissor-fuck."

"Oh, my little one, how wrong you are. I'll just have to show you how it's done. But first, Tucker need food," he grunted and pounded his chest like a caveman.

"Anything you want," she jumped out of bed.

He gasped out in fake astonishment. "Are you feeling alright?"

"Don't push your luck. I'm feeling very submissive this morning so enjoy it while it lasts," she smiled as she pulled her panties, a t-shirt and jeans on. "I'll be right back so be ready to scissor-fuck me until the sun goes down!" She disappeared out the door in the blink of an eye, leaving him to deal with his rampant boner.

Moving to the window, he peered out. The day was bright and he could hear the sounds of the wind blowing past the trees. He opened the window and the smell of fresh cut grass tickled his nose. As much as he loved the city life and the thrill of the hunt of a new land project, he also missed *this* – the serenity and peace that country life provided.

The stillness and quietness of the room unexpectedly brought on a sense of bleakness. The momentary solitude was a harsh reminder of how alone he really was. Sure he had women at his disposal twenty-four hours a day, but they provided him with nothing that he needed emotionally, and his family had their own lives to lead. He had always wanted a wife and children of his own, but after years of trying to find *the one*, he had given up. But being here with Lilliana... Maybe... Just maybe...

He knew he had a tendency to jump the gun when it came to beautiful women and he didn't want that to be the case with her, so he suppressed the ache in his chest.

He was just going to take things slowly with her. Remembering her comment about the taxes on her land, he began formulating ways of getting around that. If she would only agree to sell a portion of it, or maybe land lease some of it...

His brain was abuzz with ideas of how to solve her problem when she came back into the room with a warm cinnamon bagel smothered in peanut-butter and a glass of milk. His mother must have told Lilliana it was one of his favorite childhood foods. She smiled and set it down on the nightstand.

"I need to stop off at the Dollar Market. My snatch box will be decorated in red roses in the next few days, so I need to get some fem products. After you eat, we can go and then get right back here for a quick scissor-fuck," she beamed.

He froze in the door of his closet. "I don't shop at the Dollar Market."

"Why not?" She asked as she sat on the edge of bed to put her shoes and socks on.

"Because I don't need to," he answered curtly.

She lifted her face and glared at him with disdain in her eyes. "You unbelievable snob."

***

A shadow of irritation crossed Tucker's face. "I'm not a snob, I'm just not shopping there. You can pick any other store you want, but I am not shopping *there.*"

Lilliana walked into his closet and started digging through his shoes. *Surely he had a pair of old boots from his farm-boy days*. She couldn't believe that someone who came from the same background as she did could be so uppity.

"What are you looking for?" He asked with both hands on his hips.

"Ha! I knew it!" She blurted out when she found what she was looking for. She thrust the boots at him. "Look at these old boots hidden in the back of this closet in a dark corner like you're ashamed of who you are and where you came from. This is who you are, Tucker. Now put these on, find a pair of jeans that didn't cost you $200 and an old t-shirt, and let's go."

Tucker's eyes widened and then narrowed just as quickly, and his body stiffened as if she had struck him. "I'm not ashamed of where I came from."

"You could've fooled me."

Tucker grabbed the boots from her and tossed them aside. "You can think what you want, but I didn't bust my ass to get a scholarship at a top-notch college, bust my balls to get through six grueling years earning my Master's degree with a 4.0 average, and bust my first marriage building up my business just so I could shop at the fucking Dollar Market," he gritted his teeth.

His defensive stare was riveted on her. She hadn't thought of it that way, but still, he was being snobbish and it was grating as hell.

Just before exiting the bedroom, she glanced over her shoulder and glared at him. "I bet your parents still shop *there*."

If Tucker didn't want to accompany her then she was content to go alone. She had necessities that had to be purchased and one store was as good a place as the next to get them. With car keys in hand and about ready to leave, Tucker met her in the living room.

"Are you happy?" He asked.

She couldn't believe her eyes. Rarely had she seen Tucker in anything less than a business suit and tie. Even when he was casual he sported expensive duds, but at that moment, he was a whole lot of wet panties in old Roper's, worn, ripped jeans and a faded college t-shirt on his back.

"I'll wear the damned boots, but I'm *not* going to the Dollar Market and that's the end of this discussion. Also, I sure as hell am not shopping for feminine hygiene products. Buying tampons is a hard limit for me."

Lilliana hardly heard a word he had said. "Your ass is so amazing in those jeans," she drooled.

"Of course it is." He did a slow three-hundred and sixty degree turn, proudly showing off his glorious physique. "The last time I wore this get up was when I was in college, and it all still fits. Boo-yah! Look at this ass, Baby!" He shimmied his bottom.

She truly cherished His wit – even if he was occasionally a snob.

"I said look at it, Woman!" He jiggled his butt, slapped it and grunted. "Uh-huh, yeah," he gyrated around.

She rolled her eyes and snorted out a loud laugh. "It's *one of the best* I've seen," she joked, enjoying their verbal sparring.

He suddenly lunged at her and backed her up to the couch where he pushed her down and promptly seated himself in her lap, smothering her.

"Say my ass is the best you've ever seen!"

"Ah! You're hurting me, Tucker! I can't breathe!" She screeched when he bounced up and down.

He threw his head back and roared with laughter. "Don't be such a girl! Now, say it!"

Realizing this was Tucker's version of the cruel game 'uncle,' Lilliana gave in, just wanting him off her lap. "It's the best!" She yelled, trying to push him off.

He stood and glared down at her with teasing enjoyment in his eyes. "And don't you forget it."

She rubbed her breasts and thighs, trying to get the circulation back into them. "Is that how you treated all your former booty calls?" She asked, incredulous of his immature behavior.

He grumbled, "I'm starting to realize you have no idea what's coming out of your mouth and I doubt there's any hope for curing your sassy lip service."

"The sooner you realize that, the better," she puckered her lips in a fake kiss.

"Those women were sophisticated and proper; they'd never allow such fooling around."

What the hell did Tucker mean by that? Her amusement swiftly died down and she sat reeling. Didn't he think she was a real lady?

Standing, she pushed past him, annoyed with his unwelcome frankness. She was just a small-town girl to him who shopped at the Dollar Market; uncultured and simple. She knew it to be true, but hearing it left her inexplicably irritated.

"Whoa. What's wrong?" He asked, gripping her upper arm and spinning her around.

"I'm sorry I'm not as chic and classy as your usual main entrees, and I'm just an unstylish, unrefined side dish," she answered in a rush of words.

"Oh, hell, Lilly, I didn't mean it like that," he simpered, holding her arm firmly.

She struggled to free herself. "I'll go by myself. I wouldn't want to embarrass you with my lack of sophistication."

In an uncompromising yet strangely gentle tone, Tucker responded. "What I meant was those women were a bore. Shit, I've never kidded with any woman the way I do with you, and it's not because you're simple and unrefined. It's because you're real. Authentic beats phony every day of the week and you, Sugar Lumps, blow those women out of the water. Now, seriously, stop pouting."

He reached around and swiftly smacked her ass. And not lightly. She felt the sting immediately. A soft gasp escaped her mouth. "What was that for?" She asked, rubbing her ass cheek.

"For accusing me of such a shitty thing. Keep up that pouting and there's another one where that came from."

His eyes were narrowed, his tone was severe, and she knew Tucker wasn't fucking around anymore. She smiled timidly at him and batted her eyelashes in an attempt to smooth things over.

His right brow went up infinitesimally. "Do you want to be bent over my knee?" He asked with a deceptive hint of calmness.

She swallowed hard. *No, she didn't.* Her ass was still sore from the paddling from the night before. Bowing her head shamefully, she remained in a position of frozen stillness.

"That's better. Contrite is more appealing than insincere."

She could barely withstand the urge to roll her eyes at him. God, she hated when Tucker lectured her as if she was the student and he was the mentor. He was only five years older than she was, but still he had the countenance of an old professor. Correction: an old cranky professor who needed a corncob extraction from his ass.

His deep voice cut through her thoughts. "Whatever it is on your mind, speak up."

Guiltily, she looked around the room avoiding his stare. She seriously needed to get her facial expressions in check because they gave her away every time.

"No," she timidly whispered.

His eyes darkened and the tone of his voice was a low, deep whisper. "I don't like that word, Lilly, especially coming out of *your* mouth. Find another way to use a negative tense with me."

She thought for a moment and came up with, "I'd rather not. *Is that better?*" She couldn't help hide the cynicism in her voice, and just when Tucker opened his mouth to chastise her, his mother came in from outdoors.

"What's going on?" She asked, looking over both Lilliana and Tucker.

Lilliana quickly ratted out Tucker's temperamental behavior. "Tucker doesn't like the word *no*."

He puckered his mouth and narrowed his eyes at her, and she smirked in response.

Charlene slapped Tucker on the back and laughed full heartedly. "He never did; even as a child. Dad McGrath doesn't like it either, but life is funny in that we can't always control the things people around us do and say."

Tucker half rolled his eyes and let out a deep sigh of aggravation.

"My boy has always had control issues and he doesn't hide the fact that he likes to be in charge. But that's part of what makes him so charming, and I'd imagine what draws all those pretty ladies to him. Like yourself, Lilly."

Lilliana's insolent smile suddenly felt smug at being called out by Tucker's mom. Tucker, however, puffed his chest out; happy that his mother had just pointed out what he already knew.

"Yeah, what she said," he grinned.

Charlene sneered at him and tugged his long hair. "Lilly, was right: brash and arrogant, indeed."

He threw his hands up in defeat and sank onto the couch. He pulled her into his arms and kissed her neck. "You're a pain in my ass, Woman, but I wouldn't have you any other way."

***

Lilliana was basking in the glow of the nightly McGrath post dinner discussions. Returning from a visit to the restroom, she stepped into the doorway of the kitchen to hear Tucker's and Charlene's whispered voices.

"I haven't seen you this happy in a long time, Tuck."

"Don't, mom," he sighed.

"Don't *what*? You two are so much alike. She challenges you and that's exactly what you need. What are you so afraid of? Not everyone is like Aubrey. You have to let what she did to you go, Son."

"I know that and I have let it go. I'm not afraid of anything; I just don't want to dive in head over heels like I have in the past. Lilly isn't interested in getting married and neither am I. Let's not get ahead of ourselves, we just met a month ago."

Charlene reached a hand out and squeezed his forearm. "I knew on our first date that your father was the one."

Tucker chuckled softly. "That was different."

"Why?" She asked with her brows raised.

"Times were different," he tried to dismiss her.

"Time is irrelevant when love is concerned," she smiled kindly.

"*Love*? Jesus, mom, don't go getting your hopes up. I just want to enjoy this thing with Lilly for what it is."

Lilliana's glow faded. What was it that Tucker thought this *thing* was? And what had Aubrey done that hurt him so badly. When she shifted, Tucker and Charlene glanced in her direction.

Embarrassed to be caught eavesdropping, she made her way to the sink. "I thought I could help with the dishes."

Charlene excused herself and Tucker moved next to her. "What do you want me to do?"

"I'll wash; you dry."

She filled the sink with hot, soapy water and began to clean the few plates and silverware that were left over from dessert. She remained silent, thinking about his words.

He skimmed his fingers down her arm. "How much of that conversation did you hear?"

She didn't want to do this with Tucker. Their weekend had been wonderful so far. "Just dry the dishes."

"Lilly..."

He attempted to turn her body sideways, but she resisted. "Don't. You're right. Let's just enjoy this thing for what it is; however short term that may be."

His mouth set into a thin line and he shook his head. "I never said anything about short-term."

She turned her head to face him. "What did Aubrey do to you?"

His body stiffened and he reached for the towel. Grabbing a wet plate from her hand, he dried it. "No. Huh-uh. I'm not talking about that. I've let all that shit go and I don't need to rehash it like I'm in therapy."

"I see. So you get to know all of my dirty secrets, but yours remain hidden away? I have to live with the ghosts of your ex's whose pictures you keep close by?"

Tucker's gaze burned into her as he laid the plate down loudly. "You saw those?"

Lilliana's cheeks blushed and she averted her gaze out the window. "Yes. I'm sorry to have been nosy, but I just wanted to know more about you."

When she found the courage to look into his eyes again, he looked beyond irritated. "Fine. You want to know what happened? She bought a positive pregnancy test online to convince me that she was having a baby so that I would marry her," he snapped.

Her throat tightened. What a horrible thing for someone to do and what an awful thing to lie about. *Buying a positive pregnancy test?* She had never heard of such a thing. Silently she stood next to him, ashamed for having forced a confession out of him.

"She knew how much I wanted a family of my own. She even faked doctor's appointments. I showed up unannounced to her supposed OB physician only to be told she didn't have an appointment, and that they had never seen or heard of her. I checked her computer and found the invoice for the fake test."

"I'm so sorry, Tuck."

She touched his arm and he pulled out of her reach. "For what? I told you I'm fine. You wanted to know so I told you."

Her stomach knotted under his sad, withering stare. She wanted to hold him, but she knew by the look on his face to let him be. He tossed the towel aside and left her alone to finish the dishes. When she was done, she lingered in the kitchen, upset with herself for having brought up the subject.

Still, she was glad to know a bit of his history and what kind of despair lived in his heart. They had both been lied to and hurt by people that they loved, and it was just another thing they shared in common.

Wanting some fresh air, she stood on the back deck. The night was cool and dark. As she hugged her body for warmth, she gazed at the big dipper that was bright in the sky. *Tucker McGrath*... The name formed on her lips and she silently mouthed it as if wishing him into existence.

As if he heard her silent wanting, his arms wrapped around her body. "I don't know where this thing with us will go and how long it will last. That's the reality of any relationship. But right here, right now, I want you, Lilly. End of story."

CHAPTER 23

Lilliana was excited for the evening festivities that were planned. While Tucker dressed, her thoughts wandered to the previous weekend. It had ended far too quickly and she already missed the kindness of his family. Tucker seemed to warm up and relax after their return, and the preceding few days had been like a dream for her. On occasion she had to pinch herself just to reassure herself that he was real.

Their nights had been spent alternating between her home and his, and it seemed to work out nicely. She felt a sense of euphoria when he would gaze out longingly at the sunset with her, and she no longer had doubts about to his intentions. Throwing her suspicions to the wayside, she allowed herself to believe in Tucker.

She floated around the room on a cloud of exhilaration as she got ready for the party. She had brought a dress of her own to wear, however Tucker had surprised her one he had picked out himself. It was a sweet gesture and one that no man had ever done before.

When she opened the long box on the bed, her thrill dissipated rapidly when she was faced with a hunter-green, taffeta, strapless dress that looked to be about four inches too short, a full size too small, and as if someone had inadvertently shrunk it during dry cleaning.

What did Tucker think she was, a freakin' elf? She scanned the tag and was shocked to see that it was actually the correct size. What the hell kind of cocktail party were they going to - a leprechaun hooker convention? She didn't want to be rude but there was some 'splainin' to do.

"You picked this out?" She asked Tucker who was still in the dressing room, trying her best to hide the disgust in her voice.

"Not exactly, my clothing consultant picked it out." *Well that explained a lot.* "I asked for something in green," he continued.

Oh, it was green alright, just the completely wrong shade, wrong style, and hideous.

He poked his head out of the dressing room door, his eyes sparkling with zeal.

"Do you like it?"

"Umm… Not exactly," she spoke in a stifled and unnatural voice.

She lifted the dress up to show him when he walked into the room. She figured he would be equally as appalled, but to her astonishment, he simply shrugged as if not understanding why she wasn't pleased with it.

He was dapper as hell and sexy as a rock star in his black Valentino suit and puce tie. She didn't understand how the same consultant could have picked out his outfit and her unsightly dress.

"Does the same consultant pick out your clothing, too?" She asked, still staring at the nasty garment.

He shook his head and chuckled, "No. I'm a big boy. I pick my own clothes."

"Then why do you have a clothing consultant?"

"It's not for me, it's for…" He stopped himself and cleared his throat. A faint blush ran over his perfectly sculptured face before he disappeared into the dressing room again.

The light instantly went on over Lilliana's head. Tucker had a clothing consultant for his surfeit of groupies.

"Ewww." The statement came out before she even knew it was in her head. "You may want to reconsider keeping this so-called *clothing consultant* on payroll. Unless, of course, you enjoy your dates being dressed like high-class hookers with no sense of fashion."

She tossed the dress onto the bed and dug out the dark pink, knee-length, off the shoulder frock she had originally planned on wearing. As she dressed, she became more and more irate with the fact that Tucker would be okay with her wearing something so completely sleazy. Not to mention allowing someone else to pick out a gift for her.

She approached him as he fixed his hair. "Please don't do that again," she pleaded as gently as possible considering how annoyed she was.

"What?" He asked without looking at her.

"If you're going to give me a gift, then pick it out yourself or just don't get me anything. I don't want your gifts anyway; they make me uncomfortable. And seriously, that dress was... Good God, Tucker, did you really look at it? Is that how you want me dressed on your arm? Like a skank?"

He glanced toward her with a stupid grin on his face, and she fought the urge to slap some sense into his gorgeous head.

"But you would've been the best-looking skank there," he joked.

"I'm serious, Tucker, pick your own damned gifts and I'll pick my own damned clothes."

He sighed and gave her a faux condescending glare. "A man of my wealth and stature has subordinates to do those kinds of menial chores," he continued to kid.

Tucker was a lost cause sometimes. However, he was in such a good mood, she didn't want to ruin it. He was outright scrumptious and it was the first time she had ever seen his hair tamed. *Thinking of well-maintained hair...*

"Like manscaping your junk? Do your cronies do that kind of work for you, too?"

He closed his mouth but gave her a shit-eating grin.

"Ewww," she responded.

"Stop wielding that *ewww* like a weapon and don't you dare judge me. I like a woman's hands on me, even if it means having her groom my cock fleece."

Her voice rose in surprise. "Tucker McGrath, gross. You grew up on a farm in Iowa for pity's sake. Trim your own damn pubes!"

His mouth twitched with amusement and he suddenly burst into obnoxious laughter. "I swear you'll believe anything!" He howled while gripping her shoulders.

"Yeah, right. It's too late now, I know the truth. You wait until I tell your brothers about your little admission. Maybe they'll shame you into hedging your own man-bush."

"You better not! I was only kidding, I swear!"

***

Tucker's expression stilled and he grew serious when he saw how striking Lilliana was in her dress of choice. It was simple yet stunning, and it fit her like a glove. He outlined the curve of her waist and slipped a hand underneath her dress and into her panties.

"You look amazing, Lilly," He exhaled as he pressed his fingers into her wet pussy. He withdrew them and brought them to his lips and licked them. "And you taste even better."

Her eyes flared and sparkled. Her mouth trembled with a smile as she dragged her nails over his chest, sending tingling sensations over his torso and down to his crotch.

Inching down her body, he lifted the hem of her dress high and lowered himself to his knees. "I think a little snack is in order before we leave."

She spread her legs in response and propped herself up on the bathroom counter. Sinking his teeth into her thighs, he nibbled his way to the apex of her groin. "Open yourself for me, Pet" he ordered as he placed his hands on her thighs to hold her legs apart.

She spread her labia for him, and aggressively he smashed his mouth down onto her, sucking, licking and biting every centimeter of her sensitive and soft, pink flesh he access to.

She and shivered when he buried his tongue deep inside of her. Moving his mouth back to her clit, he began his assault on her tender nub. He sucked viciously, rolling it between his teeth while he fingered her unremittingly.

"Oh, God, Tuck... I'm so close..." She mewled.

Her legs began to quiver and he knew her end was near. She squeezed her thighs together, trapping his head between her legs, and screamed his name.

He stood, dropped his trousers and thrust into her. Snaking a hand up to her neck, he wrapped his fingers around it as she tossed her head back, giving him full access to her delicate tissue.

Dizzy with intense arousal, he exhaled a long breath. "Let me control you, Lilly. Let me own this body."

"You do, Tucker. You already do," a hoarse whisper fluttered past her lips.

Lilliana's words crashed into him like a floodtide of emotions and he released his seed into her, his cock throbbing with appreciation of its new domain. She threw her arms around his neck and pulled him into her needy and desperate kiss.

"Oh, Tuck," she muttered against his mouth.

He stood back, gently pulled out of her and flashed his teeth. "Because I'm just that good, Baby."

"Ugh," she huffed with stars in her eyes.

Tucker leaned down and kissed the corner of her perfectly shaped mouth while grinning like a juvenile. Things really couldn't get any better as far as he was concerned.

***

When Tucker and Lilliana arrived at the Grand Hyatt ballroom, the party was already in full swing. He held onto her like she was his most prized belonging, and she was. She greeted everyone politely and hung on his every word. Most of all, he loved how when he spoke, she acted as if no other man existed.

Darren made his appearance and he guided her in the other direction. The last thing he needed was for Darren to rat him out. His lies were long over with and he didn't need that kind of drama, especially considering how amazing things were between him and Lilliana.

She drifted off into the crowd as he talked business, but he kept his eyes on her at all times. When she walked to the bar, he turned away, smiling at how beautiful she looked from across the room.

***

Lilliana was in seventh heaven; somewhere between the levels of cloud nine and pure otherworldly bliss. The night was going wonderfully and everyone she met was exuberant and happy. It was probably the alcohol coursing through their veins, but she didn't care. She felt like a teenager at prom. Her dress was a little on the understated side and though she felt mildly self-conscious about it, Tucker kept reassuring that she looked nothing less than stunning.

Still reeling from all the excitement buzzing in the room, she approached the bar with her heart beating rapidly. Just as she was getting ready to place an order for a coconut martini, she felt the distinct sensation of eyes on her. She turned to find a blonde standing next to her.

"So are you from this area?" She asked, trying to make polite conversation when she noticed the blonde conspicuously eyeing her necklace.

"Mmm-hmm," the woman answered curtly as her eyes flicked over Lilliana's body.

Offering her hand, she introduced herself. "I'm Lilliana."

"I've heard," the fair-haired female responded coldly.

The stranger reached a hand out and for a moment Lilliana thought she was going to shake her hand, but instead the woman touched her necklace.

"At least three other women in this room have this exact same necklace; all given to them by the same man. Myself included," she stated with blatant bitterness.

Lilliana quickly dropped her hand to her side.

"I liken it to having worn a badge of dishonor considering the depraved and scandalous things Tucker did to us," her lips curved upward in a sarcastic smirk. "I'm not complaining. It was fun while it lasted, even if it was only for a short duration."

The woman's tone remained civil despite her look of ridicule. Standing quietly, Lilliana contemplating the blonde's words and what action to take when another woman approached them.

"Hi, Sophie," the tall brunette greeted the blonde.

Without acknowledging Lilliana, the brunette's icy eyes moved to her neck.

"Oh, so you're Tucker's new funhole?" She asked acidly, placing a hand on one of her hips.

Lilliana felt her temperature rise in response to the woman's haughty rebuke. She was so furious she could barely speak and she felt the blood drain from her face. Doing a quick inventory of the two women's attributes, she decided if push came to shove, she could take them both. And she would, too, if they didn't back the fuck off.

The brown-haired witch lifted a bony finger as if to touch her locket and Lilliana came unglued, ready to go ghetto redneck on her ass and deliver a cunt punt to her over-used snatch. "Don't even think about it," she pulled out of reach. "If you two know what's good for you, you'll turn your fake tits around and walk away before you both lose a mouthful of your ridiculously huge fucking veneers," she hissed.

Both women's eyes widened, but Sophie giggled, and the lively twinkle in her eyes only incensed Lilliana more. Sophie's chuckle promptly died down when she took a step toward her with her hand raised, ready to pluck her blue eyeballs out and scalp her like a savage.

"Lilly..." She heard from behind her, low and deep.

She whirled around to stare at Tucker, anger flashing in her eyes. They exchanged a deep, long look and the unsettled expression on his face infuriated her.

His eyes darted back to the women now standing behind her, and his gaze darkened like ominous thunderclouds. "You're dismissed," he spoke firmly.

Lilliana peeked over her shoulder to see them both looking apologetic, and something else. *Fearful?* That was twice now she had seen the look of fright on Tucker's ex's faces, and the way they both scurried away pissed her off even more. If a man had ever dared speak those words to her, she would've planted her knee firmly in his testicles, robbing him of future parenthood.

She pushed past him and went headed straight for the door. Catching up to her quickly, He abruptly caught her by the elbow and firmly escorted her to a secluded corner.

"I won't tolerate you fighting over me." His voice, though deep, was crisp and clear.

She snorted sarcastically and looked Tucker up and down scornfully. He was so damned arrogant, of course he would think such an absurd thing. "Don't be ridiculous. I wasn't going to fight over you; I was going to fight for my honor and dignity seeing as you forced my hand by bringing me to a place where your ex-girlfriends were name-calling."

He blinked rapidly as if affronted. "Lilly, I'm sorry..." He started in.

"For what, Tucker?" She cut him off. "Bringing to me a party where there are a handful of your ex-lovers without warning me or for giving me a gift that was neither heartfelt nor original?"

With shaking hands, she removed the necklace and shoved it into the chest pocket of his jacket, disgusted that he had categorized her as the same as all the rest. Tucker's eyes narrowed, but he remained silent and with his jaw clenched.

"Take me home," she whispered angrily.

He nodded back without saying anything as if not trusting himself to speak.

The tension in the car was thick like blood pudding and not even a knife could've cut through it. She seethed the more she thought about having worn the sleazy *badge of dishonor*. She knew Tucker had a reputation and what she was getting into by being with him, but that wasn't what pissed her off. It was the way he had treated the women and his choice of words.

"Is that what you do to women when you're done with them? Dismiss them?" She blurted out, her voice thick with contempt.

He remained silent and kept his eyes glued to the road.

"Answer me, damn it," she pounded her fist on the dash.

"Not until you lower your voice and show me some respect," he grumbled.

"Like the respect you showed me by buying me that hoochie-mama dress and tagging me with the same damned locket that all your other conquests have worn?"

He shook his head woodenly. "I just wanted everyone to know that you belong to me."

"Oh, they know alright. They know I'm just another member of the *Tucker McGrath-Fuck of the-Month-Club*. And when you're done with me, then what? I get to keep the accessory like some kind of award for being a distinguished member of your Ho-Bag Alliance?" Her voice rose several octaves. "What exactly are you trying to turn me into? One of your McGrath Stepford Wives? What's next on the agenda? A microchip up my ass when I'm sleeping so I'll follow all your ridiculous commands? *As you please, Tucker. How may I serve you, Tucker? May I have another spanking, please?* Thanks, but no thanks. I swear to Christ, if you ever tell me I'm dismissed, I'll put my foot up your dominant, alpha-male ass. I swear it!"

Tucker gripped the steering wheel so tight his skin squeaked against the leather and his knuckles blanched. Grinding his teeth loudly, he mumbled, "Enough, God damn it. I get it, Lilly; I fucked up."

Lilliana sunk back into the soft leather seat with her arms crossed over her chest. She was glad to hear him admit it, though it didn't make her any less angry. She had been hoping to spend the night in Tucker's arms, under his intense brown-eyed gaze and following his commands, but now it was looking like she would end up alone and without the man whose touch she craved like a drug.

As his car turned toward the direction of his palatial home, she snarled, "I said home."

"We are going home," he answered back as if his home was hers.

"My home," she clarified.

He clenched his mouth tighter, gritted his teeth, and swung a U-turn in the middle of the street. His tires screeched loudly and several horns blared when they almost rear-ended his car.

Twenty hushed minutes later, he pulled in front of her door as they both sat quietly not looking at one another. She felt the screams of frustration at the back of her throat, but she remained silent, not knowing what else to say.

As she sat with her arms crossed, she felt like crying for having thought that she was different than the rest and for having led herself to believe that Tucker felt the same way. *She met his family for Christ's sake*. Didn't that mean she was special? Or was she just a diversion like all the rest?

Tucker's conversation with his mother popped into her mind about not making their relationship into something it wasn't. That should've been warning enough of what was to come. Biting her bottom lip harshly, she forbade herself to shed any tears.

Fuck that. She had been hurt far worse by Adam and she never cried once over that worthless piece of rotten man-meat.

"Lilly, I never meant..."

She blocked out Tucker's words, fearing he dismiss her, too. *What then*?

***

"I thought I was different," Lilliana whispered sadly, cutting Tucker to the bone.

He turned to face her, his apology left unsaid. "You *are* different."

"Don't do that to me," her voice cracked.

"Don't do *what*?"

"Lie to me. I'm not a child or some fragile girl that needs to be coddled."

She wasn't fragile; she was the toughest girl he knew. When he heard her choked out words, he rapidly unbuckled himself and then Lilliana. Towing her into his arms, he buried his face in the soft spot behind her ear. He didn't want to be the reason to ever see this resilient woman weep. He had already lied to her enough, but that was in the past and that's exactly where he wanted to leave it.

"My sweet, strong Lilly, I'm not lying to you," he tried to convince her, but to his regret, she gently pushed away from him and opened the door.

"I need time…"

Suddenly, he felt panicked. "Time for what?" He reached out and grasped her wrist firmly.

"To think. I knew what I was getting into by being with you, but… I just need time to rethink things."

"Lilly, please don't do this. I never meant to hurt you, Pet," he said softly.

"I know," she said decisively as she sat up straighter. "But I'm not going to try to be something I'm not for you and what I absolutely *am not*, is a woman who is content to wear clothes that neither suits her style or personality, and that you've had someone else pick. And I sure as hell am not a women who is okay with wearing a piece of jewelry that has no meaning behind it simply because it's expensive and given to me by the most eligible bachelor. I'm not that girl, Tucker, and I don't want to be. I know I'm flawed and I don't know when to stop talking, but I like who I am. It's taken me a long time to accept myself." She sighed miserably. "I'm just sorry you feel like you need to change me."

He was dumbstruck. That couldn't be further from the truth. He loved that she didn't know when to shut up. *Most of the time*. And he liked that she was imperfect and frustrating and exasperating. She was *real* and that's what he wanted. That's what he needed.

"Just fucking wait. I'm not trying to change who you are…" He said loudly when she pulled out of his clutches and stepped out of the car.

His heart beat wildly in his chest and his stomach churned. He had never felt so frantic at seeing a woman walk away from him and he didn't know what to do aside from make a complete fool of himself, and he wasn't ready to do that just yet - for any woman.

She hovered in the door, her eyes scanning the ground as if pleading for him to stop her.

"We'll talk more tomorrow," he finally said, unable to think clearly enough to say anything else.

"We'll see," she responded back, slamming the car door closed.

Tucker watched Lilliana walk briskly to her home and let herself in. He lingered several minutes outside, staring at the house as it became illuminated, first the living room, then her bedroom. He imagined her undressing and readying herself for bed, and he wanted more than anything to be lying next to her and feeling her heart beat against his chest as they spooned.

Her bedroom window curtain shifted and he could see her peering out at him. She touched the glass and a dull nagging pain settled in his chest. When she turned away, her wet cheeks shined against his bright headlights.

He revved his engine loudly and slammed on the acceleration, spinning his back tires as he sped down her driveway. He had made her cry and he was livid with himself.

He drove for hours thinking about Lilliana and their time together, driving past her place two more times before parking at the far end of her drive way as he sat in his darkened vehicle. His actions were immature and he damn well knew it, but going back to his large, cold, empty house was unthinkable at that point.

Another hour later, he was back at his place and in the shower. He had to be up and ready for work in four short hours but he knew there would be no sleep for him the remainder of the night.

In bed, he was besieged by confusing emotions. Things had been going so well... *Too well*. He knew better than to allow that flicker of hope into his life. Angry with himself for having fallen so hard for Lilliana, he picked up his phone and texted her.

McG: Are we okay?

He didn't expect to get a response back as late as the hour was, but his phone chirped back almost immediately.

Lilliana: I don't know.

Tucker fisted his own hair and let out the breath he wasn't even aware he had been holding. He didn't know what else to say and he didn't want to push her. The nagging feeling in his chest became almost unbearable and he felt as if he couldn't breathe without feeling the smarting pain of something lost.

Laying his phone down, forced himself to sleep.

He woke late almost five hours later. He was surprised he had slept at all, let alone overslept. Before he even climbed out of bed, he checked his phone, optimistic that Lilliana had tried to call or message him, but his phone was lifeless.

He dressed without thinking and went about his morning on auto-pilot mode. He tried to remember what it had been like before Lilliana and go about his day as if he was still single and without the distraction of the woman who had crawled under his skin and right into his heart.

He was doing fair until Ariel came strolling in giving him nothing but attitude and a hostile stare.

"What's your problem?" He finally asked.

She folded her arms across her chest and narrowed her eyes at him. "You ripped that poor little bunny's heart to shreds, didn't you?"

"What the hell are you talking about?"

"You know damned well I'm talking about Lil. The Big Bad Wolf Tucker McGrath tore that pretty little bunny to pieces. I'm glad to hear she threatened to kick the Wicked Witch of the East and West's asses, at least."

"Can you please speak like we're not living in a fairy tale and as if we're both adults?" He snapped.

"Right, because you're an *adult*. You get my drift, Daddy-O. You're a terrible, nasty man," she snorted.

"Oh, fuck me." He threw his hands up in resignation. "So what's this about kicking asses?"

"Sophie is blabbing it all over about how Lil ripped her and Gemma's asses and threatened to knock out their veneers, and how *uncouth* Lilliana was."

Ariel started giggling and Tucker found it so infectious, he, too, began to chuckle.

"Lilly is one hellacious little vixen," he shook his head.

He eyes rounded and she waved in his direction. "It's about time someone gave you a run for your money."

His laughter died down and he became solemn thinking about Lilliana's last text message.

Ariel eyed him cautiously. "Did you screw things up beyond repair?"

"I hope not."

"You'd better do more than hope, Wolf-Boy; you'd better fix it," she instructed him just before she walked out.

All morning was spent thinking about Lilliana and the gloomy look on her face. He wanted to see joy in her eyes like he had when he given her the now infamous gift that lead to this whole damned drama.

During his lunch break, he mustered up enough courage to call her. Her phone rang and rang, and he was becoming more irate with each passing moment that he couldn't hear her voice. He ended the call and messaged her.

McG: I want to hear your voice.

Tucker waited. And waited.

McG: You know how I feel about waiting.

For nearly thirty minutes he sat impatiently holding onto his phone and watching the screen off and on between eating his lunch. Giving up, he slid his phone across his desk. He rose from his chair, cursing and fisting his hands.

What was Lilliana doing to him – punishing him? Did she really think she could break him by acting petulantly? Had she forgotten the simple rules he had set forth for her or was she just ignoring them in her quest to make him hurt for having fucked up?

He paced the office, his mind infiltrated with frustration. She was pushing his boundaries and limits, just as she had done since the first time they had met - and he was allowing it.

But not anymore.

He tried to pretend like she didn't exist again and went about his day, ignoring the muted ache in his heart.

When the end of the work day rolled around, his phone finally beeped. He stared at it for a long moment without responding, making her wait just as she had made him wait.

It took everything he had to fight the urge to drive past her house, knowing she would be home.

As he ate dinner by himself at his favorite restaurant and sulked, Gemma's voice was heard behind him. "Alone?" She asked. "So does that mean you're done with Lilliana already?" He turned his head to glare at her. "That was quick," she continued as she stepped toward him. "Our time lasted longer than that," she flirted, seating herself across from him .

"Did I invite you to sit?" He gritted his teeth. *She was part of the reason he was eating unaccompanied and without his woman of choice.*

Gemma simply smiled and fidgeted with the flatware on the table. "Is there any chance that you and I..." She began.

"No," he summarily cut her off.

"I can be better this time, Tucker. I'll follow your rules and be more adventurous; do more of the things you asked. I'll even allow you to punish me this time."

Gemma batted her eyelashes and walked her fingers across the table and touched the top of his hand. In a flash, he pulled it away, feeling as if he were betraying Lilly by allowing another woman to touch him.

"Our time has come and gone. Nothing can be accomplished by dwelling on the past and I wish you would stop doing it. We had fun, didn't we?" He pushed his irritation aside and asked sympathetically, not wanting to hurt the obviously fragile woman sitting across from him.

"Yes, but we could've had so much more if I hadn't been so unwilling to try the things you suggested," she whispered in a low, tormented voice.

"That's life, Gem. But there's no going back. It's time for you to move on," he replied kindly, remembering Lilliana's reprimand for the harsh words he had spoken to Gemma and Sophie the night before.

She scanned the tabletop. Looking up at him, her tone became chilly and her exotic, pretty brown eyes turned frigid. "Is it because of Lilliana that you won't have me again?"

"Even if I didn't have Lilly, it still wouldn't be you," he clarified more sternly.

She sighed as if defeated. "You're an asshole and a motherfucking liar," she murmured caustically as she stared at the tabletop.

"I never lied to you," he half agreed.

"You dick, I hope that Lilliana bitch burns in…"

Tucker swiftly cut her off again. "Don't," he growled. He was all for allowing her to grieve the loss of their relationship in whatever way she felt necessary, but there was no way he was going to permit her to speak unkindly about Lilly.

She instantly shut her mouth and her eyes rounded when she became the victim of his icy glare. He shot her a penetrating look as he rose from his chair, signaling for her to leave. "We. Are. Over. And so is this conversation," he declared with his lips set in a thin, hard line.

Her lower lip trembled as she returned his glare. She stood, slammed her hand on the table loudly causing several people to look their way before finally stomping off.

He had tried to remain civil but there was just no speaking rationally to Gemma. He never could and it was one of the many reasons he had let her go. She was not only unadventurous between the sheets, but she was catty, melodramatic, and disrespectful to him; qualities he detested.

Just as he gulped down the last of his beer, his phone chirped, reminding him of his unseen message and a new one.

Giving in, he checked it.

Lilliana: I know how you hate waiting, I'm sorry. I was busy with a work emergency. Bicuspids, molars and incisors... Oh, my.

Lilliana: Are you alive and safe?

Tucker felt like a complete douche bag, but he couldn't help but smile at Lilliana's attempt at a joke.

McG: Alive – check. Safe – check. Lonely – check. Can I see you tonight?

He assumed approval but was disheartened by her frosty reply.

Lilliana: I'm lonely, too, but not tonight.

What exactly was she trying to accomplish by keeping him waiting? His blood began to boil. He wanted Lilly and he was sick of her games. He knew he fucked up. What more did she want, a written fucking apology?

McG: What's the point of waiting?
Lilliana: Absence makes the heart grow fonder, they say.

287

He didn't believe that line of bullshit – not for one fucking second. He shot back.

McG: Out of sight out of mind, I say.

He snorted, proud of his snarky comeback, but when reread the short conversation, he kicked himself for the shitty remark. She was most definitely *not* out of his mind nor would she be anytime soon. If ever.
Gemma was right, he was an asshole.
He quickly tried to backtrack.

McG: Nix that last statement.
Lilliana: Just like that? Nix it and it goes away?

He rolled his eyes.

McG: Don't be over-dramatic. They're only words.
Lilliana: Words can hurt just as much as actions.

He stared at her response for several minutes. She was right. He could remember his father's harsh words spoken to Mason about his homosexuality and how hurt his brother was. His father had tried to blow it off but the damage had already been done.

McG: You make me act a fool sometimes.
Lilliana Sometimes? Don't blame me for your foolish actions. Own up to them. Good night.

He had fucked up yet *again*. He just couldn't seem to win.
After driving home, he changed and tried to sleep. He was dead-tired but restless. Lying on his stomach, he pulled up an image of Lilly on his phone. Tucker wanted her mouth – to kiss and fuck and whatever else he could think of. He gawped at it, imaging it was wrapped around his dick. He ground his cock

into the bed trying to alleviate the throbbing but it was no use.

Shit, he was getting ahead of himself. Lilliana was almost certainly still incensed about everything that had transpired the last two nights and he was a damned fool for thinking things would blow over so quickly. He'd be lucky if he could even get her to agree to see him again let alone suck his dick.

Annoyed with the whole situation, he dressed in sweats drove to her place, and parked at the far end of her driveway again. He contemplated walking the distance to her doorstep, kicking her door in and ravaging her, but her house was dark and knowing Lilliana, she'd probably knee him in the balls and kick his ass out for a stunt like that. Instead, he reclined his seat back, opened up his sunroof and watched the stars until he drifted into a deep sleep.

He woke to a loud knock on the window. Opening his eyes and rolling down his window, he was greeted to Lilliana standing in a robe with a hot cup of coffee in her hands. The sun was just starting to come over the horizon with vibrant yellow, orange and pink hues highlighting the sky, and he had never seen a more stunning view than the one facing him.

She eyed the foggy, frosted windows and asked, "What have you been doing out here?"

"Don't think I didn't think about it," he quipped, raising a suggestive eyebrow and motioning with his hand in a faux jerk-off gesture.

"You're impossible. And a wreck," she smiled, handing him the coffee mug.

"That's an understatement," he countered, taking the coffee and sipping on it.

God dumm, Lilly could make a mean cup of java. It was always just the right temperature and never too hot. He didn't know how she did it. He smiled up at her gratefully when she raised her eyebrows.

"Nice try."

His eyes narrowed with puzzlement. "What?"

"Your beautiful bicuspids aren't going to get you out of hot water at this hour. How many nights are you going to sit out here in my driveway?" She asked, leaning into the window.

"As many as it takes until you stop being mulish and come back home."

"Mulish, my ass. I am home, remember?"

"No, you're not home until you're under my roof, Lilly. I need you..."

She straightened up. "You don't need anyone; you just don't like being alone. If it wasn't me, it would be someone else. " She straightened up. "I'm sure you'll eventually put that necklace to good use. Now don't be a weenie your whole life. Go home."

She turned and jogged up the path back to her house, leaving him gape-jawed and utterly appalled. *She just had to bring up the fucking necklace, didn't she*? Like hell he didn't need her. Did she really believe anyone else would satisfy his longing the way she did?

He gulped down the hot coffee and drove out of her driveway with purpose. He would just have to prove that there was no one else for him.

Focused on what his goal was, his day went quickly and he was glad for it. His phone remained message-less but it was well enough. He didn't feel like debating the details of how badly he had screwed things up.

Leaving work an hour early to pick up the new item he had ordered for Lilliana, he texted her.

McG: I'll be at your place in 25 minutes. Be ready. I won't take no for an answer.

He held onto his phone waiting for some kind of come-back, but after several minutes of silence, he was content in knowing that Lilliana wasn't going to put up a fight.

The drive over was painfully slow. All the pent up nervous energy he had been suppressing throughout the day began to bubble over. Half-way to her place, he pulled off to the side of the road and stepped out into the cool Connecticut breeze. He circled around his car several times, trying to control his rapid emotions.

Was he really going through with this? What other choice did he have? To be alone and without Lilliana? She had been right in saying that he didn't like solitude, however, she was wrong to think it would be someone else if not her. He knew damned well there was no one else for him. She challenged everything about him and made him see things differently. She reminded him of where he came from and who he really was.

Yes, he was going through with this. There was no other way.

He took a deep breath in and let it out slowly, then climbed back into his car.

Pulling into Lilliana's driveway exactly ten minutes later, she was waiting on the porch and he exhaled a breath of relief. She was obstinate, but she never failed to heed his commands. When his car came to a full stop, she climbed into his vehicle without saying a word. He watched her guardedly. They stared at each other for a long moment before he reached over and squeezed her thigh. He just wanted to feel her and to remind her that she still belonged to him.

"My Pet," he whispered.

She blinked long and hard and turned her face to the window without responding. Her silence was killing him. She was still hurt and angry, and he hoped his heartfelt gift would make up for his having given her something that wasn't sincere.

He drove far too fast to his residence, but his nerves were frayed. He had been anticipating seeing her all day and driving himself crazy wondering how she would react to his peace offering.

Once at his home, he led her inside and guided her to the long lounger in the living area and seated her. Sitting next to her and he brought out a large square box from his pocket and tried to hand it to her, but she immediately pushed it away.

"I don't want any more of your gifts. All I ever wanted was you."

He was touched by her words. "I told you I wasn't taking no for an answer. Open it."

Stubbornly she sat with her hands in her lap, refusing to touch the box. He sighed loudly and opened the box himself and held it up to her face. Though she tried her best to avert her eyes away from the white-gold, halo-looking necklace that seemed to have no beginning and no end, she eventually gave in.

"It's called an Eternity Collar," he told her, his mouth dry and his words choked.

Her eyes inquisitively scanned the unusual looking choker with a D&O ring on the end before darting up to his. "Eternity?"

He nodded decisively and leaned into her ear in a wistful gesture. "As in *forever*," he whispered, unable to bring himself to say the terrifying word out loud.

She shook her head emphatically, her mouth parted in alarm and her eyes glowing with fear. "Tucker, I can't accept this…"

He put his long index finger up to her mouth, "Please don't refuse me, Lilly. Just wear it. We'll figure out the rest later."

He took the shiny collar from the box.

Her eyes sparkled when she smiled at him. "How does it open?" She asked.

Feeling a sense of relief, he reached into his pocket and removed a small L-shaped tool. "With this key."

He returned her smiled when he saw the uneasiness leave her eyes. It was only appropriate that his pet wear a true collar. He only hoped Lilliana would accept it and the role she was about to step into.

"It's a collar, Pet. Do you understand its meaning?" he asked tensely before placing it around her neck.

"Yes, Tucker. Do *you?*"

He knew what it meant. It meant this thing with Lilliana was real. It meant there was no turning back.

"It means you belong to me and only me. It means that you *are* different, Lilly, and that you're unique and only deserve to wear something as distinctive as this. You were wrong when you said if it wasn't you it would be someone else. I don't want anyone else, and I *do* need you. And I sure as hell am not trying to change who you are."

"Tucker... I..."

Her eyes filled with tears and he acted swiftly before either of them had a chance to let their fears of commitment overcome them. This *was* right and he knew it. *Lilliana* was right. She was good and true and loyal... And fucking right for him. His hands shook as he opened the necklace, and he almost dropped the small key twice.

Placing her small hands over his, Lilliana steadied them. "We don't have to do this."

Her eyes reflected sadness and a hurt that he wanted to free her from. "Like hell we don't. We belong together." He spoke with unwavering steadfastness. "You belong to me. Don't you ever question that or my decisions again."

He waited for her reply and just when he thought he would have to paddle it out of her, she responded, "Is this the part where I say, *yes, Sir?*"

A low, lusty growl rumbled in his throat. "Abso-fucking-lutely."

* * *

Tucker reached around Lilliana, placed the choker on her and closed it. When it clicked and locked into place, there was finality to it; an irrevocability that they both felt. She was scared out of her mind and she could see the same terror in his simmering mahogany eyes.

Forever.

She had already been promised that once before, but this time it felt different. It felt more powerful; *deeper*. The last two days without him had been miserable beyond anything she had ever known. Her connection with Tucker was beyond comparison. Not even with Adam had she felt this grounded to someone.

Now *this;* this collar, his discipline, his possessiveness... As much as she tried to deny her feelings, *she wanted this.* She wanted *Tucker* and she *needed* him.

Seeing him parked in her driveway and not going to him had damn near killed her. She wanted to hold him, but she had been so wounded by his actions, she couldn't. The last several days had been unbearable without his touch. She had allowed herself one good cry and then refused to do it again for fear of never being able to stop.

But here he was now, placing this thing around her neck and telling her that there was no one else for him. And his eyes... They were so sincere and bright. All her fears melted away and she threw her arms around his neck so quickly, a gasp of air left his lips. She had hardly been aware of how much she truly wanted him until that very second.

Pressed against him, her body quivered. Tucker dipped his head down and his mouth smashed down onto hers so aggressively, she barely had time to breathe as his tongue stabbed inside her mouth and caressed all the interior surfaces.

He reached into his other pocket and pulled out a leash, and her heart thudded in her chest as he clamped the end of it to the O ring. She was truly his now; his muse to rule over and dominate, and she hoped - to cherish.

"I've always wanted a real pet, Lilly. One who would surrender herself completely to me; one who would obey without hesitation and without question. Will you be that person for me?"

Tucker's usual familiar confident tone was gone and replaced by a fragile and unsure voice foreign to her ears. His need was all too apparent, and his yearning and sexual desire for her was dripping off his toned body. His eyes burned for her and scorched a path through her heart. At that moment, she wanted nothing more than to please him... But, still, the fear of complete submission was still coursing through her veins.

As if reading her emotions, he responded. "Being submissive doesn't mean you're weak. It takes a strong person to allow another to take control. I want to be that person *for you*. I want all of you and nothing less, Lilly."

"I'll do my best," she squeaked out.

He gave her a secret smile. "That's all I ask."

He ran his index finger over her mouth and dipped it in, allowing her to suck on it. Without any further hesitation, she closed her eyes and gave into her carnal desires.

Tucker tugged on the leash and guided her to the floor directly in front of him. "On your knees," he ordered, his fierce confidence now back in full force.

He held the leash tightly with no slack so that he had absolute control of her movements. Looping the end of the leash handle around his wrist, je unbuckled his belt, teasing her with his slow tempo. She could hear herself panting as she waited feverishly to pleasure him. She swallowed tightly as he slid his rigid cock out and pushed it down to meet her mouth.

"Show me how much you want me."

His voice, deep and sensual, carried a unique force that she couldn't resist if she tried. She opened her mouth wide for Tucker and he swiftly pushed past her comfort zone, making her gag straight away. She focused and licked at him, coating his dick with a thick layer of saliva as she readied herself for another try.

She brought her hands up to rest on his thighs, but Tucker had other plans. "Hands behind your back."

She didn't ask why, she simply obeyed, and when she did, his eyes lit up like roman candles. She opened her mouth again, as he gripped her head with both hands in preparation of the mouth fucking she knew he had been eager to give her. She concentrated and opened her throat to his shaft, while she dreamily watched his mouth.

She was his to do with what he wanted, and she didn't want it any other way.

Tucker slid into her mouth again, slowly and more patiently, easing his cock in and out. Her eyes watered profusely and drool dripped down her chin, but she threw all humiliation out the window in her quest to show him how much she wanted to satisfy him. With each thrust, he dipped deeper into her throat until he hit the sweet spot. At the base of her throat, his cock pulsed and swelled, and her pulse quickened with his excitement.

"Damn, Lilly," he exhaled as her throat constricted around him.

His eyes rolled back in his head when he pulled out and once again pushed himself into her mouth. Digging his fingers into her hair, he thrust harder and faster. Their eyes met and he graced her with his lusty smile, their connection purely sensual. He was happy and she loved seeing the sheer joy on his face of having given herself over to him. She squeezed her thighs together to try and suppress the ache in her pussy, but the sloppy sounds of his throat fucking were overwhelming her.

"That's it, Pet," he grunted, diving deeper yet.

Still buried deep in her throat, his movements ceased and she thought she would suffocate, but just as she reached her limit of breathlessness, he withdrew and allowed her to breathe.

When her sputtering died down, he pushed past her lips again. Just as her throat squeezed around him, he stilled, and his warm, thick, salty release hit the back of her throat as he grunted her name. She felt the movement of his ragged breathing and the throbbing of his dick, and she gagged but swallowed his gift.

"That was incredible," he moaned, throwing himself onto the lounger.

She studied Tucker while he lay catching his breath. He was so devastatingly beautiful on so many levels; not just physically but intellectually.

And she belonged to him for *eternity.*

***

Tucker gently eased Lilliana off the floor and led her to the bedroom. She wrapped her arms around his neck, her touch upsetting his balance, but the unsteadiness of his composure that she caused was a welcome one. He stood her at the foot of the bed as he undressed her, caressing each part of her body that became exposed to him. He kissed her neck and her taste overpowered all of his senses.

"Oh, Tucker, thank you," she sighed while he continued to suck at her soft flesh.

With his lips pressed against her collarbone, he mumbled, "For what?"

"For making me feel like a woman again. For *this,*" she touched the collar.

His pulse quickened with her soft spoken words and he felt compelled to ravage her. He lifted her into his arms again and strode quickly to the time-out room. He laid her naked body on the bondage bed and skillfully shackled her wrists, ankles, and neck into place.

Her breathing became rapid and unpredictable, so he leaned down and whispered in her ear, "Shush, Pet. I'm going to make you fly tonight."

He couldn't help but notice the shivers that his words sent across her skin. He ghosted a finger over her taut nipples and captured one in his mouth as he tugged at the other, her moans flooding his senses.

"No music tonight, Lilly. Only the sounds of our breathing and cries of pleasure."

She nodded enthusiastically. Sauntering over to the rack with whipping instruments, he stripped down, enjoying the way Lilliana's eyes lit up as they watched him.

He brought down a new tawse he had been itching to break in and smiled at its short length. "Just your size," he commented, the rich timbre of his voice filling the small room. Next, he picked up a feather tickler, a strip of silk, a

Wartenberg's wheel, and a blindfold. He first placed the covering over her eyes tightly, shielding out all light. "I want to hear how much you enjoy this, Lilly. Don't hold anything back. I want lots of adjectives."

The corners of her mouth curled upwards, "Yes, Sir."

His cocked twitched at the way her mouth formed the word *Sir*. He blinked several times before leaning down to kiss her. He was anxious to make her skin prickle, crawl, burn and tingle with arousal. Gliding his tongue down the center of belly to her mound, he delivered a sharp bite, making her squeal.

"So nice," she moaned.

He reached for the feathers and dusted them over the bottoms of her feet and up her legs to her pussy, making her toes curl and laughter escape her throat. "Good; so, so good," she mewled.

The silk came next. He wrapped the long thin strand around a breast and pulled it tight, then let it cascade over her skin before placing it flat against her cheek so she could feel the coolness of the fabric.

"Oh, Tucker, that feels so wonderful," she panted.

Her body writhed and squeaked noisily against the bed. She yanked on the restraints around her wrists and his fiery gaze took all of it in. He was in another place as he watched the way her body responded to his touch. He slipped a finger into her and circled it around only to remove it quickly, making her beg.

"More please..."

Damn he loved to hear her beg.

Reaching for the tawse, he slapped it against her belly, softly at first, then gradually built up to a rapid rhythm of light-to-moderate smacks down and over her thighs, and tops of her feet. She hissed and panted, softly moaned, and smiled. Suddenly, he strictly brought it down onto her labia making her shriek from the unexpected sensation. She tossed her head back and jerked her body violently.

"Tell me what it feels like," he insisted.

Ella Dominguez

"Wicked and... And... Amazing..." She stammered out breathlessly.

"What else?" He asked as he spread her labia open and delivered another lighter slap over her clit.

"Oh, God! I don't know... It hurts. No... Not pain. It feels like... I can't describe it. Good and bad and... I just want more!" She grunted as her body arched into Tucker's leather.

Tucker swore he could hear Lilliana's heart beating in his own ears. He was totally entranced by her naked body and the sounds of her breath as it left her lungs. He placed his mouth next to hers so he could feel her moist breath against his mouth. His feelings for her were intensifying by the minute, and when the shiny metal collar glinted in the light, pre-come dripped down his thigh.

He gripped the Wartenberg wheel in his sweaty palm and steadied his movements. As he glided it over a pebbled nipple, she swallowed hard and tried to clench her thighs together, but the bindings wouldn't allow.

"Yes, that... That thing..."

He rolled it over her other breast harder, almost penetrating the delicate skin around her tightened bud. She whined loudly and pushed her chest into it, causing the wheel to leave a spectacular imprint on her areola.

"My sweet Lilly, you look so stunning right now. Tell me, I want to know what you're feeling right now," he pleaded desperately.

"I feel like I'm floating, up, up... Oh, Tuck, it all feels so good. Please fuck me. Take me there. I want you inside of me. Please!" She implored.

He dropped the wheel and climbed onto the bed with her and between her legs, and plunged into her, ripping the blindfold off so he could see her eyes. The fringe of her lashes, damp with sweat, cast shadows over her cheekbones as she blinked rapidly trying to adjust to the light.

He held onto her head as he stared into her shimmery eyes and whispered with a lethal calmness, "Can you feel the bond between us, Lilly? Can you feel how strong my need for you is? I can feel your need for me, too, Pet. It's suffocating me, tightening around my throat like a noose, and it feels so fucking good to be breathless." His s strained words carried throughout the room and she almost sobbed her agreement. With his palms flat down on the leather and next to her head, he placed his ear next to her mouth to hear her velvety murmuring. "Fly, Pet, and when you do, say my name loud and clear." He pushed and ground into her tight depths, driving her body into the leather.

Lilliana's breathing deepened and halted, and then it came, loud and undeniably clear... "Tucker!"

His mind drifted in and out reality, and after several minutes of frenzied and impassioned thrusts, he got his release, and his body crashed onto the bed next to her. With the last of his energy, he released her from her bindings and pulled her roughly and almost violently onto his chest.

"My pet," he said softly.

Lilliana's hot breath touched his ear, "My Sir."

CHAPTER 24

Tucker and Lilliana had fallen into a casual yet intensely sexually heated routine. Three weeks had passed since their private collaring ceremony and all drama seemed to be behind them. He was spending more time at her home and she found her closet overrun with his pricey suits. She smiled as she eyed the bedroom that was taking on more of a masculine look. He had made his mark, not only in her home, but in her heart. She belonged to him, and every day and night was spent thinking of him and ways of pleasing him. He was kind and gentle, and never took advantage of his reign over her. When he felt she was disobedient, he guided her to rethink her actions before the heavy hand of the law was used, and she was grateful for his patience with her.

Suffice it to say, his arrogance had died down, too. Not much, but some. Despite allowing that small part of her submissive nature to come out and play, their lighthearted banter and sarcasm was still a mainstay in their relationship, and she never let him get away with being temperamental or too pushy without speaking her mind.

She had just arrived from work to find freshly picked violets and calico bush neatly placed in a vase on the table with a note, a cream-colored bear dressed in lilac-colored leather bondage gear and handmade leather and lace wrist cuffs. Her smile practically lit up the room when she read the note.

Beautiful flowers for a beautiful soul, and kinky gifts for my naughty girl. You, my Pet, deserve only the best. ~Tuck

She brought the flowers to her nose and sank into the kitchen chair and skimmed her fingers over the soft bear's nose. A small, breathy laugh escaped her lips and without warning, it popped into her head.

Love.

Her throat tightened, the word sending currents of fear through her. Sliding a hand down to her stomach, she felt the quivering that the unbidden word had caused. Her head was spinning as she ran to the front door and threw it open, gasping from hyperventilation. Stumbling to the porch, she leaned over the railing. When she had finally calmed down, she laughed at herself. *How ridiculous was she being?*

She retrieved Tucker's car keys and decided to pay him an unplanned visit at his office. She was looking forward to spending their next few days off together and she was hoping they could start their weekend early. He had called and stated he would be working late, but after her little semi-admission to herself about her true feelings for him, she wanted to see his beautiful smile.

When she arrived, she was chatted up by Ariel who was eager to go on another girl's night out. They had already gotten together twice in two weeks and she was thoroughly enjoying their new friendship. When Lilliana, Dana and Ariel had gone out they found it amusing that Tucker had tried to nonchalantly crash their little party. More than slightly intoxicated, they had demanded he do a strip tease for them, but he didn't find their proposition amusing and Lilliana ended up with a sore ass for two days for even suggesting such a thing.

Later, feeling guilty, he gave her a private lap dance and her paddling seemed well worth it after the show and thorough fucking he gave her.

She heard herself laughing out loud at the memory as she made her way to his office when she heard an unfamiliar man's voice as she approached his office.

"So I hear you've practically moved in with her. I guess you really do always get what you want. But what about what Ms. Norris wants?"

She looked through the glass to see Darren standing near Tucker's desk. *Why the hell were they discussing her?*

"Lilliana wants whatever I tell her to want," Tucker snorted with fury in his eyes.

Her heart lurched into her throat and she backed up so she was out of sight.

"And what she wants is to give her land over to you?"

"That hasn't come up. *Yet*. But when it does, I can assure you it will be off the market," Tucker countered.

"That's what you told everyone weeks ago. Now I hear you're looking into selling off acres. So what's the deal, McG?"

Her pulse pounded in her ears with what she was bearing witness to. She took a deep breath and held it for fear they would hear her heavy breathing.

"When are you going to learn to mind your own fucking business, Schumacher?" Tucker bellowed.

Darren bent down into Tucker's face. "That girl needs to know what kind of man you are and that your intentions are *not* honorable."

Tucker wheeled his chair back, his face flushed bright red with fury. "You have no idea what my intentions with her are! Now, seriously, back the fuck off!"

"I know how you work and I remember what you told me: That *nothing* was going to get in the way of you getting that land. I guess you found a way to make it happen, didn't you?"

She watched in shocked horror as Tucker stood and poked Darren in the chest. "Listen to me, I'm only going to say this once: I do whatever it takes to get the job done. If you..."

She couldn't stand hear any more and she bolted down the aisle to the restroom and collapsed on the floor inside a bathroom stall. Bile was rising quickly in her throat and she wretched loudly as she gripped the sides of the toilet. The smell of urine lingering in the stall overwhelmed her, and she puked. It was then that the tears came flowing out of her.

It couldn't be true. Tucker *was* honorable. Tucker cared for her. Tucker loved... She leaned over and gagged loudly. She couldn't bring herself to even think the word. *No, she was the one who loved him, not the other way around*.

It was all about her land. It always had been. He weaseled his way into her panties and heart thinking he could mindfuck her into giving him control of her land just like she had given him control over her body.

She wailed loudly not caring who heard her. She loved him. *She fucking loved him.* She yanked on the choker around her neck knowing full well she couldn't remove it without the damned key that was in Tucker's possession. *Tucker...* Fuck him! She stood and pounded her fists against the walls of the stall. How *could she be so damned stupid*?

She heard the bathroom door open and she sank onto the toilet and stifled her sobs. *Now what*? They were practically living together.

"Lil? Are you okay?" Ariel whispered outside the door.

"Umm... I'm not feeling well. Just give me a minute, please," she sniffed.

"Sure."

She heard the click of heels on the tile floor and the door swing closed. Her throat tightened painfully and her head throbbed with an impending migraine. It was a lie - all of it; everything Tucker had told her and made her feel. His hypnotic smile flashed before her eyes and anger swept over her, dark and ugly. It coursed through her veins and her core temperature rose to an unbearable level.

Stepping out of the stall, she splashed her face with cold water and looked into the mirror. What she saw looking back scared her. Her face was contorted and she suddenly looked years older, and the hurt and betrayal lay naked in her eyes. A tear rested on her lower lashes and she swept it away with new purpose.

She could play the lying game, too. She had learned from the best: Adam *and* Tucker. They had been her mentors in the cruel, heart consuming and soul ravaging sport. But she wasn't going down without a fight. She knew what Tucker wanted, deep down: control and utter and total submission from her. She smiled wickedly back at her own image and felt the rumble of nausea in her stomach again from the sickening and evil look on her face. She blinked long and hard, keeping her eyes closed for longer than necessary. This new person in the mirror wasn't who she was; it wasn't who she was brought up to be and wasn't who she wanted to be, but she was facing a lightless future without Tucker and a hopeless recovery from the heartbreak caused by his lies.

She stood with her head downcast as she formulated her plan when the bathroom door opened and Tucker stepped in.

"Are you okay? Ariel told me you weren't feeling well." His voice oozed concern and she clenched her jaw tightly. Her mind screamed for her to lunge at him and scratch his beautiful, lying eyes out.

With her eyes still closed, she answered. "Everything is fine. I'm just feeling a little ill."

His warm hand rubbed a small circle on her back and his touch made her skin crawl. Bile, thick and hot, rose in her throat again. She cringed and pulled away and dry heaved over the sink.

"Shit, Lilly. Maybe I should make an appointment for you with my doctor."

She stood upright and found the courage to face him. With her eyes resting on his chest, still unable to look into his smoldering eyes, she shook her head *no*. "I just need to go home and rest," she spoke without emotion.

"That sounds like a good plan. I'll leave here early and pick up a few things for you, Pet."

Pet.

She swallowed the acid that was coming up her throat at his term of endearment. Yes, that's exactly what she was to him - a pet to lead around by a collar and keep at his feet. Someone he could order around and swat on the ass when they didn't act appropriately. And she was just ignorant enough to have given him all that and more. She had wanted to be that pet for him because she felt he was worthy of her submission and devotion.

She had never been more wrong in her life and she hated herself for it.

He reached a finger up to guide her to gaze into his eyes and she pushed past him. "I'll see you at home."

She walked out the door with her spirits low but her head held high. There was sweet revenge on the menu for that night, and it was going to be served up Lilliana Norris style.

***

Lilliana looked a mess and Tucker's protective side kicked into high gear even though he was still seething from his conversation with Darren. He should have just told Darren the truth - that he loved Lilliana, but he had been pushed into a corner and just wanted that asshole to get the hell out of his face.

He swept his conversation with Darren aside. Lilly needed his attention at that moment. She had been vomiting according to Ariel and he hoped she wasn't coming down with the flu.

Or perhaps... *No.* It couldn't be *that*, could it?

His heart rate spiked at the thought of Lilly being pregnant. She had told him she was on birth control and he believed her without actually seeing the proof. She wouldn't lie about something like that. *Would she?*

Aubrey's horrible lies flashed in his mind and suddenly, he didn't feel so well either.

Back in his office, he rescheduled his last meeting and texted Lilliana.

McG: How are you feeling?

She was usually right on top of his messages, but this time he waited for more than half an hour. She must really be feeling sick or why else would she make him wait when she knew how he felt about that?

Lilliana: Fine.

He frowned. Her answer was a little too curt for his taste. And he knew *fine* never really meant fine when it was spoken by a woman.

McG: Have you been diligent with your pill?

Lilliana: WTF r u asking me? YES. I take my pill just like a good little pet.

A warning voice whispered in his head that something was wrong. He knew it wasn't her time of the month so her moodiness wasn't due to that.

McG: Just asking.

Lilliana: Whatever. Even if I was pregnant, which I AM NOT, I wouldn't expect u to do anything about It.

He flinched at her harsh response and speed dialed her number. It rang several times before going to voice mail. Quickly losing his temper, he redialed when she picked up after the third ring.

"I'm not pregnant so don't you worry your pretty little head about it," she sniped before he could get in a word.

"Jesus Christ, what the hell has gotten into you? It was a simple question. I know you're not feeling well, but, fuck."

Her response came out in a rush of vehemence. "No, it wasn't a simple question. It was an accusation."

He could hear the raw anger in her voice, and his own anger burned in his throat. "So what the hell is this about not expecting me to do anything if you were pregnant? Are you serious about that?"

"Absolutely. I can take care of myself and, if push came to shove, my own child, without any help from you or anyone else."

The shock of her statement yielded to quick fury. "Okay, listen to me: I don't know what the hell is going on with you, but I don't deserve this shit. If you were pregnant, I would step up and take responsibility for you and our child. But you already know that, don't you?"

Cold and flat, she spoke. "I think you should stay at your place tonight."

He couldn't believe what he was hearing. *All this over a simple question?* No, there was more to it than that. "That's not going to fucking happen. I'm leaving for *your* place, now."

"No. I'll just meet you at your place."

She ended their call and he questioned whether or not she would really show up. Giving her the benefit of the doubt, he drove slowly to his home. He wanted time to calm his temper before dealing with her petulance. When he arrived, he sat in his car for another ten minutes before going inside. He turned the knob and when the door opened, he was stunned into total silence at the image before him.

Lilliana was waiting by the door, naked, on her knees and with her head bowed in a perfect pose of submission. Astounded, his mouth hung open and his keys dropped to the floor next to his feet.

"I'm sorry, Sir. Please forgive me."

***

Lilliana's voice was soft and cloyingly sweet when it left her mouth, and her insolence was well concealed. She had reacted impetuously when confronted with Tucker's accusation of not taking her birth control, and needed to put her plan into action sooner than she had anticipated. She wanted to spend the night alone, thinking things through and deciding whether or not it was worth the effort to try and deceive and break him, but he had forced her hand.

When she heard his keys hit the floor, she knew she had hit a nerve with him. This is what he wanted more than anything: her absolute, unwavering obedience.

Tucker twisted his fingers into her hair and his touch tore at her heart. *God, she loved him.* Why did he lie to her? Just for money and a piece of land? Wasn't her heart, love and loyalty more important than that? *No.* It was all about how much he could accomplish and win. She inhaled and stilled. She would *not* break down and she would follow through at all costs.

Her head swept up gracefully to meet his vivid gaze. Her mouth suddenly became parched, but she choked out the words lodged in her throat. "Tell me what you want from me, Tucker. I'll do anything you desire tonight. No limits. No boundaries. I'm yours to use."

His brows furrowed and he tilted his head as his eyes scanned her face for several long seconds. His hoarse whisper broke the silence. "I don't understand. Why now?"

She couldn't think, her heart was too injured and her mind was too clouded with fury to form a coherent response. *What would Tucker want her to say?* "Because it's what you want, and I want what you want."

She suppressed the queasiness that was bubbling in her belly again as she stared into his caramel-colored eyes. For a brief moment, she thought she saw love reflected back, but knew she was only kidding herself.

She hated him. She needed him. She loathed him. It was too much. She couldn't go through with it... No...

He reached down and lifted her into his arms and she buried her face in his neck, biting back her tears, and inhaling deeply the scent that had embedded itself into her memories and very skin. She wrapped her arms around his neck, wanting to both hold him close and strangle him into unconsciousness.

Inside her bedroom, she wondered what debauchery he had planned for her. A flogging or possibly a harsh paddling? Bound and tied to within an inch of her life, maybe? Perhaps, strange and awkward positions that would test her physical limits. Or breath play? *God, she hoped not that.*

Tucker laid her on the bed and undressed slowly for her, her eyes wandering over the body that she would soon be saying goodbye to. She would miss his tattoos and firm body pressed against her. How long would it take her to get over his taste and smell... His commanding voice... His intense and protective gaze... His kind compliments... His firm touch and soft kisses... *Would she ever get over him?*

Money. Land. Lies.

An overwhelming sickness and emptiness swept over her and a surge rage came again in a flash. While gritting her teeth, she leaned back flat on the bed, ready for whatever torture he was going to impose on her. However, to her astonishment, he simply climbed in bed with her and made sweet love to her; nothing more and nothing less than beautiful.

She blocked it all out and dreamed of a better time; a time when she didn't know about his lies and she still believed there was a future with him; a time only a few hours ago when she realized that she could love again.

She went through the motions - moaning, groaning, meeting his thrusts, and crying out his name in ecstasy, all the while meaning none of it. They made love twice more that night and she gave into him in all ways. When he placed the leash that she had learned to love around her neck, it took every bit of strength not to openly weep at his feet and beg him for an explanation.

He guided her to the foot of the bed where his hands roamed over her body and he whispered words of appreciation and praise, and she kept her eyes to the floor for fear her rage and anguish would shine through.

When he lay next to her, she waited for the sound of his breathing to deepen and slow, and then stumbled into the dark bathroom. Allowing herself to finally break down, she buried her face in a terry cloth robe to muffle her misery before showering and washing off all traces of the liar she was madly in love with.

Tortured dreams kept her from sleeping that night, but Tucker slept as though he was a bear in hibernation. He reached for her several times in his slumbered haze, but she pushed him away, not wanting any more of his deceptive touches.

Only a few hours later, the sun came up. She had only slept a total of two hours and she felt weary, torn and heartsick. Her eyes were swollen from crying and her body ached from the passionate love she and Tucker had made.

His eyes fluttered opened and he rubbed them with the back of his hand. As he rolled onto his side, his eyes scanned her face. "I'm so in love with you," he whispered out as he ran a finger over her lips.

She sat straight up. *How could he be so cruel to say such a thing?* What kind of person was he? Wasn't it bad enough he had abused her trust and taken her submission, all the while knowing he had misled and lied to her?

"How dare you," she snapped, disgusted with him.

"What?" Tucker sat up, confused, his searching hers for some kind of clarification.

Her face was a glowering mask of anger and hurt. "Is this part of your game, too?"

He gave her a narrowed, glinting stare. "I tell you I love you and you think I'm playing games with you? What the hell, Lilly?"

"I know about your plan to get my land and about your lies," she blurted out.

Tucker's cheeks reddened and his eyes looked everywhere but at her. "I don't know what you're talking about."

His voice was low and discomfited, and any hope she held out for his truthfulness died the moment she saw the guilt written on his face.

"Another lie. I heard your conversation with Darren. *I heard you.* He said you only wanted me for my land."

His eyes rounded. "I am *not* with you for that reason."

"You didn't deny it, did you? You told him you did what needed to be done," she shouted. "And all those realtors and investors? You told them my land was spoken for, didn't you?"

"Yes, but... Why didn't you come to me yesterday after you overheard that conversation?"

She didn't dare answer the question.

His eyes fixed on her when she didn't respond. "Why?" He repeated loudly.

"I wanted revenge," she answered as her throat closed up with embarrassment.

"So last night... What was that?" He asked with a steely edge to his voice.

"Payback," she said even softer, knowing her admission made her just as terrible as Tucker.

He frowned, but to her disappointment he wasn't as upset as she had hoped, and it proved to her that he really didn't have any feelings for her. Her tears threatened to choke the life out of her, but she fought them back.

"I only lied in the beginning. The rest was really me," he finally said.

"*Only* the beginning? Is that supposed to make me feel better? That was the most important part. That was the part that made me believe in you. That was the part that made me trust you. I told you that lying was a deal-breaker, Tucker. I told you that up front!"

"Lilly... I should've told you, but... You once told me I never had to explain my actions to you." His usual confident voice was barely a whisper.

"That was before I knew you were a liar and a thief," she started to cry despite her trying to hold back her tears.

Tucker winced as if he had been physically assaulted. "I never stole from you."

"Like hell you didn't! You stole my heart and more than that, my trust. I gave you all of me. I gave you my submission; something that was so hard for me to do. I let you punish me! I wish you had cheated on me because I can get over that kind of betrayal. But to lie to me like you did, and for so long... And to do the things you did to me. You hurt me far worse than Adam ever did."

Tucker gasped and choked back tears. "Don't say that."

More tears slowly found their way down her cheeks. "I met your family. You said I was different. You told me I belonged to you; that I was your pet," her hard voice softened to a breathy whisper while she continued to sob, "You said forever. All for what? A piece of property? Money?"

"I meant all of that and I swear to Christ I do *not* want you for your Goddamn land!" He bellowed with possessive desperation in his husky voice.

He grabbed her by the shoulders and she thrashed to pull out of his grip. "And I'm supposed to believe you now? How much of our relationship was real, Tucker? How much of it was fake? Where did the lie end and the truth begin? Do you even know anymore?"

She turned her face away, unable to stand the look in his eyes. She wanted to believe he meant it, but she knew he was nothing but a phony and she was nothing but a damned fool for ever having fallen for the man everyone warned her about. He had sliced her heart and soul open and laid them bare for everyone to see.

"I'm such an idiot," she cried into her hands. "An idiot and a fool with a small-town mentality to think that you would ever want anything more from me than my land."

Tucker reached a hand out and touched her cautiously. "Please don't cry, Lilly..."

She suddenly became enraged. She'd never shed another tear for this man, or any man. She sucked back her tears and glared at him. "You want the land? It's yours. You know I can't afford to keep it."

"I can pay the taxes for you, Pet..."

His sympathetic eyes and compassionate tone infuriated her even more. "In return for *what*? Me? I told you I wasn't for sale. My love was never for sale!"

She stood and frantically began to dress.

"Oh, God, Lilly, please don't leave like this. We can work it out," His panicked tone came out whispered.

She laughed sarcastically at his ridiculousness. *Did he really think such a thing could be over-looked?* Was he that delusional to believe that his lies could be forgiven or was he just so egotistical to think that she would fall at his feet regardless of what he had done?

"Draw up the contract, Tucker. The land is yours. Do with it what you will. Whore it out and build an apartment complex on it like those sons-of-bitches did with your parent's land.

Sell my family's legacy, you cold-hearted, lying bastard. As for our so-called *eternity* - consider it null and void."

***

Tucker stood, naked, exposed and cut to the bone. "You lied, too. You played with my emotions and surrendered to my will under false pretenses so don't pretend like you're innocent in all of this. I fell hard for you and now you're leaving? You just ripped my soul out by admitting last night was a lie. You were a fake just as much as me. The only difference is you followed through with your plan; I didn't."

He was livid with Lilliana for having lied to him so grievously. The previous night was the best he had ever experienced with a woman. And the words she had spoken? They had meant so much to him and they were all a motherfucking lie.

As she stared back him with hurt in her eyes, he could suddenly imagine how he had made her feel.

Swallowing loudly, she turned her back to him and strode to the door. He just wanted to see her exquisite almond-shaped eyes but she stared defiantly straight ahead without glancing back in his direction.

"You're right about me following through," she finally peered over her shoulder. "If you taught me anything, Tucker, it was to win at all costs regardless of who would be hurt. But you're wrong about me giving myself to you under false pretenses. I surrendered to you willingly like the stupid fool that I am," she countered, her voice cold and exact.

He didn't know what to do or say. His mind was spinning out of control trying to devise plans and lies and ways to get her to stay.

Lies.

They were what had gotten him into this whole mess and, still, he wanted to lie to keep her. *What the fuck was wrong with him?*

"And this damned collar!" She suddenly shrieked out, tugging at the shiny metal around her neck. "Take this meaningless thing off of me!"

Again, she knew the precise words to tear him apart. It wasn't meaningless when he placed it around her frail and beautiful neck. It really had meant to be on her for an *eternity*.

Why hadn't he just told her the truth before it came to this? God damn his pride.

"Take it off!" She yelled when he sat motionless.

"I won't," he whispered.

She looked horrified. "You *won't?*"

"You heard me," he declared obstinately.

"God damn you!" She screamed while pulling at the choker.

He strode to her and tried to control her frenzied actions before she hurt herself or attempted to chew off her own leg like an animal caught in a trap. She grunted and twisted the collar around trying to find the opening.

He reached out and gripped her wrists in an attempt to calm her down, just wanting to hold her and to soothe her pain. "You're being irrational. We can work this out."

She pulled herself away with a choking cry, "I haven't thought this rationally since before I met you. You've done nothing but cloud my judgment and mind fuck me since the minute you found out I owned that land!"

"Stop, Pet, stop! I love..." His words came out strained as he tried to control her frenzied movements.

She stepped back out of his reach and slapped him harshly across the face before he got the words out. "Don't you dare say it!" She snarled.

Traumatized and stunned, his cheek blazed with the heat of her anger and tingled. He had never been struck by a woman before. It hurt, but the pain wasn't so much physically as it was emotional. A sinking anguish overwhelmed him and caused him to stumble backwards toward the bed.

Lilliana gasped out looked mortified with her reaction. She reached her hand out and started crying again when he backed away further.

She closed her eyes and swallowed hard, her hand falling to her side. "You win, Tucker McGrath," she sighed heavily, her voice filled with dejection.

He sank onto the bed. His entire life, that's all he had ever wanted to hear, and now the words tore right through him, leaving a path of destruction in their wake. He didn't want to win. *Not like this.*

"I don't want the land," he choked out.

"If not you, then someone else. And is that what you really want - someone else to win?"

Her words shook him. Would she really do such a thing? By the look in her eyes, he knew she would.

She let out a low tortured whimper. "You once told me that you would ruin me. I should've run then, but instead I believed you. I believed *in* you. I fell in love with you. You kept your word though didn't you? You've ruined me and now I'm just another notch on that belt you love to bind women with," she hung her head. "I'll never get over what you've done to me. *Never.*"

He stifled a sob, the knowledge of her admission twisting and turning inside of him. He loved her, too, with the kind of love that he had never experienced before. He needed her. His heart belonged to her, and no one else would ever come close to providing him with the kind of stability and honesty that she had.

A suffocating sensation gripped his throat. *They could work things out if she would only listen.* If she would only... He sat quietly contemplating his next move, but he blinked and in a flash, she was gone.

His pet was really gone and he had no one to blame but himself.

CHAPTER 25

Lilliana lay in her darkened room, motionless. The endless night had finally grayed into dawn. She felt worthless as she lay there feeling sorry for herself. Having used all of her vacation time after her breakup with Tucker, she now had nothing in reserve for days when she felt like hiding inside her house. Days like today. But luckily for her, she had a late start and didn't have to be to work until ten.

Dragging herself out of bed, she dressed mechanically. When she reached into a drawer to pull out a pair of clean panties, she was faced with Tucker's boxers. She stared at the silk fabric and held back tears of disappointment. She must've forgotten he kept a few extra pairs in her dresser. Bringing them to her nose, she inhaled and Tucker's scent caused a deep sob to rack her body. She dropped them to the floor and held onto the edge of the dresser for support.

Breakfast. That's what she needed.

She went into the kitchen and toasted some bread. It was all she could stomach. Seating herself at the table, the manila package that had arrived in the mail the two weeks earlier caught her attention. It was the offer Tucker had sent her on her land. She slid it toward her and dug out the paperwork to read it over again. 5.25 million dollars for the whole shebang — land, water rights, and house. She could retire on that amount and travel the world like she had always wanted to do.

She reached for a nearby pen and traced her signature on the paper without retracting the pen. She had gone through the motion time and time again, trying to get up the courage to really go through with it. She clicked the pen in and out, and then laid it back down.

Five million dollars for her family's legacy. It didn't seem like near enough.

She took a deep breath and bit into the dry, unbuttered toast before sulking out onto the porch to gaze at her land. It had cost her the love of her life and now the calico bushes that she adored so much only served as a reminder of what Tucker had done to her. A light snow had fallen the night before and the landscape took on a white ghostly appearance. Just as the tinkle of Tucker's chime whispered in her ear and she let out a pathetic moan, her phone vibrated in her pocket.

McG: I stopped by your office. They told me you had a late start. We have business to discuss. Be there in a few minutes.

Her mouth opened in dismay. She hadn't seen or heard from him in nearly six weeks. After multiple attempts at trying to get in touch with her, he finally seemed to give up.

She puckered her mouth and stuffed her phone back into her pocket. She would just have to leave before he showed up. Grabbing her coat and purse quickly, she ran to her car only to find the battery half-dead from the cold weather. *Damn.* She really missed the reliability of Tuck's Lexus sometimes.

She turned the engine over several times and pumped the gas pedal only to hear the whinny and whine of her classic vehicle's battery's demise. Allowing the battery to try and recharge, she waited a moment. She turned her key and pumped the gas pedal again when there was a loud knock on her window. She gripped her steering wheel but didn't dare look out the window.

"Lilly," Tucker's deep muffled voice could barely be heard over the wind.

She ignored him and turned the key again only to be denied by the sound of rapid clicking. *Of all days, why today?*

"We need to talk, Lilly," he stated more adamantly.

Motionless, she stared forward. The car door opening startled her and she reached over to pull it closed but Tucker was already kneeling next to her.

"Lilly, please. This is important or I wouldn't have bothered you."

Without saying a word, she unbuckled herself and pushed past him as she got out of the vehicle. She moved towards the porch with Tucker close behind her. She had just slipped the key into her door when she felt his hand on her lower back. Spinning around, she glared angrily at him. *Who the hell did he think he was touching her?*

"Don't do that again," she stated with a thinly veiled chill hanging on the edge of her words.

His mouth twitched into a frown. She rapidly turned away, unable to bear the sight of his luminous eyes hidden behind dark circles without breaking down.

When they stepped inside, she pointed toward the kitchen table where he promptly seated himself. The way he stretched out his long legs casually, she found it hard to concentrate as memories of their time together flooded her brain.

Damn, he was beautiful.

Sitting directly across from him, she lifted her chin and forced herself to meet his eyes. "What do you want?"

He tapped the offer that was still lying on the table out in the open. "This offer is expired. My new offer is four million."

Tucker spoke so heartlessly, she wondered how she ever could've loved him. "It's worth more than that," she almost yelled.

"Okay – 3.75 million." His eyes and facial expression remained emotionless – no hate, no love, just cold and blank.

She stood and slammed her hand onto the table. "You vindictive son-of-a...." She stopped herself, unable to speak badly about his mother.

He blinked several times. "Three million and you can keep the house and five acres. That's my final offer."

"I'll sell it someone else," she ground out between gritted teeth.

"No, you won't," he gave her a slow shake of his head. "We made a verbal agreement. If you back out now, I'll make sure your sale doesn't go through and I'll sue you."

A flash of hurt, loneliness and anger stabbed at her heart. She reached out and slapped him across his sculptured cheek bone and his toffee eyes blinked long and hard, but his penetrating gaze never left her.

"Take the offer, Lilliana," he stated softly.

She slumped into the kitchen chair, defeated. Feeling totally miserable, she closed her eyes.

"I hate you." She wasn't sure if she had spoken the words aloud or just thought them.

"No, you don't. You hate yourself for falling for me. I know the feeling."

The effect of his sad expression and words was shattering. She raised her eyes. No longer was his look blank, but bleak, sorrowful and grim. *So she had affected him.*

His dark brows slanted in a frown as he watched her. "For what it's worth, I still love you."

"The only kind of love you know is for money and yourself," she choked out, her gaze clouded with tears.

"You're wrong."

She bowed her head and pointed towards the door. "Just get out."

Reluctantly, he stood walked toward the door, his movements stiff and awkward. His steps slowed as he lingered in the doorway, taking a last long glance around the room and at the wind chime. "I'll send the paperwork over immediately. Lilly... I..." He sighed heavily and shook his head. "Goodbye."

***

Winter was turning out to be a cold and miserable time of year. Christmas was only a few weeks away and Lilliana was dreading spending the holiday alone. Dana had offered to take her down south to meet her family, but she passed on the kind offer. Ariel, too, had tried to coax her into spending the holiday weekend in New York with her, but her nightmares were coming at such an alarming rate, she wasn't getting any sleep and she doubted she would be good company to be around.

The sound of bulldozers in the distance had become a distracting part of her life. So distracting, she started taking the side road to exit to the main highway to avoid seeing the activity that was taking place on her land. Correction – on *Tucker's* land. Lilliana bristled at the thought and wondered if his mother was proud of her son's accomplishments now; one-hundred acres in exchange for a broken and tortured heart.

She forced herself to dig out Margo's Christmas decorations and was in the process of hanging a large handmade wreath on her front door when she heard a car coming up her drive. She turned to see a dark green VW Golf kicking up snow and dust before finally coming to a stop.

She stepped off the landing as a cold gust of wind swept past her. When the car door swung open, Mason stepped out. Her stomach did a tumble, but when she saw a smile spread across his face, she was immediately put at ease.

"Lilly! You look amazing!" Mason yelled through the loud wind.

He pulled her into his arms and his smell almost brought her to her knees. It was the same cologne as Tucker's. He pulled back and Tucker's eyes were staring down at her.

She gulped hard and bit back her tears.

"What is it, Hon?" He asked with a look of concern on his face.

"You look so much like Tucker. And your smell..."

"Oh, Lilly. I'm sorry."

"I'm fine. Every now and then it hits me that we're actually over, but... I really am fine," she lied.

Mason lifted his brows and looked her over. "I'm supposed to believe that?"

She shrugged and led him inside the house.

"Why are you here, Mason?" She finally asked as she removed her coat.

Digging out a letter from his pocket, he handed it over to her. The name of a company she wasn't familiar with was printed on it along with hers, and she promptly opened it. It was a check for just under $10,500. Her mouth dropped open. She didn't remember signing up for any kind of mail lottery.

She scanned the check for some kind of revealing information but could find nothing of importance.

She held the check out to Mason. "I don't understand."

"You know as much as I do. It was on Tucker's desk with your name and address, and stamped. I thought I'd drop it off instead of you getting it by mail."

"Why?"

"Because I wanted to talk to you and it seemed like a good excuse. Look, Lilly, I know what Tucker did to you, he told me everything, and I'm not going to make any excuses for his actions. But... Ah, hell.... Tucker's a mess. He has been for awhile now. I kept thinking he would just get over you and move on like he did all the rest, but this time it's different."

She was at a loss for words. She shook her head and scanned the floor.

"I love my brother, Lilly. He's a good man, albeit, tenacious and often times full of himself. He'll never admit it, but he needs you. He's torturing himself over what he did. Can't you just go and talk to him? He's hurting."

Mason's eyes begged for her to show sympathy, and she was warmed at the sincerity in his actions. She shuffled the check between her hands as all traces of resistance vanished. The check in her hands had served as an excuse for Mason to pay her a visit and now it could serve the same purpose for her to speak to Tucker. She needed an explanation about the check anyway. Mason's kindness touched her and if not for any other reason, she would speak with Tucker on his behalf.

"Yes. I'll talk to him."

He let out a loud exaggerated sigh. "Thank you, Lilly."

***

Tucker had his head buried deep in paperwork. He was severely lacking sleep and the upcoming holidays were wreaking havoc on his nerves. His caffeine intake had doubled in the last month and a half, and the jitters had started to become part of his daily routine.

Frantically, he looked around his desk. *Where the hell did that check for Lilly go?* He could've sworn he put right next to hIs calendar. He rested his elbows on his desk and fisted his hair. He couldn't keep a thought straight in his head anymore.

Fucking, Lilliana Norris and that Goddamn one-hundred and twelve acres.

He pushed the intercom button to ask Ariel if she had mailed the check already, but decided against it. Ariel and Lilliana had become very close in the last several months and he had already had more than enough of the redhead's nasty attitude because of what had gone down with Lilly.

He pushed his chair back violently away from his desk and stood. Staring out the window at the snow covered buildings, he smiled. He missed Lilly, but took solace in the fact that she got to keep her land and make some money on it, as well. Sure, he was alone and miserable, but Lilliana would always have her family's land.

"Tuck?"

He leaned his head back and closed his eyes. He could still her voice soft and low as if she were in the room with him.

"Tuck?"

He felt a tug on the sleeve of his jacket and he jerked his body around.

She really was in the room. His mouth dropped open and his eyes quickly assessed her body. Her hair had grown out by at least four inches and was over her ears in a short wind-blown bob with her bangs swept to the side. She was wearing a tight-fitting, cream colored sweater underneath a puffy pink winter coat and calf-high, shearling boots.

She was absolutely fucking perfect.

His mouth became unbearably dry and he felt like he had been chewing on dust when he addressed her. "I didn't hear you come in."

Her heart-shaped face had a healthy glow and she smiled shyly. Right on cue, his cock twitched in response. *Damn if that mouth didn't get him every time.*

"I just came to talk to you about this check I got today. I don't understand what it's for."

He hesitated, blinking with bewilderment. "How did you get that?"

"Mason brought it by."

Mason. Of course. He had been eyeing it when he stopped by to visit. His entire family was concerned about his well-being and had been calling incessantly to check up on him. He loved them for it, but it was getting damned aggravating.

"So what's your question again?" He asked as his eyes rested on her breasts. It was hard for him to remain coherent when she was so close to him.

"What. Is. It. For?" She emphasized every word.

"What do you mean? It's your profit sharing check," he stared back at.

Her lashes flew up and her gaze bore into him with obvious astonishment. *Didn't she know what she had signed?*

"Lilly, you act like you're surprised. Didn't you read the contract before you signed it?"

"Well, not exactly. I was still very upset with you and... I thought I sold it. I received the big check for the five acres and the house."

Her breasts rose and fell under her labored and excited breathing, and He shook his head to force himself to concentrate. His voice took on a disciplinarian tone. "You should always read anything before you sign it."

She rolled her eyes. "I'm well aware of that, thank you. I don't need another one of your lectures, Professor McGrath."

His mouth lifted in a lop-sided grin. Goddamn, he had missed her sarcasm. Lilliana did a double take before eyes rested on his mouth. In that instant, her lips parted and he could hear the sharp intake of air.

His smile. How could he forget? It was his secret weapon.

When tried to flash his teeth without being obvious, she blinked several times and her eyes became glassy. "So... Profit sharing? You mean the land is still mine? But what about the big check?"

"The large check was for the lease of your land for five standing years. It was payment up front to cover the rental of it. The smaller check is part of the profit sharing of the organic crops that are being grown and harvested there. You'll receive those checks quarterly. After five years you can choose to either renew your contract with Farm Aggregates or end it."

She threw herself into one of the chairs across from his desk.

"But you made it sound like I was selling my land. Why would you do that?" She whispered through a strained and fragile voice.

He sat on the edge of his desk, watching as her emotions played on her face.

"Because you were still angry with me and I knew you wouldn't listen to anything I had to say. I lied so I could get you to at least look over the contract. I assumed you had. Hell, you signed it."

"But... What about the original contract?" She stared at him, baffled.

"That was just a place holder until I got everything ironed out. I didn't want you running to someone else to sell your land before I could get the details sorted through."

"That's so deceiving!" Her temper flared. "What if I had signed it?"

"I wouldn't have done anything with it. And, honestly, I knew you wouldn't."

Lilliana stood and paced the office, mumbling unintelligibly under her breath. "Why, Tucker? After all your lies, why would you help me out like that?" She turned her face away from him.

He swallowed and managed a feeble but completely heartfelt answer, "Because I love you."

She whirled around and faced him with a look of denial. "You mean *loved*."

He shook his head slowly. "No. *Love*. Present tense."

Her legs wobbled and he thought she was about to lose her footing, so he lunged toward her and pulled her into his arms. The warmth of her body and divine smell overpowered him and his heart dropped to his toes, and he suddenly felt weak in the knees, too.

Pouting her bottom lip, she rested her hands on his chest. "You don't really mean that. You lied to me."

"Yes, I do mean it. I wish I didn't. Hell, my life would be easier if I didn't. But you won my heart long before you think; somewhere in between the apple crisp and the animal shelter. Maybe even sooner if I'm completely honest with myself."

The sun shining in Lilliana's eyes reflected astonishment. "That was almost the beginning."

"I tried to tell you that. That conversation with Darren... I was so pissed off that he had gotten in my face and was asking for an explanation. I felt like I didn't owe him anything so I didn't deny his accusations. I should have. Every day I regret that I didn't, but my fucking pride didn't let me."

She stared, speechless for a brief moment. "But I slapped you. Twice."

"I deserved them," he responded when her lashes bordered with tears.

"No one deserves that." She pressed her face into his chest. "I'm sorry for that."

"I think we're both sorry for a lot of things."

She met his gaze once again and nodded but a question brimmed in her eyes. "That night that I gave myself to you, why did you go so easy on me?"

He cocked his head and furrowed his brows. "Submission is a gift and I would never take advantage of that. The fact that you said no limits was enough for me. You know... You ruined me, too, Lilly."

She shook her head as if trying to process his words.

"Since I'm coming clean, I should also admit that those biscuits you ate weren't really my mother's recipe. They were store bought," he gave her a guilty smile.

Her eyes and expression softened. Wrapping her arms over his shoulders, she caressed the strong tendons at the back of his neck. "I already knew that, I just didn't want to hurt your feelings by calling you out."

His mouth curved upward in a hopeful smile. "Can we start over, Lilly? From the beginning, but without the lies?"

She swallowed loudly, then bit her bottom lip. "Yes, I want to. I've missed you so much, Tuck," her voice broke with sadness.

He felt a warm glow flow through his body that started in his buzzing brain and worked its way to his tingling toes. "Lilly of the Valley... Tell me this isn't another cruel dream. Tell me you're really standing here saying we're going to try again." Though try as he may, the desperation in his voice was difficult for him to hide.

"Yes. Try again. From the beginning. You. Me. Us. Again." Her eyes focused on his mouth as her arms clamped around his neck tighter.

His ego was instantly restored when he felt her arousal and saw the acquiescence in her eyes that he had missed like the air in his lungs. He puffed his chest out and smiled with an air of confidence. "Admit it. You got it bad for me."

Lilliana wrinkled her nose at him. "If by *got it bad* you mean I want to slap you upside your pugnacious head and..."

"Stop talking, Lilly," he whispered, his mouth inching closer to hers.

She smiled and opened her mouth, but to his absolute astonishment, it wasn't to speak; it was to accept his carnal kiss. Nipping at her bottom lip, he breathed into her mouth, "My Pet."

EPILOGUE

Tucker waited impatiently at the altar, his eyes fixated on the door at the far end of the aisle. He detested waiting and now, of all days, he was waiting for his bride-to-be. Lilliana was taking too long and he began to wonder: had he been the victim of a runaway bride?

The entry music stopped and restarted three times. Everyone was looking to him for some kind of answer, but he didn't know anymore than the guests what the hell was going on. Darren's eyes widened and shrugged his shoulders when he looked over to him for some kind of sympathy. He was glad to have worked things out with him. At Lilliana's insistence, of course.

The music started a fourth time and a mocking voice in his head hammered at his resolve. Losing all patience, he stomped up the aisle and into the back room where his future bride was hiding out. Throwing the door open, he found her sitting on the floor and mumbling incoherently. His irritation faded as he gathered her into his arms and held her snugly.

"My sweet, Lilly…"

"Oh, Tucker…" She simpered, her eyes full of tears.

"Christ, Pet, calm down. Just breathe."

He watched her closely as she followed his instructions and her rapid breathing slowly subsided. He stood, helped her up and guided her to a long couch. The fear exuding from her was heartbreaking. *Didn't she want to marry him*? He knew she loved him, so why the hesitation? She had only let on about her nervousness on a few occasions during the planning, but nothing to this extent.

"Explain to me how that over-sized brain of yours works," he tucked a strand of her loose hair back into place. "My collar around your neck is fine, but my ring around your finger is making you vacillate? How the hell does that work?"

She moved her shoulders in a shrug of confusion as if she didn't know the answer herself. She smiled but the terror in her eyes was all too evident. "I love you, please don't question that. I just... Why do we have to sign a piece of paper to prove that?"

"I want you and our children to have my name," he winked and flashed his teeth, trying to put her at ease. It worked every time and this time was no different. Her eyes moved to his mouth and she sighed.

"God, you have the most amazing molars," she whispered.

"Let's not forget about my bicuspids."

"Yes, those too," she laughed.

"So are we going through with this?" He asked, quirking an eyebrow at her.

Her eyes widened as if she had momentarily forgotten why they were there. He was growing more eager than ever but he didn't want to push her.

"When did you know you wanted me? I mean *really* wanted me?" She asked.

He knew the answer without even having to think: "The moment I saw those mysterious eyes at the dentist's office." He lifted her face and pecked her forehead. "When you told me I couldn't begin to fathom the amount of fucks you didn't give about what I wanted." Another kiss on the corner of her mouth. "The first time you allowed me to spank that heavenly ass of yours." He swiped his tongue across her lips. "Every time we shared a bed and you lay in my arms." His tongue dipped into her mouth. "When you accepted my collar." His mouth crushed down onto hers briefly. "But the real moment was when you told me that we could try again and start over. I knew then that you would be mine until death do us part." At last, he wrapped his hand behind her neck and hauled her into his deep and possessive kiss, burying his tongue deep inside her mouth. She panted when their lips separated while her eyes remained closed. "I love you, Lilly of the Valley, and I want to spend the rest of my life with you. But I'm not telling you anything you don't already know, am I?"

Her eyes fluttered opened. "No, you're not. But... Maybe we can just stay perpetually engaged. Permanently affianced.

Eternally bound by a promise. Betrothed until the end of time..."

He had heard enough. Lilliana's plea was halted by him standing so suddenly it scarcely registered on her radar. In one fluid motion, he snatched her up and heaved her over his shoulder, his arm over the back of her legs holding her firmly in place.

He was taking his bride, one way or the other, Lilly was going to be his. *Forever.*

***

"Tucker, wait!" Lilliana shrieked out of breath as his bouncing movements compressed her diaphragm and made her unable to get a complete sentence out.

"I'm done fucking waiting. We're doing this. I love you. Now stop talking."

She panted and tried to squirm out of his grip, but his muscular arms were too strong. There was no way he was really going to haul her down the aisle over his shoulder like some kind of Neanderthal, was he?

Oh, God, he was.

Tucker kicked the door open and the chorus to *On Top of the World* by Imagine Dragons promptly started and people's voices died down. Some people's faces looked shocked, some appalled, but most - amused. A low sound of merriment built up in the wedding hall and turned into a loud rolling laughter that echoed throughout the large room.

Leave it to Tucker to know just how to make a grand entrance.

Sheepishly, she grinned at a few people as he strode toward the altar. When they approached the bridal party, a whoop and a holler roared over the crowd. It was Mason and Gavin. Apparently they were quite entertained by their big brother's caveman antics.

"Take your bride!" Mason yelled.

"Get her, Tuck!" Gavin bellowed.

Tucker lowered her and gingerly placed her on her feet before. Straightening her lace, cream-colored strapless dress, he smoothed her now mussed, shoulder-length hair, and readjusted the crown veil. When the crowd broke out into loud applause, her face burned bright red.

Tucker's large hands took her face and held it gently. "Don't even think about running," he lifted a brow at her.

She felt a poke in the ribs from behind and heard Dana's and Ariel's giggles.

She became entranced in his eyes and suddenly the room became silent. The man standing before her was such a good, kind man... And so damned beautiful. She took in the handsome image before her as he stood watching her cautiously. His black tuxedo-suit, pale blue tie and newly layered cut hairdo was quite an appealing look. As the minister's words droned on in the background, she wondered what it would feel like to tear his clothing off, run her fingers through his short hair, and feel his lips on hers while officially having his name.

She remembered how hurt she had felt when she found out about his lies, but now, seeing the look of love reflected in his eyes, she let it all go. She knew Tucker would never hurt her that way again or the way Adam had, and that their destinies were forever intertwined. They were meant to be; truly for *eternity.*

They were going to grow old together on her family's land, and in the home that Tucker had renovated to make room for the large family that they wanted. A smile spread across her face at the thought of a clan of McGrath's running around their home, and in the same calico fields that her mother and Margo had once played in.

A dull pain stabbed her heart thinking about them and wishing they were present, but she shifted her eyes momentarily to look over his shoulder to see the large poster size photos of her mother and Margo prominently displayed in their honor. It had been his idea and she loved him for it. Her eyes immediately darted back to her future husband's and explosive currents of love coursed through her when she saw the galvanizing look of possessiveness in his eyes.

The pounding of her heart finally quieted, and softly breaking through her trancelike state, she faintly heard, "Do you take this man to be your lawfully wedded husband?"

She blinked rapidly when his mouth lifted into his signature, lop-sided grin as he held out the ring. A knot rose in her throat and her eyes filled with happy tears at the vision of the large emerald cut diamond set in white gold. Reaching down, he held onto her hand tightly as he slipped it on her finger. A single tear fell from her eye as she met his passionate gaze.

"This is the part where you say, *I do*," he winked.

With a contented sigh, she surrendered to his will and gave into the inevitable - *'til death do them part.* A rush of air left her lungs when she answered, "Yes, Sir, I do. I really, really do."

Tucker wrapped his arm around her waist and tugged her firmly to him. His mouth ghosted hers as a round of applause filled the room, and she barely heard him say, "And now you're really, really mine. End. Of. Story."

She smiled and touched his lips. "Oh, no, Tuck. This is only the beginning of our story."

ABOUT ELLA D.

Books by Ella D.
Available at all major ebook retailers.

*The Art of Submission (The Art of D/s #1)
*The Art of Domination (The Art of D/s #2)
*The Art of Control (The Art of D/s #3)
*The Art of D/s Trilogy
*The Art of Redemption (Art of D/s, #0.5)
*Unpublished. Revised editions coming late 2016—to be titled: Submission, Domination, Control & Redemption (The Art of Becoming Us)

Becoming Sir (An Art of D/s Novel)

Continental Breakfast (Continental Affair #1)
Continental Beginnings (Continental Affair #2)
Continental Life (Continental Affair #3)

This Love's Not for Sale (BDSM romantic comedy)

Grace Street (Chapter 8, #1)
Return to Grace Street (Chapter 8, #2)
Chapter 8: The Complete Series (with bonus material)

Altered State (An erotic psychological thriller)

Hard Candy for Christmas
The 12 Kinks of Christmas
A Cub for Christmas
F#ck You Valentine!

Adam's Apple: An Erotic Short Story
Tennessee Moonshine

Ulterior Designs (House of Evans, Book One)
Interior Motives (House of Evans, Book Two)

Biography:

In addition to being a writer, Ella is a mom, a wife, a respiratory therapist, and a lover of ukuleles and unicorns. She was born and raised in a sexually conservative, strict Christian household in the Bible Belt of the USA. This upbringing and repression contributed to her wicked imagination, and writing has become a pleasurable and satisfying outlet for her fantasies. At the mature age of forty, she mustered up the courage to share her thoughts and put pen to paper. She sincerely hopes to find her niche in writing romance in all forms, be it dark romance, romantic comedy, psychological thrillers and paranormal.

She doesn't consider herself an author, rather, an avid reader above all else and someone who simply writes the stories that the characters in her head tell her to.

Blog: www.elladominguez.blogspot.com
Twitter: https://twitter.com/ella_dominguez
Tumblr: http://literarysmutologist.tumblr.com/
Facebook: www.facebook.com/theartofsubmission
Goodreads: www.Goodreads.com
Website: www.bondagebunnypub.com
Instagram: https://www.instagram.com/ella_dominguez/

Sign up for updates and exclusive teasers:
Newsletter: http://eepurl.com/bwsvUf

For this book's playlist and all of Ella D.'s music selections, follow her on Spotify:
https://open.spotify.com/user/12146676013/playlist/1YJISOPejiqTUo2vxnCeOe